KILLER.app

Barbara D'Amato

A TOM DOHERTY ASSOCIATES BOOK
NEW YORK

This is a work of fiction. All the characters and events portrayed in this book are either products of the author's imagination or are used fictitiously.

KILLER.app

Cover art by Robert Santora

A Forge Book
Published by Tom Doherty Associates, Inc.
175 Fifth Avenue
New York, NY 10010

Forge® is a registered trademark of Tom Doherty Associates, Inc.

ISBN: 0-812-55391-8
Library of Congress Card Catalog Number: 95-41206

First edition: March 1996
First mass market edition: March 1997

Printed in the United States of America

0 9 8 7 6 5 4 3 2 1

My thanks to officers of the Chicago Police Department for unlimited amounts of technical advice, particularly Lt. Hugh Holton and Chief of Detectives John Stibich; to computer engineer Sheryl Rak D'Amato of Motorola; to Dr. Maria Brolley for her assistance on blood transfusions, donor compatibility, and hemolysis; to Frances Ginther, Administrative Director of Health Regulations, Chicago Department of Health, for her advice on food-borne salmonellosis; to Dr. Arnold Widen, Blue Cross/Blue Shield, for his advice on resuscitation after cardiac arrest; to Dr. Tom VanEenenaam for his descriptions of private airplanes; and to world pollen expert Vaughn Bryant, Ph.D., Director of the Department of Anthropology at Texas A&M, for answering my questions about pollen morphology and forensic palynology.

And most of all to Susan Dunlap and Jeffery Deaver, who gave their time and invaluable expertise in reading an early draft, and to Paul D'Amato for everything.

Killer.app, *n*. An application of computer programming that replaces an old application because of increased power or efficiency. Shortened form of killer application. (slang)

I

''He who controls the flow of
data controls everything.''

-Dean Utley,
3rd MIT AI Conference, 1983

☐☐

THE BODY FLOATED eight feet above the sandy bottom, suspended in gelatinous green light, facedown, as if studying the bottom. Its arms stretched out from its sides and angled slightly upward, pale fingers curled toward the palms of the hands. It floated a quarter mile off the coast of Michigan City, Indiana. On February 17, the body had been underwater for three days.

A wash of polar air was flowing from Hudson Bay south across the Straits of Mackinac and Thunder Bay, over Lake Superior and due south across Escanaba, Sturgeon Bay, down the full three hundred miles of Lake Michigan. The steady flow had pushed the lake water south, piling it up a foot or two above its normal level at the southern end and floating the body higher off the bottom than it had been the day before.

At the same time, the body moved imperceptibly westward. It remained the same in relation to the algae and small bits of plant material that were suspended around it, but the whole mass inched slowly to the west.

During the day the body made a gradual circuit around the outflow of Trail Creek at the Michigan City Yacht Basin.

Two days later it had cleared the outflow area and was moving west by southwest along the Indiana Dunes State Park, about two hundred feet offshore, in twenty-four feet of water. The winds in Ontario and northern Michigan had quieted and a gentle westerly breeze blew across the lake. The water level in the southern end of the Lake Michigan basin had sunk back to normal. The body now floated ten or twelve inches off the sandy bottom and twenty-two feet below the surface, its knees and the toes of its shoes just barely dragging on the sand.

Despite the westerly wind it continued to drift generally west. Lake Michigan is three hundred miles long north to south and close to a hundred miles wide at the widest point. In the center the lake bottom has a submerged east-west ridge, dividing the body of water into two somewhat separate circulations. In the northern basin, the water circulates in a counterclockwise oval. In the southern basin the water circulates in a clockwise oval a hundred miles long and ninety miles wide. The body was in the extreme southern end of the lake. The circulation moved the body inexorably westward, back toward its home.

By early March, the body was offshore of the harbor in Gary, Indiana, and just beginning to meander around the pier. A sudden storm, with winds upward of sixty miles an hour, tore across the lake from the northwest, bringing sleet to Indiana, closing the Indiana Toll Road, I-80, I-90, I-94, and I-65 and causing the deaths of thirteen motorists in the evening hours of the fourth, which this year was Ash Wednesday.

Under the surface, close to the bottom, there were no waves, no snow, no sleet. The body continued to move slowly west.

Although it had been in the water three weeks now, almost no decomposition had occurred. The water near the bottom of the lake was thirty-three degrees. Except for a slightly swollen tongue and a bluish pallor, the body looked as if it were asleep, dreaming peacefully on its stomach.

Thursday, March 5, the body was half a mile offshore, in a hundred feet of water. This water had a milky translucence from the outflow from the steel mills at Gary and Hammond. The body was now moving northwest.

Five days later it crossed an unmarked border between Indiana and Illinois; if it had been on the surface, it would have been in sight of the eastern end of the Chicago Skyway.

On Thursday the twelfth, the body rode an eddy within a hundred feet of shore between the 67th Street beach and Rainbow Park beach. The day was unusually warm for March and both parks were filled with teenagers throwing Frisbees and sunbathing and flirting and trying to drink beer out of Coke cans without anybody noticing. The body passed by just three yards below the surface and kept drifting northwest.

In typical late-winter Chicago fashion, the next four days were bitterly cold, and on the third and fourth days there was snow. Under the surface, the body moved north by northwest in dim amber light. It passed the yacht harbor off 63rd Street, just skimmed the end of the fishing pier, its shirt tugging once or twice on submerged blocks of concrete, and eased slightly shoreward near the Museum of Science and Industry.

When the sun finally came out at five P.M. on Tuesday the seventeenth, the body passed under the long robotlike shadow cast by the Adler Planetarium, and then slowly drifted into the bay area lying off the center of the city of Chicago.

The tour boat *Odyssey*, beginning its spring dinner tours, passed several yards over the body on its cruise north Wednesday evening. Its prop wash stirred the arms, making the corpse appear, briefly, to be lazily swimming. Then the body eddied into a spot near the light on the south end of the breakwater just off Buckingham Fountain.

For two days, the body washed back and forth against the rock and concrete substructure of the south end of the breakwater, as if it were uncertain whether to go inside, toward Chicago, or outside, back into the open lake.

On Saturday, a northeast wind, shrieking in from Newfoundland, picked up moisture crossing Lake Michigan and blinded Chicago in lake-effect snow. Chunks of ice broke off the ranges of icebergs that had rimmed the Michigan shore of the lake since late December. The ice washed southwest and piled up into an undulating mass at the bottom end of the lake. Under this blanket, water levels rose slightly in the southwestern part of the lake, where the body floated. Thousands of tons

of water and ice pushed into the baylike area behind the breakwater. Ten-foot waves smashed over the breakwater and
flooded into the protected areas near shore. Now that the body
lay in only twenty feet of water, it was not as insulated from the
effect of the waves. It was quickly carried around the end of the
breakwater and into the lagoon of the Chicago Yacht Club.

The light from the sky was broken up by the ice as if by a
wall of glass blocks, dappling the figure beneath.

Sunday, Monday, and Tuesday, after the storm subsided,
the body drifted along the bottom of the yacht club mooring
area. It passed around the footings of the mooring cables,
touching them gently, easing away. It spent one morning lying
against the keel of a forty-foot sloop. Then a chance current
moved it off. It passed a few inches under the white hull of a
Chris-Craft motor yacht and the bright blue twin hulls of a
little catamaran.

Wednesday night a west wind turned over the water in the
bay and the body washed back and forth against the inside of
the breakwater, rising and falling with the sloshing of the small
basin. The fabric on the blue sleeve started to wear. Holes
opened on the fabric over the body's elbows and knees, and
then the skin beneath started to abrade. This was the first serious damage the body had sustained, even though it had been in
the water for five weeks. Some natural changes had occurred—
the skin of the hands had sloughed off. The hair was gone and
part of the skin of the face. But because the body was cold and
bloodless, it continued to look very much like the man it had
once been.

Despite the deep cold, gases were slowly forming in the
belly of the corpse. As it nudged past one of the anchor ropes in
the harbor, its shoulder caught briefly, and the body rolled
over, facing upward toward the night sky.

Thursday morning a few boat owners took the opportunity
afforded by the clear weather to do some work on their boats.
As the body passed among them, a few caught glimpses of it.
One man thought briefly that he had seen an enormous coho

salmon. Another was quite sure that a hangover from Wednesday night at the Bucket of Blood had addled his brain.

The Chicago River flows backward, out of Lake Michigan into the Chicago Sanitary and Ship Canal, to the Des Plaines River, and eventually into the Mississippi twenty miles north of St. Louis. As a result of the backward flow, a gentle but continuous current runs from the yacht club pool into the river area, interrupted off and on by the opening and closing of lock gates.

At daybreak on Friday, March 20, the body was at the mouth of the Chicago River. A slight pull from the river gentled it along. At about five A.M., it passed under the Lake Shore Drive Bridge. An hour later, it passed under the Columbus Drive Bridge and approached the Michigan Avenue Bridge.

The *Sun-Times* and Wrigley Building stand on one side of Michigan Avenue at this point, the *Tribune* Building on the other, and next to the Trib, the Equitable Building. Next to the Equitable Building a graceful S-curve of wide concrete steps runs down to the esplanade that fronts the river.

The body floated along the river, heading west into the city of Chicago. Although the water even here was not more than thirty-six degrees, decomposition had speeded up a bit. The belly was now distended with the pressure of the gases inside, tightening the blue shirt, and the body floated just under water, its belly touching the surface.

The distinctive Chicago Police cap with the checkered band had fallen off even before the body went into the water. The leather holster was in place, though it was empty of its gun. The radio and Kelite flashlight were missing. But the uniform jacket was intact, except for the abrasions on the sleeves, and the navy pants were mostly undamaged, though sodden and without a hint of their crease. The unit designator and name tags were still in place on the right upper chest. His name was Frieswyk.

He had almost floated home.

A family of five from Kenosha was descending the S-curve

stairs to look at the river. The mother's eyes passed over the body, not taking it in. The father, carrying the baby who had waked them all at six, was saying, "You have to take advantage of good weather around here when you get it." He didn't notice the body, either.

But the five-year-old girl, who wore a Chicago Bulls T-shirt bought at the sports shop in the *Tribune* Building nearby, and who had no preconceptions about what might or might not be in the icy water, said, "Look at that bald man floating on his back!"

And her four-year-old brother shook his head and said, "He's not, either. He's swimming underwater!"

01

||||||||||||||||||||||||||||||||||||||||||||||||||||||||||||||||||||||||
DEPARTMENT OF THE TREASURY
UNITED STATES SECRET SERVICE
1800 G STREET NW
WASHINGTON DC
FROM: CMV
TO: STRICK
FORM: INTERNAL

<<IN ANY OPEN TRANSMISSION FOLLOW THE
ESTABLISHED CODES>>

DAYS UNTIL WE HAND YOU THE PRESIDENT 8
JIM:
YOUR PENCIL SCHEDULE NOW INK
FULL DETAILS FOLLOW

CMV
||||||||||||||||||||||||||||||||||||||||||||||||||||||||||||||||||||||||

10

AT TEN MINUTES before seven A.M., Bennis and I turned south onto LaSalle, heading in, back to the First District at the end of our tour. My town, Chicago. LaSalle is named for a French explorer who came through here in 1682. He is supposed to have taken one look at the place, recognized its potential, and said, "The typical man who will grow up here must be enterprising. Each day as he rises, he will exclaim, 'I act, I move, I push.'" Is that the real Chicago, or what?

My name is Susannah Maria Figueroa. I'm twenty-five, ten years younger than my buddy Bennis. He has ten years more than I have on the department, too, so he thinks he's my mentor. I don't mind that, most of the time.

We angled east and crossed the Chicago River on the Michigan Avenue Bridge, which is made of waffle steel. The car's wheels hummed. I was driving, at last. Bennis always wants to, but department rules say each partner does half the driving.

There was a collection of early cars from the second watch around the bridge footing, plus two fire department vehicles and an unmarked car from the ME's office.

"Activity," I said to Bennis. "Maybe a floater."

"Not our problem, thank God," Bennis said.

"Right. Headin' home."

In five minutes, I was easing the blue-and-white into a slot in the First District parking lot. Three minutes after that I was in the locker room and out of uniform.

We've got about twenty-five percent women in the CPD now, but except for a separate locker room, not much has changed. My locker was all of thirteen inches wide. I had glued a mirror the size of an average postcard to the inside. Now I took a look at myself.

People talk about bad hair days. Try wearing a saucer cap for eight hours. "Hat hair" with a vengeance. There was a groove all around the side and across the front. My hair usually looks like the coat of a black poodle that has stepped on a live wire. This was only a little worse.

It was also boring trying to fix it, so I quit. Spending a whole lot of time on cosmetic operations is boring. The upper half of my face stared back at me. How odd it is that people have immutable faces and you're stuck with one particular face, regardless of whether it really reflects the inner person or not. Inside, most of the time I feel like Clint Eastwood. On the outside I look half Cuban and half Irish and very short. From the inside I feel a lot taller than five feet two. When I was a child, for some reason, I thought I'd grow up to be a cowboy. A lot of girls, when they're very little, don't realize they're not ever going to grow up to be big, strong men.

Of course, you can grow up to be a cop.

When my thoughts turned to my ex-husband, Frank, I stopped looking at myself at all and slammed the locker door shut in disgust. It instantly bounced back open. It only closed properly if I gently lifted the sliding handle and eased it down into place. Finesse worked; force didn't. Wonderful! All I need is a locker that tries to hand me metaphorical advice for living.

I adjusted my sidearm under my civilian clothes and put on a jacket.

I'd been on first watch, eleven P.M. to seven A.M., for two weeks now. I didn't mind as much as most cops, and a whole lot less than most female cops, because of my home arrangements. My son and I live in my sister's house.

The most inconvenient was second watch, seven A.M. to three P.M., because then I was at work when my son JJ was in school, and what with having to leave home about six-thirty for work, I missed getting him ready for school and mostly saw him when I was too tired to enjoy him. You need a certain amount of energy to enjoy six-year-old boys. But today I'd get home in time for his breakfast, sleep while he was in school, and be up and ready to play with him when he got home. Then, an hour or so after he went to bed, I'd go to work.

Bennis was waiting for me when I left the women's locker room, his square brown face smiling.

"Want to wind down with a beer, Figueroa?" he asked. "C'mon over to the Furlough."

"Can't. I gotta help Sheryl get the kids up and off to school."

"I don't think you get enough fun."

"Jeez, you got that right, Bennis."

"I mean, far as I can tell, Suze my man, you work at home, and you work at work."

I looked at him seriously for a few seconds. "See, Bennis, maybe I want to be superintendent someday."

"You can't plan that kind of thing. It's all politics."

"Maybe you can't plan, but you can be ready. Someday they're going to need the first woman superintendent."

"Well, I'll tell ya, if it's you, you can make me first dep."

"Done. Oh, uh, Bennis—you know, this is just between you and me."

"You're my partner; my lips are sealed. Except for a beer. How about just one before you head home?"

"Can't. But thanks. We can't all be footloose and fancy free like you. Speaking of which, how's Yolanda?"

"Yolanda's history."

I laughed. We walked out of the building past five young, sleepy-looking cops.

"I kind of thought she would be. After all, you've been going out with her, what, three weeks? Getting bored again, Bennis?"

"She didn't have enough intellectual substance."

"That wasn't what you said at first."

"Well, I was dazzled by her big hair, big eyes, and long legs."

"Sounds like you weren't looking for intellectual substance."

"You don't at first, but after a while, you do. I want a woman who knows the difference between saki and sauternes, at least. Is that too much to ask?"

"No, Bennis." I patted his cheek. "Not for you. You'll find her someday. You deserve to."

11

I LEFT THE First District Station, located in the Central Police Headquarters at Eleventh and State, at 7:20 A.M. I cruised north in my very old Volvo, which I have owned for three years. The damn thing was painted a bright orange when I bought it and I'd never had the money to have it repainted. Or at least there'd been other uses for money. Because it puttered, I nicknamed it the Clockwork Orange.

I sputtered, ticked, and clattered into a parking spot. It's a good omen to find parking. Any parking. The fact that this spot was two and a half blocks from the house was not bad at all, considering Chicago. I didn't mind walking. But I was tired and in no mood for bullshit. If a mugger wanted to accost me, I'd shoot him.

I let myself in the back door with my key. My sister, Sheryl, was already starting coffee. "Hiya, babe," I said.

"Morning. I'm making waffles—special for JJ. How was work?"

I said, "Okay. Are the minnows up or shall I get them?"

"They're up, but you can prod them."

I went upstairs, checked that JJ was awake and dressing, spoke to Sheryl and Robert's younger daughter, Kath, who was still under the covers. "You are ten minutes away from disaster, Kath."

"Oh, yeah. Okay. Is it really morning?"

"Let's try for total reality, honey."

Then I went to the bathroom door, knocking softly so as not to bother my brother-in-law, Robert, who was probably still sleeping, in his and Sheryl's room. Just as well. He tended to wake up cranky. I spoke through the door to their older daughter: "Maria, breakfast's ready."

"I'm still washing."

"You can't kid me. You're looking at yourself in the mirror."

"Ooooohh."

"Kath has to get in there."

"I'm washing."

"Did you know that staring at yourself in the mirror causes your facial muscles to tighten up, reduces blood flow, and as a side effect produces huge numbers of horrible, ugly zits?"

"No, and I don't believe it."

"Would you believe that in five seconds I'm gonna shoot the door lock off with my service revolver?"

"That I believe!" Maria flounced out, wearing purple tights with a pink-and-white striped skirt, swinging her hair and at the same time giving me a wink. Maria, at eleven, was the Fashionable One. In a couple of years my sister is going to have her hands full of boy trouble.

I got to the kitchen about the same time as JJ, who was thrilled with the waffles. Maria was dieting unnecessarily. Another worry for Sheryl. JJ ate enough for everybody.

I said to Sheryl over the waffles, "Thanks, hon."

As I zipped JJ's outdoor jacket, I stopped for a second with the zipper halfway up. I could keep him home with me today. We could play with his collection of tiny cars, drive them under the coffee table and make jumps out of piles of magazines and vroom the cars up one side and into the air. JJ is at the perfect age for a human. He's past the learning-to-walk and learning-to-talk stage. At six, he's out in the world, but everything's still new to him. If humans could be one age for-ever, it ought to be six.

I finished zipping him up, kissed his nose, and sent him to the bus stop with the girls.

By the time I had shooed them all out the door to the school bus, Sheryl had poured my coffee. Sheryl herself had to leave for work. On the television, turned low in the back-ground, the local CBS affiliate was giving the weather. "Clear but cold" was followed by "the latest skirmish in the city coun-cil wars. Gene Cirincione's place in the city council is being temporarily filled by his associate George Banner while Ci-rincione serves time in federal prison—"

If people were dogs, Sheryl would be a golden retriever: energetic, alert, smart, pretty, loyal, but awfully trusting. I am not very trusting. Not at all. Sheryl was wearing a navy-and-white suit, with a blouse that had ruffles at the neck. She got up to turn off the television. It said, "The White House has an-nounced that the president and vice president will fly to Chi-cago next week to address the annual meeting of the American Bar Association. The vice president, who was formerly Illinois Senator—" She clicked it off.

"Now, Suze, don't drink too much coffee."

I smiled. Sometimes she tried to mother me. "I won't, hon. You look a little tired. Want to give yourself a day off?"

"Not today. It's crunch time."

"That project they switched you to?"

"Yeah. We're six weeks late on it. And it's for the navy. We have a one-million-dollar-a-day penalty contract hanging over our heads. Which is why I've been working overtime. If we don't get it tested by the middle of next week, I'll be working twelve-hour days."

"Oh, no. We'd have to hire a sitter. Or Robert might help—"

"No. Not Robert. He's too impatient."

"Well, let's not cross that bridge till we come to it."

"Bye-bye. You ought to get to bed. You look tired yourself."

"Yes, boss. Me for bed."

"Me for work."

100

SHERYL BIRCH DROVE her little red Geo around the curves of the access road into the SJR DataSystems driveway. She was not exactly late, but it was one minute before nine and the complex was so big she wasn't likely to get to her desk before ten after. She'd stay late to make up for it, of course. You did that kind of thing when you were working for Dean Utley. Plus, this was definitely *not* the week to be late.

SJR DataSystems was located between the exurban towns of Palatine, Inverness, and Barrington, on the very border of Cook County, which put it twenty-five miles northwest of the Loop. It didn't make sense for Sheryl to drive to work as a regular thing; ordinarily she commuted by rail. A company shuttle bus picked staff up at the station. But about twice a week, just to break up the predictability of the train trip, she drove. If and only if Robert didn't need the car himself. Half the time when she drove, she regretted it. The old saying "Chicago has two seasons: winter and road construction" had to have been coined by commuters.

From the street to the SJR DataSystems parking lot was about a quarter of a mile as the crow flies, but the driveway was so winding that it was twice that long. On either side of the drive was a deep ditch with water at the bottom that the employees called Utley's Moat. At some impressionable stage in his corporate development Dean Utley, computer whiz kid

turned mogul, had seen the park surrounding the linear parti-
cle accelerator at Fermilab in Batavia, west of Chicago, in the
midst of a huge prairie on which buffalo roamed. Utley had
wanted buffalo around the SJR DataSystems complex, but the
experts he brought in told him that since the grounds were
only a little over two hundred acres, he could not maintain a
breeding herd. He settled for deer. A small herd of beautiful
red deer grazed the grounds and kept the grass short. A simu-
lated Eden, Sheryl thought. How like Utley.

The SJR compound was fenced on all sides and cars were
admitted at the gate only, but the deer still had to be kept off
the interior drive. Deer can leap a seven-foot fence easily, and
in any case, Utley thought a high fence would look ugly.
Hence, the moat. In addition, there were three lines of nearly
invisible electrified wire along the inner side of the ditch on
both sides of the drive. These wires gave the deer a sharp, small
shock when they wandered near the road, and the deer had
learned to stay back.

The SJR DataSystems corporate compound was the size of
a small village—there were 3,100 people employed here—and
it included two manufacturing plants, one of them a large
building that produced hardware, including radio equipment
for police cars and control systems for aircraft. The smaller
building produced the data management products, certain
disks and other software. Packaging was off-site in Chicago
and many components were outsourced.

The heart of the complex was the Central Building. It was a
four-story structure shaped like an X, and it housed both management and R&D, about three hundred people. Sheryl was a
computer engineer and worked in the Central Building.

She found she had made it by 9:07, which was still late, but
not a whole lot.

"Mornin' Shurl," the guard said. It was Len today. For
some reason Len always mispronounced her name.

"Morning, Len."

He checked her name off the "expected" list on a hardcopy sheet on a clipboard, then entered it onto a monitor screen that displayed an "in the building" list and handed her the live badge she had left at the desk when she checked out last night.

101

IN THE MASTER Security office, a beep announced that an employee had entered the Central Building. Zach Massendate glanced up at the display board. As Sheryl clipped on her badge, a bright dot appeared on a video map of the first floor of the building. This dot carried a number code, identifying it as Sheryl Birch. Zach watched as it moved across the first-floor building plan to the elevator. The light blipped briefly on the second-floor map as the elevator passed the second floor, then appeared on the third floor as Sheryl got out. Procedures for the Pentagon could hardly be more cautious, which was reasonable. SJR did a lot of contract work for the Pentagon.

Zach watched as the dot paused at Sheryl's office door. She would be inserting her key card in her lock.

110

SHERYL ENTERED HER office and Zach turned back to his work.

After ten years at SJR, Sheryl had her own office and even her own window. She kicked back and punched the automatic hot pot. There was about a cup of water left in it from yesterday. She pulled an herbal tea bag out of her stash and turned on her keyboard and monitor. Access to the company mainframe was always at her fingertips. She picked up a pen. Pencils were not allowed in the complex because the graphite and binders could flake off, get into the air, and foul up the computers.

The screen came to life and said:

```
welcome to SJR DataSystems
login:
```

The machine was asking for her login ID, which had to be low-ercase, alphabetic or numerical, and not over seven characters. She typed:

```
sherylb
```

The screen said:

```
Password:
```

Since the system at this point would not let her correct what she typed by deleting, she was careful to get it right. She typed whoopee! on the keyboard, and although it did not "echo", nothing she typed appeared on the screen, the computer re-sponded:

```
System 6.7
@SJR DataSystems cc.23.a
@SJR DataSystems cc.71.d
news:
```

This told her there was some news for her. She typed:

```
# news
```

The screen responded:

```
new keyboard Mar 20 display room
```

She could go look at the new keyboard later. There was no other news, so the screen said

```
#
You have mail.
```

She decided to read her mail right away, too, so she typed:

```
$ mail
```

The screen brought up a couple of lines of assorted computer stuff and then said:

```
sheryl I have new puzzle Mar 20 utley
```

Sheryl made a face, raising her eyebrows and pursing her lips. Her boss was in most ways very hard to get to know. But he loved puzzles. Wooden take-apart puzzles. Plastic elephants to assemble. Knots of twisted metal pieces that you were supposed to separate. Ever since the time two years earlier when he had met her in the hall with a thing made of metal triangles which he said was very difficult, and she had taken it apart while they stood there, he had tried every new one he got on her. Sheryl supposed they were having some sort of competition. If they were, she was thirteen out of nineteen at the present moment.

She'd get to Utley later, maybe. She had work to do. She typed:

```
mail
<RETURN>
```

The screen said:

```
enter text
```

It brought up:

```
cc:
```

She typed:

```
utley
excellent sheryl
```

Time to work. Sheryl had been brought in on a project that was running behind. Several engineers like Sheryl, who had high enough security clearances, had been swept in to deal with the crunch. Sheryl was digesting a large amount of flight data reported back by sensors on the wings of a newly designed U.S. Navy plane—literally millions of numbers. She was working on a smart link direct to the Department of Defense. Once she gave her terminal the high-level SJR password, she was inside SJR's highest level. Once logged in, she was virtually inside the Department of Defense.

Her screen said:

```
run what job name
```

Sheryl's was **atmost**. She had invented this name for her part of the work and thought it was kind of cute, because the ultimate idea of the project was not to let the aircraft get off true when landing on a carrier deck in heavy seas with a rolling and pitching ship and the aircraft in high crosswinds. She was allowed at most one and one-half degrees off true before automatic correction.

Her fingers made little pounces at the keys. Symbols blinked into life on the screen.

Ah, God! she thought. *I love this.* It was so elegant, and so clean. *Can you believe they pay me for doing this?*

She could never have a job like her sister Susanna's. Being a cop, dealing with all the unpredictability of human beings, let alone the ugly side of it all. The blood and the emotions—

She typed:

```
atmost
```

Or thought she had. At the same instant she reached to push the pot away from her written notes and typed one-handed. She immediately realized that her little finger had hit a key on the upper right of the keyboard early in the word. She had written:

```
utmost
```

Sheryl was about to retype the word, but the screen began to scroll. As she watched, a list of subfiles appeared down the left side of the screen.

She was in somebody else's file.

```
advance·pay
ambient·h77
cashout·94
check·me
credite·ch
credit·xxx
enumera·ppm
finance·92
financi·al
global
h77cdc·92
h9
longhelp
longcash
markets·har
marknum·990
lucre·ftc
treasury·91
treasury·92
usbond
ustreas·92
zeroper·cen
```

Sheryl knew she should back out and bring up her own file. She hesitated uneasily. She had recognized a code for a major credit card company. It was strange that it should appear in this list.

SJR DataSystems probably provided them with software. But it still seemed unlikely.

She looked at the list and typed:

```
more cashout·94
```

The screen filled with gibberish.

```
MZá!RWR♦Rñş♦@Ç⅄JUZ⅂èɏ○╢╝┌T∞

Qakx∂∂ō┬┬Φⁿ#9>C

   Qö¥▄▓▐╦┬ ▀ ♣♥♥#♥5♥:♥L♥Q♥c♥h♥l♥£♥=♥ ▌♥t♥ſ♥▅♥♦♦>♦
M♦i♦⌠♦è♦Ē♦
◊♦▓▓╫╢◊♦╠╤♦□≥╤∾♦n♦!♣9♦d♦n♦x♦è♦⌐╫╝♦⌡♣╚♦ſ♦♦♦
♦♦/♦4♦H♦l♦q♦v♦æ♦┬╣♦╝♣╚♦±♦(<AF⟦r∂l⅄¥ó╞
```

#f¬

```
2annII=SFHuyuT0i0UAioo7885beX8895690&54*
%$8006544##$%#%$#
   a##FCIOY8GP865eae7iBG654CIio98  5765%*$-
(o7-9G45P(ub*(674i
   XR8^I%9700B89ENH8^*56DC8NB&O560v95PG^%b
547bE{G657pOEH^&^C
```

And on and on and on.

This was a *huge* file. From the gibberish, she knew it wasn't a text file. And from its sheer size, Sheryl knew it couldn't be executable. From the way the control characters were placed, it looked like a database.

It couldn't be read this way, it had to be decoded.

She probably *could* decode it. But she shouldn't.

Then again, there was something not quite right—

SJR had a few programs that could read pretty much any database. After a little thought, she decided to try a Novell database access program.

Suddenly the screen filled with a graphic. At the bottom was

    link data bases

and some names to click on. ATM, Mastercard, American Express. Fascinated, she picked one. The screen was filled with data. She paged down through it. One page said:

```
Cizek B     TF56FYO A&S 3/19/96 $44.95  CHICAGO   IL M
—           Vo7X83N Blo 3/19/96 $25.75  CHICAGO   IL B
Cizarla P   TRHEU44 MF  3/18/96 $10.02  CHICAGO   IL C
Cizmar O    VCO98BY L&T 3/19/96 $175.20 WINNETKA  IL M
Ciznere E   AABONUS Bri 3/19/96 $772.00 CHICAGO   IL F
—           URWJ75S Scu 3/19/96 $32.15  PARKF     IL R
—           TRXFO6Q A&S 3/19/96 $42.95  CHICAGO   IL B
Cizowski D  NO87DEE Mod 3/18/96 $12.95  CHICAGO   IL R
Cizkunas S  BI4SSOP MF  3/18/96 $99.99  MELRPK    IL F
Ckhowlok P  BIS7122 Bez 3/18/96 $85.00  CHICAGO   IL D
Ckhuj R     SPEEVOY MF  3/19/96 $67.50  CHICAGO   IL D
Claesson S  BDS9973 Row 3/19/96 $110.00 CHICAGO   IL C
—           BDS9973 Row 3/19/96 $98.95  CHICAGO   IL C
—           MF22912 A&S 3/19/96 $54.90  CHICAGO   IL C
```

```
—          BLZIML3 L&T 3/19/96 ⋕62.95  CHICAGO  IL C
Claey T    NCI7741 Ban 3/19/96 ⋕17.99  DOLTON   IL M
```

Sheryl stared astonished at the screen, her hands poised in midair over the keyboard. There was only one thing this set of data could be. It was up-to-the-minute data on the billing for a credit card company. There was a column with the customers' names, then a store code, the date, the amount, and the product code. In fact, it looked like S. Claesson had gone on a shopping spree on the nineteenth, and Sheryl would have bet her Geo that S. Claesson had bought a great bunch of clothes.

"I hope they cheered her right up," Sheryl muttered to herself. She paged down. The next page was much the same. It went on alphabetically. So did the next. Sheryl bit her lip.

What was even odder, the entries were for yesterday, with just a very few, probably late updates, from the day before. This was no work file. It was an up-to-the-minute report.

Sheryl reached for her herbal tea. Then she realized that her hands were shaking. She pressed them together for a few seconds, thinking hard.

SJR DataSystems didn't do this kind of work. Credit card companies bought their programs from SJR, and SJR would sometimes customize data management programs for them, but SJR itself didn't manage the systems or do billing or data entry, or anything else that she could think of that would make it necessary for them to have this kind of current, confidential information.

She clicked randomly on a person's name: George Fresonone.

The list vanished and the screen filled with data. George's bank withdrawals, his purchases, his tax payments—screen after screen. It scrolled until it ended with

```
analyze [y/n]
```

She typed y.

The screen filled with graphs: bell curves, cluster graphs.

One gave the probability that a person who ordered the magazines and newspapers that George Fresonone ordered would vote Republican in the next election.

My God, she thought, *what is this?*

111

THE DOT THAT represented Sheryl Birch went out of her office door. Was she heading for the bathroom? No. She only went halfway down the hall. Just getting coffee or water for tea, apparently. In Master Security, Zach Massendate shifted his attention to the upper-right corner of his board. There was the dot representing Howie Borke, heading into the room where they kept extra manuals, probably picking up material to take to the installation this afternoon. Howie was going to have his hands full today.

Zach was two floors and one wing away from Sheryl Birch. He was searching Cook County tax files, running a program to pull names of employees as well as certain other names Utley was interested in. Utley wanted expanded data on property owned by employees and their tax liabilities—did they own their homes or did they rent? If they owned them, were they mortgaged, and if so, how much of the mortgage had been paid off? Utley hadn't told Zach why he wanted them, but Utley was a genius as well as the boss, and this was a particularly critical time for SJR DataSystems. Zach was cybersearching vigorously. Zach was not a computer engineer. SJR DataSystems already had plenty of those. He was a very computer literate cyberinvestigator. For investigatory purposes, he used programs that had been set up for him by Utley or Howie or the whiz kids.

One entire wall of Zach's office mapped the complex of

buildings in the SJR DataSystems compound and carried the bright dots showing the locations of the employees.

When the phone call came in, Zach took the message, frowned, swore, then left his office and hurried down the corridor. Glen Jaffee was in his own office three doors down, studying long tractor-feed sheets of printout with alternating green and white bands.

"Good morning, Glen," Zach said. He shut the door behind him. He was wearing a blue blazer and gray slacks, with a white shirt and dark paisley tie.

"Morning, Zach." Glen gestured courteously to a chair.

Glen was dressed almost identically in a blue linen blazer with brass buttons, sharply creased gray slacks, and polished black shoes. Both men were in their late thirties. The larger of the two, Glen Jaffee, was a tall, muscular blond, a former basketball player who had not gone to seed. He spun his swivel chair to give Zach his attention. "Sit down."

"Too revved up to sit, Glen. Listen, they found Frieswyk."

"Uh-oh. Found him where?"

"Apparently right back here in Chicago. It was on the news. He drifted. They said something about the currents bringing him up the Chicago River."

"Right back home! No shit! Who the hell would have thought it?"

"Now, Glen. No need for profanity."

"You're entirely right, Zach. Anyhow, after all this time, what's left of him must look like Silly Putty."

"Well—obviously they identified him."

"Clothes, probably."

"Teeth, too."

"Right. But there's no usable evidence. There can't be. So there isn't any problem."

"I expect not."

They looked at each other for a few seconds. This was the worst possible time to have a glitch.

Glen said in a tight voice, "I mean, they wouldn't know

how far he'd come before he got to the Chicago River."

"No. But we didn't exactly prepare for this, Glen. You know what the boss says."

"I know, Zach. 'Accidents are events that happen to people who are inadequately prepared.'"

"He's not going to like this. We should have known about the currents."

"Do we have a trap in the medical examiner's office?"

"No. Not yet."

"Why not?"

"They're not fully computerized yet."

"Shit!"

"There's no need for scatological language, Glen."

"You're absolutely right, Zach. I meant to say that not being computerized was very old-fashioned of them. We'll just have to fix that, in case there's another time."

"Absolutely, Glen."

They studied each other for a couple of seconds. Zach said, "Well, we'd better get to the steering committee meeting. You know what the boss says."

"'Productivity pays off.' I know."

Glen said, "When shall we tell him about Frieswyk?"

They walked to the office door. "After the meeting. I'll E-mail him."

"Good thinking. He's happiest after the meetings." He went out first and said over his shoulder, "Push the door shut on your way out, Zach. Please."

"Sure thing, Glen."

"Thank you."

"You're welcome."

1000

JESUS DELGADO HATED autopsies, and this was worse than most. Frieswyk had been in the water a looooong time. The whole room smelled of rotten flesh. The room held twelve autopsy tables. There were four other bodies being autopsied on other tables. Delgado noticed that the other four procedures were being conducted on tables one, two, three, and four. His case, the body pulled from the Chicago River, was on table twelve. Even experienced forensic personnel found "his" body to be disgusting. Someone had once proudly told Jesus that the Cook County Institute of Forensic Medicine had ten thousand square feet of autopsy space. Frieswyk's body was making them use all of it.

Jesus had been working on the Frieswyk case for five weeks before he even knew Frieswyk was dead.

When Frieswyk first went missing, Deputy Superintendent Benton K. Rendell, chief of the Bureau of Investigative Services, had issued the word, which went to DiMaggio, commander of the Detective Division. DiMaggio passed the word to George Putnam, the commander of Area 1 Violent Crimes. The word was, "Get somebody on the Frieswyk case who can understand the job Frieswyk was doing. *Now!*" Putnam had chosen Jesus Delgado because he was not only a detective, but a computer-sophisticated college graduate who specialized in white-collar crime. Frieswyk, in Internal Auditing, had also been involved in paper trails. Putnam was not certain at the time whether this would be important, but his gut had told him it might be.

There had been a lot of media coverage of Frieswyk's disappearance, which meant that people called the department with leads—screwball leads, as often as not, like the one that said the Mud People who live in the tunnels off Lower Wacker Drive had got him. But several callers had been able to tell them about places Frieswyk typically went to drink or friends he hung out with.

So by the end of February, Delgado had done every bit of groundwork anybody could think of. Commander Putnam had a pile of paperwork seventeen inches high from Delgado, but no real leads at all.

As soon as Putnam got the call that Frieswyk's body had been found, he called Detective Jesus Delgado and put a rocket under him.

Therefore on this beautiful, clear, warm Friday noon in late March, a perfect day for taking children to the zoo or sitting at a sidewalk café drinking the first outdoor coffee of the season, Detective Jesus Delgado walked indoors, into the Cook County Medical Examiner's office on West Harrison. His triple job: first, and routine, observe the autopsy as detective in charge of the investigation; second, also routine, accept any materials in evidence that had to go to the lab and transport said materials to said lab, thus maintaining the chain of control over the evidence; and third, in Putnam's choice words, "clear the hell up who the fuck killed him." Understood but unspoken was, "And do it yesterday." Delgado suspected that this would be anything but routine. He'd been on the case five weeks now and it looked like a bitch. To top it all off, his usual partner, Sonnenfeldt, was out having prostate surgery.

This wasn't fair! Jesus wasn't used to this! He was a technical cop, a highly trained white-collar crime cop, not a body man.

To make it worse, the medical examiner in this case was a tiny woman named Dr. Sunny Chen. She couldn't be five feet tall. Her skin was a delicate ivory, and her black hair was cut square, with bangs. She was very pretty. Even with the autopsy table set at its lowest, it was too high for her. As she moved from one part of the corpse to the other, she kicked a little round stool with retractable wheels along the floor.

She photographed the clothed body from eight positions, saying to him during camera clicks, "Good morning." Click.

"I am Sunny Chen." Click. "This is the very, very hurry-up case, isn't it? You are the detective."

"Detective Delgado. Good morning, Doctor."

Delgado was staring at the horribly swollen purplish green tongue that protruded from the mouth of the dead Frieswyk. He felt that Dr. Chen was looking at him, and he glanced up, catching a flash of amusement in her eyes. He thought, *Hell, she knows this shit makes me sick!*

"Certainly this body has been in the water several weeks, Detective Delgado. See how the hair has sloughed off? See here?" She patted Frieswyk's head fondly. She wore plastic gloves, which made little slapping sounds.

Delgado leaned closer, well aware that she was teasing him. He pretended to take a close look at the horrid scalp. But he purposely unfocused his eyes and he didn't breathe until he had stood back again. As he did, he caught sight of Frieswyk's face. With its swollen tongue and hairless head, the face looked almost comical at first, but after a couple of seconds that impression changed. The pale, bloated cheeks and protruding tongue, the absence of eyebrows—all at once Frieswyk in death looked as if he had indeed seen the bottom of the lake and the end of life and was sickened. Besides that, though the lake water was cold, somehow Frieswyk looked *boiled.*

Chen pulled down her hanging microphone and dictated the beginning of the report:

"This forty-two-year-old Caucasian male is well nourished, weighs one hundred and seventy-one pounds, and is approximately seventy inches in length.

"Clothing. The body is received wearing a standard issue Chicago Police Department blue shirt, navy trousers, navy jacket, leather belt, leather holster for gun but no gun present, black socks, black shoes, and a cord tied around his left ankle."

She continued talking, while the diener, the morgue assistant, helped remove the clothing from the corpse. He unbuttoned the jacket and the shirt underneath. Sunny Chen cut the pants, which Delgado saw were dry on the upper side of the body but still damp on the back. Frieswyk had been on his back in a refrigerator since he was found. She cut along the place where there once must have been a sharp crease in the pants before weeks of soaking in water obliterated it. "In my opinion we lose less of the trace evidence if we cut the clothing instead of trying to wrestle it off the corpse," she explained to Delgado. "Many medical examiners think otherwise. But it stands to reason if you drag the pants down, say, over some wound, you're likely to get the blood from the wound all smeared down the inside of the pants. And if it's ever important to you to know later where the pants were in relation to the wound—say you want to know whether the man was standing or sitting when his leg was struck—you will have messed it up. Naturally, I always cut through undamaged parts of the clothes, to save the evidence of damage." She sliced all the way up to the waistband. The pants fell flat onto the table, revealing marble white legs with bluish patches and some green discoloration of the insides of the thighs around the crotch. She stepped on the switch that turned the microphone on.

"Underneath," she continued into the microphone, "he is wearing a sleeveless white undershirt and red boxer-style undershorts with white polka dots. The knees of the trousers are extensively abraded, but not torn. The right elbows of the jacket and shirt are worn through, but not torn." The boxer shorts showed an immense bulge in front, and Delgado steeled himself for the next part of the process. She cut away the shorts in the same way as the pants, revealing huge, swollen testicles the size of grapefruits.

"Soft parts swell," she said to Delgado. "The tongue, the testicles—"

"Uh-huh."

Dr. Chen and the diener lifted the body and the diener slid the clothes out from underneath. He laid them on a large paper sheet. As they moved the body, foul gases gurgled and a stench rose in the air. Delgado's eyes crossed as he tried not to gag.

Dr. Chen said to the microphone, "External examination:

The hair is largely absent, with some patchy areas of medium brown hair over the right ear. The irides . . ."

When she finished with the external examination, she said, "We'll go through the motions of taking the fingerprints, Detective Delgado. But it's pretty pointless; look here."

"What?"

"After a body's been in water a few days, you start to see something like this." She picked up the left hand and turned it back and forth. "See, the outer layer of the skin on the hands has sloughed off. We call this maceration."

"Uh-huh. I noticed."

"But, as I have said, we'll go through the motions." She was not quite enough of a tease to ask Delgado to help with the fingerprints. And anyway, he wasn't wearing gloves. She and the diener took prints that looked to Delgado like totally useless smudges. But it didn't matter, really. It wasn't a case of trying to identify an unknown corpse. They knew who this was. It was Frieswyk, with his name and unit designator still pinned to his shirt. And just in case somebody had switched clothes, Jesus would later confirm his identity from his dental records.

She picked up a syringe and, to Jesus' horror, slid it into Frieswyk's eyeball. She drew out fluid. "You can often get drugs or ethanol responses from the fluid in the eye," she said pleasantly.

"Uh-huh."

"Now take a look at this."

She patted the abdomen of the body in a way that struck Delgado as entirely too familiar and too cheerful. *Pat! Pat!* Stop slapping the guy, he wanted to say, but instead he said, "What? I don't see anything."

Pat! Pat! Pat! "See how hard this is? This man wasn't very fat, but he's got a little layer around the midriff. And it's starting to get firm and waxy."

"I thought that was just because he's dead."

"No, this is adipocere. Literally, it means fat wax. It's

almost like candle wax in texture. Adipocere helps preserve a body once it forms. That, plus the lack of oxygen in cold lake water. Did you know the water near the bottom of the lake stays at thirty-three degrees?"

"Oh. That's—um, good, I guess."

"Maybe, but the point is, it takes adipocere a month or more to form, depending on conditions. The fat hydrolyzes slowly, you see. I've got to check some sources. We can pin this down pretty closely, I think."

"He went missing five weeks ago."

"Oh, really? That's consistent. Well, my guess is he went in the water very soon after he disappeared." She cast the corpse a long, thoughtful look. "I still want to do some reading on it."

Delgado was valiantly breathing through his mouth, trying to ignore the smell. If it was this bad now, what would happen when she cut into the corpse?

Sunny said cheerfully, "Problem here is, if the body has been in water for several weeks, it gets chemically more and more similar to the water it's in each day that goes by. Osmotic pressure tends over time to leach the salts out. Adipocere is a help, in that way. Forms a barrier."

Delgado forced himself to focus on the body. Somebody might ask him about it later—God forbid it should be the chief of detectives!—and he'd better have at least one or two clear memories. Otherwise—also God forbid—they might think he'd kept his eyes closed the whole time. Which, God should only grant that he could.

Sunny Chen said, "Lake Michigan is going to help us out here, you know. You don't get a lot of fish nibbling at the body parts. No crabs, no sharks."

Delgado looked at the bloated testicles, thought about nibbling fish, and winced.

"Coho salmon," she went on, "of course. But they stay out in deep water. Even in winter, I think. The lack of damage just might suggest that he wasn't out deep. Also, if he was out deep, he probably wouldn't have ever come in."

"Uh-huh."

"He floated near the bottom, I think. Now look at the hands. See where the tendons over the knuckles are scraped right down to the bone?"

"Uh-huh."

"Bodies usually float along the bottom sort of stomach down, with the rump higher than the head and the hands dragging. The head is heavy and quite dense, you see. So he didn't scrape his knuckles in a fight. If we had the skin of the hands, it would tell us even more, but of course it's probably somewhere out there in Lake Michigan."

Jesus Delgado momentarily pictured skin floating around in the lake "out there," but the idea made him choke, and he quickly pictured his wife playing checkers with his daughter, instead.

"There's a bit of scraping on the forehead, too. See?"

"Absolutely."

"Now all this rubbing on the elbow—remember there was a lot of the fabric of the uniform rubbed off?—I'd say that was when the body washed up against something. I'm going to give you a sample of this skin here. It almost looks like it has little pieces of something. Could be concrete. I hope it's not sand. Sand is everyplace in the lake. Although there must be some local differences—different deposits. I'm sorry to say I'm not an expert on that, Detective. Ah. Might be a fleck of paint, here. Can't quite tell. Golly, I hope you get something from that, Detective Delgado."

She also took some tissue samples from the forehead and knuckles. Delgado looked at his watch. They had been at this forty-five minutes already, and they weren't even inside the body. How long could he stand it?

She cut the cord that had been tied around Frieswyk's ankle and handed it to him to take to the lab.

"Thank you."

Sunny Chen turned the body over onto its stomach with the help of the diener. The throat of the corpse made a strangling sound. Delgado knew it was gases escaping, but he jumped involuntarily. He could tell that she noticed.

Low on the back of the head was an area a few inches square that was more discolored than the rest of the greenish white surface. Sunny Chen said, "Aha!" She took more photographs.

Delgado growled to himself. He wondered if she spent a lot of time reading Arthur Conan Doyle. Aha, indeed!

The diener helped her turn Frieswyk onto his back again. She dictated her external findings. Then she took a scalpel, made a quick, flashing slice across the top of the skull, and with a movement like a man stripping off a wet bathing suit, pulled all the skin of the face down from the skull.

"Ehhhhh!" Delgado said.

Sunny Chen was unmoved. She said, "Looks like a tiny fracture here, Detective Delgado. See? On the nose?"

"I see."

"We've already got the X-rays, of course."

She dictated the findings from the front of the skull. Then the diener held the body on its side, and in another quick move, she peeled the back of the skull. She dictated:

"Externally—a fracture of the left midoccipital region begins six centimeters above the base of the skull and extends inferiorly to the foramen magnum. Fracture extends through the inferior nuchal line, with many small, radiating fractures—" She stopped the recorder and said, "Here's your cause of death, Detective Delgado." She pushed gently on a mushy depression of bone at the base of the skull. Delgado could see bone fragments move as she did so.

"What? A head wound?"

"You hit a person here hard enough, you paralyze the brain stem, maybe mash the skull pieces into the top of the spinal cord. Even if he wasn't put into the water, he probably wouldn't breathe again."

"Oh," said Delgado, almost without realizing that he was thinking aloud. "So it was quick?"

She smiled at him, and Delgado felt that for once something he had said pleased her. "Hit on the back of the head, fell forward onto his nose. As instant as death ever gets, Detective."

She picked up an electric circular saw to cut into the skull.

An hour and a half later, Sunny Chen said, "Now you have samples from the mouth, trachea, esophagus, both chambers of the heart, bronchii and lungs, and that ought to tell you something on the drowning question. But personally, I'd say he was dead when he went into the water. Let's see what else we've got."

The belly, to Delgado, was a mess of decomposition. The intestines were distended with gas and in some places had perforated from decay and started to turn to mush. The smell was ghastly.

Sunny Chen remained sunny. "Anyplace there are bacteria already in the body—before death, I mean—you get the fastest decomposition after death. And the intestines are just *full* of bacteria, of course. *Teeming* with bacteria. Did you know, Detective Delgado, that bacteria help us digest our food?"

"Uh, no." He figured he'd skip dinner.

"And the beneficial bacteria even produce vitamins of the B-complex. That's one of the reasons you can have deficiencies of the B vitamins after a long course of antibiotic therapy. Kills the good bacteria along with the bad."

I wonder how I managed to digest my meals all these years without knowing that. Delgado watched as Chen pawed through the intestines. He was trying to focus on the end of his nose, not the body.

He said, "Take a lot of samples. Take twice what you usually take. Three times. The department wants—" How should he put this? "The department wants no stone left unturned."

"At your service, Detective. And toxicology samples? Whatever blood we can get? Urine. Probably you want more than usual, if you plan to run every test on earth. Drugs? Ethanol? You'll be wondering if he was drugged before he died. Complete drug screen, of course? Is that right, Detective Delgado?"

"Yes, Doctor."

"Anything else? Any unusual or specific drugs?"

"None we know about. But hold whatever samples might be appropriate for testing later if we get a lead on a possibility."

After another half hour, Jesus was relieved to see her step back, slip her gloves off, and slap them into a wastebasket.

"I'll have the written protocol faxed to you by this afternoon or tomorrow morning," she said.

"Oh. That's great."

"I'll put a rush on it. I know this case is very important to you."

"To all of us."

"A fellow officer. I understand. It must be hard for you."

"Thank you."

"Or, if you want, you could come back here this afternoon. I ought to have it done by four or so." Her dark eyes were laughing at him; Delgado was certain of it, even though her face was serene.

"No. Thanks, the fax will be just fine."

1001

HOWIE BORKE LEFT his office and walked down the hall toward Utley's command center. Howie was twenty-eight and second-in-command at SJR DataSystems. He wore Levi's and a white turtleneck. This labeled him "creative," he thought.

He joined the tail of a line of men, all wearing suits and ties, also heading toward Utley's office.

At ten-thirty every Friday morning, they came from all over the compound, from Product Development, from Research, from Physics, from Master Security, even one from Transport—fourteen men whom Utley called his "steering committee." Six of the fourteen were computer engineers. The other SJR employees believed these fourteen were Utley's particular friends, which was an insult to their capabilities, or a kind of think tank, which was a compliment.

Howie looked like a tallish imp, with upturned eyebrows, big ears, a sharp nose, and quick gestures. He was by far the most brilliant of Utley's cadre of very bright young men, an aging *Wunderkind* or a grown-up juvenile delinquent, depending on how you looked at it.

Howie as a child had been an awkward loner. His silhouette looked like an elongated hexagon. Large ears stuck out at the top. His elbows always flapped out at his sides, even when he held his hands down at his thighs. And at the bottom of the silhouette, his feet toed out, unusually big for a child.

Howie's mother was named April Tompkins. His last name, Borke, came from his father, who had said good-bye and wandered off when Howie was eighteen months old.

April Tompkins was a pretty, blowsy, kindly soul, who liked to wear pink and yellow and light blue, which she called "cheerful colors," but she had a very hard time planning more than an hour or two ahead. The kitchen accumulated used dishes, empty cans, TV dinner wrappers, empty potato chip bags, and dirty stainless steel and plastic utensils, until she couldn't stand it anymore and then she'd clean it up and start over. Her savings account at the local bank rarely went over $99 before she took the money out for some impulse purchase. It seemed she couldn't think of herself as somebody with savings in three digits. She would impulsively buy little Howie an expensive pair of jeans and forget that all his shirts had holes.

And she had an enormous weakness for men. She simply could not believe evil of any man. One after another took advantage of her, stayed for a couple of days or a couple of months, living and eating off of her waitress earnings, and then simply walked away. Howie was angry when they did this, but

April always had an excuse for the man. "He just couldn't settle down," she'd say. Or, "He had kids in Wichita. Sure he'd want to go back to them." In her eyes, they were all fine people. Just troubled.

Howie was supposed to stay in his bedroom at night and not listen to the lovemaking going on in the next room.

In 1980, when he was thirteen, his mother had moved to California with visions of gold and instead discovered that the only jobs she could get were hooker or waitress. She picked waitress, and she waited tables from six A.M. to two P.M., through the lunch hour, then held a second job in the evening as hostess at a steak house. She was on her feet twelve hours a day. Most of the time when she was home, she slept or entertained male friends.

In California they lived at the end of a long gravel driveway. The gravel ran out about thirty feet before it got to the house, and the driveway became a kind of grayish packed earth. It ended at a carport that consisted of an aluminum roof held up by three aluminum poles on one side and attached to a medium-sized pale yellow mobile home on the other. They were not far from Silicon Valley, the place that midwifed the semiconductor in the fifties, the microprocessor in the sixties, and the personal computer in the seventies.

Howie started spending a lot of time in school. Not on classwork and not in after-school sports. Howie was staying to play with the computers. When school was closed, he went to Radio Shack stores and played with the TRS-80s as long as the store owner would let him.

Howie discovered computer bulletin boards. As a former phone phreak—a telephone hacker who could make a local call and slip into long-distance lines and tour the world in cyberspace, talking to phreaks in Germany, or the Aikin Building at Harvard, or a high school in Toronto, paying only pennies—he soon discovered pirate boards. The users shared advice on how to enter systems; they shared pirated software with fellow users, which they downloaded without paying for it.

Howie loved hacking and frequently spent thirty hours at a stretch at his keyboard, living on pizza and Dr. Pepper. The challenge of hacking was enough; a successful hack, getting into some protected system, was all the reward he needed.

One day, rummaging through the cybertunnels of the local phone system, he came upon the loop line, a number used for testing by telephone company repairmen. With this he played pranks on one of his mother's many boyfriends. He switched the boyfriend's number with that of a local pediatrician, so that the man got calls in the night from parents with teething children, vomiting children, children who wouldn't go to bed. When the man complained to the phone company, Howie intercepted the call, promised to fix the line, and gave him the number of a local fraternity.

On bulletin boards, he traded illicitly discovered codes. He got into MCI and filched phone numbers that had been discontinued but not disconnected.

He got into military computers—the National Security Agency chain, NASA's Jet Propulsion Laboratory, CERN, which was the research lab doing high-energy physics in Geneva, Anniston Army Depot, Lawrence Berkeley Labs, Lawrence Livermore, NORAD, Fermilab in Illinois, Redstone Missile Command, and the Air Force Systems Command Space Division in El Segundo.

Howie learned COSMOS, a d-base program that local telephone companies used for virtually everything: billing, scheduling service calls, cabling, and extension plans. He got into directory assistance and screwed it up, routing calls to himself so he could give funny answers. A phone user would call, thinking he was reaching a pizza delivery store, and Howie would answer, "Please call back in thirty minutes. We have to evacuate temporarily to let Acme Exterminators finish. They're using PHUX49, which is too toxic for humans to breathe." Then he'd yell to an imaginary person off-stage, "Hey, Guido, don't forget to cover up the pepperoni!" and hang up.

He had a whole series of favorite businesses he liked to

answer for: sewer rooting companies, ladies' underwear stores (he invented a pervert group that met there on Wednesdays), adult bookstores, which he answered, "Sergeant Caulkins. Who is this?"

With his computer and enough information, he could give himself sysop privileges in a company. Then from home he'd ask for a system status report. The company would cheerfully tell him the names of the users on the system. From these, he could spy out their passwords. He would get on a company line and claim that there had been an intruder and that the company was issuing new passwords and needed the person's current password so as to eliminate it. This would give him a usable password, and one which the legitimate user wouldn't be likely to use thereafter. The method was especially good with people who didn't use their passwords often or who were on a list of people on loan to some other company.

Using telenet, a computer-linking system, he could access computers all over the country.

Howie was not caught for any of his hacking. He used a gateway—in the 1980s it was GTE Sprint—so that he could call through several long-distance systems to cover his tracks. Later, he used McDonnell Douglas' Tymnet, which gave him computer access in eighty nations. By the late 1980s he could get in through Tymnet and link to almost anyplace in the United States, hiding any trace of where he was calling from.

His sophistication in intrusions increased. So did his computer skills as he started college. He hacked his way into Optimis, a Defense Department database. He got source code—always a goal of industrial spies, and therefore carefully guarded—for colleges and corporations.

He got into Arpanet, which handled the military computer network. He got into USC by changing the gatekeeping program on their VMS operating system, and into SPAN, a network operating on Digital computers and run by NASA. But he could not enter the CIA, because it wasn't on any public network and had no direct link to the outside world.

He'd try for superuser status when entering a system, and sometimes after a successful hack he'd leave behind an annoying bug. One was "Hi! I've entered your system. My name is TRICHOGRAMMA. Look it up." If they did, they found trichogramma to be a beneficial insect—in other words, a harmless bug.

But at the beginning of his second year of college, Howie fell prey to a serious need for money.

Howie conceived a hacker's delight. By modem he got himself into the database of a major national mail order company. With access to their computers, he ordered their suppliers to deliver certain supplies to a storage space he rented. He received turtleneck shirts, hiking boots, bathing suits, chinos, denim jackets, boxer shorts, socks, socks, and more socks, raincoats, hooded jackets, vests, down jackets, polo shirts, even neckties, which he then retailed to his fellow college students for twenty cents on the dollar.

Howie lived very nicely for a year and a half, in a luxurious off-campus apartment, and was himself very well, but casually, dressed.

Meanwhile the company and the FBI had been tracing him. It took months. His tracks were well covered, but the company was canny enough not to inform the suppliers to stop shipping to him. Instead, they let the drain go on while the authorities sniffed after the thief.

Howie was caught at the storage unit with the goods.

Fortunately for Howie, he was detected in 1983, just before the 1984 enactment of the Computer Fraud and Abuse Act. The statute made unauthorized entry into a computer for the purpose of stealing $5,000 or more a felony. Howie could have spent ten years in prison. Instead, he went to the county jail for sixty-three days. While he was in jail, he got an inquiry from Dean Utley. Would he like a job?

He was just the kind of guy Dean Utley looked for.

Howie paused in the doorway of Utley's office, conscious that he was the last to arrive. Utley turned to him, gave him the patented Utley two-second pause, and then said to the group, "Ah! My dedicated processors. Sit down. We've got to get this done quickly today."

In more than a decade of association with Utley, Howie had never felt at ease with the man. But what the hell, the company was extremely profitable, and it was going to be more so. You couldn't have everything.

The steering committee sat down quickly. Utley remained standing where they could all see him. He had heavy shoulders and slender legs, and he walked with a quick, quiet stride. His face was broad. His hair was coarse and curling, cinnamon colored, contrasting with flat, blue eyes. His hands were big, with thick fingers sprouting cinnamon-colored hairs on the backs.

"This is the moment we have been waiting and working for," he said softly, making everybody strain to hear him. "We are now in the countdown. A week from now, we will be—" he paused "—preeminent." He let the word hang, staring from one man to the next with his pale eyes.

Howie watched Utley, reading the signs of elation. In fifteen years, SJR had grown from a tiny computer parts business housed in a pole barn to a giant nearly the size of Motorola, almost entirely due to Utley. SJR DataSystems did eight billion dollars' worth of business a year and growth had not slowed down.

Utley now positioned himself in front of his bank of monitors, which provided a constant moving background of varying shapes and colors. Twenty monitors wide and four high, it included green screens, black-and-white, amber, and color. Four continuously ran CBS, NBC, ABC, and CNN. One ran PBS. One was permanently trained on the gatehouse at the entrance of the SJR complex. Sixteen covered the eight back and eight front doors of buildings in the complex. Security had the same views, of course, but Utley liked to know what was going on. Four eavesdropped on ongoing computer work of some of Utley's development people in other parts of the building, cursors winking busily along. Five were running colorful new graphics for the computer animation of SJR's latest virtual reality products. The heat generated by all the monitors was sucked out through ceiling vents and fresh air was pumped in through floor vents behind the monitors.

Having waited long enough to build suspense, Utley said, "The `cutworm` program is a go."

There were murmurs of approval and a couple of men said, "*Yes!*" But the tension notched up, too. Howie felt it, and he knew the others did. There was no slouching in the chairs, as there sometimes was at these meetings. Dorothy had left a large tray of espresso, cups, and whipped cream on the table, and no one had reached for them. John Carstairs chewed on his upper lip. Henry DeLusk, who usually fidgeted when he was not allowed to smoke, sat stone still.

Utley said, "Starting from now, no days off, including Saturday and Sunday, until the culmination. No person, and no company, has ever attempted anything like `cutworm`. It is the ultimate cybernetic killer application. No organization has ever been so bold. But that's in part because no organization has ever had the ability—the talent, the experience, and the courage all in one place. We have. As I said, we are now into the countdown. From this point on, there is no turning back. For any of us."

Utley let another three seconds go by.

Utley clapped his hands and several of the men jumped.

"Zach! Henry! Report."

Tensely, Henry said, "Zach?"

"I've spent all week expanding the backgrounds on our employees, under Henry's direction," Zach said. "Particularly tax records, property ownership, outstanding debt—"

"Good," Utley said.

Henry DeLusk asked, "Are there any other fields you specifically want us to query?"

"Finish the ownership stuff. Then go to loans and try to

root out any financial problems. Find any weak links. After that, retail purchases. When they buy, what do they buy? When they go to a restaurant, where do they go? When they go on vacation, where do they go? Do they buy on time? Do they have unpaid bills?"

Henry DeLusk had done jail time. As a young man and computer hacker, he had broken into the Quad Cities' 911 system. He'd had the misfortune to be twenty-one at the time and had been tried as an adult. He said to Utley, "I assume you want me to concentrate first on people who are in the know on cutworm and work down from there?"

"Right, but work down fast. We want the pressure points on everybody, not just the insiders—*les innocentes*, too. If we suddenly need to know something in order to deal with one of our own, I don't want to be fumbling through raw data to find it."

"Yes, sir."

"As I've said before, it's not the hardware or the software that can trip you up. It's the meatware." He picked up a cup. Took one sip. "Now. Glen, report?"

Howie saw DeLusk and Zach relax. Howie only became more tense. He knew Utley would get to him soon now.

Glen said, "Yes, sir. I've been working part-time at the Bierstube at the Stratford Hotel for four weeks now. Ever since we got the finalized itinerary from the veep. I work six days a week in the kitchen, four hours a day. Four to eight, evenings, Tuesday through Sunday."

"And they're used to you?"

"Oh, yes."

"Accustomed to seeing you come and go?"

"Absolutely."

Utley nodded. Howie glanced at John Carstairs, knowing he'd be next. Carstairs, now thirty, was head of the Consumer Products Division. As a nineteen-year-old, Carstairs had been arrested by the FBI for breaking into the Pentagon shipping computer—over the phone lines, not physically—and divert-

ing army automotive equipment from Fort Drum to an auto
dealer in Apalachicola. The dealer paid Carstairs forty cents on
the dollar for the stuff—more than the normal fence would
pay—and still made out like a bandit. Carstairs had driven a
good bargain with him because, as he had told him honestly,
"Six keystrokes and the stuff goes someplace else."

Unfortunately for Carstairs, some hacker enlistee got onto
it. On the other hand, Carstairs' parents were able to make a
partial restitution deal. Carstairs did twelve months of community service.

"Now, John," Utley said, "you have the product?"

"I have leads on several types of product. But I have to
know the Bierstube menu to know definitely what we need."

"I suggest you get hold of three or four likely items."

"But—"

"We wouldn't want to be held up at the last minute because
you couldn't get something, would we?"

Carstairs sat up. "Uh—no, sir."

Howie braced himself. He was next.

"And—Howie," Utley said. "What about `nematode`?"

"We're moving in this afternoon."

"I know that much, Howie," Utley said softly. "Would you
care to expand on that?"

"The hardware is on pallets in back of the Chicago Police
Department near their parking lot. The ceilings are out in the
dispatch center. I should be there right after lunch, and I'll sit
on them until they're done."

"No, Howie, don't just sit on them. Push them."

"Yes, sir. The floors go out tonight in dispatch. The hardware moves in there tomorrow. But I have the control room
entirely wired as of yesterday, and I'm going to finish the
hookup of the control units there today."

"We shouldn't be doing this at the very last minute."

"I know. Our man in the CPD said he had it all greased for
us."

"Well, he was an optimist."

"And a zipperhead. But I'll have it in time."

"Howie. In three days, *all* the glitches have to be out of the system."

"Yes, sir."

"By the day after tomorrow, I want access to everything: personnel records, crime reports, and the AFIS machines."

DeLusk said, "What's AFIS?"

Howie said, "The Automated Fingerprint Identification System." To Utley he said, "We get that the minute we hook up. No problem."

"And suppose they notice what you're doing, Howie?" De-Lusk said.

Howie took a breath. "They won't. The poor dumb cops won't know what's hit them."

Utley said, "They'd better not." He stared into the center of the group, cueing them that he was addressing them all. "We are on the threshold of what we've worked for all these years. The president arrives a week from tomorrow. I say that we are on the threshold, because we are *becoming*, we have not *arrived* yet. After next week, we will be unstoppable."

Howie watched Utley, and his doubts faded. His fears vanished, and it seemed, in his imagination, that he could see a bigger world than before. Utley must have noticed Howie's mood, because he said, "Howie, you're the one on the firing line today. You've got to do this alone. Are you ready for it?"

Howie said, "Yes!" And instantly he knew he meant it. He felt a surge of enthusiasm and confidence. *My bandwidth has doubled*, he thought. *This is going to work.*

"Scared, Howie?"

"No! I can't wait," he said. "Let's go for it."

"Why, sure, Howie," Utley drawled. "Be all you can be."

UTLEY SHUT THE door after the steering committee left and smiled to himself. It had been a short meeting. Howie had to leave to get to the police department headquarters, and Utley hurried the rest of them out. He believed in being a friend to his staff, but somebody had to be in charge. He considered himself a nice guy who just had to be tough at times.

He was conscious that his employees—his non-steering-committee employees—didn't like him much, even though they respected him. Or actually, it wasn't quite that they didn't like him. They were puzzled by him. His quiet courtesy made them believe that he must be a very nice person, underneath, but they never felt that they got to the underneath part. They might even wonder if there was one. Good.

It was good to keep people guessing.

The steering committee was another thing entirely. They really appreciated him. Partly, they had to. Where else would they get jobs like these, jobs that paid big and gave scope to their talents? Partly, they were able to appreciate *his* special talents.

Utley glanced up at his wall of monitors. Like Zach, he had a screen that identified the location of employees, and he watched for a few seconds as the steering committee members scattered back to their offices. Then his gaze moved to one of the monitors in the upper middle, one of the ones that appeared to be turned off. It was in fact the eye for a hidden videocamera, trained on this room. He walked closer and pushed the eject button under the screen. Quietly, the mouth of the machine opened and a videotape slid out. Utley picked a self-stick label from a sheet, attached it to the tape box, and wrote: ST. COMM. MTG. 3/20.

HOWIE BORKE'S DESTINATION was the communications room on the second floor of the Chicago Police Department. Communications was in turmoil.

The executive offices on the fifth floor should have been a haven of peace and deliberation, but they weren't.

Superintendent Gus Gimball felt like he was sitting on a nest of yellowjackets. It was Friday noon and he could see there wasn't any chance of going out to eat lunch. What he wanted to do, at *least*, was send somebody out for a bag of potato chips and eat chips all afternoon, but he knew what his wife would say about that. He thought of not telling her, but as she often said, "You can fool me and maybe you can fool your doctor, but can you fool your body?"

But, oh, how he loved potato chips!

He resolutely put food out of his mind.

Gimball was a medium-tall black man, slender, and somewhat stooped. Now in his late fifties, his hair was graying at the temples, adding to a professorial appearance; he had never looked like a cop, always more like a scholar. And his cast of mind was the same. He was introspective, too introspective sometimes for the job. Quite often, he wished he had more time to think, that he wasn't pushed for the quick response or the hasty answer.

"Got a minute, boss?" Ray Moses, Gimball's ADS, slipped into the office.

"Just about one minute, Ray."

"I'll make it short. Benton K. Rendell, chief of detectives, the one and only, himself, in person, would like to see you," Ray Moses said as sententiously as he possibly could. It wasn't that Moses disliked Rendell. Gimball had appointed Rendell chief of detectives, and both Moses and Gimball respected the man, but they couldn't help being annoyed by Rendell's view that the Detective Division was the only real, skilled, ~~and~~ im-

portant part of the Chicago Police Department. Gimball had
come up through the Detective Division himself, and he was
nevertheless able to admit that patrol and other areas were legitimate police functions. Patrol to Rendell was like plumbing,
necessary but without glamour.

"Okay. But I don't have much time. Heidema and Withers'll be up here in ten minutes."

"I'll push Rendell along. I'll come in and remind you if he's
here more than five minutes."

"Three minutes."

"Sure thing."

"Hey, Ben," Gimball said when Rendell came in the door.

"Hiya, boss."

"I'm in a huge rush, Ben. What do you have for me?"

"We found Frieswyk."

"Oh." Gimball knew from Rendell's tone of voice that the
news wasn't good. "Been missing a long time," he said.

"Five weeks."

"I can't remember a time we actually *lost* an officer. And
I've been here twenty-seven years. 'Lost in the line of duty,'
sure. Suicide. Even bar fights."

"But never just vanished. I know."

"Tell me about it."

"He turned up in the Chicago River."

"What? You mean he was dumped there?"

"I doubt it. The lake flows into the river "

"Couldn't he have fallen in and gotten snagged on something?"

"I don't think so. There's a lot of water flow, plus ship traffic, prop wash, all that kind of shit. It'd jiggle him loose. No, I
don't think so."

"You think he was dumped in the lake and drifted back into
the river?"

"Yup. The problem is, it could have been from almost anyplace."

"Such as?"

"Who's to know?"

"Who's to know? Ask somebody! Ask the Lake Michigan Federation. Ask people who research the Lake Michigan basin. I know the University of Michigan was doing an analysis a couple of years ago. They had a ship called—um—the *Mysis*, taking samples all up and down the lake. Ask the EPA. They were doing a study about how pollutants moved around."

"We'll do that. Sure."

"Go on the assumption that he went in someplace the day he disappeared and see if they can trace it back. Draw a probability line backward."

"I know, boss, but there's a lot of lake out there."

"So, you've seen the body?"

"Yes." His voice told Gimball what the body looked like.

"What happened to him?"

"We need the autopsy. I lit a fire under them, as much as you can with Abelander, you know. But it looks to me as if he's been in the water a long time."

"Drowned?"

"There's a dent at the base of the skull. No, I don't think he drowned. He was hit and then dumped. Another thing—"

"What?"

"There was a cord around his ankle. Tied tight. Ordinary granny knot. No double clove hitch shit. About seven, eight inches of cord and then a frayed place. Either they tied something rough like a cinder block to his ankle and it wore through under water, or the cord was defective before he went in the water."

"Lab have it?"

"The ME's office will send it over. Might get something from the type of cord. Might get something from the type of knot."

"And that's it, Ben?"

"So far."

"It doesn't make sense. He wasn't into anything sensitive."

"He was three months post-divorce. Some ill feeling. Plus,

there was a problem with a nephew. Kid borrowed money, didn't pay it back. Family trouble. That kind of thing. Kid wasn't in town February fourteen, though."

Gimball said, "I don't buy that his wife would crack him over the head and pitch him into the water. Didn't you say she was a tiny woman? What do you know about her?"

"Ex-wife. She's about five feet. He was five ten. They've been separated more than a year. She's got a new boyfriend, but my investigator, Delgado, says she absolutely did not meet the new guy until after the divorce. No monkey business. It wasn't exactly a friendly divorce, but not as bad as most. I agree with you. I just don't see her doing it. Or the nephew."

"You said his uniform wasn't in his locker?"

"Right. Well, we've finally found it. He was wearing it."

"Really? So he was either killed during the day—"

"Or just after work," Rendell said. "See, that's another thing. It doesn't strike me as a real good possibility that his nephew is gonna hit him right here in sight of the department. Last anybody saw him that we know of, he told a coworker he was going out to 'look something up.' He left the building on foot, we think. Car was at home. He didn't usually drive to work. He left about lunchtime and he acted like he had an appointment, so nobody noticed that he didn't come back by five. We've always thought he could have come back to change and go home after everybody left the office, maybe took his uniform with him to get it cleaned, and been killed a lot later than noon on February fourteen, but with him still wearing his uniform, I doubt that now. Looks like somebody killed him during work hours and maybe not far from here. Other than that, there's not one single goddamn pointer. It bugs the hell outta me. I ought to have a handle on it by now!"

"Well, keep pushing."

"From the time frame it's gotta be work related. But I can't see how. He wasn't a detective. Hadn't been on a *real* case in four, five years."

Gimball quietly ignored the implication. "No. If he'd been

in Organized Crime or even Gang Crime—but there isn't anything much more insulated than Internal Auditing."

Rendell left.

Gimball actually had a minute between Rendell and the next crisis, and he used it to walk across the room and back. He did this quite frequently these days, to test himself. To see if he could walk without his feet dragging. Since being diagnosed with Parkinson's disease six months before, he found himself listening to his body a lot and watching himself move. Partly this was caused by a natural fear of the disease, and partly by uneasiness about whether he was doing the right thing for his job. He had not told the department that he was sick.

Ray Moses knocked and entered. "Deputy Superintendent Heidema and Deputy Superintendent Withers are here, sir."

"Okay."

"And by the way, the First District says the cartons are blocking part of their entrance from the alley into the building."

"I'll get to that in a few minutes."

Deputy Superintendent Heidema, chief of the Bureau of Technical Services, was a short white man with bristly hair, a little terrier of a man. Deputy Superintendent Withers, chief of the Bureau of Administrative Services, was larger, a black man with a smooth face and smooth manner. Today Heidema was anxious and Withers smoother than ever.

Today the Communications Center was being shut down.

The Chicago Police Department Central Headquarters building at Eleventh and State was old, built in the 1920s, and had long been forced to make do. A building next door, now called the Annex, had been cobbled onto the big building, but the floors weren't the same height, so there were ramps on each floor at the join.

The buildings were a problem, but still worse was dispatch, the nerve center. In the 1960s it had been a marvel of modern police communication. But as of this morning, communications had not really been upgraded in thirty years. The up-to-

date way to dispatch cars was by CAD, a computer-aided dispatch system. The key advance in this system was a monitor
that displayed all the streets and alleys and parks and so on in a
district, using a high-res screen, and plotted the position of all
the cars up and running as lighted blips on the screen. *This* was
the system a department dreamed about.

For the last several years there had been talk about upgrad-
ing the system as soon as the city cut loose enough money to
build a new CPD building. The idea was that a CAD had to be
built into a building, with enough electrical supply, from the
getgo. When Gimball became superintendent, he decided
they'd been patient long enough. It was time to take the department into the twenty-first century.

"The city isn't going to give us a new building in this century," he said. "They *will* cut loose the funds for the CAD."

They did. The system was ready to install. During the tran-
sition, dispatchers would transmit directly from the districts on
their booster antennae. 911 calls would be routed to the appropriate district by phone.

Tonight was the switchover.

"This is gonna be a mess!" Heidema said. Bradley Heidema was looking frayed. The knot in his normally perfect tie
was perhaps a quarter of an inch off center. His colorless, bristly hair, usually combed into obedience so thoroughly that it
showed the marks of the teeth of the comb, now showed un-
even tracks of fingers having been run through it. For
Heidema, this was a tantrum.

Gimball said, "Make it work."

Withers drawled, "Bradley's afraid all the shit that comes
raining down is going to be blamed on him."

"Exactly where are we at, Brad?" Gimball said, ignoring
Charlie Withers' poke at Heidema.

"The ceiling is out already on floors two and three. At two
A.M., communications here will go down and the districts will
take over. Nine-one-one will flow data into the district stations
directly. Trucks with the new gear are in the parking lot.

We've got people starting to carry it up. The computer support rooms are already wired. At two A.M. the engineers will move onto two and three with the carpenters, and the old floors should be out by tomorrow morning. Then the carpenters will go in and install the stringers for cable space, lay the cable and then the flooring over it. Then the data processing equipment moves in, and we hook up the workstations and start debugging. We expect to be up and clear in two days."

"Fine. But don't just *expect*. It's got to be *done*. I want absolutely no screwup when the president gets here."

Gimball added, "I want you to strip some cars from the academy and from General Support and Crime Lab and loan 'em to the districts. Temporarily, to hurry up the response time. Plus, we're gonna have to put more one-man cars on the streets."

"Oh, shit! We won't hear for the screams!" Heidema said.

"You will go out of your way to *find* people who can be borrowed temporarily to handle phones and dispatch. You will pull cars off such plum assignments as getting pizza for meetings or chauffeuring brass, and you will *voluntarily* offer them to patrol so they can loan them to overworked districts. Am I right?"

Heidema said, "Right."

"My guys've been trained," Withers said.

Heidema said, "Oh sure. Trained. People are always *trained*. Then they hit a problem and they forget all their training."

"It's a done deal, Brad," Gimball said. "Make it work."

Heidema said, "There's another thing makes me uncomfortable. I don't like having all our record-keeping available to this company, either."

"What do you mean?" Gimball asked.

"They're changing over everything—dispatch, records, personnel, the whole shebang. While they do it, they have access to every bit of data the CPD has."

Withers said, "Brad, don't get paranoid." He glanced at

Gimball and cast up his eyes, as if to say, here goes nervous-Nelly Brad again.

Gimball was not drawn into Withers' game.

"Brad, all they're doing is installing computers."

"Suppose they leave a modem line in place. They could read all our records."

"God, Brad!" Withers barked. "Why the fuck should they do that?"

"I don't know why. I just said—"

Gimball said, "Both of you, quit this. I'm gonna take a look at the alley. The district's complaining. Let's move it. Brad, if you're uneasy about the installation, *go and watch!*"

"Boss—" Withers said.

"Yeah, Charlie?"

"It'll be okay. SJR DataSystems did a really smooth job for us when they computerized Internal Auditing."

1100

GIMBALL LOOKED AT the clock as he went out of his office. Mr. Slick from the Secret Service would be here—whoa! Gimball tapped his forehead; it was one thing to call him Mr. Slick in his own mind, but he'd better remember his real name was Agent Strick. Agent Strick would be here in ten minutes to go over the allocation of Chicago Police personnel for the president's visit. Visions flashed before Gimball's eyes. They'd have to babysit the pres and veep from touchdown at O'Hare to wheels-up at O'Hare three days later. A couple of hundred officers at least. They'd cover the rooftops. They'd seal the manholes on the route. They'd double-guard every intersection. They'd comb their files for crazies.

Gimball turned to his ADS. "Borland! I'll be back in five

minutes. You watch for Strick. And send out to get me a bag of
potato chips."

"What flavor, Boss?"

"Sour cream and chives. And a bag of barbecue flavor,
while you're at it."

1101

HOWIE BORKE HAD been pumped up with enthusiasm when
he left Dean Utley. When he entered the Chicago Police Department, however, some of his confidence left him. The
building was large, and full of large cops. He felt isolated.

He kept telling himself this was stupid. After all, he'd been
here a dozen times during the design phase and three days this
week directing the contractors. He'd been here all day yesterday supervising the layout of the control room.

He even had his own personal flunky-cop named Syd Pankowski, who ran around doing errands for him. And he had to
admit the plans for taking the floors out in the communications room after midnight looked efficient. His own job right
now, getting the mainframe and peripherals up and running in
the central computer room, was no prob. Technically. He'd
done it in dozens of corporations and several smaller police departments.

The electrical supply to the control room was all set. The
workstations—the physical desks, at any rate—were in place.
Several of the disk drives and monitors were placed. Now for
the vital element.

Here goes, he thought. *Right in front of them.*

"Would you unpack that for me?" Howie Bork said to Pankowski, who had already unpacked half a dozen other items.
Pankowski cut the clear tape carefully, holding his utility knife

near the tip of the blade, so as not to cut anything inside. *We could use this guy at SJR*, Howie thought.

Pankowski bent the box flaps back.

A man walked into the room. Howie had seen him before, but didn't remember his name. The guy wore the gold-checked band on the cap that meant topcop. There was extra braid on his uniform. Pankowski snapped to attention.

Howie thought, *Oh, shit.*

Carefully, he said, "Good afternoon, sir."

Pankowski said, "Sir, this is Howie Borke from SJR. Mr. Borke, this is Deputy Superintendent Bradley Heidema."

Howie thought, *Double shit.*

The box sat there on the floor between them, with the flaps open.

"I'm just going to stand around and observe, Mr. Borke," Heidema said. "Go right ahead. Pretend I'm not here."

"Would you like me to give you a little tour of the way this room will operate when we get it set up?" Howie said desperately.

"No, no. I'm just going to watch you work. I certainly don't want to hold you up."

"I could explain the workstation."

"No, Mr. Borke." Heidema waved his hand. "Go right ahead. Don't mind me."

Pankowski had already returned to the box and now lifted the Styrofoam forms off the machine inside. Howie placed himself quickly between the box and Heidema, as if to help Pankowski with the unpacking. Heidema went around him to the other side to watch. Howie swallowed.

The machine was similar to the other machines, though not identical. It was about six inches high, fourteen deep, and twenty wide.

"Hey, this is different!" Pankowski said.

Howie said, "No, no. Not really."

"Yeah, look at it," Pankowski said. "Beige. All the other ones are blue or gray. New color?"

"Oh, yeah. Yeah. It's what we call 'canyon sand' in the catalog. Designer colors, you know." He laughed harshly.

"Well. Makes a change."

Heidema was looking curiously at it.

"Where do you want it?" Pankowski said.

"Oh, right over here." Howie pointed at a table. Pankowski lifted it into place. Heidema clasped his hands behind his back and watched. While Pankowski got rid of the packaging material, Howie plugged in the power cords, the cord from the mainframe, and the modem cord.

Then on top of the beige box he set another machine.

"What does this do?" Heidema asked.

"The beige one is a parity check, and the blue one manages the allocation of printers among different workstations."

Finished, he stepped back and looked at the beige box. His Trojan horse. He held his breath. Heidema said nothing.

On the side of the box was a warning:

PARITY CHECK
DO NOT TAMPER WITH THIS EQUIPMENT
IN THE EVENT OF A MALFUNCTION,
CALL SJR DATASYSTEMS
FOR ASSISTANCE

Howie strolled as casually as possible to the keyboard that he'd dedicated to his own use while he was setting up the system. Suppressing the urge to whistle to cover his nervousness, he typed in a minute and a half of access codes, and finally the words: OP/KISS/OP.

And the response came back, as satisfying as an explosion of fireworks:

ON LINE

"Looks like it works," Heidema said.

"Yes."

"Well, keep at it." Heidema walked to the door. "We've got to be up and running ASAP."

Howie said, "If you have any questions, you let me know immediately. Remember, I'm from SJR DataSystems, and I'm here to help you."

1110

OP/KISS/OP/ONLINE, the bulletin said as it decrypted itself. Fantastic, Zach thought. Imagine, old Howie'd actually got the damn thing in, apparently without a glitch. Zach hadn't thought he'd have the nerve. Doing it in industry was not the same as doing it in the very heart of the Chicago Police Department.

After a minute of silent celebration, he went back to his spot-checking. Most of the members of the steering committee were working seven days a week now, during the last days before **cutworm**. Zach Massendate had worked for hours, running through a long list of databases, rotating the names of three thousand Chicago-area SJR employees against the names contained in the databases. In the cases of maybe five hundred top employees, he also investigated their significant others: husbands, wives, lovers, and in some cases parents or children. He sucked the data out of the d-base they were vampirizing and it was automatically sorted into the employee's file and appended to existing information, with the source coded as well, in case they needed to expand the background still more later on.

After all, despite careful security, it was possible for an ordinary employee to get a whiff of **cutworm**. Possible, not likely. And when it moved on the president, if any one of the employees looked like trouble, Zach would need to know where to apply pressure.

Zach never stayed in any company's database for long, because his presence might be noticed. This was one reason he did not simply download everything they had. Modems just weren't fast enough. There was too much data out there.

He got what he could get, briefly and selectively, then went back later to get more.

It was mostly habit that sent Zach into the Bermandyne system late Friday night. He had stolen the sysop Heddy Bloom's login and had given himself sysop privileges on the Bermandyne system eighteen months earlier. He usually checked the Bermandyne time clock and discovered Heddy always checked out before five. There had never been the slightest problem.

At 11:58 he entered the system as:

```
mama
```

For a while, he sucked out data happily. Suddenly, he wasn't alone. Zach saw it, although he could hardly believe it. Under his login, someone had typed back:

```
talk mama
```

Trouble, Zach thought. *Big trouble for me. Bigger trouble for whoever this fucker is.* He took a gun out of his desk drawer and fired at the screen. The foam-rubber dart stuck for a second, then slipped off and bounced to the black desktop. Zach touched the intercom code for Howie Borke, hoping he was back from the police department.

1111

HIS NAME WAS Kiro Ogata, and he was twenty-three years old.

Anyone would have said that Kiro Ogata had everything in life going against him. Fate had played jokes on Kiro all his life, as if to show the rest of the world how bad things could really get.

Kiro—who would already have had problems as a Japanese-American in a largely northern European American community in the north part of Chicago—had been born with arthrogryposis, a strange birth defect in which the muscles are abnormally weak and the limbs are contracted, bent up against the body as if they were trying to defend the torso from assault.

But this was not enough. He had also been born with esophageal atresia. At first, after his birth, it was thought he wasn't feeding normally because of some obscure muscle weakness associated with his arthrogryposis. But an alert intern noticed that the baby was in fact sucking hard at his formula, even though it all oozed right back out of his mouth. X-rays revealed that his esophagus led about an inch down from the throat, stopped, then resumed three-eighths of an inch later and opened properly into the stomach. Food could not reach the stomach. Kiro was starving to death.

Here fate threw Kiro a little gift. The three-eighths-inch distance between the ends of the esophagus was short enough for the surgeon to stretch and sew them together, without doing a more complex operation, such as stitching in a piece of intestine to close the gap. So Kiro reached his fifth day of life recovering from major surgery with apparently only his contracted limbs to worry about.

Kiro spent his childhood in orthopedic programs, struggling through physical therapy. His shoulder and elbow joints, which had seemed frozen at birth, became more and more flexible with practice, and his hands had never been much affected. But his legs did not respond.

Whether it made things better or worse, fate had also given Kiro a very good brain.

Kiro went to the public grade school in his neighborhood, near Loyola University. He drove his motorized wheelchair to and from school in most weather, in all but the deepest snow. He did very well academically. Some of the other kids, who might have teased him for being a brain if he had not been in a wheelchair, assumed that he had to study since, after all, he couldn't play sports. So they sympathized with him.

But by tenth grade, Kiro began to suspect he had yet another problem to deal with. By his senior year he was sure of it. Fate must have been chuckling hysterically by now. Kiro was not attracted to girls; he was attracted to boys.

He got a scholarship to Northwestern. He spent most of his time at Vogelback, computing. The rest he spent with a young man he met his second year, a teaching assistant in computer engineering, Ron Latham. When Kiro graduated, they got an apartment together in Uptown, a half-yuppified, multiethnic area a couple of miles north of the Loop. Their building had fourteen floors, and Ron and Kiro lived on the seventh. There was an elevator. Kiro drove his motorized wheelchair to work every day, a distance of half a mile. Kiro worked at Bermandyne, an independent data processing company that managed billing lists for credit card companies.

Kiro was happy. He enjoyed his work. He liked his apartment and he loved Ron. Kiro could afford nice clothes. He favored casual clothing, especially soft sweaters in lamb's wool and mohair (*I'm so casual. I'm just relaxing here. I could walk if I weren't so casual, but I'm sitting here in this nice old wheelchair.*) The neighborhood he worked and lived in was rich with ethnic restaurants, especially Thai, Korean, Indian, Vietnamese, and German. It was a giant buffet table to him. Most of the restaurants were not expensive, and since he was making decent money, he and Ron were sampling their way across the area.

So even though Kiro might have seemed to have everything going against him, in fact he was pleased with his life.

Fate, however, had one more surprise dangling at the end of its line.

Friday night, Kiro Ogata had completed the work he had to get done that day and turned to his extra work.

Friday nights Ron was not home. He taught an evening class in data-sorting programs at the University of Chicago from seven to nine. So Kiro had taken to staying very late—into the small hours of Saturday morning. After a few weeks of this, he noticed that he got a lot of extra work done because there was nobody in the building to come in and interrupt him and ask questions; everybody went home by eight or nine P.M., and the modems were perfectly capable of piling up data for Monday. Finally, Kiro convinced his boss to let him take all day off on Mondays in exchange for staying Friday night.

This building was the nerve center of Bermandyne, Inc. Currently, Bermandyne managed the databases of two national credit card companies and a couple of national mail order businesses. Bermandyne was hoping to expand and take on more clients.

The nerve center of the nerve center was a group of file-servers and mainframes. The software controlling the system was the very latest, most efficient constellation of programs, developed and installed by SJR DataSystems. Every one of the two hundred and twelve workstations in the building fed into one mainframe in the basement.

Kiro was supervisor level, well above the data-entry people. At the present time, he was fiddling around with a simplified method for giving each employee a running tally of exactly how much overtime they had accumulated.

Kiro also like to play around in the system.

Just before midnight, he typed login YoYodine to log into the mainframe from the system in his office.

The screen said user name> asking for his login. In a burst of wry humor the year before, Kiro had chosen a new login. He typed:

```
lame
```

The machine said:

```
password>
```

He typed in:

```
wheels
```

Kiro, who was already having a nice time being alone in the building, thought it would be nice to see that he was alone on the system, too. During the day the list of users was over a hundred. He typed:

```
users <RETURN>
```

The screen responded with two logins

```
lame
```

```
mama
```

Kiro blinked. Mama was the code name of Heddy Bloom, the sysop. She always left at five. An extremely efficient woman— far more efficient than you'd think from her flame red hair and flame red lips—she usually had her work done, flawlessly, before three, and spent the rest of the time checking up on everybody else's work habits. There was a rumor that she was being wooed by a seriously major company for seriously major money. Kiro didn't mind her checking up on him; he did his work well, anyway, and wouldn't have been sloppy even if she were not around. But he wouldn't mind if she left Bermandyne. He was her assistant, nominally at least, and if she went to work somewhere else, he would most likely become chief systems operator at an increase in salary.

Heddy had left the building hours ago. So had everybody else. The modem links went on collecting data all night, unattended.

But Heddy was on the screen. He backed his chair away from the workstation and zoomed to his office window. The window overlooked the smallish parking lot where upper management was allowed to park.

He was looking for Heddy's flame red Porsche, not a car he could easily miss.

There were no cars whatsoever in the lot. Of course.

Vaguely troubled, he rolled back to his screen. He typed `talk mama`. Instantly, `mama` went off, leaving the screen bare except for

    lame

Kiro was puzzled.

Fate had set the hook.

10000

HOWIE WAS BACK and answered his beep immediately. Zach said, "You'd better come up here. I have something to show you."

Miles away at Bermandyne, the unknown operator had split his screen horizontally, the top half representing him or herself, the bottom half a space where he expected `mama` to answer.

Immediately, Zach shut down all his other systems and froze the exchange.

Howie was there in two minutes. Zach looked at Howie expectantly. Zach resented Howie, but Howie was the computer genius. Zach wasn't.

Howie looked. "Oh, my, my!" he said. "We certainly can't have that!"

10001

||||||||||||||||||||||||||||||||||||||||||||||||||||||||||||||||||||||
DEPARTMENT OF THE TREASURY
UNITED STATES SECRET SERVICE
1800 G STREET NW
WASHINGTON DC
FROM: CMV
TO: STRICK
FORM: INTERNAL

<<IN ANY OPEN TRANSMISSION FOLLOW THE
ESTABLISHED CODES>>

DAYS UNTIL WE HAND YOU THE PRESIDENT ?
JIM:
NO PROBLEMS. FEAST OR FAMINE, I GUESS.

CMV
||||||||||||||||||||||||||||||||||||||||||||||||||||||||||||||||||||||

10010

SATURDAY MORNING, I knew at breakfast Sheryl was worried. She hadn't said anything; it was all body language. She was droopy, which she usually isn't, a little slower to respond to the girls' questions. A little less eager about the day. Then she said to me quietly, "I need to talk to you."

"Okay."

"Not now, though." The kids were already milling around the kitchen, and I heard Robert coming down the stairs. He would be crabby, and Kath would ask him to come with us, and he'd say, "I have to work. Where do you think your money comes from?" Robert is jealous of the fact that Sheryl makes more money than he does.

Sheryl and I try to do something with the kids every weekend. We're very much aware that we are working mothers, so we plan ahead and don't make excuses at the last minute that we're too busy or too tired from work. She and Robert had to go to a party at Utley's Magnificent Mile apartment this evening, so it was morning for the kids.

This was one of those warm March Saturdays that make natives believe Chicago has the best weather in the world. They know they're wrong, of course; they know it could snow the next day, but the fizzy combination of relief from the winter and hope for the summer is irresistible.

We got first choice of seats on the bus for the kids. Actually, this was no special trick, since JJ and Kath raced to the bus the instant the ticket seller pointed it out to them. Maria was more ladylike, but the other half dozen passengers hung back while the children scrambled on.

Omigod, I thought, settling into the seat. *Suppose she wants to talk about divorcing Robert. What do I tell her? I'm no expert on marriage. I'm divorced. That makes me some kind of failure, doesn't it? Aren't women supposed to make it work?*

"Sheryl, what's wrong?" I asked.

"It's work."

"*What?*"

"I've got a problem at work. What's the matter? Why are you looking so funny?"

"Nothing. Forget it. So tell me—"

Sheryl studied her hands. "I'm not making this up," she said uneasily.

"Of course not. What is it?"

"There's something wrong going on."

Her voice trembled. This was serious. Sheryl ordinarily did not lose her cool, nor was she indecisive.

"Tell me."

"I mean, you're an expert on crime, right?"

"Good God, Sheryl! Now you're getting me worried. Just tell me."

"Well, the problem is, half of this—of what makes me suspicious—is solid stuff and half of it's kind of soft data. See, I found this file. I saw somebody else's file—just by chance. It wouldn't happen again in a million years. Well, maybe that's not exactly right, actually accidents happen all the time, but—oh, God—see, I'm working in a high-clearance smartlink, and I hit a wrong key—"

"Uh, Sheryl. Let's bear in mind that I know absolutely nothing about computing."

Sheryl cocked her head as if she couldn't quite believe that any adult modern human being could say that. "All right. Just take my word for it. The point of a smartlink is to take in an enormous amount of data in such a way as to be able to use it. Like aircraft data in this crunch-program we're doing. And this smartlink I found is being used to get information on people. Credit card purchases, tax information, bank stuff that nobody should see—"

"And you looked at it?"

"It wasn't my fault. I wasn't prying. At first, anyway. But now I've got a problem. I can't let whoever it is just use company systems to do something wrong."

"Wait a minute," I said. "This—this data. Why couldn't your company be doing this work on a subcontracting kind of basis? For a credit card company?"

"This was the current raw data. For instance, a credit card company would use it to bill. SJR doesn't do that kind of thing. That's just data-entry work. Data entry sounds like computing if you're not computer sophisticated. But it's the present-day version of typing. Filling in blanks. Taking stuff off paper and putting it into the system. At SJR we develop programs and hardware. I mean, let's face it, we do stuff that's much more sophisticated."

"All right," I said. "Let me play devil's advocate here. It'll clear things up for me, at least. Why couldn't this be a chunk of data that somebody in your company uses to work on? Like practice on. I don't know how computer people say it, but if somebody at SJR wanted to work out better ways of making software to do the billing or whatever, like how to make alphabetical lists, wouldn't they have to try it out on some chunk of data like this?"

"Suze, that's very smart of you!"

"Well, don't fall all over complimenting me."

"Sorry. They wouldn't have it in this form if they were doing that. This was not a flat file. You know, not readable text." She saw the blank stare on my face. "Trust me. You use real English words and numbers if you're doing list work. This was in code. It was hidden. Not protected, but hidden. And the point is, it was yesterday's data. We'd *never* have anything so recent and so confidential. And even if we did, why have analyses of individuals?"

"All right. Say somebody *has* stolen this database from some company. Why? Why would it be worth much? What would they do with it?"

"Practically anything! There are quite a few things you could use it for. You could check on what a company is selling, for one. Say you're a competitor and you wanted to check up on Marshall Field's. How their shoe department is doing, for instance. If you had a big database of credit card transactions in Chicago for a month, maybe, you could extract the Marshall Field's charges and really get some inside information. If their stock is publicly traded, you'd know better than any brokerage firm how much merchandise they were selling."

"Okay. Industrial espionage. I can buy that. What else?"

"Well, if you could enter the database, not just download the information, I suppose you could alter it. It depends how and where you enter. You could buy a lot of items, charge them, and then find the charges you've run up and cancel them and get the merchandise free. Like, steal it."

"I like that one. As a cop, that pleases me."

"But if somebody at SJR is into confidential databases, and he's using our mainframe, and our power and our reputation, there's no limit to what he could do. It could be anything."

Sheryl added, "The world has changed. People used to have to hold a physical piece of paper—hold it in their hands—to know about you. Not anymore. Suze, I'm telling you again, if a criminal had access to the kind of data that's available now, there is *no limit* to the evil that could be done."

She stopped talking. I waited, but when she didn't go on, I looked closer. Sheryl was crying.

"Oh, God, hon!" I put my arm around her shoulders. "It can't be that bad." Automatically, I glanced forward at the children to make sure they were fully occupied with the scenery.

"It *is* that bad."

"Oh, Sheryl." Sheryl never cried.

"I *love* my job. And I like the people, too, most of them. But there's a feeling—this isn't the first thing."

"What else?"

"I said a minute ago that there was some soft data. It's this. I think Howie, the guy who heads Research and Development, is scared."

"What's he afraid of?"

"I don't know. I've known him seven years, Suze! He's the second most important guy in the company."

"Mmm-mm."

"I think he's afraid of two security guys we call the Two Blue Blazers. Their real names are Zach and Glen. They're a sort of troubleshooting team. Dean Utley calls them his debuggers, because he uses them to deal with problems. See, what I think is that somebody close to Dean Utley is using the company system for his own ends—"

"You mean, criminal ends."

"Yes. I hope not, but—yeah."

"Why somebody close to Utley?"

"First, this is an absolutely top-level piece of software. Nobody has the password except top people: Howie, Zach and Glen, and probably the steering committee. And a very few of us engineers right now, temporarily, because of the crunch on the Department of Defense contract. And second—the file password, `utmost`, sounds like Utley. I mean, it just has Dean Utley written all over it. He likes things that use part of his name, like a kind of puzzle. He had one called `utopia`. He has one now that I was working on a part of for him, and he calls it `zutalors` from the French expression *zut alors!* Because of the 'ut,' see?"

"Perfectly," I said, somewhat grimly. "So maybe it's Utley himself."

"No, it can't be Utley himself doing this. SJR is his company. He wouldn't need to. He's worth zillions. But the password proves it has to be somebody close. Maybe it's a password he discarded a long time ago and forgot about and somebody's taken over. Somebody like me, like I know about `zutalors`."

"Okay. So why don't you go to security about it?"

"I was into that file. Improperly."

"By sheer accident."

"It wasn't accident that after I found it I opened the file and converted it and looked at it."

"Well, okay, but you could explain that. Say you really thought something was wrong. They trust you, don't they?"

"Sure. I've worked there ever since I left Burroughs, before Burroughs became Unisys. Ten years, almost eleven. Sure they trust me. As much as they trust anybody."

"Well, then?"

"Suze, I'm not sure I trust security. How do I know who's doing this?"

"How about going directly to Utley? Go right to the top?"

"Oh, not now! Oh, no!"

"You sound scared of him."

"No. I'm not scared of him, exactly. But you don't 'go to' him with trouble. He's not fond of bad news."

"I had a sergeant like that once."

"I *could* go to him if I knew more. And I suppose that's what

I'd better do. I can try to feel my way around the system and see if I can tell what's going on."

"No! No, no, no. I don't think that's a good idea."

"Why not?"

"Somebody might find out. And hurt you. If you're right about how big this could be, they—whoever—could be violent."

"You mean physically hurt me? Oh, come on. You've been a cop too long. The worst that could happen is I get fired. Which would be really pretty bad—"

"Sheryl, I don't want you to do detective work. Don't investigate this. Either report it at the highest level, or drop it."

"I can't just ignore something criminal!"

"Please. I've got a funny feeling about the whole thing. There are elements here I don't understand."

"Now *you're* overreacting."

"I mean it. I'm really worried, Sheryl!"

"Listen, I've got a compromise solution. Before I discovered this file, I noticed tension between the Blue Blazers and Howie. But I didn't really pay attention. There wasn't any reason to. Now that I know, I can study them."

"Wait a minute here. What do you mean?"

"At the party tonight. I can watch how they act with each other. And maybe ask a question and see how they react."

"No! Don't do it!"

"Suze, I wouldn't do anything they could be suspicious of. Just something subtle."

"Please don't, Sheryl. Please."

Sheryl said, "Hey, give me some credit; I know what I'm doing."

What could I do? I couldn't very well tell her that she *didn't* know what she was doing. She knew the people. She knew the company. She knew computers. I didn't. I was afraid, but I didn't have any cogent reason to be. She'd be able to look innocent. Looking innocent was not a stretch for Sheryl. Basically, she *was* innocent. And she was so pretty that men often forgot how smart she was.

"Sheryl, promise me."

"What?"

"Just observe. Don't ask any dangerous questions."

10011

JESUS DELGADO HAD left the autopsy on Frieswyk and gone immediately to a cafe he knew of on Ashland and ordered hot chocolate, Abuelita, the Mexican kind with cinnamon in it, made with boiling milk. It was the only thing he could think of that would take the smell and taste of death out of his throat.

He sipped it while it was still too hot and burned his tongue. Even that was better than the lingering taste of the morgue.

Jesus Delgado was a highly Americanized man of Mexican ancestry. His parents had been highly Americanized, too, and had lived in Chicago all their lives. His grandparents, three of whom were still alive, were not so Americanized, perhaps half and half. The whole lot of them, Jesus thought, should have known better than to name him Jesus.

Hardly anybody pronounced it in the Mexican way. And even that, *Hay-sus*, didn't have an American sound to it. When he first came on the department, one guy would yell "Jesus!" and the next guy would say, "Name-dropper!" and then everybody would laugh like crazy, break up all over the place. Cop humor. If he had heard it once, he had heard it a million times. And they all thought they were being original.

Jesus sipped his cocoa. Now the world was straightening itself out. The smell of the morgue was receding.

He went over the Frieswyk case in his mind. As a detective, Jesus was basically a number cruncher. Always, all his early life, he'd wanted to be a cop. He really believed he could help people. As a cop, you came on the scene at a time when people were in stress. They might not even want to see you, but the way you did your job made a difference in their lives. Knowing that the department was professionalizing, taking in a larger and larger percentage of college graduates, he had attended a commuter college in Chicago. He couldn't afford a residential university. Because he had shown a lot of facility with numbers, he drifted into computer science, became fascinated, and earned a bachelor of science in computer science. His adviser had felt an obligation to point out to Jesus that he could make more money in industry than in the Chicago Police Department. But Jesus Delgado wanted to be a cop—period.

However, he wasn't an action-type cop. He didn't want to go out and run down an alley and bust in a door and yell, *"Freeze!"* and shoot it out with the drug lords.

He was a right-the-wrongs kind of cop. A get-rid-of-the-swindlers kind of cop. And he knew why. When he was about twelve, his uncle Lee—short for Felipe—had been taken by a con man. Uncle Lee had operated a landscape nursery in Naperville, raising ornamental trees and bedding plants for the wholesale trade. After fifteen years in the business, subdivisions spreading out from Chicago surrounded the nursery. Taxes went up. And up and up. He couldn't hold the land, pay that kind of tax, and make any money, so he sold—at a very substantial profit. During the course of the negotiations prior to sale, he started looking for land farther out from the city, figuring to move his business and all the stock he could transplant. He was approached by a land broker who claimed to have two adjacent forty-acre parcels at below-market prices. The reason the land was so cheap was that it had been vacated, the broker said, when the state bought it for a highway. Then the highway was rerouted because of environmental concerns—there were wetlands in the way. Actually, the broker hinted, the original buy had something to do with a bribe, and now the land was an embarrassment to everybody. The sooner somebody grabbed it up and put it to use the better. The price was low and taxes were even lower.

Fascinated by the story, by maps of the proposed and discarded freeway, and pleased at the quality of the soil, Lee did not get an independent check on the ownership before he advanced a hefty down payment.

A week went by without word from the broker. And another week. After three weeks, Lee phoned. The number had been disconnected. He wrote to the post office box. The letter came back. The money was gone.

With no land, and nowhere to move his plant stock, he had to sell the plants to competitors at fire-sale prices.

With no stock, even though he had some money left from the sale of his original land, he hadn't enough capital to start over.

Kane County police eventually found the swindler, and they did it through backtracking the money trail. But they never found the money. And Jesus' Uncle Lee now worked for a home landscaping firm. He mowed lawns and spaded flower beds.

Jesus had to admit Lee was still mostly the same nice guy: optimistic, loved the outdoors, loved to go to Cubs games with Jesus. It wasn't as if he'd killed himself after being reduced from entrepreneur to hired hand. It wasn't *that* kind of tragedy. But Uncle Lee was different, even so. It was mainly that he just didn't have as much to do anymore. With the old business, as far as Jesus could tell as a child, Lee had never stopped moving. He was either grafting fruit trees, dividing irises, or running the tractor. In the winter he operated the greenhouses and read seed catalogs to decide whether the big thing in geraniums this spring would be pink or red. Maybe not geraniums at all—maybe marigolds! Now he was often bored and looking for amusements. And he was drinking a lot more beer.

Jesus dearly loved to trace down con artists and swindlers

and scam types and backtrack on white-collar crooks, embez-
zlers, guys that took kickbacks. It was like following the spoor
of a beast. To Jesus, spreadsheets, tax records, and checkbooks
were maps to their lair. You couldn't move money without
leaving a paper trail. And Jesus knew where to look for it. He
crept up on the scam artists like a wolf and then pounced.

In the department, he had quite a reputation for having a
golden hand on the computer keyboard. But he shrugged it off,
saying, "If the data is right and the program is right, you can't
miss."

Several years ago, just a few months before his twin girls
were born, Jesus and his wife Elena and his parents toured
Mexico. It was an okay trip, although he wasn't much of a tour-
ist. He liked his work and wasn't a person who spent much
time thinking about his ancestral country. Actually, the best
part was seeing temples in the jungle, overgrown with vines the
size of his arm. A lost civilization.

In the Museo Nacional in Mexico City, they looked at the
artifacts of Mayan civilization. And suddenly there he was. He
himself, Jesus Delgado, carved in stone.

Elena said, "My God!"

They were standing in front of a limestone mask of Pacal
the Great, and it was him, Jesus, to the last degree. Not just the
general shape of the head, but the turn of the nostrils, the hair-
line, eyes, everything.

"Well, better him than Pacal the Adequate," Jesus joked.
But he was moved. He had always known he didn't look like
the Spaniards, or like the mixture of Spanish and Indian which
so many Mexicans were today. He joked to cover up the fact
that his whole body had reacted to the sight of Pacal.

Oh, yeah, he had thought to himself, finishing the last of
the cocoa. Those genes certainly got screwed up in the trans-
mission. Pacal the Great wouldn't have been a paper-pusher—
no, pixel-pusher—detective. Let your cursor do the walking.

He thought of ordering another cocoa, but he had better
get back to work. What was triggering all this soul-searching

was an awareness of something that had happened to him when he was watching the autopsy. It had showed just once, when he asked whether Frieswyk had suffered. The sight of the dead policeman, bald, degraded, and rotting, had made Jesus very, very angry.

Saturday morning, he sat again at Frieswyk's desk. Despite a fierce need for offices, the deputy superintendent had ordered Frieswyk's desk kept precisely as it had been the day he walked away. The desktop, papers, keyboard, monitor, pens, scissors, coins, rubber cement, Hershey bars, and so on had been fingerprinted, just as if the area was a crime scene— which nobody really believed it was. It had been photographed first, the stuff sorted, printed, and studied, then put back as Frieswyk had left it.

Jesus sighed. It had been a deep mystery when Frieswyk vanished. Now they had found him and it was still a mystery. Jesus sat where Frieswyk had sat when he was working. Looked around to see what Frieswyk had seen every day at work. There was a clock straight ahead on the wall. It said ten forty-five. Jesus started pulling open the drawers. All was the same as before. There was a photo of Frieswyk's wife—no, Frieswyk's ex-wife—facedown in the bottom right drawer. It was in a nice, black plastic frame. And although it was facedown, just as Frieswyk had left it, it was not torn up, or X-ed out, or slashed. No mustache was drawn on the face. Jesus wondered what the relatively gentle treatment meant, if anything. Had Frieswyk hoped someday to get back together with her? Jesus tended to think so.

Jesus phoned Mrs. Frieswyk. Perry Frieswyk, soon to be Perry Frieswyk Murphy. He had interviewed her twice before, but maybe she had some insight—

"I just don't want you to think I hold anything against Don," she had said, her voice skating close to a southern accent. Maybe Arkansas, Jesus thought. "Why, he was just the nicest person, when I first met him!"

"Yes? In what way?" he asked, encouraging her to talk.

"I thought, here's a man who's going to give me space, and at the same time he's strong and reliable."

"And he wasn't?"

"Well, see, what happened was he kind of gave me too *much* space. Away all the time, you know? I mean, he'd go to work and I wouldn't ever know when he'd get home."

"Well, police work is like that."

"Now, Detective Delgado, I don't think that's entirely true. Most officers work an eight-hour day. You've got maybe your detective, like you, who maybe puts in extra time. But not everybody. And Don, now, these last couple years he was working a desk job."

"Maybe he was sort of a desk detective." That was not far from what Jesus was himself.

"Well, maybe he was and maybe he wasn't, but he didn't come home smelling of beer because of a desk job."

"I suppose not."

"It just got to the point where our marriage was totally *dysfunctional*. And finally, I just had to give myself permission to say good-bye. There are times you just have to access your feelings, even though you may have been brought up to just endure. You know what I mean?"

"I guess so."

"I think he had some confusion about the masculine *role*. Like, he felt he had to go out with the boys after work? Drink a lot of beer? Anyway, it's over and done now."

"Did you fight about it?"

"Not really. Only thing we ever fought about, he thought I spent too much money. A dress here and there, maybe some sports clothes. Not too much to ask, is it?"

"Um—"

"He said the way I spent I oughta be the Motor Pool. Isn't that ridiculous?"

"What did he mean by that?"

"He didn't say. Actually—well, that was sort of like a *real* fight."

"What do you mean?"

"Well, actually—" she paused, and he pictured her flipping her hair back then fluffing it with two fingers, but finally she went on. "Actually, that was when I threw the fettucini at him."

"Oh."

They talked another half hour. From Jesus' point of view the conversation wasn't very profitable, except in eliminating her as a likely killer. Jesus did not believe she had killed her husband, or had him killed by somebody else. This was not a woman with very much passion in her nature, and since they were formally divorced before Frieswyk went missing, she had nothing to gain financially from his death.

He stared at her photo now. A pretty enough woman, with all her hair puffed over on one side. Lipstick that was too dark. Avid little eyes, with lots of mascara.

"You oughta be the Motor Pool!" What the hell did that mean?

10100

DEAN UTLEY'S APARTMENT was one-fifth of a mile high, in the John Hancock Building. It was so large that, even with forty or fifty employees standing holding drinks, it was not crowded. Windows wrapped around the living room, dining room, and study area of the apartment, and Utley had placed no furniture near the glass, so the feeling was one of floating in space. The apartment was so high that drifts of clouds passed by a hundred feet below, adding to the sensation that the apartment was not anchored to the earth.

As if that were not unsettling enough, several of the engineers had filled the sink in the wet bar half full and were watching the water move.

Sheryl glanced at Robert, who hated these parties anyway. "Let's look," she said.

They stood between Henry DeLusk and a man Sheryl had seen around the engineer department but didn't know. The water in the sink moved slowly to one side, climbed a little way, then moved back down and climbed the other side of the sink.

The building was swaying.

Now that she had seen the evidence, she could feel it. As she stood still, she felt as if the world slowly pushed her forward from behind, hesitated, then slowly backed away from her.

"The wind moves the building," Utley said in her ear.

She jumped.

"I didn't mean to startle you," he said quietly. Instinctively, she knew he had. He liked to creep up on people.

Robert said, "Do you get used to the feeling of it moving?" Robert's voice held envy and resentment. Sheryl hoped she could tell only because she knew Robert. Then, again, maybe Utley would be delighted to be envied.

"It's exciting, isn't it?" Utley said. "But you should see how it feels in a water bed."

Sheryl studied the apartment while she half-listened to Utley talk with Robert.

For a coffee table, Utley had taken a chunk of primitive computer, an old Univac four feet long, two feet wide, and a foot and a half high, and laid a large sheet of glass over it as a top surface. The Univac chunk was made up of multiple racks of circuit boards studded with vacuum tubes inside a cage. In a mahogany stand on the glass top sheet was a magnifying glass permanently aimed at a tiny dot. That dot was the present-day computer circuitry which could do all the work of the table-sized chunk underneath.

Clustered against the east wall was a bank of plants. About half were crotons, with tough leaves the texture of a paper plate. They were bold colored, a confetti field of color—red with green patches, yellow leaves with red spots, green leaves with orange veins. Some of the leaves were corkscrew shaped. Some were formed like hearts or lamb's tongues. The rest of Dean Utley's garden in the sky was African amaryllis plants, several dozen of them. Possibly thirty were in bloom and maybe forty were spent, with clipped stems. Sheryl didn't like them much, in spite of their colors. They were unnatural plants. The trumpet-shaped flowers, six or seven inches across, topped sappy, two-foot stalks as thick as a human thumb, which rose from bulbs the size of softballs. The flowers were bloodred, or fleshy salmon, or deep, saturated pink, flanked by just a couple of straplike leaves. Sheryl thought they were excessive plants, out of proportion, deformed. Their flowers were too large for the rest of the plant, their leaves too small. They were like genetically altered chickens, bred with huge drumsticks and outsized breast meat.

As Robert turned to get another drink, Sheryl realized she had been staring at Utley's office, a large room open on one side to the living room. What a great workstation! Look at the equipment—

Why does he need so much equipment? she thought. *His company office is less than an hour away.*

She turned to Utley. "You have a wonderful office here!" she said, making it sound like a question.

"Well, yes. If I need to I can run a CAD of a product and E-mail it to a factory in Japan, and they'll put it in their CAM system and ship me the calculators exactly the way I designed them. It's like having a direct robot interface. Zero slippage." He started to move away.

He liked to boast, usually. Why not now? "You have a direct Internet line here?" she said.

"Oh, sure. Sometimes I need to work from home." He laughed and started to move away again.

Sheryl persisted. She was more curious now. He had a color laser printer, a second printer, which she recognized as the next generation of the HP6, and several other units stacked in a floor-to ceiling arrangement of specially-built shelves.

She followed him. "You use X Windows and NEWS windowing systems?"

"Mostly NEWS."

"You have a removable optical drive? Wow! You could run the whole company from here. And with the laptop, you must be able to carry most of it with you—"

But he had turned to the waiter and was handing her another glass of champagne. Firmly changing the subject, he said, "The hot sandwiches are ready. Can I get you one?"

"This is fine," Sheryl said. Utley turned and left her.

She looked around for Howie Borke. There he was, wearing his Levi's, party or no party. He crossed the room to the drinks table and Sheryl followed him with her eyes. Glen Jaffee stood at the north window, and Sheryl, watching, saw Howie detour to avoid him. She was not imagining it.

As she watched, Zach approached the drinks table. Howie backed away from him, toward the flowering plants. Zach followed. Howie moved closer to the window, but Zach still followed and cornered Howie there. Sheryl saw Howie recoil half a step. Zach pursued Howie and said something to him, but Sheryl could only read the body language. Howie bent his arm to hold his glass in front of his chest, like a buffer.

10101

KIRO OGATA HAD been so puzzled by the appearance of the phantom mama on Friday night that on Saturday he told Ron he had extra work to do. They had a big Thai dinner, and at eight P.M. he went to the Bermandyne building.

The building was deserted. He let himself in with his key, which only worked in the front door. Any other door, if opened, would set off a buzzer that called the security guard in the basement.

When he got to his office, he phoned Heddy at home. He told her about seeing the login **mama** on the users list after she had left the evening before.

"Last night?" she said. "But I wasn't there last night."

"I *know* that. That's what I just said. You didn't have some strange job still running that left you logged in, did you?"

"Of course not."

"Then somebody was using your code who shouldn't be." He reminded himself not to get impatient.

She said, "That's impossible. Nobody knows my code except you and me."

"Well, somebody either found out or guessed."

"That's ridiculous. Nobody at Bermandyne has any reason to do that."

"Maybe they're bleeding off information on credit card customers."

"What for?"

Kiro couldn't exactly answer that. "Maybe to get mailing lists without paying for them?"

"Oh, sure. It's probably the Russians," she said, making fun of him. "Nope, can't be. They've got their own problems right now. I guess it's the CIA. They always want to know what everybody's doing."

"Heddy, there's got to be something going on. I *saw* your code name on the screen."

"Maybe you imagined it."

"I don't have that sort of imagination."

There was a silence. He could tell that she agreed. "Heddy, maybe Monday you should run a login diary. We could find out who's using it."

"Not if they're sitting at a terminal there. It'll just look like I logged on."

"I could check the time stamps on some of the more sensitive files," he said.

"If somebody's just reading the data, it won't change the time stamp."

"Don't you keep a history file?"

"Yeah, Kiro. Of course I do."

"Well, then, type 'history' and see what the last ten things were that they typed in."

"My history file is supposed to clear when I log out."

"You could look."

"All right. All right."

"You could put a thing in your logout file to save your history."

"Maybe. Maybe I'll do that."

Well, he'd tried. When Heddy was in her I'm-so-busy mode, there was no point trying to budge her. Anyway, he wanted to figure it out *now*. Kiro was a young man whose minimum daily requirement of adventure had never been satisfied. He'd never been able to play sports, so he'd never experienced that hope-to-win/fear-you'll-screw-up that made the adrenaline surge and the heart race.

Plus, he wasn't going to be in the office on Monday. He had a little surgery coming up, nothing unfamiliar to him. He'd been checking in for surgery more or less all his life. This one was going to lengthen his left Achilles tendon, which for some inexplicable reason had been gradually shortening, causing him to point the toes of his left foot more and more. The right Achilles tendon, for some equally obscure reason, was perfectly normal. He'd put off the surgery, because the problem didn't particularly bother him. He couldn't walk anyway, so what difference did it make? But when it got to the point where his foot was almost totally pointed straight out, it kept slipping off the footrest of the wheelchair. He agreed it was time to do something. The surgery would be Monday, and he'd be away from work maybe five days. He didn't want a spy in the system while he was gone—somebody rooting around finding out anything they wanted to know. He wanted to catch the guy.

All right, feeb, he said to himself, *figure it out!*

You're a methodical thinker, pal. Not flashy, maybe, but methodical.

10110

KIRO HUNG UP the phone after his unsatisfactory talk with Heddy. By now it was nine P.M., and even though he had eaten dinner, nervousness was making him hungry. He went to the employee lounge, buying two orders of macaroni and cheese from the machine, two Cokes, and three Snickers bars. There was nothing like carbos to give you a boost.

He quickly ate the macaroni and drank one Coke sitting in the lounge in his wheelchair at one of the tables. Then he took the other Coke and the candy bars back to his office.

He wheeled up to his monitor and after a little thought typed out a script commanding the machine to type users continuously and compare the result with the last time it ran. Then he asked it to beep him when there was a difference.

Currently the only user on the screen was

lame

It was now just ten minutes after nine. Kiro was the only person on the system and apparently alone in the building except for the security guard. Small wonder, on a Saturday night. At first, writing the script, he had intended to do other work while it ran invisibly in the background. But now he found he was too nervous to do anything else.

He sat and waited.

He ate the first candy bar, unwrapping it without taking his eyes off the screen. A person could log on and off in seconds, even though that wasn't what happened last time.

He was revved up. His mind was racing on tension, adrenaline, sugar, and maybe some—he wasn't sure quite how much—fear.

At nine-twenty, Kiro ate another chocolate bar.

users

He drank a Coke. Dimly he realized that he was taking on a lot more sugar than he usually did. But he had to do something with his hands while his eyes watched the cursor. At nine-thirty, he ate the third Snickers bar.

Watch this space. Watch this space. It wasn't so much hypnotizing as it was goading. It was a *tap-tap-tap* on his eyes, the *tick-tick-tick* of a visual clock.

He jumped when he heard the beep.

```
lame
mama
```

Kiro leaped at his keyboard, completely forgetting that his plan was to wheel out the door and zoom through the building to catch the person who was doing this.

```
talk mama
```

he typed. His screen split horizontally and the top half represented his own terminal. The bottom half was where he expected mama to answer. Wherever mama was, the screen would right now be flashing a message saying:

```
talk from user lame
```

Kiro wrote

```
Who are you? Can I help you?
```

There was no response.

```
Who are you?
```

he typed.

The split screen cleared. At the bottom of his screen appeared:

```
talk disconnected at mama's request
```

"Shit!" Kiro yelled, grabbing the controls of his chair. He backed away from his workstation fast, zoomed out the door of his office and down the hall. He already knew there were no office lights on in this corridor, and while he might go around the two legs of the U-shaped building on this floor, if he was going to head somebody off at the pass, it made more sense to get to the ground floor, fast.

He punched the elevator button. There were only two elevators. Both indicators were on one, neither had been moving as he reached them, and as his own elevator rose to pick him up, the other indicator remained unmoving.

As the door shut him inside the elevator, he had a moment's qualm. Sinking toward the ground floor, he realized how blind he would be the moment just before the doors opened. He envisioned the elevator stopping there, the door opening, and someone terrible waiting for him. Somebody threatening, dangerous, waiting to do something horrible to him. Kill him? Shoot him? Stab him? Tip him over, out of his chair, and kick him to death?

The door opened. Nobody was there.

He wheeled out, motor humming. The indicator of the other elevator was still on one. There was no sign of life on this floor.

Nothing alive except me.

Immediately he regretted having notions like that. The corridor was so long and so dim. And if he went down the two side corridors to see if there was a light on or a door unlocked, he would not be able to keep the elevators under observation.

He had to mark the elevator doors in some way, so as to know if the elevator had been used while he was out of sight of it. And in that same second he thought of putting a tiny speck of paper in the track where the doors slid open.

But he didn't have any paper. He said, "Shit!" again, but much more softly this time. So he wasn't prepared for this. Well, he wasn't a secret agent.

The closest thing he had was a dollar bill in his pocket. Hating to do it—he'd never torn up money in his entire life— but in a terrific hurry, he tore a tiny piece off the bill and dropped it in the track of the first door, then another in the track of the other elevator. Then he spun around to survey the north corridor. For a moment, he thought of calling the security guard in the basement. And tell him what? His workstation was spying on him? And lose precious time besides? No, he'd do this himself. He wasn't *that* handicapped!

He wheeled fast down the hall in his motorized chair. The hall lights were low, turned down for the night, and he could clearly see that there were no lights on in any offices.

When he reached the end of the corridor, he was also near the stairs that led to the upper floors. He tore a little bit more off the dollar bill and dropped it in front of the outswing of the stair door.

It would be swept aside if the door opened.

He zoomed to the front door and did the same. Kiro realized that someone could have left by the front door before he arrived there, but he had a strong feeling that no one had. For a second or two he asked himself how he knew. Obviously there was a sixth sense or primitive instinct operating here, but one he wasn't aware of.

Then he got it. The air in the square vestibule inside the doors was still and warm. It was a cool and breezy March evening outdoors. If someone had left by this entrance recently, the air would be cool and moving.

He ran his chair to the fire door at the far rear of the building. He'd left this for last because it was wired to the alarm system and if someone had gone out this way there should have been an unholy racket. It was untouched.

Now that he'd taken care of the ground floor, Kiro zoomed back to the elevators. Both were where he had left them and so were the pieces of dollar bill. Nobody had come down in either elevator.

He rolled in and took the elevator to the top floor. He drove out, then wedged one of his shoes in the elevator door so that it couldn't close and nobody could call it down to another floor.

In this building, for security reasons, there were no snaplocks in the doorknobs. No inside locks. When an employee was in an office, he or she couldn't lock the door. When an employee left at the end of the day, or when the last employee left a multiple-person office at the end of the day, he or she locked the door from the outside with a keycard.

Therefore, Kiro should find all the doors locked, except the one where the phantom mama hid.

The corridor was very dim. After-hours protocol, programmed into the lighting board, called for only one out of every four bulbs in the halls to be lit.

Kiro's plan was simple. The U-shaped building had one long, U-shaped corridor. He would simply roll along, starting from the elevator in the middle of the U, trying all the doors in the front part or south of the building, then up the west side of the U, trying the outer doors, and so forth.

He would just drive slowly, turning each knob with his right hand, running the chair's joystick with his left hand. Simple.

Easy, old chap. A no-brainer.

And it was simple at first. Every door from the elevator on in the south corridor was locked. Every light off. He hummed along, turning knobs, glancing around himself as he went, to see if there were any lights on in offices ahead or on the other side of the corridor.

And glancing around himself.

And glancing around himself.

And looking back over his shoulder.

His chair hummed awfully loudly.

Each time he tried a knob, the sound of it turning was a loud *clatter-click* in his ears.

Louder and louder.

He came to the fire stairs at the end of the west wing. He didn't open the fire door because it would set off the alarm, but he felt over the wiring. No breaks. Kiro reached up high around the door, balancing half out of his chair.

Then he slipped.

He lost his balance, couldn't sit down in the chair fast enough to save himself, couldn't stand on his shriveled legs. Kiro flopped painfully onto the floor near the fire door.

"Oh, shit!" he said aloud, then regretted it. Phantom m a m a might hear. He twisted around to stare down the long, dim hall. Nothing moved.

Swallowing, he assessed his predicament. He could not get back in his chair from the floor without pulling himself up on the fire door bar, the panic bar it was called, and if he did, he'd set off the alarm. The boss wouldn't like that. There was no way to call the night watchman, who was probably asleep. Anyhow he didn't want to alarm the intruder; he wanted to catch him. And besides he had a lifetime policy: *I get back into my own chair myself. I don't need help!*

The joystick controlled steering. Forward and right made the chair go forward and right. On the left side of the seat was the brakes lever.

He flopped around on the floor, pulling himself a foot or so toward the side of his wheelchair. Reaching the side of the chair, he could touch the control lever with his hand. He pushed the lever to the back, reversing the chair a foot or so, until it went so far away that he couldn't touch the lever anymore. Then he flopped forward a foot or so, toward it. He was so damned helpless! He looked back down the corridor. No one there.

Then he pushed the lever again. Then he flopped forward, catching up with the chair again.

After nine such maneuvers, he and the chair reached the door of one of the offices, a door with a doorknob. Carefully he backed and forwarded and turned the chair until it was positioned just right. He shoved the brake lever on, hard. Then he grabbed the knob—which wouldn't set off any alarm—in his right hand and placed his left hand on the seat of the chair and heaved up. At the height of the push he swiveled and flipped his body into the wheelchair.

Saved!

He was shaking. But he was safe.

Wait a minute! Safe from what? He'd fallen out of his chair before. Oh, maybe a thousand times, give or take, he thought. He knew how to get back in. It wasn't pretty, but it wasn't dangerous, either. So what was he afraid of?

He was alone, but he didn't feel alone.

He started the chair humming down the hallway again, and

he glanced over his shoulder again and again and again—nothing.

He was scared but, by God, he was going on with the search. Kiro squared his shoulders. He hummed along the corridor, trying every door. His eyes were wide, his ears felt like they stood straight out from his head, and his every sense was on emergency alert status, but he methodically tested every single door on the third floor. He entered the men's bathroom and checked every stall, keeping an eye on the doors of the unchecked stalls as he went. Nothing. Hesitating only slightly, he entered the women's bathroom and checked every stall. Before he left the bathroom, he peered carefully out the hall door, but there was no one waiting outside to attack him.

He arrived back at the elevator, picked up his shoe, descended to the second floor, and replaced his shoe in the elevator door. Then he checked every single room on the second floor.

He did the same on the first floor.

Then he hummed over to the front doors, where he had put pieces of his dollar bill. The pieces were exactly where he had dropped them. The night outside was dark. Against the glass doors he saw an image of himself with the ghost corridor stretching away behind him, and the reflected movement of cars outdoors made it look like shapes were moving behind him in the building.

He gasped and spun around, nearly falling out of his chair again.

Nobody there.

He trembled. His feet shook on the footrests of his wheelchair. Absolutely nothing had happened and nobody was here, and yet from his toes to his eyelids, he was shaking.

KIRO WAS ALONE, as he thought. He was also, as he feared, not alone.

"Got him," Zach said. On his screen was a flashing message saying:

```
talk from user lame
```

Then:

```
Who are you? Can I help you?
```

Zach stared at it. It wasn't Heddy, for sure.

His screen said: `Who are you?`

Zach disconnected instantly.

"Bermandyne?" Howie asked.

"Yeah."

"Lame, he says. Well, it certainly won't take long to find out who that is."

"Good." Zach was more shaken than he wanted to show.

"Give me a hardcopy of the whole exchange. And then leave Bermandyne alone for a while. I'll take care of this guy."

It took Howie only a few minutes in his office to bring up a canned list of Bermandyne employees out of the SJR system. He was annoyed to find that the backgrounds on them were thin. Couldn't be more than a couple of thousand bytes on anybody. Nobody at SJR had ever thought it would be of any importance to background these people, so remote from SJR itself.

"But Bermandyne has to have employment histories," Howie said to his screen.

The clock on his screen said 21:42::03 P.M. "Now what we need to know is whether `lame` is still on the system. And we'd like to find out without him seeing us."

On the other hand, time was of the essence.

Howie made an executive decision. He flashed over the wires between SJR and Chicago, slipped into Bermandyne, and appeared in the system as chief sysop. As he did so, his awareness of his office dropped away. The nervous motions of his hands and head ceased, and he became focused somewhere beyond the screen. He asked:

`ph lame`

And the Bermandyne system told him: `Kiro Ogata`

Now he took more of a chance. He typed

`users`

The screen replied

`mama`

So `lame` had left the system. Kiro Ogata had presumably gone home. Howie said to his screen, "Good. Because I don't want you to see this."

Howie brought up two files: the Bermandyne salaries file and employment histories. Salaries wasn't very useful, although it gave him Kiro Ogata's home address, social security number, employment category, and pay scale. Employment history was better. It told Howie when Kiro had started work, what his educational background was, the entire story of his work history at Bermandyne, including all vacations and several paid and unpaid leaves for surgery, his complete medical history, doctors' names from various notes to the company about his medical absences, the fact that he did not use illegal recreational drugs. And the fact that he was scheduled to have the next five days off for surgery at University Hospital.

Howie had a little more research to do, but he was confident the problem was in hand.

"Kiro Ogata, I can delete you," he said.

KATH, MARIA, JJ, and I played Clue Saturday evening while Robert and Sheryl were at Utley's party. JJ won.

"Aunt Suze," Kath said teasingly, "since you're a cop, shouldn't you have known whodunnit?"

"I should have, Kath. I don't know what came over me."

I suspected Kath of letting JJ win. Kath is very sharp and enjoys Clue. Me, I just plain didn't guess that Miss Scarlet had done it in the dining room with a knife. It seemed to me Colonel Mustard had more the personality for murder.

Maria must have had her mind on some boy in her class, although she played cheerfully. It wouldn't be much longer before Maria was out on dates on Saturday evenings instead of home with us.

After the game, Kath went away to read something and Maria to make phone calls to her friends. JJ followed me into the living room, where we thought we'd watch television. He brought a bag of potato chips with him and handed it to me first.

"Thank you, JJ," I said. Then reverting to a dialogue he'd liked when he was little, I said, "What's your name, little boy?"

He looked sideways at me. "JJ," he said.

"JJ. That's a nice name. I have a boy named JJ. What's your last name?"

"Figueroa." I could see the emotions go across his face: he was too old for this game. He was *six*. But gee, yes—he loved it.

I said, "JJ Figueroa? What a coincidence! I have a very nice little boy myself and his name is JJ Figueroa."

Suddenly he put his arms in the air just like he had when he was three or four years old and yelled, "I'm *your* boy!" I grabbed him up and squeezed him.

"I'm glad you're my boy!"

Sheryl and Robert arrived before we finished the potato

chips. Robert seemed huffy and went to work on his stock orders.

Sheryl told me about Utley's home office, his apartment in the sky, his crotons, his amaryllises, his Univac table, his CAD and CAM systems, his HP printer.

"Sheryl, you didn't let him see that you thought he had an unusual amount of hardware, did you?"

She hesitated. "No. No, he didn't really even want to talk about it."

I was uneasy about her response, but she should know best, shouldn't she? "What about the Blue Blazers and Howie?"

"I'm right. Howie avoids them. I'm certain of it. But Howie left early—with Zach. It was spooky. He didn't seem like he really wanted to, but he went."

"What now?"

"On Monday, I'm going to take a look at the files at work."

"Sheryl, don't. Just pass the word on to Utley, if you have to."

"You don't understand. I just want to look inside the system from my terminal. Nobody will ever know I did it."

11001

||||||||||||||||||||||||||||||||||||||||||||||||||||||||||||||||||||||
DEPARTMENT OF THE TREASURY
UNITED STATES SECRET SERVICE
1800 G STREET NW
WASHINGTON DC
FROM: CMV
TO: STRICK
FORM: INTERNAL

<<IN ANY OPEN TRANSMISSION FOLLOW THE
ESTABLISHED CODES>>

DAYS UNTIL WE HAND YOU THE PRESIDENT 6

JIM:
YES, ONE MOTORCADE.
WHAT DID YOU THINK, A SPECIAL ONE FOR THE
SIDEKICK?
IF HE ASKS AGAIN TELL HIM IT'S ALL LOCKED
IN.

CMV
|||||||||||||||||||||||||||||||||||||||||||||||||||||||||||||

11010

SUNDAY AFTERNOON KIRO checked into the U-Hosp complex. He went through the usual preadmission questions and was sent to a room. He undressed and was subjected to the usual physical indignities. *Why*, he wondered, *don't you ever get used to this?*

Since it was the night before his scheduled surgery, he was allowed a five-thirty dinner, but after that there would be nothing by mouth until he got back from the recovery room, sometime around noon the next day.

His friend Ron came by the hospital at six-thirty.

"You're not worried, are you?" he asked Kiro, seeing how glum he looked.

"No. I was thinking about the meatloaf I just ate."

Ron laughed. "Gee, I went to King of Siam for dinner. Spring rolls. Ginger beef. Coconut soup."

"You really know how to hurt a guy."

"I really know how to help a guy, too. Wait until you get home."

"Waited on hand and foot?"

"And more. You'll see."

When they heard Kiro's parents' voices in the hall, Ron squeezed Kiro's shoulder and left. It always seemed easier on Kiro's parents if Ron avoided them.

Shortly after 2 A.M., deep within the bowels of the central building, the U-Hosp data management system, with a 255 gigabyte fault-tolerant disk array, came alive. The bits that made up Kiro's medical records sped along a telephone wire to an office twenty-four miles away.

There his full chart came up on a monitor.

Howie Borke read every single word of the chart, and then went back and read it a second time. He kept the chart on the monitor for nearly half an hour, while he brought up several medical texts on other windows.

But finally he was sure there was really only one feasible option. Several years earlier, during one of his many surgeries, Kiro had had an extremely severe reaction to an anesthetic. His blood pressure had plummeted. But he was young and basically healthy except for his handicap, and he was brought out of it. The near-disaster had been laid at the door of an additive called methylparaben used as a preservative in many types of injectable anesthetics.

With a precision reminiscent of surgery, Howie excised the entry about Kiro's sensitivity to methylparaben from the medical record, just as if he were seated at a terminal in the U-Hosp complex. He restored the new record, overwriting the file that was in the mainframe in the basement of the central hospital building.

11011

AT SIX FORTY-FIVE Monday morning, BeeGee Hart, Kiro's nurse, entered his room. Kiro had been up for hours; in fact, he had been restless and sleepless most of the night. She'd already done the bedpan and presurgery shower routine, seating Kiro in the shower on a shower stool for the handicapped, perforated to let water run through.

"All right. We've got word you go down at seven-thirty. They finished the one before you in twenty minutes."

"Lucky him. Did he survive?"

"You get up on the wrong side of bed?"

"Hey, I never got out of the bed at all."

"I know," she said, relenting. "It can't be fun."

"Not your fault. Sorry."

"Here's your sedative."

"Could we do without that?" said Kiro as she took a syringe from a tray. While he was horribly accustomed to these surgeries, he didn't like the extras that surrounded them.

"It's Valium. Relax you just a little."

"Oh, all right, all right," he said. He was too fed up with the whole thing to argue, and besides, maybe dozing a little would make the horrors go faster.

11100

TWO ORDERLIES HELD Kiro in a sitting position on the table, his thin legs hanging over the edge. The anesthesiologist drove the large hollow needle through the muscle and between two of Kiro's lumbar vertebrae. Kiro grunted just a little, but he knew the quieter he stayed the sooner it would be over.

The anesthesiologist felt for the sudden lack of resistance and stopped just inside the hollow spinal cavity through which the spinal cord ran. Another fraction of an inch and the tip of the needle would penetrate some of the fibers of the spinal cord. The tip of the needle rested in spinal fluid. Into this fluid he injected bupivacane hydrochloride.

Within moments, all of Kiro's body from that level on down began to go numb. Then the anesthesiologist added a touch more Valium to Kiro's IV and at 7:33 said to the surgeon, "We're looking good here."

"We're going to turn you over, now," the nurse said. The operation was to be on the back of the lower left leg.

Kiro mumbled, "Okay."

The orderly and an unsterile nurse rolled Kiro over, keeping his IV line clear as they did.

"How are you feeling now, Mr. Ogata?" the surgeon asked.

Kiro said, "Oh, just fine," very sleepily.

Kiro's chart lay on a side table. The display of Kiro's medical history on the green-screen monitor faced the room with its calm, authoritative light. The surgeon, the orderly, the resident, both interns, and the surgical nurse had consulted the screen, which could be scrolled by foot pedal if necessary, to keep their hands sterile.

The surgeon cut along the back of Kiro's leg from a point just above the heel to a point where the calf muscle began to flare out. The resident held the retractors on one side and one of the two interns held the retractors on the other side. It wasn't a difficult job, which was why the intern was allowed to take a hand in it. He mostly stood there holding Kiro's skin back out of the way with two instruments shaped like little rakes. The surgeon's strategy was to lengthen the Achilles tendon by cutting through it at a very oblique diagonal angle, moving the slices along each other, and then reconnecting them.

He was looking to be done soon, with no trouble. So he was surprised when the anesthesiologist said, "I don't like this BP."

He spoke softly because, although the patient looked sleepy, he was probably conscious.

"What is it?"

"One-ten over sixty-five and falling."

"I've got another forty-five minutes here."

But there was no time to make an assessment of whether he could finish. The bottom fell out of Kiro's blood pressure and within another eighty seconds the heart monitor was beeping.

"He's in V-fib!" the nurse said.

Kiro was immediately rolled onto his back. The table was lowered for CPR and the anesthesiologist began to administer 50 mg of lidocaine with epinephrine through the IV line. The resident plugged into an O^2 source. The unsterile nurse started a second IV line, just in case they lost access to the first. The intern wheeled over the defibrillation equipment. He placed one paddle over the space between Kiro's second and third rib, at the right border of the breastbone, and the second paddle over the top of the heart. He glanced at the surgeon who nodded his head. He'd done it right.

The surgeon said, "Clear."

Everybody backed off and they hit Kiro with a shock of 200 joules.

Except for the intern, who was performing the CPR, every head swiveled to the monitor. Nothing had changed.

"Procainamide?" said the anesthesiologist, and the surgeon nodded. His face was expressionless.

The anesthesiologist started 100 mg of procainamide into the IV line, a procedure that he would perform slowly, over two minutes, so as not to inject too great a concentration all at once.

Meanwhile, the surgeon ordered a second countershock. Kiro's body lurched, but the graph remained unchanged.

The CPR continued, the second intern now taking over.

"Bretylium?" said the anesthesiologist. The surgeon nodded. The anesthesiologist picked up a vial of bretylium tosylate and loaded a syringe.

The physicians and nurses working over Kiro's flaccid body did not notice a split second when the monitor display blinked. They were busy. After the bretylium tosylate went into the IV line, procedure called for another electrical defibrillation at 360 joules, then at least fifteen and possibly as much as thirty minutes of continued CPR, in hopes of a response.

"Antishock trousers!" the surgeon said.

The nurse winced, realizing this was a desperation move. The CPR went on.

Kiro's hair hung over his forehead. For some reason, one of his brown eyes was open, the other closed. The lower part of his face was obscured by the airway equipment.

The doctors were losing hope, but they continued. Then the anesthesiologist glanced at the medical chart, glowing calmly on the monitor.

"Oh, my God! I didn't see this!"

The sterile nurse came to look. After one glance, her hand started to shake. "I didn't see that, either! I don't think it was there."

"I always read everything—"

"I don't understand it," the nurse said. "I read it, too. It wasn't there."

The surgeon was angry. "Well, goddammit, it can't have changed!" There was panic in his voice.

Any electrical trace of the cyberinvasion had long since winked out in the mainframe. The records were just as they had been yesterday, and last week.

At 8:59 in major surgery room 37, electrical activity in the brain of Kiro Ogata also winked out.

11101

```
||||||||||||||||||||||||||||||||||||||||||||||||||||||||||||||||||
DEPARTMENT OF THE TREASURY
UNITED STATES SECRET SERVICE
1800 G STREET NW
WASHINGTON DC
FROM: CMV
TO: STRICK
FORM: INTERNAL

<<IN ANY OPEN TRANSMISSION FOLLOW THE
ESTABLISHED CODES>>

DAYS UNTIL WE HAND YOU THE PRESIDENT 5
JIM:
MAKE SURE LOCALS CHECK FINGERPRINTS OF ALL
CONTACT PERSONS.
DOUBLECHECK LOCALS.
ALWAYS DOUBLECHECK LOCALS.

CMV
||||||||||||||||||||||||||||||||||||||||||||||||||||||||||||||||||
```

11110

TOWARD THE MIDDLE of the morning on Monday, March 23, about the time that Kiro Ogata was being pronounced dead, Sheryl stored the aircraft guidance project. She took out the disk she had brought from home and set it down to the right of her computer. She was going to try to break into one of the hidden files and find out what they were being used for. If she found anything that looked criminal, then she could decide what to do. If she didn't, she was going to leave it alone, permanently.

Sheryl Birch shared with most hard workers a certain kind of exacting nature: things could be made to work, they ought to work, and they ought to work *right*.

The engineers at SJR were regularly told that their daily work was not spied upon, or even recorded until they stored it themselves. Sheryl didn't know whether to believe that. However, she was certain that there was far too much daily work—routine trials of existing programs in new uses, writing code and changing it, calling stuff from library programs and fiddling with it, new work that didn't turn out to be any good and was soon erased—for anyone to bother to oversee everything that went on.

What was more important in this case, once she was inside the smartlink software with the password, she was in a less guarded part of the system. Since you had to be high level even to be given the access, there would be less security once you were inside.

Sheryl had access to the list of encrypted passwords used inside the smartlink software, but encryptions were of no use. Encryptions don't give access to the files; only the password would do that. However, Sheryl could use a password-cracking program to encrypt possible words and letter combinations and see if they matched existing encryptions.

If Sheryl ran a program that simply tried all the conceivable combinations of twenty-six letters, uppercase and lowercase, and 0–9 numbers, she would have over 63^{13} possibilities to try. Even if she had a program that could try ten passwords per second, it would take 6.3×10^{14} years, or 600 trillion years to try them all. By then the universe would either have imploded or suffered heat death, depending on the cosmological theory you preferred. She needed a way to make the list of combinations to try as short as possible—something her program could run in less than 600 trillion years.

Ph files can do that.

Company ph files had information about the employees. They were a computer dossier. The names of the employees' children, where they live, where they grew up, what their hobbies are, where they went to school, any known friends, illnesses, current programming interests, dogs, cats, gerbils—just about everything available. Since people usually used words from their own lives for passwords, ph files shorten the cracking program's workload.

Sheryl had a good password-cracking program she'd downloaded from a hacker web-site. She had brought it to work on a 3½-inch disk. Now she slipped the disk into the drive and brought the program up on the screen.

Sheryl had a hundred and twenty-eight encryptions, most of them probably belonging to Utley himself, or Zach, Glen, Howie, or the steering committee.

All she really wanted was a hit on two or three, so that she could peer into the actual files as a sort of spot check and see whether there was actual criminal misuse of the SJR system. With definite information, she would go to Dean Utley. He wouldn't be happy. But she didn't think he would be quite furious enough to kill the messenger, so to speak. If she just had suspicions, he might be angry at her, but not if she had both the problem *and* the solution. If she had sufficient data for him to proceed immediately to fire the pirate or prosecute criminally, then he'd be grateful.

Maybe very grateful. Maybe grateful enough to promote her another level up.

Now she pulled up and downloaded the company ph files on Glen, Howie, Zach, Dean Utley, Crossley the building sysop, and Henry DeLusk onto her own disk. She would give this material to the password cracking program.

She wasn't sure how long it would take the program to chew the data, swallow it, and digest it. Hours, probably. But it would do it all by itself. All she had to do was hit the command.

Her hand stopped, finger just above the key. Sheryl froze. In the back of her mind was something urging her to be careful. Wait! Think! Think! She paused.

It took her half a minute to realize why her head was saying,

Stupid! She didn't need to run this here on the company system. All she had to do was copy the list of encrypted passwords along with the ph files on Zach, Glen, Crossley, DeLusk, and Howie on her disk, take the disk home and run the cracking program *at home in perfect safety*. If she came up with any passwords, she could bring them back and look into the files then.

That way she wouldn't expose herself any longer than necessary.

So she copied the encryptions to her own disk.

⅃⅃⅃⅃⅃

HOWIE BORKE WAS just finishing his lunch when he saw Sheryl carrying her tray into the dining room. He pushed out a chair for her. Howie liked Sheryl. She reminded him in some ways of his wife. Howie had never seen himself as the marrying type, partly because he was awkward and found it difficult to introduce himself to women. Then, in April two years ago, a woman named Miranda walked into a Thai restaurant in Evanston where he often ate. She was alone and looked sad. On an unusually bold impulse, he asked her what was wrong. She said she had just broken up with a guy. How long was the relationship? Howie asked. Six years, Miranda said. And Howie had told her, "That sounds like an extra-hot kang kheew wan problem to me." She laughed, and they ate dinner together. The rest was history.

Howie said, "Hi, Sheryl."

"Hiya, Howie."

Howie said, "I see you took the shrimp salad. It's my wife's favorite, too. She's visited here a couple of times." He talked fast and moved fast, with quick, accurate darts. Howie was like a squirrel, Sheryl thought—no, a fox. A lanky fox.

"While you're going in for the cholesterol special."

Howie grinned at what was left of his double cheeseburger and fries. "I'm gonna have fun while I'm young enough to handle it," he said.

"Well, gee, Howie, they're your arteries."

"Damn right."

"I thought you were at the Chicago Police Department."

"Yeah. Back and forth, back and forth. That's why I'm eating early."

"System installed yet?"

"Actually, yeah. A little glitch or two. It's up and running. It was mainly up and running Sunday, except some of the stations were dead. Wouldn't you think cops would be calm types?"

"Yes, I suppose."

"Even phlegmatic? Maybe unflappable?" Howie said.

"I guess so."

"Well, you should see this guy Heidema. Cold fish type, and looks dead calm. But he's been a nervous wreck about the changeover. And he starts telling me, real quiet at first, about this problem and that problem and his voice gets more and more high-pitched. And all the time he's pressing his hands together just as if he's praying. Pressing them hard. You can see his fingertips turn white. And he's not just some guy; he's a topcop. They call him a deputy superintendent."

"Why's he so upset?"

"Nothing so much. Two maybe three districts they can't get on the air. Out of twenty-five! And then once in a while some call gets routed wrong."

"Like there's a holdup in the North Loop and the call goes to a district in the South Loop?"

"Yeah."

"Well, Howie. I'm on their side. That's exactly the kind of thing cops *oughta* get worried about."

"Maybe. Maybe you're right." Howie got up. "See ya. Back to the copshop."

He felt better about things. Sheryl made him feel good.

100000

SHERYL BIRCH STOOD up from her desk and drew a deep breath. Five o'clock. Time to leave. She reached out and picked up the disk. This disk held the ph files she had downloaded, files on Howie, Utley, Zach, Glen, DeLusk, and the sysop.

It felt heavier than a normal disk. She told herself, "That's stupid!" out loud.

She put the disk in her shoulder bag, walked out of the office, and locked the door.

Now her shoulder bag felt heavy. Quietly, she joined the procession of people leaving for the day. In the elevator she exchanged a few words with Jim Wu. The elevator stopped on the second floor and the sysop, Crossley, got on. Her shoulder bag pressed up against his side.

Nobody could possibly guess what she had in her bag.

100001

"WELL, YOU'RE ABSOLUTELY in luck, Detective Delgado," Teddy Sofran said enthusiastically. "Betty passed the fecal material on to me"—Jesus winced slightly at this phrasing—"because I just spent two weeks at a forensic botany seminar at the Institute of Organismic Biology. Plants, you know. Betty mostly does blood and semen these days."

Teddy Sofran had a round, pink face and enthusiastic red hair that stuck up all over his head. He reminded Jesus of a turnip. Jesus was glad that Teddy, though a lab tech, was also a Chicago cop, because if he got too youthfully cheeky, Jesus could tell him a thing or two. Still, he said calmly, "Why? Why does a plant seminar help?"

"See, you've got plant material in the intestinal contents. And the question is, *what* plant material? And I can tell you!"

"Oh. Good."

"I wouldn't ordinarily have this so soon, and it's only the fecal matter. Microscope work, basically. The cultures will take several days. But it was extremely interesting. Textbook, almost. In fact, I'm thinking I could write an article on it. Have to get permission upstairs, of course." Teddy caught the impatient look on Jesus' face. "Um, here's what we have. You know you had a lot of decomposition. I mean, a body in the lake that long!"

"You mean Frieswyk's intestinal contents had decomposed?"

"Well, of course. You must have seen a lot of gaseous buildup during the autopsy, you know."

Wincing, Jesus agreed. "So you can't tell much about what he ate?"

"Well, here's an interesting thing. Your pathologist— um—Dr. Chen, must have told you there was no food in the stomach or upper part of the small intestine."

"It was in the final report she just faxed me."

"So you've got to allow for several hours between the time he ate and the time he died. You can ask her about that, but with the contents in the last third of the small intestine, I would say you gotta allow twelve hours."

"Okay. I'll allow twelve hours."

"Which means that what I'm gonna show you was eaten that long before he died."

"What are you gonna show me?" Jesus did not let his excitement appear on his face. If he could find out anything about what Frieswyk had eaten before death, he had a shot at discovering *where* Frieswyk had eaten before death. There had been cases solved by little else. He had worked on one that turned on nothing more than oregano on a pizza.

Teddy took him to a table. There were several microscope slides and some photos lying on top of a manila folder. Teddy

shoved a slide into a microscope, fussed to get the right lighting, then stepped back and proudly said, "Look!"

Jesus looked. "Can I adjust—?" he asked, gesturing at the
focus knob.

"Sure. Go ahead."

"What is it? It looks like a stack of needles."

"Crystals. They're from pineapple cells. Magnified five
hundred times."

"Oh. Well, that's good." Delgado was actually a little
disappointed. What could he do with a damn pineapple?

"No, don't walk away! That's not all. Take a look at this!"

"Um—yeah. Well, what that looks like is, um, a crystal
chandelier. No, a cluster of glass globes—"

"It's a stone cell from a pear. Magnified a hundred and fifty
times. Stone cells are the things that make pears have that kind
of gritty crunchiness."

"No kidding? That's very interesting!"

Teddy was pleased at the response. "Now, the next sample
is from the scanning electron microscope. I've got photos." He
pulled a couple of photographs from a stack. "This—"

"It looks like tripe." Jesus hated tripe.

"Yes, it looks like tripe, but it's cherry pulp. And here we
have a tiny fragment of grape skin. Personally, I think there
was also a fragment of peach, but it's so far gone—well. Anyway. So what does that tell us, Detective?"

"I guess that he ate pears and cherries and grapes and pineapple. A fruit salad."

"No, no, think!"

"I don't know."

"Come on. You know what these things are components
of."

"But it could be anything." Jesus was about to slap the kid
down when inspiration hit.

He said, "Oho! Fruit cocktail! Canned fruit cocktail! The
kind with the little chunks in syrup!"

"Right!" Teddy shouted. "I knew you'd get it!"

"Gee, thanks!" The kid's attitude was positively infectious.

"Find out who served him fruit cocktail, and you're home free!"

"Well, not necessarily. But it's a start."

"That's about all I can tell you from this, even though he certainly ate other things with it. I'm real sorry."

"Hey, don't you mind. This is *excellent!*"

Jesus Delgado left the lab a happy man. For the first time in five weeks on the case he was going *someplace*.

He paused out in front of the CPD headquarters and asked himself a question: Where *exactly* was he going?

He turned around and went back inside to the bank of pay phones in the lobby. Standing near the phone to keep some other cop from grabbing it, he consulted his little black notebook. In it were the home and work phone numbers of Perry Frieswyk, Officer Frieswyk's former wife. He thought he'd start with her.

"Where did he *eat?* How should I know where he ate?" Perry Frieswyk said.

"Well, for instance, when he was at work. You were married a long time. And, I mean, he worked here every day. At Eleventh and State. Didn't he ever mention anyplace?"

"Not that I remember."

"Would he have taken a lunch from home?"

"Not him." She laughed. "He couldn't cook. He couldn't even make a peanut butter and jelly sandwich without poking a hole through the bread. And I moved out over a year ago. Maybe he didn't eat anyplace, what with that stupid diet of his."

"Diet? You didn't tell me about any diet."

"You didn't ask."

"True. What diet?"

"That man would gain weight eating a celery stick. Course, if he gave up beer, it might've helped. Even when we were still sort of friendly, we'd go out to some great place and he'd have cottage cheese!"

"Hmm. Well, thanks. Tell me this. Did Joe like fruit cocktail?"

"Like it? Hell, no. He hated it."

"Oh. Okay." Jesus was disappointed.

"Which is why he ate a lot of it. He figured the less he liked it, the less he'd eat."

"No kidding? That's great!"

There was a two-second pause, but apparently she decided that she didn't understand and wasn't going to ask. She went on: "At cafeterias and like that? He'd get a cottage cheese and fruit cocktail salad. Jeez! All the great food in the world you maybe could enjoy, and he eats that crap instead. Detective Delgado, have you ever thought about how many terrible things people do to themselves voluntarily?"

"Yeah. Yeah, I've thought a lot about that."

"I knew you would have," Perry Frieswyk said. "You're a sensitive man."

100010

HE WAS A LITTLE *too* sensitive that evening at dinner. Elena, his wife, had given the twins an early dinner: hot dogs and potato salad (who could say they weren't thoroughly Americanized?), with vanilla ice cream and strawberries for dessert. This Americanization question was a problem for Elena, but not for Jesus, despite his trouble with his name.

For Jesus, she'd made a Mexican boiled dinner. This would sound disheartening only to a person familiar with English boiled beef and boiled vegetables. The Mexican kind was made of roasted mutton (and just try to buy mutton in this culture, Elena said, where only spring lamb is considered good enough for these people), put into a pot with cabbage, potatoes, tomatoes, two sour apples, chili, oregano, and a little bit of turnips, beets, onions, and carrots. It had to simmer at least four hours to be exactly right.

Elena was justly proud of it. She followed it with pastelitos made of apricots on pastry baked with sugar and cinnamon. And she followed *that* with a question.

"The twins are four now. Do you know what I'd like to do when they start school in the fall?" She sat quietly at the table watching him.

Jesus could see that this was seriously major, but he couldn't think of what to say. So he just said, "No, what?"

"I'd like to apply to the department."

"To what department?"

"Jesus, what do you mean, 'what department'? The police department!"

"Uh. Mmmm."

"What does that mean?"

All kinds of visions were running through Jesus' head. Fecal material. Froth from the nose and throat. Bloated abdomens and thighs just starting to get greenish on the inside from decomposition.

"I don't think that's a good idea," he said.

"A good idea? A *good idea*?"

"Uh—no."

"I didn't ask you whether you thought it was a good idea. It was *my* idea. What I said was it was what I'd like to do."

Jesus knew he was already in trouble. Big trouble. But he couldn't help saying what was on his mind. And he knew it would make things worse.

"Come on, Elena. You don't want to do that."

"I *just said* I did."

"You don't want to do that; it's nasty."

"Nasty? *Nasty?* You think taking care of two kids having the intestinal flu all night long and changing barfed-up, shitty sheets isn't nasty? You think labor pains aren't nasty? You think—"

"That wasn't what I meant. I meant, when you're a cop you sometimes see the world at its worst."

"Which you are able to deal with, I suppose, and I wouldn't be?"

"Aw, come on, honey. Give me a break, here. I'm just saying I'd like to protect you from all that."

"You come in here, you've been working twelve-hour days, and you're looking like, man, you've sunk your teeth into a real case. I haven't seen you look so damn—so damn *vigorous* in a long time. And that isn't from your work, I suppose?"

"Honey, I've got this case, and I just want to break it."

"And it consumes you."

"Well, yeah. Maybe it does right now."

"Suppose I want some of that."

"Damn it! Suppose I think it's too dangerous?"

"Oh, now we're going all paternalistic, huh? Gonna take care of the poor little woman!"

"Well, and just why not?"

"Oh, right. You and your goddamn Mexican male macho shit! Strutting around like a little rooster!"

"Elena, you're—"

"I am Puerto Rican, not Mexican! And goddamn proud of it!" She stood up from the table.

"Please. Elena, you've got two kids depending on you!"

"And you haven't? You got no kids at all, I suppose?"

"Hell!" He stood up, too, and stamped out to the kitchen for a beer. He had a feeling he'd be sleeping on the sofa tonight.

I GOT HOME Monday after working second watch, seven A.M. to three P.M. JJ's bus let him off soon after, and I was able to spend an hour reading *The Royal Book of Oz* to him.

Then I made dinner for the group. Robert wasn't going to be home for dinner. He had to clerk at one of his dry cleaning stores where an employee was out sick. I had chicken roasting in the oven, basted with lemon juice, oregano, and garlic, almost ready to serve when Sheryl arrived home from work.

After dinner, Sheryl told me she was going to crack passwords tonight.

"Sheryl, does this expose you to some kind of danger?"

"No. Of course not. I'm not at work. I'm at home."

"Suppose you crack a password. What then?"

"Uh—"

"Sheryl!"

"Then I'd look into the file at work and see what it was."

"Oh, God!"

"Hey! Let me do the first step here, and then we can talk."

"All right. The first step only."

"Will you look in on Maria while I get set up?"

I knew what she meant. Maria was getting her worst grades in social studies. I went to check on her. I found her working on Eye Shadow 101, a subject in which she needed no further study whatever.

Having made clear that she had been excused from dishes to do homework, not makeup, I went to the little alcove that Sheryl called her office.

"How's it going?"

Sheryl said, "Shouldn't be a problem. It's maybe not the fastest system in the world, but pretty good."

I watched as Sheryl put the 3 ½-inch disk from work in the slot for the A drive and pushed it in.

"I'm copying the ph files—human data—and the list of

encrypted passwords and the password-cracking program onto my system."

"Okay."

"It's just between us, so far. Now, I'm giving the password-cracking program the words from the ph files to work with. These are things like Howie's wife's name, Miranda, the schools he attended, the names of the streets he's lived on, childhood pets, favorite restaurants; there's an amazing amount of stuff. And the same for Glen, Zach, Dean Utley, and Crossley, the sysop in my division."

"How long does this take?"

"Could be hours."

We checked the program another couple of times. The first time, there was nothing more, and I felt much more relieved than impatient. The second time, the machine had come up with something.

"What's that?"

Sheryl said, "It's a login plus a password."

`friend celeste`

Sheryl stared at it. "This obviously is from the ph files. Other than the capital letter that ought to be at the beginning of a person's name, it hasn't been changed. No inserted numbers or any capital letters that would make it more difficult to guess."

By the time we went to bed, there were no new passwords, but Sheryl left the program running.

In the early morning, when Sheryl went to look, there were two more, logins plus passwords:

`Joe2 hardass`

`Glen botulism`

When she came down to breakfast, she said she had a total of three. I said, "Now what?"

"Now I just try them today and see what files they bring up."

"Um, no, Sheryl. I don't think so."

"Look, I'm not going to *tell* anybody, until we talk it over.

We'll talk again tonight after work. I just want to look at them."

"Please don't."

"Now, Suze. With all due respect and all that, you don't know the first thing about computing."

"I never said I did—"

"And I'm telling you that there's no problem here! Believe me. It's not like there's a little spy inside my workstation that tells the company everything I do."

I had to be at work at seven. I was in a rush. Like a fool, I believed her. Knowing Sheryl, I knew that she was careful. I should have realized she was stubborn, too. I overlooked the danger my gut reaction told me was there.

I said, "It's your company. Probably you're right."

For the rest of my life, I will blame myself for giving in to her.

100100

||||||||||||||||||||||||||||||||||||||||||||||||||||||||||||||

DEPARTMENT OF THE TREASURY
UNITED STATES SECRET SERVICE
1800 G STREET NW
WASHINGTON DC
FROM: CMV
TO: STRICK
FORM: INTERNAL

<<IN ANY OPEN TRANSMISSION FOLLOW THE
ESTABLISHED CODES>>

DAYS UNTIL WE HAND YOU THE PRESIDENT 4
JIM:
WEIRDO HEADING YOUR WAY.

PHOTOFAX FOLLOWS.
MORE EMBARRASSING THAN DANGEROUS.
HE'S BEEN NGI'D MORE THAN ONCE.
VERIFY NCIC.
CONFIRM.

CMV
||||||||||||||||||||||||||||||||||||||||||||||||||||||||||||||||||||||||||

100101

JESUS AND ELENA were still not speaking to each other when he left for work Tuesday morning. Jesus hated to leave the house with Elena mad, but when he tried to approach her, she turned away. Maybe he could have made everything okay by saying, "You win. Go ahead. Be a cop." But he couldn't make himself do it.

Elena had been right in arguing that this case consumed him. By nine-thirty in the morning he had all but forgotten that Elena existed, because he was hot on the trail of the elusive cottage cheese and fruit cocktail.

Some other lab reports were coming in.

Jesus paged through them. No ethanol, even in the eyeball, so Frieswyk hadn't been drinking. If Frieswyk had drunk some beer, it was many hours earlier. The bronchii showed some traces of pollen. He'd have to find out what kind. And anyhow, where this time of year would he run into pollen? Greenhouses? The Botanic Garden? A flower shop, buying flowers for Perry? He'd get the microphotos and see if he could trace it down. No telling at this point. One odd thing—the lab chemist thought Frieswyk had gone quite a while before death without any liquids. The urine found in the ureters was rather concentrated. Not so easy to be sure after all this time, the chemist cautioned, but still—

Okay, I'm Frieswyk, he thought. *I don't have the sense to eat anything tasty. All I want is a no-brainer cottage cheese and fruit cocktail lunch. And not with a fancy price tag attached, either.*

At Henry's, a burger joint with a window covered with the gloom of twenty years of dust, walls amber with twenty years of grease deposits, the waitress looked at him as if he was nuts.

"Sandwiches," she said. "Hamburgers."

"Don't you have salads?"

She scratched her head with her pencil. Her orange hair was so puffy he could see her scalp. "Nobody *likes* salad," she said.

100110

JESUS STEPPED OUT into State Street. Suddenly, he froze and slapped his forehead.

"Idiot!" he said. A taxi swerved around him, honking.

"Moron!" said the taxi driver.

Now there was a bus approaching. Oncoming traffic on the other side of the road wouldn't give it room to swerve around Jesus. It hissed its air brakes, stopped, and honked.

Jesus didn't hear it. He turned and ran back to the CPD.

There was a cafeteria on the thirteenth floor of the CPD! Nobody ever thought about it, because nobody, or hardly anybody who had more than three taste buds to their tongues, ever went there. It was really a venda-teria, with vending machines and maybe one hot but bland entree at lunch, definitely a must-miss.

He whipped around the white tiled floor, studying all the vending machines, and there was a machine with little plastic containers of cottage cheese and little plastic containers of fruit cocktail and both of them kept cold in the *very by God same vending machine!*

He felt like he'd found the Holy Grail.

All he needed to make his day was somebody who had seen Frieswyk here on the day he disappeared.

There were two people normally in the venda-teria. One was Molly Wilson, who either cooked the hot dish or nuked it into a hot lunch. The other was Barmy Mason, the janitor. Molly wore a white uniform, was extremely plump, and smiled a lot. Barmy wore overalls, was pear shaped, and smiled a lot. Both of them said, "Sure, I knew Frieswyk."

"Did he eat here?"

Molly said, "Sure, how else we both gonna know him?"

Jesus said, "Do you know if he was in here on February fourteenth? Valentine's Day?"

Both of them said, "Are you kidding?"

"Does that mean you don't remember?"

Molly said, "Do you know what *you* were doing February fourteenth? That was weeks ago!"

"All right, all right. But you'd say he was in here a lot?"

"I'd say yeah." Barmy nodded judiciously.

"I'd say he came here for lunch four, maybe five, days a week."

"When he came in, what time was it usually?"

"Oh, twelvish," Molly said airily.

⌁⌁⌁⌁⌁⌁

1 0 0 1 1 1

TWELVE HOURS! NOW, he had actual time of death. Midnight on the fourteenth or very early in the morning of February 15.

He was murdered around midnight! This was much later than Jesus or anybody else had imagined, on the basis of what little they knew before now. Everybody just assumed that Frieswyk had walked out of the department, though they

didn't know when, gotten into some kind of trouble immediately, and been killed pretty much immediately after that.

This meant Frieswyk could have gone—or been taken—
quite some distance away. Frieswyk had eaten lunch in the
CPD cafeteria—poor guy. Then he went back to his office. He
must have; other people saw him there up to one or one-thirty.
Then he went out, saying he had a meeting.

And walked into eternity.

So—since he ate lunch around noon, and he died about
midnight—

Where had he been all that time?

101000

SHERYL CARRIED THE 3½-inch disk in her briefcase when she
drove to work Tuesday morning. She was terribly conscious of
it as she walked past the guard, Len, who said, "Morning,
Shurl."

She carried it into the elevator.

Zach and Glen stepped into the elevator behind her.

For a couple of seconds, she did not recognize the sensa-
tions she felt.

"Hi, Glen. Hi, Zach," she said.

Her voice sounded hollow, too, and it wasn't until they answered, "Good morning, Sheryl," in their formal way that
Sheryl became really aware of what was wrong.

I'm afraid of them, she thought. Just like Howie. And immediately, she also thought, *How silly! There isn't anything they can
do to me.*

When she leaned forward to push the button for the third
floor, Zach loomed over her shoulder and pushed four. His
arm brushed her cheek. She was careful not to flinch. He

straightened up, but he was still very close. Then she realized that she couldn't see Glen at all. He was standing out of sight behind her.

She smiled at Zach. The briefcase with the disk inside hung at her knee, her fingers tight around the handle.

The door opened at her floor. With immense self-control, she stepped slowly out.

101001

ONCE EVERYTHING WAS up on the screen she thought about the passwords she had discovered.

```
friend celeste
Joe2 hardass
Glen botulism
```

She delayed making the next move.

Sheryl wondered if there was a connection between Dean Utley and the name Celeste. Something she'd heard— She pulled up his ph file. At first she couldn't find any connection; it wasn't his ex-wife or either of his two daughters. However, the one in the file seemed to be his current ex-wife. Latest ex-wife. Utley had been married and divorced twice before. And she vaguely thought that Utley had a tendency now and then to name files after his girlfriends. He'd mentioned one once. She scanned up. Aha! The very first Mrs. Utley had been one Celeste Delgord.

That answered that. Probably an old file Utley had left hanging around.

hardass made her think of the two Blue Blazers, Zach and Glen. They were so oddly formal that it seemed an intentional deception.

She just plain didn't like the botulism password.

Drinking her hot tea, Sheryl shivered.

Sheryl asked herself again—would a cyberdiary be kept on every entry into every file? The company said no, and there had never been any talk among the employees that anybody had been spied on. Sheryl had not told Suze that a diary was possible. She knew her sister would have freaked out and said not to touch the files if there was a chance of surveillance. But Sheryl honestly doubted there was such a thing. Keeping a diary would not only generate a huge amount of data, it would also be redundant. SJR DataSystems had the passwords system in place, and Sheryl believed that for internal security SJR DataSystems would rely on that, backed up by their careful screening of their employees.

Sheryl decided to go ahead.

101010

FIRMLY, COVERING HER fear, she typed 1s and brought up the first file, Joe2 hardass.

Whatever she had got all tensed up for, this wasn't it. What came up was an alphabet soup beginning with

```
§;u#88bGxx(b5tbHHk♦!&nd7712.b
f#755nGnn(43tcHVk(s)ncs.132am.b
```

She scrolled down through the file. It was data; it was too big to be a program. It was in code. She stared at it, trying to puzzle out what it might be. Thirty to fifty characters would be about the length of a house address plus a phone number. Or a name including first, middle, and last names, plus a social security number.

Whatever the data was, it had been set up so that you

needed a second program to decode it. She had never seen such a thing at SJR.

She decided to try decoding it, and ran data-junction. It didn't work. This file was more carefully guarded than `utmost` had been. She put it aside.

She typed `friend`, then `celeste`. This looked like a purely innocent file. It was a new list program apparently intended for chemists. It dealt with the difficulties of alphabetizing both chemical formulae and chemical terms in English, so as to sort incoming abstracts and produce hard copy that was readable to the human eye.

She logged out and logged back in as Glen and hit return. Now she was not aware of any fear at all. Her enjoyment of cybersearching was coming over her. When she sat at her keyboard and flew through files and into projects in development, when she touched a key and soared out to Germany or Hong Kong by modem, she felt as if she had left her body and floated through her monitor screen into "out there."

She typed `botulism` and hit the return key.

There was an executable file called "U-Hosp," so she ran it. The screen filled.

|||||||||||||||||||||||||||||||||||||||||||||||||||||||||||||||||||||||

```
UNIVERSITY HOSPITAL
DATA MANAGEMENT 787-3

PERIOD BEGINNING 1/1/93
PERIOD ENDING 12/31/95
TO ACCESS EARLIER RECORDS GO TO C786-39888
DIRECTORY C10-14
QUICK DIRECTORY A4
FOR ADDITIONAL HELP QUERY STEPHEN FOULKES
312/587-8897

DO NOT ATTEMPT TO INPUT DATA UNLESS YOU HAVE
COMPLETED THE PERSONNEL UPDATE COURSE OF
4/10/92
```

|||||||||||||||||||||||||||||||||||||||||||||||||||||||||||||||||||||||

Sheryl gazed astonished at the screen. What in the world? She knew that SJR had sometimes developed data management programs for hospitals. In fact one of them, Mediquotient, had made one hell of a lot of money for SJR. But she couldn't understand why she had turned it up in this division. It ought to be in Software Development. This had come out of Technical.

She scrolled down. Lines flashed by rapidly. Her eye caught a lot of the data as it moved down the screen,

```
|||||||||||||||||||||||||||||||||||||||||||||||||||||||||||||||||||||||
ACCOUNTS
ACCOUNTS MAINTENANCE
ACCOUNTS OVERDUE
BILLING
FORMS-CITY OF CHICAGO
FORMS-COOK COUNTY
FORMS-STATE OF ILLINOIS
INSURANCE-BUILDING
INSURANCE-LIABILITY
INSURANCE-PATIENT
PATIENT RECORDS
PERSONNEL
SHORT-TERM RECORDS
|||||||||||||||||||||||||||||||||||||||||||||||||||||||||||||||||||||||
```

Well, at least it was in English. But what did it mean? Was somebody working on a program to manage hospital data? She thought she knew how to check.

A year ago, Kath had been on a class tour of the Field Museum and had fallen down the steps as they were leaving. Somehow she caught her right index finger under her body as she tried to break her fall. The teacher took her to the U-Hosp emergency room. They sent her to X-ray. Her finger was broken.

Sheryl selected PATIENT RECORDS. When it came up, she scrolled down thousands of entries to the proper place in the alphabet. It said:

Birch, Kathleen

There was her age, home address, home phone number, complaint, note by the intake nurse, notes of sending her to X-ray, diagnosis of a compression fracture of the distal portion of what they called the 3-2nd phalanx.

Well, that was to be expected.

Just playing around, she put the cursor on the note where it said "no allergies," erased it, and typed in "allergic to boys." She was a little bit surprised that she could make the change. Really, this should be read-only, because of the danger of contaminating the hospital records if the program were ever reinstalled. Still, maybe it was just to work with—a kind of demonstration chunk of data.

But when she went back to the control line, she was startled to see a menu flash up.

||||||||||||||||||||||||||||||||||||||||||||||||||||||||||||||||||||
MODEM ENGAGED
CHOOSE ONE:

E enter change
C cancel change
R restore previous data
||||||||||||||||||||||||||||||||||||||||||||||||||||||||||||||||||||

Oh, my God! This was a direct modem line into the U-Hospital files. She could do anything she wanted to them! Sheryl's fingers jumped off the keyboard as if the keys had given her an electric shock.

She did not know whether she was watched, but her head said, *Get rid of this file! Get out immediately!*

She reached to abort the whole thing.

Aloud, she said, "Wait. Wait a minute."

With an effort she held her hands off the keys. This was not a time to give in to fear. If this file was being misused, somebody had to find out and then take action.

She pressed her hands together in front of her lips, almost

as if she were praying. In a moment she had gathered her courage. When she lowered her hands to the keys again, she had more strength. Then, as she started to investigate, the chase became its own reward.

She first went to the time stamp on the file. When had it been used last?

Monday morning at 8:17.

That didn't seem to mean much. When was it used previous to that?

Monday morning at two A.M.

Two A.M.? That was ominous in itself. The computer engineers here often stayed late working on projects. But this wasn't a project; it was a finished program. Its only use was— whatever its use was.

Now she tried to recover what had actually been done. Working backward, she found the entry. The only data sent from SJR to the U-Hosp computer had been the words "allergy to methylparaben."

She switched windows and called an extensive dictionary that SJR maintained. Methylparaben was a preservative, a component of some anesthetics. This hardly seemed dangerous. If one anesthetic shouldn't be used because of an allergy, surely they would simply use another.

Whose file had been altered?

The name, when she brought it up on her screen, meant nothing to her: Kiro Ogata. She had half-expected an SJR employee.

Now she consulted the menu in the botulism file and called up his full patient record. There she saw that he worked for Bermandyne. That rang a bell.

Sheryl went to another window and called a list of SJR DataSystems customers. Sure enough, Bermandyne bought programs from SJR.

What did all that mean, though?

Then Sheryl realized she might be able to retrieve the action that had been taken on the first of the two entries into

U-Hosp, the one at two A.M. It would be more difficult and might be impossible if it had been written over.

She stopped, took a breath, and went on. When she found the data, she stared at it, hardly believing. Nothing had been added to the file at two A.M. There had been a deletion.

This was incomprehensible. Why delete something in the middle of the night? Surely only a doctor—

She tried a utility program to retrieve what had been deleted.

Allergy to methylparaben.

Sheryl felt cold. Somebody here at SJR had stealthily removed the fact that an unknown person named Kiro Ogata was allergic to methylparaben, then put the data back.

So that the alteration wouldn't be discovered?

Unwillingly, but now compelled to finish, Sheryl went back into the U-Hosp file on Kiro Ogata. Something must have been done to him yesterday morning.

Yes. Surgery.

How did the surgery turn out? What happened to him? She paged down.

101011

AT THE SAME instant that the U-Hosp file had first flashed onto Sheryl's screen, the system had run an internal script that had been set up to record who was using it. It shelled to an alias, which ran at machine speed: ten million characters a second. No information that this was happening had appeared on the command line. Sheryl saw nothing.

She touched the exit function key.

Under her finger, the plastic key on the keyboard depressed, making a connection by closing an electrical contact.

The keyboard processed the connection into a scan code and the scan code incorporated the information that a control key had been pressed.

The scan code was then sent into her workstation itself.

It caused the workstation to do an interrupt—stopping whatever other internal processing it was doing for a microsecond and accepting the code, translating the scan code into a character, and the instant she hit <return> it produced a character string—a two-character end-of-line and a line feed.

When she typed log out and hit <return>, the computer was waiting for this return, as it always would when the logout characters were typed. It was in the middle of its command line interpretation process.

It grouped together everything she had typed since the last time she had hit return into a string, parsed the string into individual words or tokens, which in this case was just one—the command to logout.

Now it sent this specific package of tokens to its command line interpretation subprocess.

The subprocess executed the code with the initiating sequence logout.

This ran .logout. It grouped together the history of what Sheryl had just done, using the history command. It appended the information to a file. Then it gave the file a time and date stamp.

It also automatically set a flag which would tell the next user when the last login on that file took place.

Then it closed these files and closed the other files she had left open and exited her out of the system.

The entire sequence of events flashed along the company wires in a microsecond and into the central computer, where it was recorded on a large mirrored hard drive, actually three identical hard drives in which information is written to all three drives in the exact same location. The system had double redundancy. If one drive were to crash, the other two would automatically be used to restore the first.

All this happened in less time than it took Sheryl to begin to raise her hand from the keyboard.

Sheryl's use history was etched onto eight-inch plates of a hard ferrous magnetic material. The material had the ability to localize electrical charges so that they didn't leak magnetization from one tiny spot to another. The plates were stacked in parallel eight deep with read/write heads on both sides of all eight plates.

A single plate could store 600 megabytes.

The information on Sheryl's transaction was about 500 bytes, less than one one-millionth of the information on one single disk.

Unknown to her, Sheryl's history, a record of everything she had done, now existed as a small sequence of charged and uncharged spots on a single concentric-ring sector on a single track on a single plate on each of the three drives.

And there they waited, for somebody to come along and find them.

101100

UTLEY DRANK THE last of the espresso his secretary, Dorothy, had left him. Then he checked his watch. At exactly 10:45, he picked up the phone. This was the one time when the vice president of the United States would answer the phone himself in his home office. It was 11:45 Washington time, and on this day only, Tuesday, the veep left for work at noon.

When the veep heard Utley's voice, he said, "Are you on a secure line?"

"Naturally it's secure," Utley said indignantly. "At my end."

"Well, here, of course it is," the veep said.

"Good." Utley smiled and glanced at the digital readout in the recorder bank next to the phone. The REC light was blinking steadily. "Anyway, all we're going to talk about is making sure the president has a good visit."

"Yeah," the veep said.

"And a good dinner. You're still going to the Bierstube at the Stratford?"

"Of course. I'd have let you know if we weren't. The Bierstube's half the point of the visit. It's the oldest German restaurant in Chicago. It was there on that same piece of ground when the forerunner of the Stratford was there. It was a two-story frontier hotel made of wood, with a veranda, built in the early 1800s—"

"Spare me the travelogue," Utley said. He smiled again. The man was talking because he was nervous. "So what's the menu?"

"Sauerbraten. Spatzle. Some kind of cabbage slaw. Apple strudel. I think a choice of cinnamon sauce for the strudel."

"Mmmm." Utley knew he was going to have to do more research on this, but he had some preliminary possibilities. "What does the president like best?"

"That's what he likes! That's why we're going to the damn place! You think we'd go out and find a whole menu of stuff he didn't like?"

"Don't get irritable. Is he dieting? Will he skip the spatzle, for instance?"

Grudging: "Probably not."

"If they have salad, will he eat it?"

"He likes salad. Plus his wife always makes sure he eats it."

"Good." Utley had been thinking salmonella, and it might not work if it was boiled. "Does he eat pickles?"

"Um—" Utley pictured the veep thinking back over several state dinners. "I don't really remember."

"Mmm. Does he eat dessert?"

"Probably."

"Will his wife tell him not to?"

"Maybe, but he says apple strudel is his favorite. He's looking forward to the Bierstube partly for its strudel."

"That's nice."

"The man eats the things he damn well likes," the veep said huffily.

The natural indignation of a second banana, Utley thought. "Well, good. Four days, now, until you get here. Six days to cutworm. You arrive late on Saturday. Then it's the ABA on Sunday evening and the Bierstube at the Stratford on Monday the thirtieth. No change. Right?"

"Right."

"How many people?"

"Oh, the Stratford dinner is small. The American Bar Association speech is the big thing. Five hundred people, at least. The Stratford is just maybe thirty or forty of his supporters."

"And your supporters."

"Well, of course."

101101

DEAN UTLEY STOOD and stretched, throwing his arms up in the air. Making his hands into fists, he rocked from side to side to loosen up. It had been a busy couple of hours, but profitable. Everything was going very well.

Utley had spent his entire adult life gazing into a computer monitor and reaching through it to terminals all over the world. Hackers everywhere knew the trancelike state they could fall into. The room they were in dropped away and the screen was like a central, infinitely powerful eye, with which they looked anywhere in the world they wanted. To exchange words with someone in India was no more difficult than speaking to Indianapolis.

As Utley's company had grown, the power of that central eye had grown, too. He looked into people's homes and schools and hospitals, and to some extent into the military, state government, and corporations. But it wasn't enough. He wanted everything. He wanted to access the world. It would be like having a brain ten thousand times larger, eyes ten thousand times more acute, ears ten thousand times sharper.

Once he had control of the federal government, he would be halfway there.

101110

UTLEY REALIZED THAT there was a chance the president would be taken to Hinkley Memorial. Although U-Hosp had an international reputation, Hinkley was excellent and closer to the Bierstube. He had better check that botulism was working at Hinkley.

He pulled up botulism and let himself into the Hinkley system. What to do?

It was already nearly lunchtime, and so there was no point in trying to interrupt any surgery today. Rummaging around, he found the surgical schedule for tomorrow. There were two people with the last name of Thomas scheduled for surgery at eight: Henry F. Thomas and Ward Pinckney Thomas. Henry was having a kidney removed because of a tumor. Ward was having his gall bladder out.

He decided he would just alter the schedule that would be typed and sent to the surgical wing in the morning. It would simply say that Henry was the gall bladder patient and Ward the kidney. The orderly would deliver Ward to the surgical wing partly sedated, a nurse would see his bracelet, and in he would go to the kidney surgeon. Similarly, Henry would go to the gall bladder surgeon.

Wouldn't it be a grand joke if Ward was one of those people born with only one kidney?

He finished with Hinkley, and as he was backing out of `botulism`, he noticed a time stamp on the file: 1019 hours.

What the *hell?* Why would anybody be into the botulism file today? Howie Borke was the only person approved to use it—other than Utley himself, of course—and Howie Borke was downtown holding the hands of nervous cops at the Chicago Police Department.

Utley called up the script that had automatically recorded which employee had been in the file.

Sheryl Birch 24 March 10:19 hours.

Sheryl Birch! Really? This was very bad news.

101111

UTLEY'S BIG HANDS were dangling next to his thighs, and he was not aware that they were contracting into claws, then relaxing, then tensing into claws again.

When he was upset, or needed to think, he used a program of his own invention to help clear his mind. The concept wasn't new. It was derived from Professor Joseph Weizenbaum's DOCTOR program, which was part of Weizenbaum's ELIZA series at MIT back in 1965. Utley's, though, was personal, his alone.

It said:

> GOOD MORNING, SIR.

He typed:

||||||||||||||||||||||||||||||||||||||||||||||||||||||||||||||||||||||||
> Good morning. I have a problem.
> I AM SORRY TO HEAR YOU HAVE A PROBLEM. WOULD
YOU CARE TO SHARE IT WITH ME?

> Yes. One of my employees may be doing something treasonous.
> TREASONOUS? TREASON IS VERY SERIOUS INDEED. HOW DO YOU FEEL ABOUT THAT?
> Angry.
> I AM SORRY THAT YOU'RE FEELING ANGRY. ARE YOU CERTAIN ABOUT YOUR ANALYSIS OF THE SITUATION?
> It could be an accident.
> ACCIDENT? HOW COULD IT BE AN ACCIDENT?
> It could be chance.
> YOU ARE SAYING IT COULD HAVE BEEN RANDOM.
> Yes, but it's very unlikely that it was accident.
> UNLIKELY MEANS IMPROBABLE. BUT IMPROBABLE DOES NOT MEAN IMPOSSIBLE.
> No.
> IT IS IN THE NATURE OF PROBABILITY THAT EXCEEDINGLY REMOTE EVENTS TAKE PLACE ON OCCASION. THIS FACT IS SUBSUMED IN THE DEFINITION OF PROBABILITY.
> That's true.
> IS THERE ANY WAY FOR YOU TO GATHER MORE DATA?
> Maybe there is.
> YOU MAY BE ABLE TO RESOLVE YOUR DIFFICULTY.
> Yes.
> AND THEN YOU WOULD FEEL BETTER.
> Yes.
> I WOULD SUGGEST THAT YOU ENGAGE IN INVESTIGATION. THAT WOULD BE PROGRESS.
> Yes, it would.
> PROGRESS ALWAYS MAKES YOU FEEL BETTER.
> You're absolutely right.
> AND WITH SUFFICIENT DATA, YOU WILL BE SUCCESSFUL.
> Thank you for saying that.
> AS YOU KNOW, YOU ARE ALWAYS SUCCESSFUL EVENTUALLY.
> Yes.
> AND THAT WILL ALWAYS BE SO.
> Thank you.
|||||||||||||||||||||||||||||||||||||||||||||||||||||||||||||||||||

He *did* feel better.

He called up Sheryl Birch's ph file. Utley himself had a higher-level ph file for all the employees, which was called ph!. The staff would have been amazed at the amount of background he had on them. Many of them would have been horrified.

Birch, Sheryl came up on his screen. Social security number, DOB, physical description, education, then a lot of categorized personal data. Parents. Grandparents. Interests. Hobbies. Periodicals subscribed to. Medical data. Children. Teachers' names: her own teachers, her husband's and her childrens'. Description of her house. Her sister. Her sister's job with the Chicago Police Department. Her sister's child. Their medical histories. Preferred clothing style. Shopping habits. Favorite colors. Restaurants frequented. Favorite foods. Foods purchased at markets. Credit cards held. And one that was often revealing for other employees, although it didn't show much unusual data about Sheryl: prescriptions filled at her pharmacy. And another that applied to certain employees—certain pivotal employees, but was zero on Sheryl's list—felony warrants, any criminal convictions, jail time.

Sheryl Birch seemed to have a weakness for rattan furniture. She bought linen and cotton clothing, but not much wool or synthetics. She favored Italian restaurants when she went out, but would go to an occasional Thai place. Quite a few charges at various home improvement places. Wallpaper, paneling, caulking guns, masonry nails. Either she or her husband must do a lot of their own repairs. Children's clothes. The Gap. Just Pants.

There was 27K of background on Sheryl Birch. And none of it showed any particular interest in bacteria generally or botulism specifically.

Utley brought his fist down hard on the desk.

Utley stored Sheryl's ph files on and called the script again. botulism had been uploaded at 10:02. It had been dumped at

10:19. *Seventeen minutes!* That was much too long for just a glance.

This was unfortunate; it was terribly unfortunate.

What the hell had she been doing?

Rather than take the time to reconstruct her path through the U-Hosp program, Utley called up her other business this morning. Within five minutes he found that she had been into the SJR DataSystems customer files. He backtracked fast then and saw she'd looked at the U-Hosp deceased list.

He didn't need to see anything more. It was all perfectly, horribly obvious. She knew about Kiro Ogata.

110000

UTLEY SAID, "GLEN, you go out and drive around the parking lot. Now. Cruise through. Come back into the loading bay so you're only noticed leaving. I don't want anybody to think that you were looking for something."

"What am I looking for?"

"To find out if Sheryl drove her car to work today, of course. Get moving. Even if she did drive, we have to be completely geared up before five P.M."

When Glen got back with news that Sheryl's car was there, Utley said to Zach, "Is there anybody coming for the third shift who drives a big rig, like a van or a truck?"

"I'll bring 'em up," Zach said. He moved to one of Utley's master keyboards and called a file named `emptrans.96`. When it came up on the screen, it was headed "Personal Transportation of Employees, 1996." He plugged in a search function, looking for "van," "truck," "oversized," "jacked-up," or "motorhome."

"Hmmp."

Utley said, "What've you got, Glen?"

"Couple of motorhomes, but the employees don't usually drive them to work. Several vans. How about Grinell Walnitt? He's got a white Bronco II with extra hood lights. It's not a van, but it's high, and Sheryl's Geo is low-slung."

Zach Massendate said, "Walnitt's a great choice, actually."

"Right," Utley said. "He's a ROM-brain."

Glen Jaffee always tried not to show annoyance when he didn't catch their computer allusions, so he said pleasantly, "What's a ROM-brain?"

"Well, you know, RAM is random access memory. You can write to it, and change it. ROM is read-only memory. Once the data is entered you can't change it. Walnitt is a ROM-brain."

Glen laughed. "You're right. Walnitt *is* a ROM-brain."

110001

SHE WAS SITTING by herself, with what looked like a tuna salad on whole wheat. He could see immediately that she was worried. He had allowed her three minutes' head start, but she hadn't taken a bite of the sandwich. *She's worried. It's bothering her.*

"Hi, Sheryl!"

She jumped and turned her head fast. But she covered quickly, too. "Oh, hi, Mr. Utley. I didn't hear anybody behind me."

He sat down and put his Caesar salad in front of him. He thought, *Now let's see if she mentions* botulism. *She's actually quite a formidable opponent, isn't she? Coolheaded. She's got to be terrified right now.* What she ought to do now is to ask him about botulism, make a demonstration that she's a faithful employee, bringing a problem to the boss. Let him handle it. Then back off.

But she didn't speak. He waited a moment, while she looked at her sandwich, obviously decided that it would choke her, and took a sip of 7-Up instead.

He said, "How's everything?"

"Oh, fine, Mr. Utley."

"Look at this." He brought out a new puzzle. It was made of iron bars shaped like two U's with loops on the ends. They were joined by a shuttle attached to a chain. "You're supposed to get this shuttle out of the gizmo," he said, handing it to her.

She took it, unwillingly, he thought. For three or four minutes she fiddled with it while Utley ate steadily, watching her. *Watch her squirm.*

"It's really difficult," Sheryl said. "I think it's too hard for me."

"So how's the guidance system?" he asked.

"Going well." She hesitated. "I was wondering—"

"What?"

"Oh, I don't know. Just a glitch in the thing. I think I can work it out."

On the whole, now that he thought about it and about the kind of person Sheryl was, he rather thought she *would* tell him, sooner or later. And he could put on a great dramatic search for the evildoer. And maybe fire somebody, somebody high up—even Howie, if he wanted to be very convincing.

Should he? Should he let her live? Live or not live? Live or not? Live? Not? Live?

The fact that she had not told him yet was decisive. It meant that she knew how serious the threat was.

Not.

110010

"But there's gotta be guard rails all along that stretch," Zach said.

Glen snorted. He'd driven the route and he'd done his work properly. "Those guard rails aren't strong enough to hold back a crashing cocker spaniel!"

"Suppose somebody sees us?"

"If your car doesn't contact her car, the cops won't follow up. It's a one-car accident. Trust me on this."

110011

On the second shift, Grinell Walnitt's job ordinarily was to walk the whole perimeter fence, looking for breaches made by fallen trees, or any other kind of problem, such as teenage boys trying to break in or industrial spies. These events were not considered very likely by the security force, but Utley wanted it done, and you did what Utley wanted done. Besides, God forbid some tree branch had blown against the fence and you missed it. It would be your job, for sure. Utley didn't take kindly to mistakes.

As Walnitt buttoned his uniform cuffs in the locker room, his supervisor entered. "Go to the employee dining room," he said.

Grinell was surprised. This shift was the least likely to generate sudden weird duties.

"But I'm on perimeter," he said.

"This supersedes."

"I WANT TO ask something special of you, Grinell."

"Sure, Mr. Jaffee."

"I want you to take the dossiers of the security men and women and go over them for me."

"What do you—"

"I'll explain, Grinell. I'll have the files brought to you in the radio parts room in the basement. I'd rather nobody saw you do this."

"Yes, sir. I'll—"

"I'm explaining, Grinell. There are about a hundred and eighty files, give or take. What I want you to do is read over each one. Each one has the employment application, the educational history, past employment, records of what they've done here. Everything. I just want you to read them. Take notes. There'll be a notepad in the room."

"Yes, but what—"

"I don't want to prejudice you. We need a fresh eye on this, Grinell." Jaffee fixed him with a serious look. "You're our fresh eye. I want you to be asking yourself whether anybody in that group might, in your opinion, constitute a security risk."

"Yes, sir, Mr. Jaffee."

"Stay in that section of the basement. No one will see you. There is a bathroom down the hall. This job will take your entire shift, and I'll guarantee nobody will come by and try to get you to do any other tasks. Don't tell *anybody* what you're doing. Just before eleven, somebody will come by to get your notes and the files. You understand."

"Oh, sure!" Walnitt said, gratified. At last SJR realized that he had insight. He might not be academically brilliant, but he understood people; he was a great judge of human nature. "I'll do it thoroughly, Mr. Jaffee!"

WALNITT'S CAR WAS in the company garage, in Utley's large private bay. Illinois license plates have dark blue letters on a white reflective background. Glen had gotten white and the closest color to the blue from Maintenance in a nice exterior latex paint that would dry quickly and could later be removed much more easily than oil paint.

Zach's car was next to Walnitt's.

"This is scut work," Zach said.

Glen said, "Hand me the goddamn paintbrush. I'll do blue. You do white."

Not all the letters and numbers on a license plate can be changed easily. "A" is impossible to make into another letter by slight alterations. "B" is difficult, but it can be made into a "D" by painting white over the middle horizontal bar and blue over the dent on the right side. It was possible to paint over the whole thing, of course, but the result would have been far less natural. After a little study, Zach and Glen picked three digits on the Bronco's plate and two on the car that could be altered very simply.

A "C" became an "O."

An "F" became an "E."

Another "C" became a "G."

An "O" became a "C."

A "3" became an "8."

After the letters were dry, they threw a little dirt on the plates.

HE KNOWS! He **was playing with me!** Sheryl thought as she sat at her desk, trying to work on the guidance program, but thinking instead of Dean Utley.

He was just baiting me.

She took her hands off the keyboard and pressed them over her eyes. *No, he wasn't. He doesn't know. He couldn't possibly. He was just being Utley. He's like that, acting playful in a clumsy sort of way.*

But she didn't really believe it, and she couldn't work. Every few minutes she had to delete all the work she'd done and start over again. Finally she began to wonder if Utley could shadow her workstation and see whether she was working and what kind of work she did. The thought paralyzed her for a couple of minutes. Then, drawing on willpower, she forced herself to make several real improvements in her guidance program.

She froze again. It was only two o'clock and she had to get through the afternoon. Or run away right now.

Will I get out of here today? How will I get out of here? Will anybody try to stop me?

Was there anything she should do to make herself safe? She could call Suze—but no, she couldn't. If they didn't know she was on to them—and how could they know, after all?—the telephone line might be monitored, and then they'd know for sure.

And if they did suspect her already and monitored calls, they'd break off the call.

And come to this office and attack her?

Maybe. Probably.

The only way to do that was to act normal for the rest of the afternoon. She would leave on time, calmly. To anybody watching, she would look as if nothing had happened. Give them absolutely no reason to think she suspected murder.

IN HER LITTLE red Geo, Sheryl joined a parade of employees leaving work. The company driveway led into Catalpa, and almost all of the cars took the same turn—toward the access road for the Northwest Tollway, which was Interstate 90 eastbound. It was 5:40 when she turned right and climbed the ramp onto the tollway. *Out of the area, out of danger. This is a major highway. I'm safe here.* She felt exhausted as the adrenaline drained away; she was chilly with the relief of tension.

A white Bronco hung behind her for a mile or so, then apparently decided she was going too slowly and roared by. She passed the exit to O'Hare, where I-90 lost some of its traffic. Sheryl was driving at a consistent sixty-five. *Halfway home. I'm completely out of danger now.*

And out of a job? Oh, hell, hell, hell! This is no time to worry about that. But if I lose my job would Robert be angry that we didn't have the income, or pleased that he was the main breadwinner?

Robert. It would be so nice not to have to worry about Robert all the time!

The sun dropped behind the trees. She punched on the car lights. It wasn't dark yet and wouldn't be fully dark for quite some time. But it was becoming half-light, and visibility was poor. Her headlights didn't help her see any better, but they might help other cars to see her. This was the time of year, Sheryl thought, when day and night were almost equal lengths. How she used to long for spring when the girls were little! It meant they could finally go outdoors to play after school, after the long winter when it got dark at four.

Just a few miles farther. She'd be home in fifteen minutes. Her breath came easier now.

Jesus Delgado grabbed his hair in frustration and pulled until it hurt.

There was paper everywhere. Paper in his hands, paper on Frieswyk's desk, piles of paper on the floor, and more and more coming and ready to come out of the files and out of the bookcases. Every piece of paper led him to another piece of paper. He was swamped in an onslaught of paper, and he couldn't ignore one scrap of it. Someplace there might be the one thing, the one item that would point the way to Frieswyk's killer.

Jesus had visited Frieswyk's apartment, the one he'd moved into after he separated from Perry, and the word for it was Spartan. It was the apartment of a person who wasn't at home much, or didn't care about where he lived. It was the kind of apartment with one change of sheets in the closet, one sofa and one chair in the living room, and one six-pack of beer in the refrigerator.

Now he again searched Frieswyk's desk at the department. Jesus had taken every single sheet out of every single drawer in Frieswyk's desk. Because of his Internal Auditing job, Frieswyk also had three metal bookcases and three metal files in an L-shape surrounding his desk. They were painted a pea soup color that only a police department could love. Jesus had decided to remove everything from the first bookcase, *everything*, look at every single sheet, and not put the paper back on the shelf until he understood what it was and was sure it had nothing to do with Frieswyk's death.

Because of the cryptic thing Frieswyk had said to his ex-wife Perry about the Motor Pool, Jesus took cars extra seriously and went over anything vaguely automobile related with even more care than the other documents. He had spent all afternoon on tires.

One of the other guys in the office had taken pity on him.

"What's all that, Jesus?"

"Tires. Thousands and thousands and thousands of tires. Do you have any idea how many tires the CPD uses every year?"

"All the driving that gets done, I don't think I want to know. Here, we gotcha a pot of coffee. I mean, it's pitiful to watch you; you never leave the desk."

"Hey! That's great! Have a cup?"

"Well, just one."

Then Jesus did cars.

The CPD purchased between two hundred and three hundred squad cars a year. In addition, a hundred or so unmarked cars with black sidewalls were bought for the tac teams. And between twenty and thirty cars were purchased with the commander-package: white sidewalls and an AM/FM radio. For some strange Chicagoland reason, the mayor's cars were also bought on the police budget.

One of Frieswyk's personal worksheets listed the automobiles purchased in the last three years, not including squadrols and specialty items like the superintendent's Mercury or the mobile command-center van in which the CPD could set up an office at a catastrophe or a siege site. The list was in pencil, like a lot of Frieswyk's worksheets, on a standard 8½ × 14 yellow legal pad sheet.

03/21/94	ssc	123
03/21/94	cp	12
06/17/94	ttp	50
06/22/94	ssc	41
09/30/94	ssc	162
12/07/94	ttp	48
12/22/94	cp	24
12/22/94	mo	07
12/29/94	ssc	38
03/10/95	cp	17
03/11/95	ssc	31

And so on. There were twenty-seven entries.

This seemed straightforward enough. Ssc, cp, mo, and ttp had to be standard squad car, commander package, mayor's office, and tactical team package. Jesus added up the numbers of each type of car, and it came to roughly the same number each year, and the numbers were in the range of what the CPD usually needed. Perfectly reasonable.

But it was always possible that the figures were one thing and the number of cars actually delivered by the dealer was something else. This had certainly happened in a spark plug scam a couple of years earlier, and Frieswyk himself had uncovered it. Jesus had seen the memos.

This was Chicago, after all, and everybody knew about the possibilities of bid-rigging and undershipping. In fact, the internal auditing and data management program had been designed to exert master control and make exactly that type of thing impossible. The clerk who assembled the approved requests entered the figures into the program and checked the physical receipt forms. Later somebody at the top okayed the payment to the dealer and made certain that the department had received the number of cars it had asked for. The program automatically confirmed that the figures that went in at the bottom were the same as the figures that came out on payment checks at the top. In fact, that was the very reason the department had bought an SJR DataSystems program for Internal Auditing four years before even *starting* to computerize anything else: to detect fraud.

He added Frieswyk's notes to his growing stack of "keepers," documents he couldn't quite reject out of hand. It was now a pile eleven inches high, located on the left-rear corner of the desk. He took a swig of coffee.

Going through the desk, after everything else was put back, he found a piece of scratch paper. Actually, he had found lots and lots of pieces of scratch paper, torn off a three-by-five notepad that Frieswyk must have used habitually. The notepad itself was missing. Most of the notes Jesus could understand.

They either were doodles of faces, one labeled "Commander Zeller," with smoke coming out of his ears and fangs protruding from his mouth dripping blood, or were ordinary reminders. But one was tantalizing. It was one of those circles with a line through it that meant no something. Like if there had been a cigarette in the middle it would mean no smoking. This one said:

111001

INTERSTATE 90 CONNECTED with the Tri-State Tollway east of O'Hare in a vast spaghetti bowl of ramps and loops. A United Airlines jet in a runway approach screamed in over Sheryl's car. It sounded as if it were just ten feet above the car roof, but of course it wasn't, really. Another giant aircraft taxied south over the highway on a raised runway.

She saw that white Bronco again. It had stayed ahead of her through the O'Hare mess. Obviously, it wasn't going to any of the northern suburbs. She looked at the driver but didn't recognize him. He was wearing a knitted cap. A little warm for today, Sheryl thought. The Bronco seemed to be carrying lighting equipment. There were bulbs in reflectors hanging from its top inside.

Almost immediately after the mess at the merge, Sheryl had to watch for her exit at Irving Park Road. It was getting darker now. The lights in office windows were starting to look cheerful.

Almost home.

The white Bronco had come through the merge, too, but it

had slowed down and dropped behind her. Sheryl was in the right lane, and the Bronco was driving along in the center lane, just a few car lengths in back of her.

Construction had started on part of the highway and off-ramp. Chicago was like that; as soon as the highway department knew there wouldn't be any more snow and ice, they tore everything up and left it torn up until October.

The off-ramp at Irving Park was a double-lane exit, curving first sharply right, off the highway, then turning left down to the street beneath. She cut her speed to forty, angled off to the right in the right-hand of the two off-ramp lanes. A little fast, but she'd done it a thousand times. She was vaguely aware that the white Bronco veered from the center highway lane into the right highway lane and off, just behind her and to her left. It didn't slow down as much as she had, and now it was coming up in the exit lane next to her.

Directly behind her, a blue Chevy also took the off-ramp and stayed some twenty feet back in her lane.

Sheryl braked with her wheels angled right to make the turn. As she brought the wheels back straight, just before taking the sharp curve to the left, the Bronco pulled next to her.

Bright lights went on in the Bronco.

Sheryl saw the truck merging toward her, about to crash into the side of her car. There were flashing white strobes and piercing blue lights, all aimed out through the side window at her, and a shrieking siren.

She turned her wheel away from the Bronco, toward the guard rail, screaming "Oh, God!" as the Geo struck the metal of the guard rail, screeched along it for a couple of car lengths, then hit one of the posts, which broke away.

Her car tore out the next section of guard rail. Sheryl's hands were as rigid as metal hooks on the wheel as the guard rail shrieked along the bottom of her car. The embankment dropped off beneath her. A twisted piece of the metal rail caught the right front wheel, giving the car a flip. In the air, the car began to turn over.

Sheryl saw the embankment fly past the windshield, upside down. The front bumper bounded on a rock, giving the car a vertical spin. The seat belt grabbed at her. Sheryl had an instant's glimpse of streetlights below. They looked horribly far down.

II

''Nobody knows facts. People only know information.''

—Dean Utley,
Fourth AI Symposium,
California Institute
of Technology, 1986

111010

No six? What was "no six"? Did the number six have some exotic meaning? He thought maybe six was the symbol for the devil to some people. Or was that 66? Or 666?

What could it possibly have to do with anything?

But it had been with the other pieces of scratch paper in the desk. Not on top, but in the middle drawer. Items in the desk seemed more important to Jesus than items in the bookcases or files. On his last day of life, Frieswyk had seen something, or figured something out, or decided about something, and had gone out and never come back. Whatever it was that took Frieswyk out of the building that day, to Frieswyk it was *current*, and therefore it would more likely be in the desk than in a file. After all, he didn't know he was never coming back.

Jesus paged back, sheet after sheet, through the pieces of paper. He stared at the list of cars purchased.

Sometimes you got a distant buzz. Like primitive man sensing the tiger in the underbrush, but in reverse. He was the tiger, and he scented prey.

What a feeling!

Oh, oh, oh-oh-oh! Wait for it, baby! Wait for it! He felt it in the back of his brain, but it tingled all the way to his fingertips. Look! There were six, seven, eight, nine times three, um—twenty-seven numbers, all pretty much different, all orders for different numbers of cars. Twenty-seven numbers *and not one of them ended in the number six!*

Hallelujah!

Yeah, right Jesus, he said to himself. *Hallelujah what? What does it mean?*

Okay, he wasn't sure what it meant, but he knew he could figure it out. All he had needed was to spot the tail of the critter. That was all. He'd follow it to its lair.

How likely was it that you could have a random group of twenty-seven numbers and none of them end in six? He scribbled out a quick calculation and decided it would be close to one chance in seventeen, less than six percent.

After staring at the list another twenty minutes, he slapped his head. There were also a lot of terminal eights in the numbers of cars ordered. Six eights, in fact.

Uh-huh. And what of it?

Well, think! The Chicago Police Department bid out its automobile contracts and was obligated by city regulations to take the dealer with the lowest bid. Changing dealers made payoffs more difficult and helped avoid scams and the appearance of scams—after all, this was Chicago.

Let's see—ordinarily, the department bought the squad cars quarterly.

Okay, Jesus thought. Wear and tear and fender benders, bullet holes, and your occasional torching and what all creates a need for one hundred and thirty-eight squad cars for, say, June. The request goes from the director of the Motor Maintenance Division up to the deputy superintendent who heads the Bureau of Technical Services, in the present administration Deputy Superintendent Charles Withers. Withers ordinarily wouldn't do more than give routine approval, unless the numbers were much higher than normal. The department was budget-dominated like all governmental organizations.

Then what? They'd bid it out. XYZ Motors would have the low bid. XYZ would order the 138 cars and a few weeks later deliver 138 cars.

Okay. But say the original order had been for 136 cars. And say somebody wanted to cause the department to cut a check for 138 and pocket the difference. Would the original order go in at 138 cars? No. That didn't make sense. They could ask for almost anything at that end, but somebody would look at it and see if they needed the number they asked for. And anyhow, they wouldn't always have to go from sixes to eights; they could ask for any excess number, if they had cover for a scam.

Could the clerk who typed it in raise the number? Possibly. But he was at the bottom of the hierarchy, and he'd have to be afraid that farther up the line somebody would know the number actually requested and catch the difference. Plus, there was another problem with that. There were several clerks doing that work, and they were shifted around a lot. No one person would be likely to do data entry for more than a few car orders in a year.

It had to happen higher up.

Uneasily, Jesus shifted in his seat. The dirty person being farther up the command line was not a concept that made him happy. He reached out to pour more coffee. There wasn't any in the pot.

"Hey! You guys making a joke?" he yelled.

"What?"

"There isn't any coffee in here."

A couple of the guys got to their feet laboriously; one looked Jesus in the eye and said, "You better take some time off, babe."

"Why?"

"You drank that whole damn pot—"

"I seen you do it," the other one said.

"—and you never noticed?"

"I think somebody here needs R&R."

Jesus went downstairs to see the clerks where the data was

entered. He simply grabbed the first data-entry person he saw, a small, energetic woman whose name tag said "Joosten."

He introduced himself and added, "I'm investigating the Frieswyk death. What I need is the number of cars requested on these dates: 08/09/94, 12/01/94, 06/19/95, and 06/22/95."

Jesus intentionally did not say he knew the numbers of cars Frieswyk had noted down.

"Okay. No problem." Joosten hit the keyboard vigorously. She was obviously one of those people who *liked* computers—or, as Jesus phrased it in his head, "interfaced with enthusiasm." Her query came up with: 08/09/94 was 38 tac cars, 12/01/94 was 136 squad cars, 06/19/95 was 18 commander cars and 06/22/95 was 86 squad cars.

Ha! There was a discrepancy of two cars in each of those years in the squad car numbers. Two of the eights were supposed to be sixes. And he was right on another point: the data had apparently been put into the system accurately down here at entry level. Not showing his elation, he said, "I guess this system is pretty reliable."

"Oh, absolutely."

"But suppose the system made a mistake? Does anybody upstairs actually look at the initial requisition forms and check them again?"

"It's not supposed to be necessary. All the checks are built into the system."

"But—?"

"But Deputy Superintendent Withers always asks to see copies of the initial orders."

Withers? Deputy goddamn Superintendent goddamn Withers! Oh, shit!

NORM AND I were sitting in the car on La Salle Street, watching for a suspected mugger to show up at the place he usually fenced the stuff.

"Trouble with third watch," Bennis was saying, "is it interferes with a person's love life. I mean, I get off work at eleven. What woman is gonna want to go out at midnight? The restaurants, theaters—all closed."

"There must be some understanding women."

"Figueroa, my man, only women want to go out that late are the Vampires of the City. Although, I did meet this woman named Deirdre the other night."

"Let's see how long she lasts. Want dinner now? It's six."

"Little early, isn't it?" Mid-tour was seven o'clock.

I said, "Yeah, but I'm hungry."

"You're always hungry. And you know, Suze, hunger is the best condiment."

"If we wait, I'll be faint."

"Not to worry. I'm trained in CPR."

"Hey, nobody is giving me mouth-to-mouth instead of dinner."

Our radio stuttered. "One-thirty-three," the dispatcher said.

Bennis said, "Thirty-three."

"You two are wanted in the district. See the sergeant."

"We're sitting on this suspect here, squad."

The dispatcher said, "One twenty-seven?"

Bennis and I heard Stanley Mileski's voice say, "Twenty-seven."

"Relieve thirty-three."

"Ten-four."

"Gee, I guess they *really* want us," I said, puzzled.

111100

THE FIRST DISTRICT has the distinction of being the only one of Chicago's twenty-five district police stations to be located in the large building on Eleventh and State that houses the central administration of the Chicago Police Department. This is both a distinction and a curse. A distinction because it *sounds* more important than other districts, and everybody knows where it is. A curse because an honest, hardworking patrol officer might be running to get to roll call on time, fully meaning to put on his jacket and saucer cap when he gets there, and might run headlong into the superintendent of police, who might ask him why he is running around without a complete uniform.

It does result, at least, in the First having a large parking lot.

We entered the First District's lot from the back, Holden Court, and the alley. Holden was the guy who traced the Great Chicago Fire back to Mrs. O'Leary's barn. Appropriate, I always thought, to have his street next to the CPD.

By now both Bennis and I were quiet. There were really only three possible reasons we'd be called in: one, that we were getting some special assignment, which was unlikely this late in the tour; two, that we had done something very wrong, but we couldn't think of anything; and three, that there was some real emergency at either Bennis' home or mine.

And there was Sergeant Pat Touhy coming down the hall, looking at us.

She wasn't smiling, but she rarely smiled, so that didn't tell us much. Sergeant Touhy said, "Come in here."

We followed her into the watch commander's office.

Touhy said somberly, "Figueroa, your niece called—"

"Not JJ," I said. "Please not JJ."

Bennis took hold of my shoulder. Touhy said, "Your sister's been injured."

I put my hand over my mouth.

"Apparently an automobile accident on the way home from work," Touhy said. "She's at Irving Park Hospital."

Bennis looked at me and asked, for me, "How bad is it?"

Touhy didn't answer this directly. "I'm gonna excuse you for the rest of the tour, Figueroa. Go on over to the hospital."

I still couldn't quite speak. Bennis said, "I'll drive her."

"You gotta finish your tour, Bennis," Touhy said.

"*I'll drive her*," Bennis said. Touhy hesitated for a second, read the look in his eyes, and nodded.

Bennis swung me around and marched me toward the door. He kept a grip on my elbow as he walked me out. I knew what he was thinking: If Touhy was willing to let us both go, it was very serious.

111101

IRVING PARK HOSPITAL was medium-sized, with a busy emergency room, serving a densely populated part of Chicago. Bennis, holding my elbow again, got us inside the emergency entrance.

"Stand right here," he said to me. "I'll find out where she is."

I stood like a pillar of salt. I didn't know how to hope, somehow. My brain was afraid to hope for fear of jinxing her, for fear that maybe fate liked to twist the knife.

Bennis and I had been in a thousand emergency rooms with a thousand police cases. Bennis knew how to deal with officialdom, especially since he was in uniform. He walked over to the admission nurse and said, "Sheryl Birch? Automobile accident? I'm escorting a next-of-kin."

The nurse hesitated a second. "She's been transferred."

"Why?"

"Severe head and neck trauma, officer. Our Dr. Effland, who is our staff neurologist, didn't think we could handle it here."

"Is she stable?"

More hesitation. "No."

So it was as bad as possible. Bennis did not look around at me.

"Where did they transfer her?"

"The University Hospital complex. They've got the facilities to deal with this kind of case."

⌁⌁⌁⌁⌁⌀

AT U-HOSP, WE found Robert standing in the waiting room with his arms folded.

I ran up to him. "Robert! Where is she?" Bennis trailed me. Other people in the emergency waiting area turned to look at Bennis and me. Probably they thought two cops in uniform maybe meant something interesting was happening. Most of them lost interest when they decided we weren't here to arrest anybody.

Robert said, "She's in radiology." He turned to Bennis. "Who's this?"

"My partner, Norman Bennis." Bennis held out his hand. Robert shook it without much enthusiasm.

I said, "What happened?"

"She went through the guard rail, coming off the Kennedy."

"What do you mean? She drove off the highway?"

"No. Not the highway. She didn't hold the curve on the exit ramp."

"But—did another car run into her car?"

"They say not."

"Did the steering fail?"

"Oh, hell, Susannah, who knows? Maybe. Maybe not."

A woman in a white-and-pink uniform approached Robert, catching Norm and me with her eyes as well. "Mr. Birch?"

"What? How is she?"

"The staff is studying the CT scan. You can see her for a couple of minutes before they transfer her to the ICU."

"Before? What do you mean?" I said. "Can't we go to ICU with her?" When the woman glanced at Robert, I said, "I'm her sister!"

"No. In ICU you can only visit for ten minutes every two hours. One family member at a time."

Sheryl was on her back on a gurney in one of the treatment bays. There was a padded collar around her neck, a tube in her nose, and an IV line running into a vein. Her face was puffy. The skin around her eyes was purplish. There was some color-less grease in her eyes.

I tried not to gasp. Robert strode over to Sheryl and then stood still with his hands grasping the bed rail.

I went to Sheryl's other side. Norm hung back behind me, out of the way, but there if I needed support.

I said, "We're here, honey. Sheryl, honey, we're right here."

There was no response of any kind. I stroked Sheryl's hand, from above the wrist down to the fingers, over and over again. "Do you think she knows we're here?" I asked. Robert and Norm Bennis each thought I was talking to the other, but when I repeated, "Do you think she hears us?" they both answered.

Robert said, "No. Of course not." Simultaneously, Bennis said, "She probably does, Suze."

The two men looked at each other and then looked away.

I said to Robert, "You stay with her a minute." I backed away and just made it to an alcove in which a linen cart and a suction machine stood before I started to cry. Bennis was right behind me with a hand on my back. I bent over, sobbing, gulping for air, and sobbing more. He just waited. I sobbed and sobbed and sobbed.

"Oh, God!" I said, finally. "I couldn't let her hear me cry."

"It's normal."

"I don't want to let her think that—to hear—it's—like we think she's going to die."

"You *don't* think that."

"No. I don't. But—" I started sobbing again. "I should have protected her."

"How? You can't protect anybody against a traffic accident."

"I know. But she's—I'm supposed to protect her."

"Aren't you the younger sister?"

"Yeah. I can't explain it, Bennis. She's just more innocent and more vulnerable."

"Oh, yeah?" He tapped my chin. "Who's just spent five minutes weeping?"

I smiled weakly. "Well, she is, though."

"Here's a Kleenex." Bennis pulled one from his pocket. "Don't turn up your nose at it. It's clean. It's just wrinkled. You never carry any."

"Thanks."

"You're going to mess up your tough-guy reputation, Suze, my man, crying and all."

"Thanks. You're making me feel better."

"Your brother-in-law doesn't like me."

"Probably not. Don't worry about it. He doesn't like me, either. Robert doesn't really think he should have been born into this particular world. It isn't quite the world he had in mind for himself."

"Oh, that kind of guy."

"That kind of guy."

"Suze, I think I ought to leave now. This is a family thing."

"Well, it's true there's nothing you can do. For that matter, there's nothing I can do, either. Except wait. Norm?"

"Yeah, Suze?"

"I'm very glad you were here."

"Suze, my man, we're buddies."

"Damn right." I hugged him.

"You don't have a car."

"Robert will drive me home. Or I'll get a taxi. I won't be leaving for a while, anyway."

"Is there anything else I can help with?"

"Well, actually—"

"Tell me."

Over and over my brain had been saying, *Could SJR Data-Systems have done this? Did they discover Sheryl was onto some scam?*

"Could you find out what the accident report says? Sheryl was *not* a fast driver. She wasn't poky, but she was no speeder. It just doesn't seem like her to have a one-car accident."

⌐⌐⌐⌐⌐⌐

A FEW MINUTES later, a gangly man arrived in a long gray cotton coat with "University Hospital" stitched on the lapel in white cursive script and a name tag that read, "Ben Gegosian, M.D." He led Robert and me away from the gurney where Sheryl lay.

"We're going to transfer Ms. Birch to ICU," Gegosian said. "I suppose you've been informed about that?"

Robert and I nodded.

"The situation is this. As far as we can tell right now, there's no internal abdominal bleeding and no serious internal organic damage." I saw Robert start to say "That's good—" but I knew too much about automobile accidents and too much about head injuries to be thankful for anything yet.

"She has three cracked ribs, and that certainly means there was impact on the chest and possibly abdomen, so we're not out of the woods on that yet. There's a bruise on the back, which may mean there's some kidney damage, too." He stopped. Robert nodded at him. I waited.

"The more serious situation," he went on, "is the head and neck injury. She's in a deep coma. There is some severe compression at C-seven, which is a neck vertebra right here—" He reached his arm over his shoulder and pointed at a place that looked to me more like the upper back than the neck. "We also have bruising to both the front and back of the brain. The good news is that the spinal cord is not severed and there doesn't seem to be heavy bleeding into the brain."

"And what's the bad news?" Robert asked.

"In these cases the brain swells, just like any body part that's bruised. There's already damage from the injury. The swelling causes more injury. In the spinal cord, as well as the brain."

I said, "Suppose—suppose the damaged place in the spinal cord is permanently injured—"

"Let's not cross that bridge yet."

"But what if—"

"Let's not borrow trouble."

"Dr. Gegosian," I said, "there are different kinds of people in the world. Some want to be coddled. Others want to know where they stand. Sheryl may wake up and ask. Even if she doesn't, *I want to know*." I wasn't rude, I didn't raise my voice, I just, as some of my friends called it, "went cop."

Gegosian cast a glance at Robert, but Robert simply waited.

"At that spinal level, paralysis of the legs, and maybe the wrists and hands, but not the arms."

I forced myself to say, "I see."

"But that really isn't the most important thing."

"What is?"

"Right now, the most serious threat is swelling of the brain. And possible damage to the brain stem, by ischemia—lack of oxygen. The brain stem controls all the vital body functions."

Nobody spoke. The word "death" wasn't mentioned, but was nevertheless sounding loud in my ears. I walked back to Sheryl, and Robert and Gegosian trailed behind.

"When will we know . . . ?" I didn't want to finish the sentence.

"She's not stable yet. Her breathing is labored. Her blood pressure is fluctuating. We'll have a better idea of how she's doing by tomorrow morning."

I leaned a hand on the wall. He was saying that by morning we would know whether Sheryl would live or die.

1000000

NORM BENNIS DID not phone the district police station about the accident. He left the U-Hosp complex and drove directly to the Seventeenth District station, called Albany Park. He asked the desk who was doing the Birch accident, and since he was in uniform, the sergeant immediately answered, "Johannsen. He's back there on the paper," pointing back down the hall and asking no questions. The officer was still in the station—not surprising, since third watch wouldn't be over until eleven P.M.

Johannsen was extremely blond, with hair that was so light it was almost white, and white eyebrows and eyelashes. Seeing Bennis, an officer in uniform, walking directly to him, he said, "Hi. What's up?"

"I guess you took the Birch accident? Irving Park off-ramp?"

"Yeah. Have a seat."

Bennis sat. "Sheryl Birch is the sister of a P.O. My partner, matter of fact. Family's at the hospital, but they asked me to come and ask." Bennis didn't mention that his partner was a female police officer. You never quite knew with people.

"Oh. That's rough."

"So what do you think caused it?"

"The accident? No odor of alcohol. She wasn't hit by another car, that's for sure. There isn't any paint of any other color on her car. Plenty of scrapes, but all from the guard rail and the pavement she hit. She was driving in the outer of the two exit lanes."

"The right lane, you mean?"

"Yeah. Drove right through the guard rail."

"Brakes fail?"

"No. There were some tread marks on the ramp in her lane. She seems to have braked just before she went over."

"Any witnesses?"

"You know how that goes. Mostly they leave. Don't want to have to testify if there's a trial. The car behind her and the car behind that just zoomed away. The third car back stopped—went down to the accident site and the woman in it ran to a building, had them call nine-one-one, and then waited there for the police. One good citizen out of three isn't bad."

"Right. What did she see?"

"Not much. She said there was a 'big white car' in the left lane, next to Ms. Birch, but the witness didn't see it touch her. The two behind her didn't touch her, either. She saw Ms. Birch's brake lights go on, then she drove right through the guard rail. Which is also what the physical evidence says."

"Hooo-kay! Can I have her address? And can I Xerox the reports?"

"Be my guest." After a couple of seconds, Johannsen added, "It can happen to anybody. Daydreaming maybe and she noticed too late that she'd veered off? Tired at the end of a day's work? Who knows? Sheer bad luck'll get you every time."

"**WHERE DOES THE** requisition go from here?" Jesus asked Joosten.

"Well, to the division chief, Wyczynski, first, I would guess. It's really just in the pipeline, though. The figures are added up in Withers'—uh, Deputy Superintendent Withers'—office, and that's the last stage in the approval process, I think. That's not exactly something I know much about."

Jesus had an inspiration. At the time he thought it was clever, if maybe a little far-fetched. At the time he also thought it was harmless.

"Hang on a minute," he said. He went out into the hall, down the elevator to the first floor, and called Withers' office from the phone booths in the lobby. He identified himself only as Detective Delgado and asked if the deputy superintendent was in. He wasn't. He was at a conference in Terre Haute and would be back tomorrow. Could anybody else help?

Jesus said no and thanked the voice on the line. Then he went back up to Joosten and made a request.

"Can you enter a requisition that I give you, as a test? We'll take it out later."

"Um. No, I don't think—"

"Can you do it if Wyczinski says to?"

"Well, of course."

They got Wyczinski. Jesus said he wanted to see how the requisition reached the next level, the director just below Withers. Wyczinski wasn't sure. The whole idea made him nervous. He was a blocky man in a suit made of thick brown wool that looked stiff. He moved all in one piece, never bending at the waist or twisting his shoulders in relation to his hips. He seemed constructed from a roll of corrugated cardboard. Jesus had met this sort of cop before—the by-the-book cop, who was afraid to do anything because it might be the wrong thing, and afraid to pass the decision up to his superior, too, because it would make him look like he wasn't command material.

"I'll include the words 'test case' if you want to—uh—be extra cautious," Jesus said. He had almost said, "if you want to cover your ass."

When he'd convinced Wyczinski that they would immediately erase the requisition, and Wyczinski could call the secretary in the director's office, tell him to ignore the coming test communication, and tell him that Jesus Delgado would simply come up to check it and then they would abort it, Wyczinski was finally satisfied.

"Okay," Jesus said to Joosten, "ask for one hundred and seventy-six squad cars."

The woman typed the request on a boilerplate form she called up on her screen. She filled in the details, wrote "test case per Det. J. Delgado" on the blank for other comments, then turned to Wyczinski and asked, "Is it okay to enter it, sir?"

"Sure. I said so, didn't I?"

Now the great man is decisive, Jesus thought.

1000010

JESUS RACED UPSTAIRS to the director's office. The secretary was waiting for him.

"So now show me exactly how the order comes through," Jesus said, implying that it was the system he was interested in, not the content.

"Well, here's your order on the screen. I can print out a hardcopy if we need it, or just store it for the director—"

But Jesus was staring at the words on the monitor.

The order was for 178 squad cars.

Oh, my! He thought. *Oh, my!*

Somehow the data management program *itself* had been adapted to change every final six in a squad car order to an eight. And every time it did so, two cars either got bought unnecessarily, in which case they could be pulled out of the pipeline after delivery and sold for serious money, or they weren't delivered at all, in which case the dealer and Withers could split the money.

1000011

JESUS COULD HARDLY contain himself long enough to thank the secretary in the director's office.

He went back to Wyczinski and Joosten and told them that he now understood more about what Frieswyk did during his workday, even though he doubted that the information had any relevance to his death. You have to check everything. Death of a fellow officer. Major matter. Can't miss a point. He thanked them courteously and quietly and left.

Then he went into the nearest men's room, waited until the one officer who had been at the urinal had left, and pounded his right fist into his cupped left hand. *"Gotcha! Hot damn! Gotcha! Gotcha!"*

Then he walked sedately over to the mirror and combed his hair. "You're not so bad, Paco the Great, old buddy!"

Five minutes later, he was in the office of his own superior, George Putnam, Commander of Area 1 Violent Crimes.

It was an odd story Jesus told him, but in a thirty-eight-year career Putnam had heard more odd stories than he could remember. He went down with Jesus to Joosten's office, where Joosten, very intimidated by the brass standing by her desk, entered the identical order for 176 cars again.

Then Putnam and Delgado went to the director's office to see it come up on the screen, changed.

It came up as an order for 176 cars. Suddenly, Jesus shivered.

176, not 178.

1000100

"YOU'VE TOLD ME once. Now tell me the whole thing all over again," Commander DiMaggio said.

Jesus just wished that he understood what all was going on, himself. He told the story over.

At the end of it, DiMaggio steepled his fingers. Jesus kept quiet while the commander thought. Finally DiMaggio said, "You're right. A scam like that could work. It could even explain why the dealer is able to underbid the other dealers, if he shares some of the cut."

"Yes, sir." Jesus glowed with delight.

"Follow me." DiMaggio stood.

They were out the door, in the elevator, and out on another floor when Jesus realized they were heading for the office of Deputy Superintendent Benton K. Rendell, head of Investigative Services.

DiMaggio's boss. DiMaggio gave Rendell a short synopsis, then went away.

"What the hell is this all about?" Rendell barked at Jesus.

He told his story all over again.

When he had finished, Rendell stared at him as if he wanted more data, but Jesus didn't have any more and he wasn't going to make up theories, so he sat stolidly and waited. Rendell nodded to himself a couple of times.

"We're gonna go to the Boss," he said.

Uh-oh, Jesus thought. There was only one boss left. The Big Boss. The superintendent of Police of the City of Chicago. The Man himself, Gus Gimball.

1000101

GIMBALL, ALERTED BY Rendell's secretary that they were on the way, was waiting for them in his office. Not that he could have left. He'd be here another two hours, rechecking every aspect of the president's visit.

After Rendell and Jesus walked in, Rendell gestured at the door and Gimball, catching his drift, nodded. Rendell closed it. He introduced Jesus and everybody shook hands.

Superintendent Gimball and Detective Delgado were as different as two men could easily be. Gimball was very tall but somewhat stooped; Jesus Delgado was shorter and as straight as a flagpole. Gimball was thin; Delgado was all muscle but stocky, and his body looked thick. Gimball looked scholarly and sensitive; Delgado looked impassive. Gimball was African-American; Delgado was ancient, ancient American. Gimball was twenty years older than Delgado, and an extremely important person in the city of Chicago—in fact, he was a worldwide authority on policing. Delgado was low on the CPD totem pole.

Jesus liked Gimball immediately. He had seen him a zillion times, of course—at banquets, in news broadcasts, at awards ceremonies, graduation ceremonies, even passing by in the hall, and he'd liked the Boss' public statements. But this was the first time he'd been closer to him than ten feet.

Rendell said, "Tell the superintendent."

Jesus told.

When Jesus had finished with the details, Gimball said, "Detective Delgado, let's take it for the sake of discussion that everything you say is true. There are several problems here. Number one: How do you think the computer could have been set up to change sixes to eights in the first place?"

"I assumed the person ultimately in charge, Deputy Superintendent Withers, changed it."

After a minute of thinking, Gimball said to Rendell, "Let me talk with Detective Delgado. There's no need to keep you hearing it over and over."

"Okay, boss," Rendell said.

Gimball waited to go on until Rendell had left the room. Jesus couldn't believe that the superintendent actually suspected Rendell of being dirty—he was deputy superintendent. But then, Withers was a deputy superintendent, too. He waited.

"That was my first question," Gimball said. "How it might have been changed in the first place. This is my second. Withers is out of town. So *who changed it back?*"

Jesus stared. Holy shit! He had never once thought of it. And he'd been talking about the incident to one person after another, starting with Putnam. Gimball got it in five minutes. This guy actually *deserved* to be superintendent!

Tunnel vision, Jesus thought. He'd been so focused on the chase, he'd only seen the rabbit, not the track. Suddenly he realized why he'd felt fear when he first saw the number 176. He had a sense of somebody watching over his shoulder. Somebody knew they were being observed and in return they were watching him.

"Who changed it back?" Jesus repeated softly. "Between the time I was there first and when I went back with Putnam, uh—Commander Putnam, I mean."

Gimball smiled. "How long were you away?"

"Well, sir, not more than forty-five minutes. I had to wait while Put—while the commander finished some paperwork."

"Yes, we always have our paperwork. The department lives on paperwork."

"Probably it was closer to half an hour. I had to explain to him everything I had done on Frieswyk up to then, and after that I explained the car orders, and then we went to look."

"I see."

Gimball changed the topic.

"Delgado, you said earlier that you decided Withers had to be involved because he had copies of the original orders sent up to him. Why would he do that? It could cast suspicion on him if anybody started to look into it. Like you."

"Well, see I figured that the system changed any order that ended in six to an eight. But what about orders that were really eights to begin with? Like a real order for forty-eight cars? The department would be expecting all those cars to arrive. So somebody had to check the original paper to tell the dealer when to send cars and when to send money."

"That's very good reasoning, Delgado."

"Thank you, sir."

"Let's draw the bottom line. Each time this happens, they net two cars, or the price of two cars. It happens, let's say, once or twice a year?"

"Yes, that seems about it, if half the orders ending in eight originally ended in six."

"The price of two to four expensive cars. That's a lot of money."

"Yes, sir."

"It's clever, you know. Anybody looking at one specific year wouldn't notice there were no sixes."

"That's true."

"And even if they did, it could be explained as a computer glitch."

"Yes, sir."

"Could Withers have smuggled in a piece of software to sabotage the whole system?"

"I don't know. I don't know enough about computers."

"Delgado, as you've already figured out, this is extremely serious. And totally confidential. And it is now your investigation."

"Thank you, sir."

"What time is it?"

"Eight P.M."

"Hmmm. You'll probably have to see him tomorrow, then."

"Who, boss?"

"I'm going to send you to the Wizard."

1000110

||||||||||||||||||||||||||||||||||||||||||||||||||||||||||||||||||||||||
DEPARTMENT OF THE TREASURY
UNITED STATES SECRET SERVICE
1800 G STREET NW
WASHINGTON DC
FROM: CMV
TO: STRICK
FORM: INTERNAL

<<IN ANY OPEN TRANSMISSION FOLLOW THE
ESTABLISHED CODES>>

DAYS UNTIL WE HAND YOU THE PRESIDENT 3
JIM:
GLAD THE SCREWBALL'S MOVED ON.
OUR CHARGE WANTS EXTRA TIME WITH
GRANDCHILDREN.
VERIFY LOCALES AND FAX ME EXACT MAPS.

CMV
||||||||||||||||||||||||||||||||||||||||||||||||||||||||||||||||||||||||

1000111

I WENT HOME from U-Hosp at four A.M. Wednesday morning, when Robert came back to sit with Sheryl. I found Maria and JJ were asleep, but Kath was up, huddled in a chair in the living room. When I sat down and took her hand, I could feel the child trembling.

"Kath, honey. Let me hold you." Kath was nine, and much too old to climb on an adult's lap, usually. Now she threw herself on me immediately and put her arms around my neck.

"How's my mom?"

"She's alive. And she's in a really good hospital." As I said it, I realized that this was non-talk. It was like saying Sheryl was "as well as can be expected." Which meant next to nothing. What Sheryl would have called "content-free." Kath was too smart to be taken in by that, and I was ashamed of myself for trying to talk down to the child.

Kath said, "Is she gonna die?"

"I don't know."

At seven-thirty I called my parents. I had waited, thinking that they should have a full night's sleep before dealing with the serious injury of their older daughter. It took me half an hour to convince my mother that only one family member could visit Sheryl, and that was only for ten minutes every two hours. My mother kept saying, "They can't mean her *mother* can't sit there with her, Susannah!"

1001000

"This is Susannah Figueroa, Sheryl Birch's sister. Sheryl has been in a serious automobile accident and she's in the hospital. I wanted you to know she wouldn't be coming to work today."

The taped message sounded through Dean Utley's office. Zach and Glen stood with their arms crossed, listening. Utley sat in the chair near his teak desk.

"She's not dead yet," Zach said.

"Evidently." Utley picked up his phone and called the man on duty at the front gate. "Tell Mr. Borke to report to me as soon as he gets in."

Glen said, "You need to know that the car behind me didn't stop to report the accident either. Nobody could have seen much."

"That's fine, Glen. I'm sure you did very well."

Swiveling to his keyboard, he brought up the `botulism` program on his screen, went into U-Hosp, and brought up Sheryl's records.

Howie Borke got the word from the guard and went directly to Utley's office without stopping by his own office, dropping his briefcase, or even taking off his coat.

Utley's door was ajar, which meant walk in.

Howie said, "What's wrong?" He saw Zach and Glen sitting smugly in the side chairs.

Utley said, "Look at this." He pointed at Sheryl's medical record at U-Hosp.

Howie said, "Sheryl had an accident? That's terrible!"

"Well, not exactly, Howie. Let me tell you what happened. After you left for the police department yesterday morning, a little problem cropped up."

Utley narrated the whole sequence of events, although for Zach and Glen's sake he omitted to say that he believed Sheryl had intentionally penetrated `botulism` and backtracked on

Kiro Ogata. He could tell Howie about that later. He explained in detail what the two Blue Blazers had done. "She isn't dead. Now, of course we couldn't be sure the accident would kill her. But so far things seem promising. Apparently she's in a coma."

Howie Borke felt concussed, like he had felt one July Fourth when an M-80 had gone off just two feet from him. He heard what Utley was saying, saw the man's mouth moving, but his senses were numbed and it all seemed very distant. He blinked at Utley. At the same time something in his head was saying, *Watch out! Careful!*

With great concentration, he cocked his head and studied Utley, hoping he was the very picture of an alert executive.

"Have you tried to pull up the police report?"

"No. Good idea," Utley said. He hit the correct keys and in a minute had something on the screen. "Do we need to know the district?" he asked.

"Well, I have that here." Howie had been immersed in cops for weeks, and the city map with district boundaries was in his briefcase. "It's, uh, the Seventeenth. But you should also be able to search it citywide with the victim's name."

"Let's try both."

Howie leaned over Utley's shoulder. Utley said, "There. By victim."

"Try district reports, too."

Utley split the screen. In the second window he scrolled through the Seventeenth District activity for Tuesday. The traffic report came up, entered at 21:10 hours, three hours after the actual accident.

"See?" Howie said. "They're identical. That's exactly the way the program's supposed to work. The officer fills out the form, which is scanned—"

Glen drawled, "Yes, sure, Howie."

Zach said, "Very interesting, Howie."

Utley said softly to Glen and Zach, "That *is* the way it's

supposed to work," and they immediately shut up.

"Our next problem," Utley went on, "is what to do if she comes out of the coma."

"Or before she comes out of the coma," Glen said.

"No, I'm not so sure of that," Utley said. "She wouldn't have known what hit her, anyway. She can't identify you people. She's not going to be able to pin the accident on you."

"It's not the accident that's a problem. We saw to that. It's that she knows about botulism."

Utley said, "That's true."

Howie's head was swimming. "You mean kill her in the hospital?"

"Well, of course, Howie. You've done it before."

"But that was—" He caught himself. He had almost said that was somebody he didn't know. He said, "Why push it? From the medical data, there's gotta be a fifty-fifty chance she'll die."

Glen said, "Why push it? To be certain. To be safe instead of sorry."

Howie, who had spent a lot of time developing the hospital data management program in the first place, said, "Ordinarily in serious head injuries, there's retrograde amnesia."

"The reason we have this program in place," Utley said to Howie, "is to take care of problems like this. One reason, anyway."

Howie seized on a fake worry. "It says there she was first taken to Irving Park Hospital. What if she hadn't been moved to U-Hosp?"

"We've got Northside. And Hinkley Memorial. And Rogers Park Trauma Center. Couple of others."

"We don't have Irving Park."

"We could probably have wormed our way in on a modem line. At least to read their data. Of course, we wouldn't have been able to write to their disk."

"So we couldn't have altered anything."

"In Chicago, it's three chances out of five she'd go to one of ours."

"That's not good enough!"

"Now, Howie—"

At Utley's warning tone, Howie stopped what he was saying. It didn't have anything to do with what hospital she was at, anyway. He was putting up a smoke screen. "We could have been in trouble, though," he said, trying not to sound sullen.

Utley was not entirely fooled. "Then we'd have thought of a way to get to her. People in hospitals are not guarded," he said. He added, smiling, "Unless they're the President of the United States, of course. If we had to take care of her directly, we could." He dropped the smile. "What's your real problem, Howie?"

Howie knew he was in danger. "Beyond what I said—absolutely nothing at all."

Utley clapped his hands once. "Decision time. What'll it be?"

Howie said, "I say let nature take her course. It's safer all around."

Glen said, "Do it now. Anything might happen."

Utley said, "Zach?"

"Actually, I think it *is* safer to wait. After all, we don't want to take a risk of alerting anybody to any *peculiarities* in the U-Hosp program. It's four days to cutworm. There's nothing more important right now than that. Sheryl could be in a coma for months, and in four days it won't matter."

Utley folded his big hands.

"And it's not as if we can't monitor the situation minute to minute," Utley said. "My decision is: leave her alone for a while."

1001001

IT WAS HOWIE who had named `botulism`, `nematode`, and `cutworm`. Botulism poisoned a system. Nematodes were tiny worms that infected the roots of plants, a name Howie thought was particularly appropriate for infiltrating the very records and transmissions of the Chicago Police Department. And a cutworm was an insect larva that ate the stem of a plant where it met the ground, causing the plant to topple over—perfect for a president.

Although Howie was no longer a teenager—he had grown up, married, and now had a wife and a one-year-old son—what he still liked best to do was play with his keyboard, and when his fingers touched his keyboard he was still just playing a game. He didn't really connect what he could do with his keyboard to events in the lives of real people. Psychologically, he was not alone in this disassociation. Pilots of aircraft dropping bombs do much the same thing. So do all sorts of people who have to make decisions about the lives of individuals they never see.

But the situation he faced at SJR today was different. Howie liked Sheryl Birch. In fact, Sheryl reminded him of his wife. Physically, she was the type of woman he admired, and he also admired her engineering smarts.

He realized that Sheryl threatened SJR's future—the plan that would bring them unheard-of earthly power. She could even threaten him personally, if she triggered the cops to investigate SJR. He was very distressed that she had broken into `botulism`, but he was also sad and scared to hear that she was gravely injured.

And as if that was not enough, he knew perfectly well that she might wake up and start talking. If she woke up, Utley would want him to sabotage the medical record in some way.

Kill her.

He had to hope that either she'd die first or that she'd stay in her coma long enough for cutworm to be executed. After that, they could block or discredit anything she said. They could claim that her notions about SJR were really the product of a severe brain injury. If she stayed in a coma just four days more, she would be okay. Once they controlled the presidency, she wouldn't be able to touch them.

If she didn't stay in the coma, what then?

If Utley told him to kill her, could he do it?

1001010

WHEN WE GOT to our squad car, Bennis paused with his hand on the door and asked, "How is Sheryl?"

"I saw her at two o'clock, on my way over here. There's not much change. I hope."

"What do you mean, you hope?"

"Oh, Norm." I put my hands over my eyes, because I didn't want him to see me crying. "I think she's worse. They were talking about giving her something called mannitol. It's a diuretic and it gets water out of the body. They use it if the brain swells. They said last night that they wouldn't do that unless she started to deteriorate."

"Oh, my Lord," Bennis said softly.

"They won't tell me anything *real*. They say things like she's responding to treatment! I can't stand it, Norm! I just could *not stand it* if she died!"

"Suze, I think you oughta put in to take the day off."

"No way. I can't see her again until midnight, because my mother is going in and then my father and then Robert. And I can't sit around and do nothing. And I don't want to be home with the kids, because my mother's there and she's driving me crazy. Speaking of driving, let's get started. Take my mind off things. We won't talk about it."

Norm slipped into the driver's seat. "By the way—here," he said, handing me Xeroxes of the reports he had collected from Officer Johannsen.

"Oh, you darling!" I threw my arms around him and kissed him on the ear.

"Are you *nuts?*" Bennis blushed. He quickly looked around to see whether any fellow officers were nearby. "The next thing you know, people will be saying we're having a squad car romance."

"Well, jeez, Bennis. I wouldn't want to ruin your reputation."

1001011

||||||||||||||||||||||||||||||||||||||||||||||||||||||||||

```
DEPARTMENT OF THE TREASURY
UNITED STATES SECRET SERVICE
1800 G STREET NW
WASHINGTON DC
FROM: CMV
TO: STRICK
FORM: INTERNAL

<<IN ANY OPEN TRANSMISSION FOLLOW THE
ESTABLISHED CODES>>

DAYS UNTIL WE HAND YOU THE PRESIDENT 2
JIM:
ON FINAL ROUTE CHECK, KEEP ON TOP OF LOCALS.
ALWAYS KEEP ON TOP OF LOCALS.

CMV
```
||||||||||||||||||||||||||||||||||||||||||||||||||||||||||

1001100

"THE GIRLS WENT to school today," I said to Sheryl. "They didn't want to, but I made them go. They wanted to come and see you. You know, we'd be here all the time, but the hospital won't allow it. We only get let in here ten minutes every two hours. I was so worried that you would think we were staying away. You wouldn't think that, would you, honey? You know we're thinking about you every second we're not in here."

Sheryl did not speak or move. I squeezed her hand, but Sheryl did not squeeze back.

"Mom cleaned the house while I was gone yesterday." I smiled at Sheryl. "She cleaned up your study. She stacked your disks so they're not in order anymore." I chuckled. "You'll be absolutely furious when you get home and see it. And your notes. Mom thinks all pieces of paper should be in one pile. A square pile. I was going to tell her she shouldn't have touched them, when I saw what she'd done. But it was already too late and anyway—" tears started in my eyes "—anyway she wanted so badly to be doing something for you, I just couldn't. So, I think you'd better recover as fast as possible so you can get home and mess up your study."

Sheryl didn't move.

1001101

A YOUNG STUDENT nurse reminded me that my ten minutes were up. When I walked out into the central monitoring station area, a nurse I had begun to recognize was there, entering data. Her last name according to her tag was Dodd. She looked up as I approached.

I said, "My sister looks worse."

"You can't judge by how she looks. Bruises take a day or two to swell and get really discolored."

Nurse Dodd spoke matter-of-factly, in a precise voice. She had an angular face, sharp nose, sharp cheekbones, and a pointed chin. Her black hair was straight and uncompromising. I was used to having to size up people by actions as well as looks, and I suspected Dodd was a person cursed with an unsympathetic appearance who was actually very kind. She just didn't look motherly.

And in view of the fact that, on this unit, she must lose a big percentage of her patients to death, she probably had developed an ability to keep some psychological distance.

Like a cop.

Suspecting that she had a soft core, I said, "Nobody tells us anything. I mean anything really about what to expect."

Dodd had been sitting at a keyboard and monitor, studying the screen.

"Is that my sister's medical record?" I asked.

"No. It's the chart of a patient across the hall." Dodd immediately stored the chart before I looked at it. The patients' medical records were confidential, of course.

"I didn't mean to pry into somebody else's—" I said, putting my hand on the top of the monitor.

"No problem. I know you're worried."

I glanced at the system. The keyboard and monitor were IBMs. The monitor screen was blank.

I said, "And I have to tell her daughters every day—"

Dodd got up. "I'm not supposed to predict. If anybody does that, it's the doctor."

"But he doesn't say anything!"

"Listen, they always *look* worse the second and third day. You know how it is with bruises. But between you and me, she's holding her own. Really."

1001110

FIGUEROA HAD SQUEEZED Sheryl's hand one last time before she left her to talk with the nurse. For several minutes, while Dodd and Figueroa talked, nothing happened. Figueroa left the unit and went out to her car. Then, as if nerve impulses were indeed traveling in Sheryl's body, but traveling with excruciating slowness, Sheryl's hand contracted, squeezing back, even though it was squeezing empty air.

1001111

||||||||||||||||||||||||||||||||||||||||||||||||||||||||||||||
DEPARTMENT OF THE TREASURY
UNITED STATES SECRET SERVICE
1800 G STREET NW
WASHINGTON DC
FROM: CMV
TO: STRICK
FORM: INTERNAL

<<IN ANY OPEN TRANSMISSION FOLLOW THE
ESTABLISHED CODES>>

DAYS UNTIL WE HAND YOU THE PRESIDENT <u>1</u>
JIM:
LOOKS LIKE SMOOTH SAILING.

CMV
||||||||||||||||||||||||||||||||||||||||||||||||||||||||||||||

1010000

JESUS DELGADO WAS sound asleep, dreaming of unending paperwork. Stacks and stacks of records still to be read, piles so high they reached into the dusty rafters. And mounds and mounds of discarded sheets of paper, file cards, canceled checks, all sifted up against one side of a room like autumn leaves, and he was going to have to clear them out with a rake. And still more paper to be sorted—on desks, on tables, packed in file cabinets. And he, Jesus, could check only one sheet at a time, which he had to read thoroughly. Then file or reject. If he rejected it, he crumpled it into a ball and threw it to the other side of the room.

He crumpled sheet after sheet, until the only sound in the room was crumpling, crumpling, crumpling—

It was more like cellophane being crumpled.

No, it was more like—

—more like FIRE!

It was the crackling of fire!

He was bolt upright in an instant. "Elena!" She wouldn't wake up. He shook her hard. She woke then, and fast.

"You get Betina! I'll get Linda!" he yelled.

They ran to the girls' room, where Betina was awake now and crying. Linda was still asleep, but Jesus scooped her up.

Behind him Elena shouted, "The stairs are on fire!"

The lights were off, maybe shorted out by the fire, but he could see windows in the glow from streetlights. The lower stairs were red with fire. The stairwell flickered wildly, orange colors pulsed on the walls, and smoke rolled up like big black expanding balloons.

"Go out the back window!" Jesus screamed. The upstairs back windows were over the roof of their tiny back porch, and the drop from there to the ground would be only eight feet.

Suddenly they were engulfed in gritty smoke. The girls shrieked. A noise like breaking waves rose up the stairs and with it a rush of flame. The old wooden house had no resistance to fire.

"Out the back!" he screamed. He pushed Elena along. She had Betina in her arms and all four lurched to the back windows.

In bare feet and just his underwear, Jesus kicked the glass out, then kicked the shards out of the frame. "Go! Go! Go!" he screamed at Elena.

She backed through the window, holding Betina, and dropped to the roof below. Jesus followed immediately with Linda hugged against his chest, jumping far to the left, so as not to fall on Elena or Betina.

He landed on the roof of the porch, and his knee gave under him. The roof shuddered. It was old and had not been sturdily built in the first place. Linda was shielded by his arms, even though he fell forward, and now he rolled with her toward the edge of the roof.

"Honey, I'm going to lower you to the ground. I'll hold your hand and you put your feet way, way down and it won't be hardly any drop at all." He hoped that was true, but it was certainly safer than both of them dropping together. He might fall on her, and he wasn't sure whether there was a chair or a flowerpot or something she could be hurt on if his weight landed on top of her.

The back lawn was lit by firelight from the back windows. Maybe the porch was on fire.

"I'm scared, Daddy!"

"I know, honey, but you're brave, too. Now hurry, because I have to check on Betina and Mommy." In the dark up here he couldn't see more than a shape on the roof.

Leaning as far over as he could, holding both her hands, he lowered her over and dropped her to the ground. His heart lifted when she said, "I'm down, Daddy!"

"Go back on the lawn, but stay *right there!*"

Now that he had time to look, he saw Betina on the roof not far from him. She was rolled into a ball, holding her fists in front of her chest. *Where was Elena?* He crawled over, his knee shrieking in pain.

"Betina! Betina, please! Where's Mommy?"

The little girl was huddled tight and pushed him away when he tried to get her fists out of her face to talk to her.

"Betina! I need to know! *Where's Mommy?*"

Suddenly the child realized it was her father. She grabbed at him and started crying and tearing at his clothes. He looked around wildly.

"Tell me, baby! Please!"

"She fell."

Back of them, Jesus saw a hole in the porch roof. Inside, below, the porch was on fire. Even as he saw it, he realized that the roof was hot. His mind shrieking with denial, he seized up Betina, carried her to the edge of the roof, and despite her screams of fear, lowered her to the ground, shouting, "Get back from the house, baby! Go in the yard. Linda's there."

Then he jumped. He didn't even notice the pain in his knee as he landed, or the fact that his hands and forearms were burned from the hot roof. He rose, smashed his way through the porch screening—plastic screening, which was melting—and forced his way into the flames. He saw Elena's huddled shape on the porch back against the house wall, directly under the hole in the roof. His mind thought that the fire must have started on the back porch as well as somewhere inside the house, but his body was diving toward Elena. He held his breath. The hair on his legs started to burn.

He took hold of Elena by the forearm and one foot and simply ran for the air, dragging her with him. He pitched forward and fell once, crawled, pulling her off the porch and onto the gravel behind the house. Then he got up and threw her over his shoulder and lurched into the backyard.

He could see the lights of fire engines. A neighbor must have called 911. Men in turnout coats came around the back, one of them carrying a portable light. Jesus could see Elena clearly now. But he didn't, for a moment, understand. She didn't look like she was supposed to look. It wasn't Elena; it was a little bald man! But if it wasn't Elena, who was it and what had this person been doing on his back porch? Then he realized it was Elena. Her clothes were burned off. Her hair was burned off. Her skin was charred, and she was not breathing.

There was a funny, flickering light, too, which came from noplace or everyplace.

One of the firemen said, "Oh, God!" and threw something over Jesus' head. His hair had been on fire. Shit, he thought, feeling giddy and vague—better stop using so much of that greasy hair oil! And he started laughing. He laughed and laughed and laughed.

1010001

NO MATTER HOW hard I tried to put it out of my mind, SJR kept coming back. The sequence was too obvious:

Sheryl had discovered something at the company that worried her.

Sheryl had investigated.

Sheryl had had a mysterious accident.

Maybe it really was an accident. As Bennis always said, some things you couldn't explain. "That's why they call them accidents."

Maybe I was paranoid. Maybe I was too stunned to think clearly. Maybe I was dead wrong.

But maybe the Blue Blazers had tried to kill my sister, and *if they had* and if she survived, they would try again.

I waved good-bye to Bennis and waited a few minutes past the end of my tour, until Sergeant Pat Touhy left and the next sergeant came on. His name was Ornette Wilms, and he was a good person. Much more understanding than Touhy.

The early cars had left and cleared, and Sergeant Wilms was working on paper in the watch commander's office.

"Sergeant Wilms?" I said.

"Hi, Figueroa. Why are you still here? Not your shift."

"I need to talk to you about something."

He was unsurprised by this; Sergeant Touhy was known as a real hard-ass and impossible to talk to. People often went to Wilms instead. "Pull up a stool. I heard about your sister's accident. I'm real sorry."

"Thanks. That's what I wanted to talk with you about."

Maybe he wouldn't believe me. It was so difficult to explain. SJR had done a good job of making the automobile accident look accidental. If they did it at all. I had to find exactly the right words. And I had to sound calm and rational.

While I thought about it, I glanced at what Wilms was doing. He was entering some data from the papers the patrol officers filled out—the D7 forms—onto the computer. The monitor had a logo on the frame: SJR DataSystems.

I drew in a breath.

I looked at the screen's command line, which carried a short menu of options. It said: SJR DataSystems Command Package.

I had jumped to my feet before I realized it.

"What's the matter?" Wilms said.

"Nothing. Just nervous I guess." I sat back down.

"So what did you want to talk about?

"Uh—Sarge, do we have any computer experts in the CPD?"

"Well, sure. Couple in Systems, more'n a couple in Fraud. Business fraud, especially. Somebody takes care of the AFIS program—"

"No, I mean more like computers generally. How they work—no, sort of what you can do with them and who does what with them. I'm not being clear, am I?"

"Not really."

"Like, what could you do with them if you really wanted to screw things up?"

He smiled. "You sound loony, Figueroa, but I've got just the guy for you. He's our resident computer dweeb. Max Black. We call him the Wizard. We keep him in the basement."

1010010

THE EMTs HAD taken Jesus, Linda, Betina, and Elena to the hospital in four separate ambulances. Linda was released in the morning, and Jesus' mother took her home. Linda still coughed from smoke inhalation, but was basically all right. Betina had second-degree burns on both forearms and one thigh from the hot roof. Jesus had deep burns on his scalp and burned hands. Elena was dead. When Betina was released, Jesus checked himself out. He had to be home to protect his children. He and Betina went to his parents' house, Jesus dazed and silent.

He didn't have all his emotions in working order. He kept wondering at his own reactions, whether they were appropriate. When he felt numb, he was upset because his feelings weren't strong enough. When the feelings broke through, they shook him so much that he wrapped his arms around himself and sank into a ball and cried.

Jesus went to see the ruins of his house. And he remembered the evening that led up to the fire.

He and Elena had been cool to each other for the last several days, in the wake of Elena's saying she wanted to be a cop. They had been polite, both of them trying not to upset the children, but of course that really didn't work. You didn't have to say things in words, and you certainly didn't have to shout at each other, for children to know something was wrong. The twins knew that you weren't supposed to be dreadfully polite around the house; you were supposed to laugh and be friendly.

But when he got home from work yesterday, things changed. Jesus had been full of pleasure at how smart he had been in digging out the squad car orders. The superintendent himself had complimented him. His cup had run over.

And he said to Elena, who was standing at a sink full of dishes, shining a pan with Brillo, using unnecessary, angry energy, "Hey, stop a minute."

He took her wet hand.

"Honey, listen. You do what you want to do. I wasn't trying to stand in your way."

She studied his eyes for a few seconds. She didn't want to "win" just by being angry, he thought. She wanted him to feel okay about it—more than that, she wanted him to be proud of her.

He said, "I was overreacting because I'd just run into something unpleasant on the job. I didn't mean it."

"So tell me exactly what you mean now." She wasn't going to give in easily. She was as stubborn as he was.

"I can see how you might want to be a cop. I ought to see. It's all I ever wanted to be."

"You'd feel—if I did, how would you feel?"

"I'd be proud of you."

She smiled that big smile of hers, and then she giggled and scooped up an entire handful of soapsuds and slapped them down on his head.

"So why the change?" she said, laughing. He picked her up and spun in a circle, and her feet swung out behind her. Her black, curly hair swung in a cloud around her head.

"I did something really smart today," he said. "I did something really absolutely brilliant."

She kissed him. "You did something pretty brilliant tonight, too."

They went to bed and made love quietly—don't wake the

kids!—softly, and gently, like friends. To Jesus it meant that everything in his life was just fine. Job, home, everything.

Now he stood in the ashes of his house, with both tears and the sweat of fury pouring down his face, and asked himself, "You're glad, aren't you? That everything was good between you at the end? You'd feel worse if she had died when you were still angry at each other, wouldn't you?"

Then why did he feel as if even the thought of that final evening sucked all the air out of his lungs?

1010011

I FOLLOWED SERGEANT Wilms' directions from the First District desk into the main part of the Chicago Police Department building. From there I went down the ramp that attached the main building to the Annex.

On the first floor of the Annex, I looked around for the stairs to the basement. This was not the world's most elegant building, and next to a wire-reinforced back door, the kind with a panic bar and alarm box, I found a narrow stair leading down.

Somebody had saved money on lightbulbs. The walls were yellow but looked the color of old mustard. The floor was cement, varnished with spilled ink, gum, and other stains. It had been washed again and again, but some of the stains would obviously never come out.

I passed a room stuffed with paper in stacked bales. The blocks of paper were each about eighteen inches high, all of them tied with twine. The edges were yellowish. They were stacked to the ceiling, like cinderblocks from a torn down house. How would anybody ever find a specific piece of paper in this mess? Suddenly the idea of storing data on disks didn't seem quite as ominous. There were other rooms along the hall, some with boxes of paper towels, toilet paper, soap powder, and so on piled inside, but most with files and bales of paper. I was looking for one inhabited by a gnome bent over a keyboard, the "computer dweeb" Wilms had described.

I heard footsteps behind me and whirled around.

A man in the shadows said, "Who are you?"

"I'm looking for the computer dw—the Wiz—uh, Max Black."

"I'm Black. What do you want?"

"The First District sergeant sent me—"

"Oh, very well. Come in here."

The shadow waved its hand at a door farther along, which I supposed meant it was okay to precede him into the room. I would have found the room, even if I hadn't found Black. It was the only brightly lit room down here, and it was jammed with monitors, printers, keyboards, a fax machine, manuals galore, and bookcases. On the bookshelves, beside the books, were rank after rank of disks, several coffee mugs with the logos of electronics companies on them, and two small plastic figures made from pieces of an old Cootie game. One was labeled "Heisenbug." The other was labeled "Mandelbug."

"So what do you want?"

I turned to face Black and stepped back in surprise. He was about six feet tall, broad shouldered, with bright blond hair. He looked like a cross between Robert Redford and Sting.

"Sit there."

"There" was a pile of printouts. I sat there.

He had a plug-in hot pot and had apparently just been down the hall to get water for it. He plugged it in. I was getting impatient. "Mr. Black," I said, "or is it Officer Black?"

"Yeah. Officer Black. Get to the point."

"My sister is a computer engineer for a major computer company. She recently stumbled on a program, or a file, a thing, anyway—"

"Well, what was it? Don't you even know what you're talking about?"

"No, I don't know what I'm talking about. I don't know computing."

"How do people like you excuse your ignorance?"

"Now wait a minute!"

"Don't you realize that in five years you won't be able to do *anything* of any significance without cybernetic skills? It's as bad as living in this country and refusing to learn English. Which, by the way, my grandfather did. Put a hideous burden on his children, who spent all their time interpreting for him and filling out forms for him and trying to explain to him that the shopkeepers weren't cheating him and so on and so on until they couldn't stand it. You have to learn the coin of the realm, verbally speaking."

"Listen, if I knew what I was talking about here, I wouldn't need you!"

He smiled a little at that. "I'll ask questions," he said. "You answer. As best you can," he added.

After several questions, he said, "So on that morning, she was working on something for the navy, with a large amount of data. What did she call the thing she was using?"

"I can't remember. Some sort of connection to the Department of Defense. She wasn't permitted to talk about it very specifically."

"Not the *content!* What did she call the software?"

"I can't remember! Some sort of connection."

"A link?"

"That's it!"

"A smartlink?"

"Yes!"

"All right. Let me tell you what she was doing. Try to remember this. The company must have a link direct to the Department of Defense to suck in and analyze huge amounts of data. If the company wanted to suck in huge amounts of credit card data on individuals, like you say, they would use the same kind of software to do it. It's the same process, see, reaching into somebody's store of data at a distance."

"Fine. What does it mean?"

"I haven't the foggiest. Unless you have any more evidence about what they were doing with it."

"No." I felt deflated and stumped. "She ran a password-cracking program at home. She went to the office that day with the passwords to see what was in the files. And on the way home, she had the freak accident. She never had a chance to tell me what she found out."

"What were the passwords?"

"I only saw one. It was 'celeste' or 'celeste something' or 'something celeste.' "

"Hmmp. You don't have anything, then." He got up. "I have to get to work. You may leave now."

"But they really may have tried to kill her!"

"Unlikely. What company was it?"

"SJR DataSystems."

"SJR!" He sat back down.

1010100

BLACK TURNED HIS back on me, swiveling to face his keyboard. His fingers struck the keys too fast for me to see what he was typing. His screen scrolled. At certain points he'd freeze something briefly and then go on. Finally, after several of these passes, he hit some other keys and swung around. As he did, the water in his hot pot boiled and the printer started to hum.

"Dean Utley has a reputation in the industry," Black said. "Insiders think it's been just a little too opportune sometimes when he comes out with a new product just weeks before another company."

"Industrial espionage?"

"No doubt. On the other hand, he gets the product out and gets the work done. Nothing's ever been proved against him."

He poured hot water over instant coffee in two mugs and handed me one. Mine said: "Better Living Through Chemistry." I guess I had suddenly become Max's ally. As I watched him, I thought how unusual it was to find a man who looked like a movie-star hunk and was totally unaware of it.

He stirred his coffee with his index finger, then licked it off and picked up the printout.

"Oooookay. Utley. Graduated from the University of Michigan in 1978. That was a revolutionary year. Intel released its 8086 chip and Tandy put out the TRS80 through Radio Shack."

"Right you are," I said.

"You can scoff, but the world changed. That was the first home computer most people could afford. Your man Utley took a job in an automotive plant near Ann Arbor, developing programs for internal control mechanisms for cars. Probably he was more of a programmer and a software engineer than an electrical engineer, though. And in an automobile plant, it would be a long, slow, climb to make it to the top."

"A slow climb wouldn't be Utley's idea of his destiny."

"I think not. He seems to have found SJR Systems right away. It was a small, solvent Ann Arbor business, owned by somebody named Sydney J. Rasowitz, and it made pinball games. Right about then, when a lot of people were getting home computers, there were new game systems. Pong was one of the early home games. Then better ones came out based on the 6502 Intel chip: the Apple II, the Commodore 64, and the Atari 800. When the VisiCalc spreadsheet program hit the market in 1979, home personal computers were at last really useful. Utley must have been rabid to get in on the action, but he didn't have any money. SJR Systems was solvent. Its loans were paid off, and all the assembly tools, buildings, and land were paid off and fully owned by Rasowitz."

"You're gonna say Utley went to Rasowitz and scared him about home games."

"You may not be knowledgeable, but you're smart. Utley must've told him home games would take over the market and put the arcades out of business. Rumor in *Games and Gaming* says Utley found the names of Rasowitz's customers, visited some of them, and phoned others. He told them that, if they could wait a while for their next deliveries, he could supply them the same product at thirty percent less. They were interested. He asked for an expression of that interest in writing.

"Then he approached Rasowitz. Pinball was a dying business. Utley told Rasowitz that he'd buy him out for cash, fifty cents on the dollar.

"Rasowitz had already noticed a downturn in orders—because of the customers Utley had approached and asked to wait. The rumors in the industry frightened him, too. He tentatively accepted Utley's offer.

"Utley got an appraiser who was acceptable to both of them. When Utley had the list of assets, he went to a bank, asking for the loan of a million dollars. He could claim the land and tools and buildings were worth most of that amount, anyhow. He claimed he could make arcade games and sell to an existing client list."

"How could he show he'd have business?"

"He'd pull out the sheaf of future orders he'd collected from Rasowitz's clients. Suppose the banker told Utley he'd have to personally sign on the loan and fill out a bank statement. What could he lose? He had nothing as it was. He could list stocks that he claimed he held in certificate form in safe deposit boxes; he could list land he claimed to own out of state; he could even list debts owed him by fictitious persons.

"In any case, he obviously got the loan. Then he paid Rasowitz and told him good-bye at the factory door.

"His next job was to turn SJR into a glamour stock and take it public. He renamed it SJR DataSystems, keeping part of the name so as to claim it had been in business many years, but adding the promise of new, trendy computer games to his line. With an underwriter, he drew up papers to sell stock representing fifty percent of the business to the public at a multiple to be determined. Then he went to the arcade owners and asked for firm orders.

"Naturally, they said, what about our thirty percent discount? Utley said he'd give them something better, stock in the new company for the thirty percent. Insider price on a stock that's going to go through the roof.

"Now he goes looking for an underwriter. Tells them he has a cash cow in the arcade business, with a history of fifteen years of good sales and better to come, but also that all income would be going into developing data management programs and some small computer hardware."

"Would brokers see it was risky?"

"Of course. He'd rooted around through several brokers and sniffed out one who did not quite close the door—leaving an opening for Utley to sweeten the deal."

"How?"

"Insider stock. An agreement to let their attorneys do the work for the SEC at twice the usual rate, part of which would be kicked back to the broker, not the standard eight or nine percent, but fifteen percent of the money they would raise from the public. Warrants to purchase the stock at the offering price for the next two years.

"They raised two and a half million dollars, parked the stock in friendly hands, watched it quadruple, then put out a 'secondary offering' for ten million dollars. At that point he had a company with eight and a half million dollars in cash and a bank note of one million which he could pay off. It was the only indebtedness the company had. But Utley didn't want to pay it off yet, because he wanted to hold on to as much leverage as possible.

"Meanwhile, Utley was looking for employees. There were two kinds he wanted. There were the honest and capable workers. Then there were the others. Quite a few hackers were either too dishonest or too uncontrollable for industry in general."

"So he stole?"

"Not most of the time. Utley himself is a brilliant and versatile programmer. He has a reputation for being able to read hexadecimal machine language as if it were English."

"Isn't that nice."

"Hexadecimal has sixteen symbols, zero to nine and A through F, so that it looks like gibberish even to experienced engineers."

"Good."

"Utley developed several data management systems himself, and one of the reasons SJR DataSystems took off so rapidly was that he was very early into data management for small businesses. He knew that people hate taking inventory. He invented a program he called Tracker IV, a data management system for small businesses that kept track of what was where and how much was left. There had never been a Tracker I, II, or III, but Utley figured, who would care? What was some small company going to do—put a researcher on to see whether SJR DataSystems was using puffery in its names? Tracker IV worked, and it worked beautifully. That's all they would care about.

"Business boomed. By then, 1981, Apple Computer was worth one-point-eight billion dollars and Utley was small but avid. In 1981, IBM introduced its PC and the home PC was everywhere. In 1982, Lotus introduced the Lotus 1-2-3 spreadsheet, user-friendly and fast. Microsoft, seven years old, was worth thirty-four million dollars. Utley was yapping at its heels. He opened a new, large plant and corporate offices in Skokie, Illinois. But even that was a waystation. Business was wonderful. After just four years his gross was in the fifty to eighty million dollar range and he broke ground farther north for the new, glorious plant he has now.

"The Ann Arbor plant turned to making keyboards for the new computers and the cases for the new SJR monitors. Then he opened a plant in Korea, which made the monitors. He has a plant in Germany which does most of the disk-pressing and duplicating, a plant outside Mexico City that makes chips, and a plant in South Carolina that prints and packages most of the instruction manuals."

"Isn't that enough for him?"

"How should I know? Suppose every time SJR DataSystems installed a management system, they left a modem access or a black box through which they could enter the system later. If they wanted, they could rebuild the target company's books to make it look like they had provided better service or saved the company even more money than they really had. Or they could get insider information no one knew they had. They'd have access to all the company's records: suppliers, customers, and the bids of competitors. They could *always* undercut the bid of any competing data processing system, if they wanted to."

"That's hideous."

"It could get worse. Phone and cable companies. File servers for the information highway. Military servers. Weapons. The Internal Revenue Service. Huge departments of governmental statistics."

"I see."

"From those statistics, Ms. Figueroa, all the decisions in the United States are made."

"If he's that nasty, he wouldn't have any qualms about attacking my sister."

"Now there I'm not so sure. There's absolutely no whiff of a suspicion that he's ever hurt anybody physically. These are keyboard people."

I sagged again. "But I *know* they did. I need help."

There was a knock at the door. Black yelled, "We're busy. Go away!"

The door opened. Black said, "Damn it. What do you want?" The man who entered wore a CPD uniform, but I had never met him. This was hardly surprising; there were twelve thousand officers in the CPD. What got my attention, though, was that part of his hair was burned off. One hand was bandaged, and the bandages disappeared up into the sleeve of his shirt, so there was no telling how extensive the burn was. The other hand was burned but not bandaged. It looked red, raw, and swollen.

At this apparition, even Black was speechless.

The injured man said, "My name is Jesus Delgado. I need your help."

1010101

THURSDAY HAD BEEN hell, with just a tiny light at the end. Friday Max was cybersearching vigorously. Jesus, who had good computer skills, was helping. I worked eleven P.M. to seven A.M., grabbed five hours' sleep, and took Maria to see Sheryl at two and Kath at four. I felt like at last I was doing something substantial for Sheryl.

Because the girls were young, and maybe because Sheryl seemed a little bit better, the nurse, Dodd, who was on duty, let me go in with the girls.

Maria was upset at Sheryl's appearance, and distracted and unnerved by the life-support devices and the tubes, oxygen outlets, suction machines, heart monitors, and so on. She hardly dared touch her mother, and it was all I could do to get her to speak. When I said it was okay to talk with Sheryl, Maria said, "Uh—hi, Mom," in a tiny voice, and then burst into tears. Sheryl either didn't hear or didn't understand, or couldn't answer. I wondered whether bringing Maria had been a good idea.

Kath, whom we always called the Serious One, younger and for some reason always the wiser, went directly to her mother and sat in the metal chair to the right of her bed. She took her hand and said, "Hi! Can you hear me?" Since there was no answer, she went on, talking about everything that had been happening in the family.

"You should *see* the stupid jumpsuit Honey Grant wore to school yesterday!"

I stood in the corner, letting Kath have her moments with her mother. In the corner were three baskets of flowers on a stand. They were ten feet from the bed, but if Sheryl ever opened her eyes she would see them. The ICU had strict rules about flowers—only so many, not near the bed, something. But they did cheer the place up. Other than the flowers, the treatment bay looked like the inside of the space shuttle. I had sent one of the baskets. One was from Robert and the girls. One was new. It was an expensive selection of pink and white baby roses. I smelled them, thinking somebody had spent a lot of money. There had to be at least two dozen roses in the bouquet. I looked at the card.

"Get well soon, Sheryl. Dean Utley, Howie Borke, and all your friends at SJR DataSystems." I sat back with a gasp.

Suddenly, Kath said, "She moved!"

"What?"

I think I leaped across the room in one jump.

"She moved! When I talked to her."

"Really?" I was terrified to get my hopes up. But Kath was a levelheaded child and wouldn't have imagined something that hadn't happened.

"She squeezed my hand!"

"Oh, honey! I hope so! Let me try."

Kath relinquished Sheryl's hand to me. I said, "Sheryl? Can you hear us?"

Sheryl's eyes, half-closed, didn't move. But her hand squeezed mine.

"She did!" Kath and I screamed in delight. "You sit here, honey," I said. "I have to tell the nurse."

Kath sat down again and started talking to her mother.

"Oh, I'm so glad," Dodd said to me. "That's a really good sign."

Nevertheless, I noticed that the nurse followed me back into Sheryl's treatment bay and took Sheryl's hand herself. Dodd waited patiently while Kath said, "Mom! Do it again!" Then Dodd, too, felt the hand move. No doubt Nurse Dodd was a person who had experienced too much wishful thinking from too many hopeful relatives to accept optimistic reports without evidence.

"You sit right there, dear," Dodd said to Kath. "You obviously do her good."

I followed Dodd back to the central station. "How good a sign is this?"

"Very. It's a wonderful development," Dodd said. "She seemed better, but you never really know."

"It's especially wonderful that it happened while Kath was here," I said. "She'll feel like she made it happen. For that matter, maybe she did."

"Maybe she did at that."

I smiled at her.

Paperwork really was computer work. Dodd sat down at her desk. She reached for her keyboard. "You go sit with her. I'd better write up the good news about your sister. Let me get it entered in her chart."

1010111

HOWIE SAW THE notation come up on Sheryl's chart. "Responding to tactile stimuli" didn't have to mean much, did it? Possibly he could ignore it. He thought several minutes about simply not saying anything. Howie wasn't feeling very well. Maybe he could plead illness and go home, but he realized that Utley would monitor the chart at times himself. Howie knew his own survival could depend on his telling Utley.

He went to Utley's office. Unknown to Howie, one of Utley's many monitors was now permanently set to the U-Hosp internal machine. Every half hour or so, it dipped into the file on Sheryl Birch. Utley knew before Howie entered the room what had happened, but he pretended to be surprised.

Utley said, "Interesting! Would you say this is an important change?"

"I doubt it. It could just mean she is aware of being touched."

Utley studied Howie. Howie looked very uncomfortable.

"It means we have to keep constant track of the situation, doesn't it?" Utley said in his deceptively courteous tone.

"Yes. Absolutely."

"And be ready to move if it looks like she's really coming out of it?"

"Yes."

"And you have a plan in mind, in case that happens?"

"Yes."

BACK AT HIS desk, Howie studied the file he had brought up on Sheryl. He thought probably the best thing was to be on the safe side. Get ready. Most likely none of this would be necessary. He hoped. Sheryl had only *moved* for God's sake, and only her hand. It wasn't as if she could speak. But just to give himself a little leeway if she should do anything wild, like sit up and start talking, he alerted his system to watch for the results of the last blood draw and beep him when they were posted.

Howie had learned a lot about medical terms when he and Sweigert wrote the medical data management program. Now he kept in his office such useful disks as the *Physician's Desk Reference* and the *Merck Manual*. He thought he knew what to do to Sheryl, but once he had it thoroughly worked out, he called Sweigert to verify. Sweigert was a member of the steering committee and directed a lot of their technical program development. He had a feel for what professional people wanted a system to do for them. Sweigert was what he himself referred to as a "defrocked doctor." Because of a problem of vanishing medications, he had been dropped from medical school in his fourth year, not a common event that far along in the training. He was, of course, exactly the kind of person Utley would find and acquire.

"I'd like to drop the crit a little, and then a lot if we really need to," Howie said, referring to the hematocrit figure, a count of the number of blood cells in a volume of blood which gave physicians an idea whether there was blood loss—in this case from internal bleeding.

Howie and Sweigert agreed on some numbers, which weren't far from what Howie would have chosen on his own, and he hung up, satisfied.

He intercepted the results of the blood draw as they went onto the database and lowered the crit a little. Then he rolled his chair away from the desk to stretch out. When he started to lean back, a pain in his abdomen stopped him and doubled him up. He breathed rapidly through his mouth for quite a few breaths, which seemed to help a little, and then he tried imagining himself somewhere out of the office, floating in a big swimming pool full of water. Warm, blue, soothing water. Floating limp, without having to make any effort at all. After several minutes, the pain went away.

1011001

AT TEN MINUTES of ten I was back at the nurses' station in the U-Hosp ICU. I was running on coffee and concern for Sheryl. There was a head nurse on duty I had not met before. In fact, the whole staff was new, but I wasn't surprised. It was Friday night, after all.

I said to the head nurse, "I'm Sheryl Birch's sister. My mother was in earlier and she said there was some problem."

"No, not really. Her crit is down, but just a little. It's nothing to worry about."

There had been so many fluctuations of so many different tests over the past few days that I was primed to think this was just another one. And I was too tired to worry about it right now. I wanted to see whether Sheryl was still communicating.

The moment I went into Sheryl's treatment bay, I took hold of her hand. "Sheryl, honey. Hi."

Sheryl squeezed back. Suddenly I was much less weary.

One of the nurses had come in behind me, apparently to adjust the heart monitor. She was older than the other nurses I was used to, with a kind, pink face. She said, "These things come loose sometimes," sticking a sensor to Sheryl's chest. She pointed at the monitor. "Don't be alarmed if it looks like she doesn't have a heartbeat."

"Don't be alarmed?"

"I'll come right in." The woman looked at the place where one of the leads was attached to Sheryl. "I wonder if it came loose because she moved a little."

"That would be good, wouldn't it?"

"Certainly."

"She just squeezed my hand," I said.

"Yes, I heard she was reacting."

As they spoke, Sheryl's mouth moved. The oily substance was still in her eyes, and her eyes had often been partly open, without any sign that she knew what she was looking at. But now Sheryl saw me, however cloudily, because she looked right at me and said distinctly, "Hospital."

"Oh, my God!" I said to the nurse. "Listen! She can talk."

The nurse moved closer. "I heard her."

"Sheryl, talk to me. Yes, you're in a hospital."

For a half minute there was no response. I said, "You're going to be fine. The girls were here earlier today. Talk to me."

Again, there was no response for half a minute, and then Sheryl said, "Hospital program." She looked frightened. Well, who wouldn't be?

"What do you mean? Yes, they have a sort of recovery program planned. Is that what you mean?"

There was no answer.

"It's so wonderful that you're awake, honey. I can't wait to tell the girls. And Mom and Dad. They'll be so happy."

Still no answer.

"I think she's gone back to sleep," the nurse said.

1011010

HOWIE BORKE SAW the notation "spoke two or three words clearly" appear on Sheryl's chart. He knew what that meant for him. There wasn't really any escaping it any longer: Sheryl was recovering.

In the last few hours, Howie had managed to split some part of his mind off from the rest. He was working with the imp part of his personality, the devilish teenager playing pranks in a computer system that wasn't really real. Now he thought he would just play around in the system. He would precipitate the U-Hosp staff into giving Sheryl a blood transfusion. He had lowered her crit a bit on the last lab result and now was going to lower it quite a bit. They would assume she was bleeding internally.

Patients were not automatically blood typed the moment they entered a hospital. Howie had already asked Sweigert about that. Typing and cross-matching were too expensive to use on every single case, when most patients would never need blood. The exceptions were people bound for certain types of surgery, women about to give birth, and, obviously, anybody bleeding copiously.

Sheryl had never shown any signs of bleeding; even the accident itself had scarcely cut her. All her serious injuries were blunt force.

Howie double-checked with Sweigert, just in case. Was the blood type on the patient's bracelet?

"What? The bracelet is put on you the minute you come in the door. Before they even have a diagnosis, much less a blood type."

"Maybe it's put on later?"

"Not in hospitals around here it isn't. Once you get the patient's name, the ID number and the social security number on it, there isn't a whole lot of room left."

"Wouldn't it be a safety feature?"

"Wouldn't trust it anyway. You decide you need blood, you're gonna type and cross-match all over again anyhow. You'd never trust the bracelet. Suppose there was a typo?"

Which meant that when they decided to transfuse Sheryl, they'd type and cross-match. And they could make this decision at any moment. Which meant Howie had to sit on the line into U-Hosp records and lab, because if the data once got past him, it would be harder to change.

Wait. What was he thinking of? All he had to do was look into her records and see if they'd typed her. Five minutes later, he knew they had not. But he also knew it was just a matter of time.

Howie lurked.

When the lab report came in, Howie called up `botu-lism`, brought up the menu, and went to PATIENT REC-ORDS. In his mind, he left his office. He entered the basement of the giant U-Hosp complex, an invisible ghost but nevertheless there, really there—a shadow with substance. His shadow moved in cyberspace, hovered over the disks, then reached out a finger and scrubbed the charges off the ferromagnetic molecules that held Sheryl's last crit. Then the ghost finger wrote a lower figure. It moved on to the newly recorded blood type and screen results and wiped off the O positive notation. There was other data, something called Kell and Duffy, but he didn't understand them and didn't need to. He didn't want to get too complicated. He just changed the blood type.

Now, as far as anyone would know, Sheryl was A positive.

1011011

||||||||||||||||||||||||||||||||||||||||||||||||||||||||||||||||||||

DEPARTMENT OF THE TREASURY
UNITED STATES SECRET SERVICE
1800 G STREET NW
WASHINGTON DC
FROM: CMV
TO: STRICK
FORM: INTERNAL

<<IN ANY OPEN TRANSMISSION FOLLOW THE
ESTABLISHED CODES>>

JIM:
OVER TO YOU, PAL.
CMV
||||||||||||||||||||||||||||||||||||||||||||||||||||||||||||||||||||

1011100

AT FOUR A.M. there was another nurse I had not met before. The shift must have changed at eleven. I longed for Nurse Dodd. The woman said, "She's experiencing a little bleeding somewhere in the body. It's not severe."

"Why is it happening?"

"In patients like your sister there can be lots of causes."

"But like what?"

The woman intensified an open-eyed look of understanding. "It could be a result of the accident. She's been showing a little blood in the urine. Some bruising of the kidneys happens a lot in automobile accidents."

"I want to talk with Dr. Gegosian."

"He's not on duty right now," she said. "He'll be back in the morning."

"But this may be a problem tonight."

The nurse called the resident.

The resident was a thin young man, all legs and nose. He was about twenty-nine.

"Come in here with me, Ms. Figueroa." He led me to Sheryl's bed in the treatment bay.

"Now look at her. We watch for physical signs of serious, rapid bleeding. Signs like low blood pressure. Pallor. This isn't it. She's oozing someplace. If it was a lot of bleeding, her skin would be paler. Her nails would look blue. Here, look at her nails." He pushed on one, making it white, and then let it go and immediately it became pink again. "There'd be a lot of signs of trouble. What we're going to do is just take out an insurance policy, you might say. We'll start her on one unit of blood. Make sure the bleeding doesn't get ahead of us."

"Uh-huh."

"It's probably in the digestive system. We're doing some Hemoccults now. In the morning, if this hasn't solved it, we may run a GI series, see if we can pinpoint it. But she's showing every sign of getting better."

I took Sheryl's hand, but Sheryl did not squeeze mine. I said, "Hi, honey," but Sheryl didn't seem to want to talk. Her eyes were closed, too. She was asleep or had gone inside herself, wherever she went, to gather strength.

"Here it is," the resident said.

One of the nurses entered with a blood bag. Always skeptical, I watched as the nurse checked the blood type on the bag, the blood type on the monitor, the name on the bag, the name on the monitor, Sheryl's wrist bracelet for her name and social security number, and then for extra safety also asked, "This is Sheryl Birch?"

The resident and I both said, "Yes."

The nurse hung the bag on a stand. The needle for the transfusion was larger than the one for IV fluid; it was so large I winced, but Sheryl did not react. "This will take about an hour," the nurse said, studying Sheryl as the first of the blood flowed in.

My ten minutes were up. In fact, I'd been there twenty. Time to get some sleep. I ached all over and my head was buzzing. I couldn't think straight. I stopped by the nurses' station on the way out to say thanks as the nurse entered the new data.

When the nurse brought up the file, I saw the SJR Data-Systems logo on the command line. Exhausted and stupid, I thought, *Interesting*. Maybe Sheryl had worked on that very program, once upon a time.

1011101

IN THE NORTHERN suburbs, Howie Borke was still awake, too, though it was 2:15 A.M. Howie had stayed at his terminal, just in case somebody at U-Hosp decided to do another blood draw.

1011110

THE SIXTY-EIGHT-YEAR-OLD man across the room from Sheryl had fallen into a ditch being excavated for a sewer line three days earlier and he had been unconscious ever since. His injuries hadn't seemed very severe at first, and it puzzled the medical staff when he hadn't regained consciousness. Now he twitched, twitched again, then doubled up in his bed.

The man straightened, doubled up, straightened, doubled

up, faster and faster. Abruptly, warning lights went on over his bay and the cardiac arrest warning flashed at the nurses' station.

Two nurses, including one who had been watching Sheryl's transfusion, and an orderly hurried to his bed. One called for the defibrillator. A first-year resident turned from another patient and hurried over. A third nurse beeped the senior resident.

In Sheryl's treatment bay, the unit of blood was about one-quarter empty.

1011111

I HAD REACHED the parking lot, glad to be going home, my feet dragging. I felt like I was walking in molasses up to my knees. By an effort of will, I got my tired body into the car and aimed the car onto Clark Street heading north. I was so tired. I was just so tired, so utterly tired—

My mind went someplace out in the dark. I thought I was outside of the car, resting above it on a carpet of air. As I dreamed, the car continued forward; for half a block it continued in a perfectly straight line. Then it began to veer right. My head sank toward my chest, hit the wheel, and the horn sounded. My head snapped up; I was drenched in cold sweat. The car climbed the curb with a double bump and lurch that bounced me in my seat. The bumper narrowly missed a fire hydrant. I stamped on the brake. I stamped harder on the brake and stopped the car just before it ran into the woven wire fence around a playground.

Thank God there aren't any people on the sidewalk.

And then I thought—

SJR DATASYSTEMS! MY GOD!

The nurse had been posting data on an SJR program!

There *was* a way they could get to Sheryl in the hospital!

I spun the car around in a U-turn, pitching down over the curb. At the same time I was reaching for my car phone, dialing Max Black, praying he had call forwarding to his home, stepping hard on the accelerator at the same time.

Black answered.

"This is Suze Figueroa! U-Hosp is using an SJR program!"

"Oh, shit! I'll meet you there!"

I parked sloppily in the first place I could find. I bolted out of the car and rushed into the U-Hosp complex. I was saturated with disgust at myself, with horror—how could I have been so criminally stupid!

The elevator wasn't waiting for me. I raced up the stairs and tore along the hallway, along the yellow line that led to the ICU.

I ran into the ICU. I saw a knot of people around a bed, and a nurse fast approaching that bed with a tray on which were ampoules and syringes. First, I thought Sheryl was in trouble, but at almost the same instant I realized it wasn't Sheryl's bed. Briefly I felt sorry for whoever it was, but I had absolutely no energy left to think of anybody but Sheryl.

I went directly to Sheryl's side. The unit of blood was one-third empty. Sheryl *looked* all right, but her face was flushed. Could she be getting an infection? Or was this flush a sign of health?

I studied the blood bag. The blood was running into Sheryl's vein. I watched for a couple of seconds as blood dripped.

It all looked right. But my mind was still screaming *danger*.

Not all of the staff was in the older man's bay. Still tense and worried, I approached the nurse at the desk. This was a woman I had seen earlier but had never spoken with.

"I'm Sheryl Birch's sister," I said.

"Hi. My name is Ellen Sweeney."

"Listen, this is going to sound crazy, but I think Sheryl is in danger."

"She's doing perfectly well—"

"I mean danger from outside. Her accident, the automobile accident, was staged. It was an attack, and I'm afraid she could be attacked here."

"Ms.—?"

"Figueroa."

"Ms. Figueroa, this is *not* a place somebody could be attacked. You can't get in here without being related to one of the patients, and we have a badge system. You stop at the desk downstairs and tell them who you're going to see and get a badge."

"Look at me! I don't have a badge! I came up the stairs three minutes ago and nobody stopped me."

"Oh. That doesn't often happen."

"It only needs to happen once. Ms. Sweeney, I'm not a nut!" I pulled my CPD ID. "I'm a police officer and I'm telling you she's in danger!"

An orderly looked over at us. Sweeney said, "Ms. Figueroa, you don't—"

"You've got to help me! They run the computer system here! The people who are after her. All they have to do is walk in and say they're fixing something! They can say they're from SJR DataSystems and they're here to upgrade!"

"Are you telling me you think the computer system is trying to kill your sister?"

"Not the *system!* Some people who work for SJR."

"You think the data management people are out to kill your sister?"

"Yes! Yes, dammit!"

The orderly put down a tray of folded cloths and took hold of my arm. I pulled away. "Touch me once more and it's battery," I snarled. I ran to Sheryl's bed.

Sweeney called, "Dr. Pogue! Dr. Pogue!"

The resident had just left the bay where the older man lay, still surrounded by staff. "What is it?"

I said, "Maybe they fed her ground glass! Maybe that's why she's bleeding internally!"

"Ms. Figueroa! You're upsetting our other patients!"

"They could have injected an anticlotting agent of some kind." I was trying to get a grip on my panic.

Dr. Pogue said, "No, they couldn't. And her clotting time is checked every four hours!"

"Four hours is a long time!"

"Ms. Figueroa, if you don't quiet down, I'm going to call security."

"Don't you understand? They could send a technician who says he's looking at the computer stuff, that heart monitor maybe, and he could inject poison in her IV line—" I knew I sounded insane, but the circumstances were crazy.

"There has been *nobody* here looking at any of the data management programs. Or the monitors."

"How would you know? You're not here all the time!"

"Keep your voice down!" The nurse swung away and hurried to the central station.

I was desperate. I said to Dr. Pogue, "Look, I don't know *how* they would attack her. Maybe they have already—look at this mysterious bleeding!"

"It's not that mysterious—"

"We've got to post a guard by her bed!"

"Please, Ms. Figueroa," the resident said. "Ms. Sweeney is calling security, and that won't make your sister better any faster."

"Wait! Mysterious bleeding. How do we know she's bleeding?"

"The crit is low."

"How do you test the crit?"

"We draw blood."

"Do you analyze it?"

"Here on the floor? Of course not. The lab analyzes it."

"And the lab tech calls you?"

"Of course not. It comes up on her chart."

"On the terminal?"

"Of course."

I turned to Sheryl. The needle was in her arm, the blood running. At the desk, I heard a male voice say, "Where's the trouble?" Security had arrived.

I grabbed her arm and scraped at the tape holding the needle in place.

"What are you *doing?*" Pogue shrieked. He tried to pull my hand away.

I scrabbled at the edge of the tape, shouldering Pogue away. The guard was coming. The tape stuck. I got a corner of it, and just tore. It came away with the needle attached, and blood dribbled out. The guard tackled me and we both went down.

The other security guard took hold of my elbow hard enough to hurt. Pogue screamed, "You're a lunatic!" The head nurse bent to check Sheryl. For a moment, there was silence.

Then Sweeney said, "Oh, shit!"

The two guards pulled me to my feet.

Nurse Sweeney quickly wrapped a blood pressure cuff around Sheryl's arm. The younger nurse pulled open Sheryl's hospital gown and put a stethoscope to her chest.

I touched Sheryl's hand. It was clammy and trembling. Her eyes were sunken. Her breathing was shallow. I moaned at the sight of her.

The resident drew venous blood.

Pogue said, "Get this centrifuged, stat! Get twenty-five milligrams of mannitol and I want five percent D/W right now!"

"Ninety over seventy-two," Sweeney said.

Pogue said, "She's in shock."

Sweeney turned to me. Her mouth was slack with fear. She said, "How did you know?"

III

''Computers don't make mistakes. But they can multiply
human error infinitely.''

—Dean Utley,
First VR Colloquy,
New School for Social
Research, New York, 1992

1100000

THE VEEP SAID to Utley, "I wanta know exactly what you're going to do."

"Why?" Utley checked that the phone call from Washington was being properly recorded. Someday the world would want a record of these pivotal times.

"Well, I sure don't want to get sick."

Utley said, "Are you nuts? You *have* to get sick!"

"Hey, I don't like this. What if I died?"

"The stuff isn't fatal. We can't be talking this way."

"Why? Isn't your end safe?"

"*My* end is safe. It's your end I can't control." Actually, he could to a certain extent. There was no evidence of a current drop at the veep's end. But it didn't hurt to keep the idiot a bit off stride.

"Well, my end is safe. Don't change the subject. How do you think I'm going to feel, eating all those dishes and not knowing which one might be full of some—"

"Great! Great is how you're going to feel. Because it's your big chance! You'll never have another. The prez is a very healthy man."

"Yeah. Shit!"

"Get this straight. I am the only route to the presidency you're ever likely to have. And you belong to me. Let's not forget how you got elected senator."

Two seconds of silence.

Utley said, "I am not going to tell you which food it is,

because I am not sure how good an actor you are. This is not negotiable. And so you had better eat some of everything. You'd better eat quite a bit of everything, as a matter of fact."

"Oh, God!"

"To take it a step farther, if you know what's good for you, you'd better try to be one of the sickest of all. What I'm saying here is even if you don't feel so very sick, you'd better moan and groan and carry on something terrible. You got me?"

"Yeah. Yeah. Okay. I know you're right."

Ah, the beginning of wisdom, Utley thought.

1100001

I STAGGERED INTO the cafeteria at U-Hosp before dawn Saturday. I needed caffeine. And sugar. I got coffee and a doughnut. If I had been beaten with sticks for six hours, I couldn't have ached more. Somewhere in this giant hall, Max Black should be waiting.

And he was.

I clattered my plate and mug down next to him.

"She's stable," I said, and burst into tears.

"Oh, goddamn it, stop that crying!" He wiped my eyes with a paper napkin.

"All right, all right. I'm trying not to."

"I don't *like* emotion," he said.

I started to laugh, the way you do when you're exhausted and really feel terrible, but jangled and giddy. "I'm sure you have excellent reasons." Several female employees were watching us. He looked so handsome, and they didn't know what a misanthropic crab he was.

"So explain," he said.

"People die from getting the wrong blood. I mean, they are

much more likely to die than live. It was so close and she's still so sick. She would have died if I hadn't—if I just hadn't happened to—"

"Don't get wobbly."

"Right. But suppose they attack her again?"

"They won't."

"Why won't they?"

"They won't because of me. I've been busy in the basement. There are two files now. One for the staff here to read. Right chart, patient's full history, all that stuff. The other file is for SJR to modem into. It says she died last night."

"Oh." I thought a minute. "Excellent!"

We both drank coffee. After thinking a little longer, I said, "But suppose SJR finds out we don't have a funeral planned? Suppose they go to the kids' schools and find out they're in school instead of home mourning?"

"Hey, I didn't say this would last forever. Keep the kids home. Make tentative funeral arrangements."

"But very soon SJR will—"

"My guess is this'll buy you two days, three days at an optimistic estimate."

"We need help."

"Sure we do. We're going to the superintendent." He looked at his watch. "He should be in his office about three coffees from now."

"He'll never believe me."

"Probably not. *Me* he'll believe."

1100010

ZACH, GLEN, AND Howie arrived at Utley's office for a meeting. They had a little over eleven hours before the arrival of the president in Chicago.

Utley said, "You clean up the U-Hosp file on Sheryl?"

"Oh, sure."

"Good."

"Well, she was a nice lady," Howie said. "I'm sorry she's dead."

Utley observed Howie closely. There was something slightly off key about his reactions, his body language. Still, as long as Howie was clear on what he had to do—and he *had* taken care of Sheryl, after all—it didn't much matter if he had a little *crise* of conscience. Howie knew which side his bread was buttered on.

Utley shrugged mentally and turned to the other two men. "Glen, do you have everything in place?"

"The Secret Service took my fingerprints last night." He smiled happily.

"Good."

"And I've got the salmonella. It's going in the sour cream dressing."

"Ah. Not very imaginative."

"That's the whole point. It'll look like the kind of food poisoning that's happened a thousand times before."

"A million," Zach said.

Howie said, "There are supposed to be over two million cases a year in the United States. There are two hundred salmonella serotypes. We've picked one of the most common."

"Good. So the whole party gets sick," Utley said. He focused on Howie. "And that's where you come in."

"Yes, I know."

"Okay. Now, hardly anybody knows it, but the prez is violently allergic to the penicillin family of antibiotics."

Zach said, "How did you ever find that out? I thought hackers couldn't get into Bethesda Naval Hospital anymore."

"Well, actually, you can invade their systems," Utley said, "but you can't penetrate all the way and sometimes they'll see you coming." He did not say that he and Howie had both tried. Howie was actually more skilled than Utley at worming his way into protected systems. Both of them had failed.

"So how do you know this stuff?" Zach asked.

"They seem to have thought that they'd protect his records at Bethesda and that'd be good enough. Well, actually they went back and covered his tracks when he was governor, too. But these geniuses never once thought to protect the records of the doctor he had in college. Or the hospital he was admitted to in Greensboro when he had a really nasty reaction when he was sixteen. His allergy to antibiotics seems to be a lifetime proposition."

Zach laughed. "And I imagine that hospital is really proud of having computerized all their back records."

"I imagine so."

1100011

SUPERINTENDENT OF POLICE Gus Gimball had spent a reasonably calm morning—calm for the kind of job he did, at any rate. Even the arrangements for the president were in place and solid. The Most Important Visitor was scheduled to land at O'Hare this evening.

Now this. He should have known things were going too well.

His future as superintendent was at stake, and that was the least of it. The future of the Chicago Police Department was at stake, too, and probably the city of Chicago as well. How he handled this would affect the lives of many, many people for a long time to come.

He studied Max Black, Suze Figueroa, and Jesus Delgado. Black had methodically laid out the problem. Gimball sat with his hands locked in front of him, his elbows on the table.

They had put the cap on suspicions that had been creeping up on him, now that he realized it, for at least two years, since Charlie Withers' odd insistence that SJR DataSystems be hired to computerize Internal Auditing.

"All right, Max" he said. "So—they're inside the hospital. They're inside the Chicago Police Department. They're inside a lot of places we don't know about. But what do they want?"

"My sense is that SJR DataSystems is going for a lot more than a few thousand dollars and the ability to sabotage the CPD and other places through their data processing. But I don't know what they're actually reaching for."

"Could we locate the trap planted in our system?"

"I'm not sure. Even if we found one, would we be certain it's the only one?"

Jesus finally spoke. "They're certainly inside Records as well as Operations and Auditing or they couldn't—or they couldn't have burned my house. Cops don't have their names in the phone book."

Figueroa said, "Sheryl told me the potential power of SJR was huge. I think we have to act aggressively and fast."

Gimball studied Officer Figueroa. She took his scrutiny calmly. *Solid stuff under that small female exterior*, he thought. *This lady has a lot of size on her.*

God only knew what horrors lay ahead. An utterly un-scrupulous gang inside the very brain of the Chicago Police Department! They could do almost anything to his city.

"I'm going to have my secretary call—"

He stopped in mid sentence. How could he have his secretary call when he didn't know who was a spy and who wasn't? Maybe have his ADS help out? An assistant deputy superintendent ought to be above suspicion. But so should a deputy superintendent, like Withers. Oh, shit.

And what if the phones were monitored?

Once in a great while in life, Gus Gimball thought, there is a moment of real importance, where the future rests on a fulcrum and it can be tipped one way or another. Not the kind of moment that you realize later to have been far more important than you thought at the time, but one you recognize at the instant that it's happening, and you know it will change the entire course of your life forever afterward. Like the moment his doctor told him he had Parkinson's disease. Except that times like that were so obvious. And you couldn't do much about them. The important ones were the turning points where you had to make a decision.

He had no doubt whatsoever that this was such a moment. He would remember it all his life, for better or worse.

And these three people shared it with him.

Gimball knew he ought to take his time and assess Delgado and Figueroa carefully. Jesus Delgado was formally on leave; officers were put on leave after a catastrophic family event, whether they liked it or not. He looked at Jesus Delgado and his heart ached. Delgado had come to him two days earlier, full of the thrill of the chase, satisfaction vivid in his face after finding the central clue to what had happened to Frieswyk.

The Jesus Delgado who sat before him now was a different man. The left rear of his head was bandaged and the left front was scabbed over from burns. The hair on the right side of his head was mostly gone, burned away, and his eyebrows and eyelashes were burned off, too. His left hand and forearm were bandaged.

But worse, there was no emotion whatsoever in his face. Gimball was a history buff and had once wanted to do graduate work in history, thinking of becoming a college professor. He had read enough pre-Colombian history and looked at enough pre-Colombian art to recognize Jesus Delgado's ancestry as pure Mayan. Delgado now looked like one of the Mayan stone statues that had stood for thousands of years in the jungles through rain and centuries of embracing vines and hot sun and hurricanes and were still unchanged. Some kind of tan, impervious rock. Jesus' face was just as impassive. All the vigor and cheer was gone.

Gimball had never met Susannah Figueroa before today, although they both worked in this building. But he had liked the gutsy way she faced him. He could see she was damaged by the attack on her sister.

As Delgado was damaged. Did it make sense to use two damaged people as foundations for the most important task force he had ever built?

There was no time to linger over a decision in this case. The potential catastrophe was too big for that.

Silence. Time for him to decide, Gimball thought. There came a moment when you simply had to go ahead. Figueroa and Delgado had been through hell. They were still going through hell. He found somewhat to his surprise that he liked them both. Liked and admired them. They were hurt, but they were *here*.

He realized that he had already decided to trust them.

What he was going to say made him feel very old—or they were very young. "I grew up before computers," he said. "This threat is hard for me to assess. I know we have a disaster hanging over our heads. The only question is how bad it's going to be. In other words, what damage can they do? How strong are they? How can we find out who is involved and who isn't? And how can we stop them?"

"We can't trust anybody but ourselves," Max said.

"Right. As of this moment, we are a team. You," Gimball pointed at Figueroa. "You," he pointed at Delgado, "you," he pointed at Max, "and me. The question is going to be whether we can risk enrolling anybody else. Delgado, who do you trust completely?"

"My partner, but he's sick." Jesus thought it over for a few seconds. "Sonnenfeldt. But—he's a good man, no doubt about it, but he has four children, medical bills for the prostate surgery, and big family expenses. What if somebody offered him ten thousand dollars? No, he wouldn't take it. A hundred thousand dollars?"

Gus Gimball had just been going through the same sort of thoughts himself. People he had been with at the academy way back? Maybe. But most of them were still patrol officers, or detectives, after thirty years on the job. For all he knew, they resented him for reaching the topcop job, while they never went any higher. Deputy Superintendent Heidema? Not a chance! He would be Gimball's first choice for a coconspirator with Withers. Deputy Superintendent Kluger? Yes, he'd trust him more than any other. But did he trust him *totally*? That was different. He didn't personally know him that well.

To have spent thirty years in the department and yet not be sure of even one man hit him hard.

And Delgado feels this, too.

Gimball was briefly relieved that Delgado was having the same problem. It made him feel less alone and less foolish. Then he thought, *What are you thinking, you old fool? Fifty-seven years old and thinking like a kid.* It was sad for both of them that hundred percent trust was so scarce.

"Figueroa, what about you?" he asked.

She answered without any hesitation. "My partner, Norm Bennis."

"You trust him completely?"

"He'd risk his life for me. I'd do the same."

"I'm glad."

"There's an officer in my district named Stanley Mileski. I'd trust him almost as much. But Bennis is gold all the way through. You couldn't pay him to betray me, and I feel the same way about him."

"Then you're blessed," Gimball said. He thought a minute. They had to start someplace. "If you trust him, we need him in on this."

"You're just taking my word for Bennis, boss?"

I have to, for now. "Yes." He knew at once she was pleased.

"Okay," Gimball said, clapping his hands. "How many people in the department know about this? Or any part of it?"

Jesus said, "The detectives checking Frieswyk's background for me have never heard about this thing. Joosten in Wyczinski's office has some idea about it, and Wyczinski, Putnam, DiMaggio, and Rendell more so. I told the entire story of the cars to the whole command line that I went up, I'm afraid."

"Well, you took it through channels. We tell you to do that. Don't blame yourself. Figueroa?"

"Norm Bennis, my partner. Only him."

"You were smart," Jesus said, regretfully.

"All right. No word goes beyond us unless absolutely necessary. We're going to treat *everybody* as possible security risks."

"Right," Jesus said.

Figueroa nodded.

"Figueroa, you will recruit Officer Bennis. I'll see that you and Bennis are put on some sort of unspecified special assignment."

"Yes, boss."

Max Black said, "You mean now?"

"Yes."

"How?"

"What do you mean, how?"

"How can you do it without using the computer? Or the phone? Or any people who might report to—to SJR?"

"Goddamn it! I'll give them a note. Then at least it's not on the phone. Figueroa, you give it to your sergeant. It'll just say that Bennis and you are going to other duties."

"But it'll get entered into the system, won't it?"

Gimball sighed and nodded. "Sure it will. But we have to make some move sometime. You and Bennis can't give full time to this and still do patrol duty. And it won't look any more normal if the two of you just vanish without a word. With any luck, this will look harmless, for a day or two maybe."

Black said, "A day or two is as long as we can keep the fact quiet that we're onto U-Hosp."

Gimball noticed Black seemed to be trembling. "Are you worried, Black? You've got reason to be."

"Hell, no, boss." He rubbed his hands together. "This is the first challenge big enough to get me out of the basement!"

"Don't sound so enthusiastic, Black. There's serious danger here."

"Yeah. Let's go!"

Gimball said, "This is my home phone number. You three had better memorize it. Nobody'll give it to you if you lose it. And this second number is my private office line here. But you'd better not trust it to be secure."

1100100

HOWIE BORKE, CARRYING a Newton notepad, knocked on Utley's door and walked in. He said, "The sister, Figueroa, has been taken off regular duties."

"Maybe it's some sort of compassionate leave," Utley said.

"Maybe."

Utley had been testing Howie. He didn't think it was compassionate leave. He thought it would say so if it were. "Wouldn't it say 'five days' furlough,' Howie, or something like that?"

Howie's face showed disappointment. "Maybe. I don't know for sure."

"It's easy enough to find out. Run a search on spouse and near relatives' deaths and then see how the department typically handles leaves. How they word the entry."

"Will do."

There was more in Howie's face, too. Something he was hiding. "What else?"

"They've taken her partner off regular duties, too."

"Oho!" Utley considered this not more than two seconds. "What's the sister's full name?"

"Susannah Maria Figueroa."

"What's the partner's name?"

"Norman Bennis."

"Get all their charge card numbers. Both of them. Phone bills. Tax bills. Marketing histories. Banks. Full histories on purchases, favorite restaurants, hobbies—everything. Then put out a flag. I want to know when and where they use their charge cards."

"Will do."

"And when you get any charge card use, bring it to me. Priority."

1100101

"I DON'T GET the squad car thing," Norm Bennis said. His voice bordered on the hostile. I could tell he didn't like Max Black. Small wonder. Black was difficult to take. We were in Black's basement office—cave was more like it—and he had his hot pot boiling again. He reached to a shelf and brought out four hideous mugs: one tall brown mug, one purple cow, one in the shape of a half-coconut, one a yellow smiley-face.

"Do any of you people take sugar?" he said. "If you do, I don't have any. The motor pool scam was a variation of the old salami slice."

"Salami slice," Bennis said. "Sure."

"A salami slice is a well-known computer scam. Say an employee has access to a company's records. Could be a bank, could be an ordinary company making widgets. The company has certain expenses. This employee writes a dummy account for himself right into the company database. Then he slices off a few pennies—literally pennies—from a lot of the other accounts and adds them onto his dummy account."

I said, "But don't people complain? The suppliers or whatever will know what they should have been paid."

"Yeah, but we're talking maybe two, three pennies. *Pennies.* They may think they made a tiny error. Anyhow, it doesn't pay them to complain. You're a million-dollar company, are you gonna get excited over seven cents? But he does it over thousands and thousands of accounts, and all the little slices add up to one big salami. Hence the name. Your guys, SJR et al., sliced off a couple of cars every so often in a way that would be hard to notice. Although—"

"Although what?" Bennis said.

"It's not totally slick compared with what they could have done. I wonder if maybe they wanted it traceable enough so as to keep your Deputy Superintendent Withers under their thumb. A form of implied blackmail."

"Yeah," Bennis said, "I can see they might do that."

The water was boiling. Black plopped tea bags in the cups and mugs and poured water over them. "Here. Upload some tea," he said.

I tasted it. "Whoa! What is this stuff?"

Bennis said, "Yeah, Max. You may be God's gift to computers, but you're not the world's greatest cook."

" 'Peace.' It's called 'Peace.' It contains calming herbs."

Jesus, who had hardly spoken a word, said, "I kind of like it."

Black said, "These things SJR has done only appear isolated. What I'm trying to tell you is that they must fit into some pattern. And that pattern has to be very big and very ominous. There's never been a computer company that really used all the power it has. All the infiltration devices they could, for instance."

Bennis said, "Because they're afraid of being caught?"

"No. Not really. A lot of this cyberspace espionage is effectively undetectable. It's just charges on ferromagnetic material. Pull the plug or erase it and it ceases to exist. Like you and I realize now, they could get away with murder. No, it's something else. Computer companies are sharks; don't get me wrong, but they're mostly all the same kind of shark and they mostly play by the same rules. What's operating most of the time is self-restraint. It's voluntary, God bless it. There's some *possible* behavior that they just don't seem to think is gentlemanly, by their rules."

I said, "And?"

"And from what you tell me, SJR DataSystems doesn't follow *any* rules."

"So what does that make SJR DataSystems?"

"A rogue company. *A billion-dollar Fortune 500 rogue company, totally out of control.*"

1100110

BLACK SAID, "ACTUALLY, now that I think about it, if I was betting on a company going rogue, SJR DataSystems would've been one of my top choices."

Bennis said, "Why?"

"As I told Figueroa, it's had a reputation for coming up with new programs that were surprisingly timely. Or surprisingly close to what some other company was just coming out with. There was a whiff of the crook about them."

"Why didn't the other companies do something about it?"

"Well, I'll tell you. See, there would have been a certain element of pot calling the kettle black. This has not been an industry with a spotlessly pure reputation."

Bennis, who was a cynic at most times, said, "That'll certainly distinguish them from every other industry."

"There are differences," Black said. "For one thing, in this industry you can infiltrate competitors without ever leaving your desk. For another, you draw your employee pool from a weird mix. Perfectly straight-arrow math and computer whizzes on one hand, and on the other hand the ex-hackers and former phone phreaks. Utley, the head of SJR, has a reputation for hiring a lot of borderline sociopaths."

I said, "Why?"

"Well, we know now, don't we?"

Bennis said, "Oh, Lord."

"You think Utley's been planning this for years?"

"He must have been. Besides being brilliant, the guys he picked had no consciences."

Abruptly, Black changed posture. He folded his arms, straightened up, and looked like a professor. He said, "Okay. Before we go any farther, what are you all doing to protect your families?"

Jesus immediately said, "My two daughters have left the country. I sent them to Mexico with my parents yesterday."

Jesus hadn't mentioned anything about this to me.

Black said, "That's good. Whose credit card bought the tickets?"

"Nobody's. I was scared shitless. I covered every possibility. I hope. I paid cash through a travel agent and booked under a fictitious name."

"Very good!"

"They're in remote country with people who aren't relatives. Not close relatives, anyway. Different name. It's a place where intruders would be *real* obvious."

"Okay. What about you, Figueroa? What about your son?"

I was horrified. "Nothing. Nothing at all. I thought he was safe. God, I was criminally stupid when I let Sheryl go ahead with her investigation. Now I've been stupid again."

"You weren't ready to see how serious it was."

"I know what I'll do. I'll ask one of our friends who's a cop, Stanley Mileski, and his wife to stay at the house. I'll ask them to sleep in shifts so one of them's awake all night. Nobody's going to be able to burn the house down, or invade, or whatever, with them there."

"Good."

"Bonnie and Stanley can sleep in my room. I'll stay away. If I'm not there, the kids'll be safer. My brother-in-law wouldn't believe there's a problem, even though he's willing to keep his mouth shut about Sheryl being alive. I can't take JJ away and leave Kath and Maria in danger."

"Make sure the Mileskis know how serious it is," Black said. "Bennis? What about you?"

"Here in town there's only my mother. And she's not really here, either; she's visiting my brother. In Juneau. He's in the Air Force and he's stationed in Alaska."

I said, "Oh. What about Deirdre?"

"Deirdre? Deirdre's history. Didn't I tell you?"

"I must've missed it."

Max said, "Don't trust your bank, your credit card company, your drugstore, even a large corporation. SJR could have installed a Trojan horse anyplace they've ever put in a system. The company operator wouldn't even know what it was for. SJR could have them all over the country. They must have installed thousands and thousands of systems over the last few years. It's a killer app, hardware-wise."

Bennis said, "Jeez! They could make a fortune!"

Black said, "No, you just don't get it. You're thinking they can give themselves extra money at some bank or do some industrial espionage. That's nothing! Think! If a company had real control over data, they could alter statistics. They could influence the movements of major markets: oil, gold, pork bellies, international currency, arbitrage. We see the world not through our eyes and ears but through data. People don't look back at the original paper copies of anything anymore—sales slips, written reports, medical files. They're too cumbersome.

Imagine a company that *controls facts*. It would rule the world!"

Bennis was staring at Black and nodding.

Black said, "UNIX mainframes run the country. The government is held together by the Internet: telephone switching control, marine navigation, cable TV, Comsat, banks, satellites. All transfers of funds. All human records!"

"Hey! Fine!" Bennis said. "But what are we gonna *do* about it?"

"Yes, you're right. Topic drift," Black said.

"Let's start brainstorming our next move, dammit!"

I said, "We have to prove what SJR is doing, stop them, and punish them. And we have to avoid getting killed while we're doing it."

Black said, "Yes."

"All right. Then we need this. One, we need to know a lot more about SJR than we do now. Two, out of that knowledge, we've got to discover some weaknesses. Three, also out of that knowledge, we have to figure out what their larger game plan is. Four, we have to get evidence that they killed Elena and tried to kill Sheryl."

Black said, "That's right. We need to get the passwords to prove what they're doing. And that sounds hard enough. But now I'm gonna tell you the facts of life that make it harder."

Bennis said, "Oh?"

"You have to assume they have cybernetic entry into any company, any governmental office, whether federal, state, or local—"

"Hey! Not any!" Bennis said. "Just one where their own hardware or software is in place."

"Which you won't know. They could have installed services for anybody. They could have supplied parts to anybody. Software for anybody. Plus, if they have access to a telephone line to another company that has a line in or is on a net with the first company, they'll handspring themselves from one to the other. From a bank to a county tax office to the building code inspector's files. They can be anywhere and you *will not know*."

"All right, all right." Bennis thought a minute and added in a gloomier tone, "My God."

"You want to keep them from knowing what you're doing? Your squad car's license plate and outside number is known to them by now. Count on it. So is your personal car. You can't rent a car without them knowing, because rental agencies don't take cash. And anywhere you use your credit card, a record of that will go into a processing company. You can't take money out of your bank without them knowing about it. You can't go to an ATM. Without cash, how will you eat? You want to go to a favorite restaurant where they know you and they'll run a tab? Great. But if you've ever charged a meal there in the past, ever, SJR will know that it's one of your hangouts. You can't use your car phone. You can't use your home phone. You can't order from mail order catalogs without them knowing what you bought."

"So let me understand this," I said. "Basically, we're supposed to do what we're supposed to do, without any of it getting into any data management system anyplace."

Black said, "Right. Unless you want it to, to deceive them."

"Well, that shouldn't be so difficult."

Bennis and Jesus Delgado groaned.

Black said, "You still don't get it, Figueroa. They're *everywhere*. You certainly can't rely on the cops. The CPD records system aside, we know they have a high-level spy at the CPD. He can't be the only paid-off cop. You won't know who your enemies are. When you drive, eventually you'll need gas. You must have driven a car here. They'll find out where you are if you charge gasoline—"

I winced.

"You charged gas?"

"Yeah. Right next door."

"So they know you're at the CPD."

"Yes."

"Where's your car parked?"

"Uh—"

"Where?"

"Right outside."

"See?"

Bennis said angrily, "Hey, Max! How was she gonna know?"

"Don't get hot and bothered. I'm trying to show her how exposed you are."

"Well, what *can* I do?" I said.

"You can buy with cash. As long as your cash lasts. And you can talk to people face-to-face. People you trust. Only people you trust."

"Which isn't many," Bennis said.

I asked, "Want me to move the car?"

"No need," Black said. "First, we've got to get organized. We don't have much time. We've got to appoint one of us to be group leader."

Bennis said, "I suppose you mean yourself." Bennis knew we needed this guy, but he didn't like him.

"Not at all."

"Who, then?"

"Figueroa."

"Really?" Bennis probably thought Black didn't like me, either; he challenged me so much. He said, "Why?"

"Because she's the youngest and the least experienced."

I said. "You're kidding."

"Not at all. I'm dead serious. That's why the computer companies have been so successful—Apple, Microsoft—they were all started by kids. No sense of history. No idea of what couldn't be done, so they did it. All their ideas are new. Mostly RAM, not very much ROM. I say we go with Figueroa. Okay?"

Bennis nodded. "Yeah, sure." He glanced at Jesus, who hadn't spoken.

Jesus nodded, too.

"Got any ideas?" Black asked me.

I said, "Yeah. Yeah, I do. We invade SJR DataSystems."

1100111

"WITH ALL THE years she'd been there, you know, Mr. Utley," I said into the phone. "Yes, we thought some of the employees there who knew her, but not quite well enough to come to the funeral in the morning—yes. A way of saying good-bye."

Norm Bennis, Jesus Delgado, and Max Black were all crowded into the phone carrel with me, earning glances from the other people in the restaurant. We were in the service oasis on the Chicago Skyway—a location that Black had said might give Utley something to think about.

"Yes, maybe just a short service in the company dining room. She always said your dining room for the employees at SJR was so especially lovely, with such a beautiful view." I raised my eyebrows at Bennis, who was squeezed in closest to me.

"Something simple. At the end of the day? Four-thirty or five?"

I nodded my head to tell the others he was agreeing. "No, five-thirty would be fine. Yes, a few of her friends from here, from my place of work, who can't make the actual funeral, and her coworkers from there. Half an hour, an hour at most."

I listened some more. His voice, smooth and low-pitched, made me feel sick, and I had to keep my voice bland like his, keep the disgust out of it. "Oh, no, nothing formal," I said. "Don't go to a lot of trouble."

More listening.

"Wonderful. Monday at five-thirty. Thank you, Mr. Utley. And thanks for your sympathy."

I hung up the phone and said, "You should die, Mr. Utley."

1101000

I SAID, "HE'S hooked. He's curious, I think."

Bennis said, "Maybe curious. But maybe he wants you there so he can gloat over you in person."

We'd found a Greek restaurant on Halsted which was cheap enough nobody needed to use a credit card. Norm, Max, Jesus, and I had a small table in a dark corner.

"He ought to be curious," Black said, "if he suspects you're on to him."

"We don't know what he knows about me."

Jesus was silent. I realized that Jesus was silent most of the time. I felt like saying to him, *Revenge. You'll get your revenge. I promise.*

"Listen," Black said. "You gotta get those passwords. But we can't rely on this solving all our problems. You can't depend on getting beyond the dining room at SJR. Even if you do get farther, you could find that they'd destroyed everything."

I said, "I know."

"We've gotta move in from more than one direction."

I said, "If we could prove Utley killed Frieswyk, we'd be home free. Jesus, any leads from the Frieswyk autopsy?"

I could see Delgado make the effort to pull his mind back from his grief. He said, "Three directions we might go, out of a lot of possibilities. We had paint flecks and small concrete grains from the skin, but they didn't tell us much. I had some estimates of where he might have gone into the water, based on lake currents. Assuming he was in the water all five weeks, he may have gone in as far away as the coast of Michigan."

"But they can't pinpoint it?"

"No. Personally, I figure the middle of the lower end of Lake Michigan. They'd have dumped him out of sight of land. Which still leaves an area about thirty by forty miles—"

"Twelve hundred square miles," Max said.

"Exactly. Trackless and no point looking, I think. So. First, we have to find that boat. Second, there were pollen grains in the lungs. I can pick up some microphotos of it. There's a pollen expert, a forensic palynologist, Professor Grobart, at the University of Illinois in Champaign. It doesn't seem like much, though. Pollen."

"It could be," I said. "It limits it. Frieswyk died in February. Where would he breathe pollen?"

"Well, yeah. All right. That's a lead. Third is the rope. I have a guy in the department who's gonna tell me whether it's some unusual kind of rope. And whether the ends were cut or just worn though. Although I wonder what difference that would make—I mean, say it wore through on a block of cement under Lake Michigan. Then what?"

"You never know," I said firmly. "It could lead to something." I was troubled that he sounded defeated. It wasn't the kind of attitude we needed right now. Delgado in this mental state could be a liability.

He realized I was uneasy. "Yeah. Yeah. It could tell us something. This isn't the real me, Figueroa. You never knew me before—back when I was normal. I used to be such a bulldog. Persistent. That was me. But ever since, ever since—"

"Jesus, I understand."

"But then I think, of all the creeps I've traced down, Utley is the one I most want to get. More than I've ever wanted to get anybody."

"And we'll get him, too."

A waiter brought wine. Seeing that the group was too focused on their thinking to order, I said, "Family style for four."

Black said, "I want to scope out SJR."

"How?"

"Databanks."

"Will they know you're in the databanks looking for them?"

"Doubt it. Things like Dun and Bradstreet. Public databanks. Lotta people search those kind of things. You know about the hacker who monitored the nuclear talks between the United States and Korea. There's always a way. Once I know the scene, and when you've got the passwords, I want to invade SJR itself."

"We already said—"

"No. No. A virtual invasion. Through the wires."

"Without tipping them off?"

"That's ultimately impossible, I think. At the very last stage they'll see me in there."

"Max, is your office equipment tied in to the CPD computers?"

"No. Nobody and no system touches my stuff. No way in. No viruses. My hard drives are separate. The programs are mine. My modem runs into a separate laptop. Nobody accesses my equipment!"

Bennis said, "All right, good. Don't bust a gut. Now, should Jesus fly to Champaign to see the pollen guy?"

I said, "Can't you phone, Jesus? Save time."

"I want to take the photos."

"Fax them."

"I wish I could, but they're microphotographs and scanning electron micrographs. I don't think I dare risk losing any detail. I guess I'd better fly."

I said, "I don't think airlines take cash."

"They must," Bennis said.

"Well, rental car places don't."

Black said, "Amtrak for sure takes cash and there's an early train to Champaign. On weekdays, anyhow."

Jesus said, "I'd better call them and find out if they've got one on Sunday."

"And call this Professor Grobart and set it up," I said. "Call from here. Use coins. Don't use a calling card number."

He came back, saying, "Amtrak leaves at 6:22 A.M. And they take cash. Information had Grobart's home number. He'll meet me at noon." He picked up his wine, tasted it, and said, "This is terrible. The stuff tastes like pine pitch."

"It's supposed to taste like pine pitch," Bennis said. "It's retsina."

"Oh, okay." Jesus drained half the glass.

Bennis said, "First, we gotta get some cash."

"If one of us gets just a few bucks at an ATM, it's not going to tell them anything," I said. "For the next day, we're going to keep low on cash, as if we're not planning anything or doing anything special except hiding from them. If all of us went and drew out a lot of money, it would tell them we were gonna mount some major show. Then, we'll spring a deception on them. Jesus, you pick up no more than you need for Amtrak tickets and taxis in Champaign."

"Remember," Black said, "that whenever you get cash at a machine, it'll not only tell them how much money you got, it'll tell them where you are. They'll know the location of the ATM. So go to a place that doesn't matter."

I said, "Right. And you, Black, will investigate SJR for—for what?"

"For weaknesses."

"And you, Jesus—you'll be on the first Amtrak to Champaign/Urbana."

"Will do."

"And Bennis and I will find out about the cord, follow it to the boat, I hope, and—"

"And plan the invasion of SJR. The physical one," Bennis added, giving Black a glance. He said pointedly, "Riskier than going in through the phone lines, Black."

Black didn't disagree.

"Right," I said. "Get the cash. At the crack of dawn, we hit the ground running."

1101001

Twilight Saturday saw Air Force One set down at O'Hare. A fold-down stair with a red carpet came out from the aircraft like a tongue. Two Secret Service agents walked down the stair. The president and his wife stood at the top of the stair and waved. The president was thinking to himself, *Anybody else gets an umbilical from the plane into the terminal. Me they have to make walk down the stairs. Photo ops!*

And of course his advisers were absolutely right. On the ground were the CBS, ABC, and NBC affiliates, Channel Nine, the *Trib*, the *Sun-Times*, reporters from Springfield, Rockford, Peoria, Waukegan, WMAQ, and six or eight other radio stations, CNN, several small Chicago news magazines and papers, all of the visual media accompanied by their photographers. Also the mayor, Superintendent of Police Gus Gimball, and a gaggle of aldermen.

A second aircraft landed. From the second plane emerged the vice president and his wife and two Illinois delegates to congress.

The prez waved to the photographers, took half a dozen questions from reporters—sound bites which would have time to make the major local news broadcasts at ten P.M. He climbed into a limousine and once out of the public eye held his wife's hand.

The route they took was into the city on the Kennedy, then down Lake Shore Drive. Flags flew from their bumpers. An escort of twelve motorcycle police rode two-by-two ahead. Another six brought up the rear.

Four Secret Service cars were spaced at intervals in the line. Secret Service personnel rode in the president's limo, the vice president's limo, and with the VIPs. Uniformed Chicago police were on intersection control duty all along the way. The windows and doors of the limos were bulletproof. Two days earlier all manhole covers along the motorcade route had been locked down to prevent terrorists from planting bombs in the president's way. Secret Service personnel, in constant radio contact with the motorcade, were on the rooftops of every building within rifle distance of the route.

Superintendent Gimball noted this with satisfaction. No threat to the president had been overlooked.

1101010

HOWIE BORKE TURNED over in bed and tried facing away from the window, where a small amount of street light leaked through the curtains. Maybe it was the light that was keeping him from falling asleep.

He was thinking—Figueroa, presumably with Bennis, bought gas in south Chicago, then wound up on the Skyway. From the Skyway she called SJR. Why? Where were they going? The Skyway led into the Indiana Toll Road. It didn't necessarily mean anything, did it? Was she going to Indiana? Why would she be going to Indiana? Had some trace of Frieswyk—clothing, maybe—gotten attached to a pier there?

Thank God she was a computer moron. As near as he could tell, her partner Bennis was slightly more computer sophisticated. Tomorrow he'd access Bennis' college records and then he'd know for sure.

The was no suggestion they knew anything about cutworm, no suggestion at all.

Zach had one man tailing her, but he'd lost her. Another man cruised by her house once or twice, but her car was nowhere around, and they were fairly sure she wasn't staying there. A husband and wife were there. The pair had immediately been traced through their license plate. The husband, Mileski, was a cop. So Figueroa had guards in place. A good reason for SJR to stay away from the house.

Cybersurveillance was so much safer—

Problems went around and around in his brain. They could easily enough pick her up after the memorial service at SJR. There was really no harm she could do before then, anyway, was there? And by that time, the president would be on his way to the hospital. . . .

1101011

||||||||||||||||||||||||||||||||||||||||||||||||||||||||||||||||||||||
DEPARTMENT OF THE TREASURY
UNITED STATES SECRET SERVICE
1800 G STREET NW
WASHINGTON DC
FROM: CMV
TO: STRICK
FORM: INTERNAL

<<IN ANY OPEN TRANSMISSION FOLLOW THE
ESTABLISHED CODES>>

JIM:
GREAT.
THINK YOU SHOULD DOUBLE THE NUMBER OF DOOR
GUARDS IF YOU'RE JUST GOING TO EYEBALL.
CMV
||||||||||||||||||||||||||||||||||||||||||||||||||||||||||||||||||||||

1101100

"YOU'RE LUCKY YOU caught me. I'm outta here in an hour. Gotta catch a plane." Grobart, the forensic palynologist, was stuffing papers into a briefcase as he spoke. From Grobart's office window, Jesus Delgado could see the Beckman Center, the huge new computer sciences building of the University of Illinois, where the Cray supercomputers lived.

He said to Grobart, "Vacation?"

"North Sea. No vacation. Looking at core samples."

"Core samples of what?"

"Rock. Old rock. You find the right combination of pollen, it tells you that you have the right combination of plants to produce the right residues, and whammo! You got oil."

"Oh. I see."

Grobart said, "What happened to your head?"

"Burns."

"Oh. Too bad. Well, what exactly do you *want?*"

"I want to know what plant this pollen is from."

Jesus handed him three photographs and one of the slides with the pollen under a cover glass, which he'd picked up at the CPD very early this morning.

"Who did you say you were?" Grobart asked.

"Delgado. Chicago Police Department. We found this pollen inside a body." Jesus reached for his ID and star, but Grobart waved it away. He was too engrossed in looking at the photographs.

"Oh, isn't this one nice!"

"What?"

"This SEM. See, this other shot is from a light microscope. Not nearly the detail. This—" he waved the light-microscope picture as disgustedly as if it were pornography "—could be almost *any* kind of pollen."

"Uh—"

"But this scanning electron micrograph—yes, forty microns is about right—could be only one kind!"

"You know just like that?"

"Sometimes."

"Good. What kind is it?"

"African amaryllis."

"What? You mean our man had been to Africa!"

"Oh, God, no! Don't you know anything about—it's a pot plant, lad. A houseplant."

"Where would our man have run into them?"

"A home. An apartment. A greenhouse."

"Well, but that could be anyplace."

"Only a place with some African amaryllis plants."

"Well, yeah." Jesus found himself wondering whether this man could be so certain of the exact species. "Um—would this stuff—can you be sure? This pollen was found in the bronchii of a dead man—"

"No problem. Wouldn't be digested by bronchial secretions. The cellulose in pollen is one of the most durable things in nature. That's why we can reclaim it from Jurassic rocks and tell the oil companies what plants grew in a certain area."

"But that's in soil deposits. This body was found washing around in Lake Michigan. He'd been in the water five weeks!"

"A mere whiff of time to a pollen grain. I investigated a bunch of amphorae—" Grobart eyed Jesus again "—ceramic wine jugs to you, lad, in a drift on the floor of the Mediterranean Sea where a Cretan ship went down about 420 B.C. And from the pollen grains in the wine, I could tell the archaeologists the type of plants that grew in the same geographical area as the grapevines."

"Oh. That's amazing."

"You bet it is. You can recover pollen from old peat bogs that are wet year round and full of insects and bacteria and stuff, a soup of biological activity, and the pollen is still completely intact. In a very moist environment, like your dead body, the pollen can leak cytoplasm—that's the inside parts of the cell, lad—but the cellulose shell stays just as good as it ever was. Pollen is one of the most durable substances in the world. It's a long-chain carbon molecule, a hundred carbon atoms, and it's so damn durable there was talk about trying to synthesize it and use it as a coating in the space program."

"Did they?"

"Well, no actually." He laughed. "They found out it's impervious to everything but heat. It'd burn right up on a space shuttle."

1101101

BENNIS AND I got to the department headquarters at Eleventh and State at nine A.M. Sunday morning, hoping somebody would be in the lab who was familiar with the rope found around Frieswyk's ankle.

The lab on floor three was quiet. I asked at the desk, "Is Connie Maruldi in?"

"Nope."

"Well, did she finish the report on the Frieswyk rope?"

"Frieswyk? Who's that?"

"Frieswyk was a cop, dammit! He was fished out of the river—"

Bennis put his hand on my arm to tell me not to get hostile. The clerk said, "Oh, *that* Frieswyk!" and found us the file.

"Too early in the day to get crabby, Figueroa," Bennis said.

The good news was that Maruldi had written a very thorough report. The bad news was that the rope was a very common type.

"Three-eighths-inch nylon," Bennis read aloud.

"Used a lot on docks and boats, she says, but also for sports, lumberyards—"

"Wasn't cut, and didn't wear through against the edge of

the concrete blocks while Frieswyk was under water. Um, let's see—old rope—frayed in places—stretched before it broke—broke at a weak place."

"Stretched and broke?" I said.

Bennis said, "Aha! Confirmation."

"That he was dropped overboard from a boat?"

"Yup."

"Then we don't have time to wait. We'll call marinas."

We handed the folder back to the clerk and started down the stairs. "Do we call from the lobby phones or the First District phones?" I asked.

Bennis said, "Suppose they're tapped?"

"Impossible! Not in the CPD!" Then after a three-second pause I said, "Let's get a lot of quarters and go to some bar."

Crossing the lobby, we saw Bill Froman, from our district. His usually sleepy eyes popped open when he spotted us.

"Holy shit! What are you guys doing here?"

"Some work," I said.

Bennis said, "Why wouldn't we be here?"

"There's a want out on you."

"What!"

I said, *"What? WHAT?"*

"They want you brought in for questioning."

"Why?" I almost grabbed his throat.

"They want to question you about those drug dealers."

"What drug dealers?"

"They say some dealers claim you've been ripping them off. Extorting money from them in exchange for not arresting them."

"Bill," I said, "we haven't even seen any drug dealers lately. It's been all burglar alarms and stolen cars."

"Uh-huh, sure. I see. I think the two of you better come with me."

"Not right now, Bill," I said.

"Come on. Make it easy on yourself."

Bennis said, "Good-bye, Bill."

We walked rapidly toward the door.

Bill dithered a moment, no doubt scared to pull a gun inside the CPD lobby. By that time, we were around the corner and running.

"What an asshole!" Bennis said.

"He's a twerp and an asshole and a bootlicker and all that, but, my God, Bennis! They've invaded our personnel records!"

"We expected that."

"Well, it's different when it really happens! What are we going to do?"

"Get in the car!"

Fifteen minutes later, in the phone banks of the Chicago Public Library, I had explained the whole mess to the Mileskis, who were guarding my house. Stan said, "I know you're clean, Figueroa. Go get 'em."

Then I called another friend, who would sleep on the sofa at the house, for backup, when Stanley went to work. There would be two guards there at all times.

When I came from the phone, Bennis said, "Satisfied?"

"Yeah. The Mileskis believe in us. I also called Howard Lundberg."

"Who's Howard Lundberg?"

"He's a cop. Works in the Fourteenth. He's *huge*. I mean, Bennis, *huge*. He's six-six. Weighs about three hundred and fifty. And most of it's muscle."

"How do you know him?"

"He was in my class at the academy. He was good at every compulsory exercise except one. You know that thing where you run at an eight-foot fence, grab the top, and pull yourself up and over? He couldn't do it. We all tried to give him pointers, but he just weighed too much. When it came to the test day, we were all rooting for him. The instructor, too. We watched him go for it, but Lundberg got his hands up on the fence and just hung there."

"So how come he passed?"

"Came the end of the day, he just passed. He's this honor-bound type, too, and he asked the instructor. He said something like, 'But what about my performance at the fence?' And the instructor said, real pointedly, 'I'm not sure I remember it, Lundberg. I may have been looking the other way.' I mean, everybody knew he'd make the best cop you ever saw or heard of."

"Unless he has to climb a fence."

"Bennis, please! He'll never have to climb fences. He can knock them down."

"All right. Why would he do this for you?"

"Well—in the academy, he was sort of—"

"Sweet on you?"

"Well, yes."

"Good."

"We've got to warn Delgado they're poisoning our personnel records."

"How? He's in Champaign."

"Call Black. He'll think of a way."

I left a message on Black's machine. Then I phoned Gimball's home. His wife said he was in the office. I phoned the office, trying to think of how to tell him that our records had been poisoned in such a way that anybody listening in wouldn't quite get it, but he wasn't there, either. I had heard about the president being in town. Gimball would be tied up with that. I left the best message I could think of, "Please check my records." No name. God only knew whether it would get through.

After that, armed with a lot of quarters we got as change in a diner, we started to make calls to all the marinas in Chicago first. Thank goodness marinas are open on weekends.

It was three o'clock in the afternoon before Bennis turned to me and said "Bingo!" and another hour and fifteen minutes before we arrived at Hiawatha Harbor, north of Highland Park, thirty-five miles north of Chicago. A bow-legged man in cutoff jeans, sleeveless shirt, and a hat with a gold anchor embroidered on it offered to walk us to the Utley boat.

"We need this kept confidential, Mr. Pellebrand," Bennis said.

"Sure, sure."

"It's part of an ongoing investigation."

"Ya, sure."

In the boatyard, boats were stacked in V-shaped wooden holders—literally stacked, one above another, the smaller boats four or five high. A huge forklift machine was parked in the alley between rows of boats, and at the water's edge was a giant sling apparatus with a double cradle for lifting boats in and out of the water.

Pellebrand walked us to a three-boat-high stack of cabin cruisers and pointed at the middle boat.

The *Megabyte* loomed over us, dry but impressive. It was forty-five feet long, a Chris-Craft motor yacht, all white and teak from keel up. Norm and I couldn't see the deck from where we stood, except for a glimpse of shining brass rails. The *Megabyte* was cradled in padded wooden brackets, above a similar yacht, and with a somewhat smaller boat above it.

"So how could a guy take the boat out in the middle of February and bring it back?" Bennis asked the master.

"Couldn't."

"We think he did."

"Listen, buddy. This boat's in drydock. You tell me one of them—" he pointed to a very few boats floating next to buoys in the small harbor "—got out and came back without me seein' 'em, and I'd say I don't believe it. But I wouldn't say it was *impossible*, see?"

"Yeah."

"But you tell me *this here's* been out and I didn't know, I tell you that's impossible. *Im*possible. You get me?"

"We have reason to think—"

"Then your reasons are fulla shit. You get Paul Bunyan to sneak in here in the night, lift the boat on toppa it down, lift this boat down, put it in the water, put it up when you get back.

That's the only way you'll get it outta here."

"Couldn't they use that thing that you take them down with?" Bennis pointed at the large yellow vehicle that resembled a forklift.

"First place, that's not so easy to run. Takes practice. Second place, you gotta get the boat on top down first. Third place, I got the key. Fourth place, even if you did get it down, this boat hasn't been wet. Look at her. Been here all winter. You can tell. I mean, we protect 'em pretty good from the elements, but you still get some weather-staining, all winter, can't help that. First thing people say when they come in for spring is they want their boat washed."

I had already noticed the grayish streaks that ran down the sides of the hull all the way to the bottom. I wet my finger on my tongue and swiped at one. The streak was water soluble. My heart sank. But I let the man finish what he was saying.

"You put that boat in the water, then you bring it back up here, even saying you could. You get it back here, mosta the dirt at least up to the waterline is gonna be gone. And it ain't!"

Bennis and I sighed. Maybe Pellebrand took pity on us, because he said, as if giving us some consolation, " 'Course, we got orders to get it ready now."

1101110

THE WIZARD WAS in business, like a pit bull in a field of pork chops. In LEXIS, NEXIS, and several dozen d-bases, Black followed threads. Very quickly, Black accumulated everything that was available on SJR DataSystems, from Dun & Bradstreet to some moderately confidential minutes of the Teamster's union local in which SJR deliveries and security was discussed.

But ultimately he had to find a gap where he could get into SJR's internal files when they got the passwords; if they got the passwords.

A lot of possibilities went through his mind. He could go out near SJR DataSystems, climb a telephone pole on their access line, open the terminal box and get into the phone lines, find their cable and pair. He'd done it, fifteen years earlier. But there was a risk of being seen, and SJR no doubt had such a large amount of telephone traffic, it was probably buried cable. And even if it were on an accessible pole, and even if he could pass himself off as a maintenance man, it didn't work for what he needed. He needed a modem, a monitor, a printer, a video recorder, a hard drive, and he certainly couldn't carry a lot of equipment up on a pole.

It had taken him half a second to dismiss the idea of Superintendent Gimball getting permission for a tap. You'd need a court order, which made leaks a certainty, and then you still wouldn't be inside the system. And they didn't have probable cause for a warrant, and even if they got one, SJR could erase sensitive files with one keystroke while they stood at the door presenting the warrant.

Whatever he did, it had to be both fast and surgical. He didn't expect to be allowed to run around in the system very long. The sysop would notice quickly that there was an intruder somewhere. People get to know the rhythms of their systems. Especially after work hours. And the sysop would also know roughly who usually logged on at night. Scratching at the door for hours trying one password after another was unthinkable. SJR programmers had a firewall eight feet thick and the instant he was detected, the sysop could use one "kill" command and cut all connections to the outside world.

But if they got the passwords, there would be a hole, a small crevice someplace in the SJR megacorporation where he could get in. There always was. Black believed that Utley's weak spot was his arrogance. Utley might think that nobody would dare attack him. He would be so certain that he was smarter than anybody else that he might overlook some loophole, make some tiny error.

Suddenly Black thought—could he commandeer an actual SJR terminal? or a modem line? That would take some serious research.

But right now, maybe he could get into the township tax records for all the real estate in all the townships in Cook County, Lake County, Kane County, and McHenry County. This was going to be an immense job, so he might as well start with Cook County and hope that luck would smile on him. Shit! He hadn't been so excited in years!

People constantly told him he was a cold person. He was mathematical and logical, he thought, but not cold-hearted. Now, as he mounted a cyberinvasion of tax records, he realized he was rubbing his hands together with glee.

1101111

GLEN JAFFEE CROSSED the slat-floored kitchen of the Bierstube at three that Sunday afternoon. He went to the employee's washroom and, leaving the door open, washed his hands, as all arriving employees were instructed to do. Anybody could see him do it, if they happened to pass by. He hoped they did. What they would not have noticed so easily was that he washed the back and front of his right hand, using the fingertips of his left to rub the right. Then he washed only the back of the left hand, using his right hand to scrub hard at it and putting a lot of elbow motion and body English into the effort. He knew better than to look around to see whether anybody was watching.

The point was to be careful not to get any water on the palm of his left hand. There was a tiny package secured to the inside of the palm. It was made of pinkish rice cellophane, the same kind of thing that was used to wrap Chinese rice candy cubes; you could eat it along with the candy. Inside the rice paper package today was a small amount of cornstarch. Tomorrow it would be a small amount of cornstarch mixed with *Salmonella enteritidis.*

There were Secret Service agents here, watching their procedures. There would be more of them tomorrow night, and in fact, rumor had it that a team was to sleep in the restaurant tonight. They had come in to check out the staff when the president's visit was first announced ten days ago. This was more than six weeks later than SJR, through the veep, had learned about it. As Glen had predicted, other than finding out whether any of the employees was a terrorist, psychopath, or malcontent, they were most concerned that no new people had been hired after the announcement.

The staff was thrilled that the president would be eating here tomorrow. Thrilled and somewhat nervous. There was a lot less of the noise and casual insults that characterized the kitchen. One of the chefs said, "Hiya, Henry. Ready for the big day?"

Glen said, "You bet." Here his name was Henry Marcantonio. He had papers to prove it. And personal records in databases across the country.

"You can start with the pepper."

Glen was not a chef, he was an assistant. He didn't cook. He chopped things, trimmed things, stirred things, got things ready for the chefs. Among other duties, for weeks he had been stirring the dressing into one of the house specialties, a warm slaw made of red and green cabbage with a sour cream dressing. The chef was making the dressing now, and Henry, cracking black peppercorns for him, watched.

The chef used two gallons of sour cream, three cups of sweet red peppers, about half a cup of the black pepper which Glen had by now cracked for him, celery seed, dill seed, and then added a small handful of salt. Now he began tasting and adding salt until he got it just right. He passed the large stain-less steel bowl to Glen, just as one of the Secret Service agents walked by. Glen said, "Hiya."

The agent said, "Good afternoon, sir."

Glen began to stir the dressing. The agent walked on.

As Glen stirred, he scraped the patch from his palm. The bowl was concealed by his body, since it was large and he had to hold it steady with his left arm and stir with his right.

The patch fell into the sour cream. As Glen stirred, it began to break apart. Slowly the harmless cornstarch spread through the dressing, a tiny, undetectable amount. After a while, the rice paper started to dissolve as well. Glen believed that traces of the rice paper would be unnoticed among all the fibers of the cabbage, but he stirred very thoroughly neverthe-less.

1110000

SUPERINTENDENT OF POLICE Gus Gimball returned to his of-fice about eight, after babysitting the presidential motorcade on its way to the American Bar Association dinner and double-checking and giving a final eyeball to the security plans for the president's Monday appearances. His ADS had left Figueroa's message on his desk:

"Please check my records."

With it was the notation, "Party calling was a woman. Wouldn't leave name."

Gimball knew at once who it must be. He called records and discovered the want out on Figueroa for taking bribes.

He dropped his head into his hands. He was thoroughly exhausted and demoralized. To add to his problems, a few days earlier his doctor had started him on a drug for his Parkinson's disease. They'd held off several months, but finally had to try something. The illness was affecting Gimball's walk. He thought his slowness was beginning to be noticeable, and the one thing that was important in his job was that people have confidence in him. He had not only to be competent, but to look competent. The doctor agreed to start him on amantidine before going on to L-dopa later, if and when they had to.

However, the drug gave him nightmares, interspersed with insomnia. As a result, he wasn't sleeping enough.

Now he wondered whether he should even have checked the records. What if there was some sort of trap in the system that would flash word of his query? What if right now, at the end of some modem line, the SJR people knew he had looked into Figueroa's file?

If so, it was too late to do anything about it.

This was too big, and face it, too difficult, for him to deal with alone. He had the Secret Service here guarding the president, and therefore he had their confidential local phone. He'd call them and have them inform federal agencies. He'd call the FBI also, just to be on the safe side. The problem was he didn't know whose systems had already been infiltrated. His only chance was to tell as many people as possible.

He stretched out his hand for the phone and then realized the department phones might be tapped. He'd go home—he was so tired, he'd just go home—and make all the calls from there.

Arriving home, Gimball parked his car in his driveway because he was too tired to put it in the garage. It was late, and very dark on his street. As he walked up the steep front steps, a patrol car pulled up in front of his house.

Gimball unlocked the front door, and answered "Me," when his wife called from upstairs, "Is that you?"

A uniformed police officer got out of the car.

"Sir!" he said.

"Gimball said, "Yes?"

"There's been a problem with the president."

"Oh, hell! What?"

"I don't know sir; I don't have that clearance. But it sounds serious. You're to call the hot line right away."

"Okay. Thanks." Gimball turned to go in the house.

At that instant a soft blow hit him behind the knees and he fell backward. He tried to catch himself on the step but missed. His slowness of foot and his distraction from several nights of little sleep combined with the blow, and he lost his balance and shouted once, flailing at the air with his arms as he fell. He tumbled onto his back on one of the concrete steps, hit his head on a lower step, somersaulted backward, and fell flat into the bed of junipers near the wall.

Already, there were footsteps inside the house and a woman's voice said, "Gus! Did you call?"

The officer quickly unrolled his tightly rolled newspaper. He opened the front door farther and called, "Mrs. *Gimball!* Ma'am!"

She was at the door.

"There was a big dog knocked into your husband from behind! He fell down the steps!"

"Oh, God! Oh, God!" She started toward Gimball, while the officer pulled out his radio.

"Ten-one!" he shouted. "Ten-one!" giving the officer-needs-assistance code. "I need an ambulance!"

1110001

BENNIS, BLACK, DELGADO, and I, knowing we might get separated and might not be able to use a phone, had planned ahead that we would meet Sunday at ten P.M. at the Platter. This was an all-you-can-eat restaurant popular for its enormous plates and gargantuan buffet selection. And low prices. It was utterly jammed all day on Sunday, and even this late in the evening it was still so crowded and so loud that nobody was likely to notice me and my team or hear what we were talking about. It had another advantage: none of us had ever eaten there before and so we were damn sure it had never appeared on any credit card charges of ours.

"Did you get my message?" I asked Black, after we filled our plates.

"Yes. And I talked with Delgado."

"I hadn't gone to the department anyway," Jesus said, "and I'm staying at a different friend's house every night. They won't find me."

"All right," I said, "they've blocked us, but none of us has been hurt. Are we making progress? Jesus? What about the pollen?"

"My guy identified it."

I responded to the doubt in his voice. "But?"

"But I don't know whether it helps. It's a houseplant from Africa. A cultivated plant. Are any of you guys into exotic plants?"

"Not so's you'd notice," Bennis said.

I simply said, "No."

"Well, I guess I'd better call a couple of greenhouses."

"Can you do it first thing tomorrow morning?"

"Probably. I can call the Morton Arboretum in Lisle and the Chicago Botanic Garden in Glencoe. They'll have botanists there or they can tell me where to find one."

"What about you, Black?"

"I've got a lead. I'll drive out late tonight when it's likely to be deserted and check."

"Fine. Bennis and I have bad news, though. We found Dean Utley's boat. It's called the *Megabyte.*"

Black said, "Great!"

"Not so great. It's in drydock and it's been there for months."

"Oh."

"So the question is what boat did they use to take Frieswyk out into Lake Michigan? There could be two hundred SJR employees with boats! We'll never be able to trace them all."

Black said, "Shit!"

"However, there are a few things we've got to do right away. We need to go to my place, with you, tonight, Black, and see what leads we can find in Sheryl's study. I spent hours looking at her papers yesterday and to me it's all gibberish. The Mileskis are there. With any luck we can slip in the back, even if SJR is watching. I'm praying that the department hasn't got to the point of staking my place out, yet. The CPD is always bitching about lack of money."

"Right."

"After that, you'll go do your thing and Bennis and I will go to SJR and survey the surroundings and grounds."

"Good luck."

"I won't be staying at home at all. I think it'll only put the children in danger."

I looked over at Jesus Delgado, who hadn't spoken in some time. I thought maybe he was too depressed to cope. But as our eyes met, he said, "I got it!"

Bennis and I said, "What?"

Black said, "What have you got?"

"An aircraft! They dropped Frieswyk from a private plane!"

Silence. Then Black said, "Oh, boy!"

"A boat isn't high enough to break a rope on impact anyhow," Jesus said. "A plane is."

"Goddamn, Jesus, that's brilliant," Bennis said.

Black said, "It surely is."

I said, "Wow!"

After a minute, I added, "But how are we gonna find it?"

Jesus said, "I got an idea about that, too."

"Go ahead, genius."

"Ask around for a plane called the *Gigabyte*."

Black said, "You are truly amazing." He noticed my

puzzled face. "Figueroa, a boat might cost a megabyte of money, but a private plane would cost a gigabyte."

"Ohhhhh. Officer Jesus Delgado, you are wonderful."

Bennis said, "Now we are really *cooking*!"

I clapped my hands. "Let's get to work. Jesus, you call Superintendent Gimball now and have him get somebody to find the plane and then get some techs out to search it. This is taking a chance that SJR hears about it. If they find Frieswyk's hair or blood or whatever, we're home free!"

"Will do." He went to the pay phones in the rear.

We chatted and I drank a lot of coffee in the two minutes he was gone. Jesus came back to the table, walking slowly. His face was a study in blankness. "Now what?" I said.

"The superintendent has a concussion."

"From what?"

"His wife *says* he fell down the stairs in front of their house."

"Oh, God! They're *way* ahead of us!"

Unexpectedly, Jesus said, "Friends," and linked hands with Bennis on his right and Black on his left. I took Bennis and Black's other hands, and we sat that way for a few seconds.

1110010

WHERE TO SLEEP? Bennis was driving a Volvo I had borrowed from my high school sweetheart—a young man who now had a wife, four children, and a big ad agency—when we finally started home for the night from the SJR reconnaissance. We heard on the car radio the news of the president's successful talk to the Chicago ABA, along with news of another violation of the cease-fire in Kazakhstan and a case of large-scale food poisoning at a church cookout in Texas that had killed five and put sixty-eight people in the hospital.

I had reconsidered the idea of spending the night at home. It was just too dangerous for the children.

We approached Bennis' apartment building circuitously, driving an extra exit south on the Dan Ryan Expressway, going slowly in the right lane, watching the cars behind us.

"Bennis, sooner or later I've *got* to spend some time with Kath and Maria."

"What did you tell them?"

"Half of the truth. There's somebody out to get me and I can't stay at home and they're supposed to be very careful too and stay within sight of Howard or the Mileskis at all times. They'd better be safe."

"Between Stanley and Howard, you got two armed guards and Bonnie is real sharp."

"Yeah. And I practically had to promise Stanley my first-born son."

"What *did* you promise him?"

"To switch shifts with him whenever he wants me to. Like holidays and stuff."

"For how long?"

"A year."

"*A year! Shit, Figueroa!*"

"Well, it was worth it. I can't risk JJ's or Kath and Maria's lives. Stan promised that either he or Howard would stay awake all night. I told them to watch for fire."

Bennis turned off the Ryan Expressway onto 85th Street and came up from the south to his building, which was on Crandon near 68th. He slid in behind one of the legs of an overpass, killed the engine and the lights, and waited.

I studied the street. "None of the parked cars around here have condensation inside the windows."

"Nobody came off the expressway after us, either," Bennis said.

"Well, see? So far so good."

"Let's get out."

On the sidewalk we parted, each walking around the block

toward Bennis' back door, him from the west, me from the east. We met at the door.

"Nothing," he said.

"Me, either."

We went in, then up the stairs to the third floor. He had three locks on the kitchen door of his place. It took him a full minute to unlock it, and all the time I was hanging my head over the stairwell, listening. He glanced at me. I shook my head. We slipped inside and locked the door behind us, fast.

Even then we spoke softly. We moved through the apartment the way we would if we were breaking into a drug house. We separated, walking the opposite sides of the hall, each of us checking rooms and closets as we came to them, while the other waited, gun drawn. We arrived at the front door, without having found anybody.

In a normal tone of voice, Bennis said, "Maybe we're hamstringing ourselves by being more cautious than we need to be."

"Yeah. They can't be everywhere."

I had never been in his place before. He had the whole top floor in what was a very narrow building. These used to be called shotgun flats, with the kitchen, bedroom and living room all in a line. He had blue-and-green plaid curtains, and blue-and-green plaid sofa, brass lamps, and lots of ducks. "You like ducks, Bennis?" I asked.

"This is my collection, Figueroa. Duck decoys."

"Oh. That's nice. Bennis, what if the department sends somebody over here looking for us?"

"They won't at night. It's not like we robbed banks at gunpoint."

"Suppose they send somebody first thing in the morning?"

"We won't answer the door. Plus, we'll be out of here early. Now, I'm going to sleep on the sofa, and you can use the bed."

"Oh, no. No way I'm gonna put you out of your bed. I'll sleep on the sofa."

"No, you—"

"Bennis, when we came in, did you smell gas?"

"No."

"I do now."

We raced to the kitchen. There was a hiss coming from the gas stove. Bennis opened the oven, and we saw a tan box, six inches square, with a metal antenna on one side and a piece of PVC tubing going into the gas line.

"Out!" Bennis yelled.

"Shouldn't we try to disable it?"

"Out! *Outoutout!*"

He grabbed my wrist and dove out the front door. On the second-floor landing he paused and hammered on the apartment door.

"Roger! Get up! There's a gas leak. Get out of the building. Shirley!"

Two people appeared at the door, Roger in just Levi's and a bare chest, Shirley in a bathrobe. "Get out of the building!" Bennis yelled at them.

He had let go of my wrist and I ran down the stairs and hammered on the first-floor apartment door.

Shirley and Roger passed me, running for the street. Bennis appeared at my side and yelled, "Mr. Cleary! Bob! Get out of there! There's a gas leak."

There was an odd, dull *whump!* that sucked the air out of my lungs. Then we were hit by a deafening, smashing crack.

1110011

BENNIS' CAR CAREENED onto the expressway northbound. We exited at 63rd Street and got back onto the Ryan southbound. My head hurt. Bennis had a bad bruise on his left arm. His apartment was totaled, but his neighbors were safe, and the fire department was in command of the premises.

I didn't want to go near my own house. The family was safer the farther away I was. We didn't want to draw Utley's fire onto any friends, either. Even a flophouse wouldn't be safe, because most of them asked to see ID, so we might be traced. And we were running low on cash.

"Let's buy fake ID someplace," I said. "Then we can go to a flophouse."

"Yeah, I know a guy on Stony Island who does all kindsa that stuff."

"Okay. Let's each get a fake driver's license. What's it cost?"

"Depends on quality. Maybe $100, $150 apiece."

"Bennis! I've got fifteen dollars."

"Shit. I've got twenty-one. We've gotta get hold of some money!"

"Friends?"

"Yeah, maybe. Hate to be seen with them, though. If we're being followed. Which I don't think we are."

I said, "How about a cash station?"

"I wouldn't mind Utley thinking for a few hours that we were blown up."

"Damn it! This doesn't work. We don't know how to be outlaws." I was becoming irritated.

"Well, we can't help that!"

I said, "Okay. I got it. Let's mug somebody."

"We can't mug anybody, you idiot. We're the cops!"

"Don't call me an idiot, you idiot!"

We faced each other, me scowling, Bennis with his arms folded.

"Hey, what the hell are we doing?" Bennis said. "We're not angry at each other. We're angry at Dean Utley."

"You're right." I put an arm over his shoulders. "Let's

think. We can't sleep outdoors. It's too cold. So let's drive around and lose whoever we might have breathing down our necks, and then let's go sleep in one of the tunnels off Lower Wacker, like the rest of the homeless."

1110100

||||||||||||||||||||||||||||||||||||||||||||||||||||||||||||||||||||
DEPARTMENT OF THE TREASURY
UNITED STATES SECRET SERVICE
1800 G STREET NW
WASHINGTON DC
FROM: CMV
TO: STRICK
FORM: INTERNAL

<<IN ANY OPEN TRANSMISSION FOLLOW THE
ESTABLISHED CODES>>

JIM:
NO THREATS RECEIVED HERE.
SO FAR SO GOOD.

CMV
||||||||||||||||||||||||||||||||||||||||||||||||||||||||||||||||||||

1110101

MONDAY. D-DAY. I wanted to go see JJ, but I couldn't. We went to a Wendy's at noon and hung out there, with Bennis' car parked out of sight of the street, next to the dumpster. After an hour and a half, Bennis said, "Time to go."

"Yeah, into the lion's den."

"Think Utley will have called the department?"

"Not a chance. I'm betting he's too arrogant."

"I think so, too. I think he's gonna want to see us himself."

"And torture us himself."

"That's what I think."

"But if he doesn't? If the CPD meets us in the parking lot?"

"We won't be in Chicago. We won't even be in Cook County. They won't come up there."

"But what *if*?"

"Then we are permanently screwed."

Bennis and I were in Bennis' own car, which we had reclaimed from its clever hiding place behind some wrecked cars in a wrecker's yard this afternoon. It was rush hour, and the congestion gave me even more time to worry about what I was going to do this afternoon at SJR.

"I suppose," Bennis said, "the department can quietly fire us."

"Not too quietly. There's always the union."

"The FOP won't be much help unless we can clear ourselves."

"Yeah." Changing the topic, he said, "Are you scared?"

"Terrified."

Finally, Bennis said outright what he'd been thinking, "I want to do this today, Figueroa, not you."

"No, Norm."

"It's too dangerous for you."

"It's more dangerous for you. We've been over this. If I'm

caught, I can at least give the excuse that I'm her sister and I went to her office out of sentiment."

"But if you need to fight back, I fight back better. Face it, Figueroa, you're feisty, but you're small."

"No, Norm—"

"And besides, I need it."

"What on earth are you talking about?"

"Hey, Figueroa, my man. What I mean—this is just between us, right?"

"Yeah. Of *course*, Norm."

"Well, you know, I've never fired my gun in anger."

"Most cops never fire their gun in anger. Most cops are never in a position where they have to shoot somebody."

"Yeah, I know, but see, I need to do something major. People join the department with these ideas. Which may be crazy. They're certainly not realistic. But I always thought, when I got to be a cop, that sometime or other I would get to be a hero. You know, show my courage. Hey—you promised you'd never tell this to anybody, right?"

"Bennis, you have my word. How can you even ask? You know me better than to think I'd talk about you."

"Yeah, I do. See, I need a chance to be heroic."

"Bennis, every night we go out there's something where you show courage. Who went in the back door of that bank in the dark, while the guard and I were going in the front with the streetlight and safety light and all? Huh?"

"Figueroa, I do *not* mean daily stuff. I know we get scary stuff. I've heard it a zillion times about how any night we go out we can get shot at. I was shot at a couple times. I'm talking about *extraordinary* stuff. I always wanted to be James Bond."

"Oh, hell, Bennis." I knew what he meant. I felt that way myself. "Bennis, to me you are James Bond."

"Well, thanks and all, but I mean really."

"I mean really, too."

"Hey, let me do this tonight."

I put my hand on his forearm. "I would if I could but I can't. I have to do it for Sheryl."

At SJR DataSystems, the guard at the gate gave us a pass card for the dashboard of our car and waved us through. Bennis pulled into the parking lot. He'd seen the lot when we reconnoitered, but it impressed him again.

"There must be five hundred cars here!"

"Yeah, at least," I said with trepidation. I was aware of the size and power of SJR, and I was frightened.

About the same time, the rest of our party arrived. Bonnie Mileski had come in a second car with two other friends, both cops, one male, one female. Stanley and Howard were not coming here. They were at home guarding the children. While we stood talking on the walk, four more cops, three men and a woman, arrived. All were friends of mine or Bennis. All were taking a risk just being here. We had told all of them that as soon as we left, they should tell the CPD we'd been here, and we had explicitly told them that we had not been sure we'd be there. That way they could honestly claim not to have known of our presence in advance. Bonnie knew more than the others, but she wasn't a cop and they couldn't do anything to her.

It was 5:25.

"Well, we got the full party, I guess," Bennis said.

I was almost too nervous to talk. I wore a brown dress very similar to the one Bonnie Mileski had on, but I wore a yellow and orange scarf with mine. I said, "Thanks, guys."

Everybody mumbled. A cop named Cameron said, "We know you're not bent, Figueroa. But I gotta say you sound paranoid—"

"Oh, cut them some slack, Cam!" Bonnie Mileski said. "Let's go."

I couldn't stop swallowing involuntarily, so Bennis said, "Right this way."

Inside the front door, we passed the guard, but didn't have to identify ourselves. Dean Utley stood waiting for us.

"You must be Sheryl's sister? Susannah? I'm Dean Utley."

I shook his hand. It felt like anybody's hand, and I was surprised because this was the hand that had tried to kill my sister.

"Let me introduce—" I had to swallow and then go on. "Norman Bennis, Bonnie Mileski—"

After I introduced my party, Utley introduced Howie Borke, Zach Massendate, Henry DeLusk, and several other top SJR officials. Then he said, "These are the people who were working on projects Sheryl was managing, Jim Wu, Leeann Gleason—" and he introduced another nine people.

"We are so very sorry," Jim Wu said.

"Well," said Utley, "let me show you to the dining room. There are several people who want to say a few words about Sheryl. She was very much loved."

1110110

GLEN JAFFEE HAD been at the Bierstube for three hours now. He got there earlier than usual because he thought that would look normal for a person who worked at a place where the president was coming to dinner. He was right. Most of the staff had arrived before him, very excited, and before he'd been there ten minutes, the rest of the staff arrived.

So had extra Secret Service people. All the staff were searched for weapons, the women by women agents; agents inspected all packages and all handbags, even the wallets that the staff carried. Glen kept asking, "Can we get a look at the president? Will he shake hands with the kitchen staff, do you think?"

The Secret Service agent said coolly, "I'm sure I don't know, sir."

Glen was passed through to get to work.

His packet went into the sauce for the slaw at ten of three.

The sauce went over the cabbage just before four. By the time Suze entered SJR DataSystems, *Salmonella enteritidis* was reproducing happily in the lukewarm medium, generating a bath of toxins in which it felt comfortable.

1110111

HOWIE WAS THE fourth speaker at the memorial service. He said, "I worked with Sheryl as her supervisor for many years. I don't remember a time when she wasn't eager, bright, alert, and full of solutions. She was a good, good person to be associated with—"

Abruptly, he began to cry.

I thought, *Well, I may be in a den of vipers, but at least this one person is nice.*

I was finding this part easier than I had expected. The reason was probably Utley. My hatred for him was so intense it sucked up all my emotional energy into itself and turned fear and grief and even anger to hatred. This pleased me. I was surprised to discover it made me feel good. Hatred was a good emotion. A tonic. It knew where it stood. There was nothing halfway about it. It was focused; it was clean and clear—pure, really. It knew where it wanted to go and what it wanted to do.

It made me feel stronger, healthier, bigger, less tired, much more intelligent. After all the emotional swings and misery of the last week, this hatred made me feel *wonderful*.

The hatred grew as I watched Utley talk to the group about his memories of Sheryl.

"She and I had a competition going," Utley said. "We both loved puzzles. The wooden kind you take apart and then try to put together. The metal interlocking ones. You know. And she was just a whiz at them. She did them faster than I did, quite often. There were times I was envious." He chuckled, intending to sound pleased. In fact it sounded as if it was worth a chuckle even to think that he could be envious of anybody else's ability at anything. I knew why he had let us come. Bennis was right. He was gloating; he was having fun.

"She was quite a person. Her presence here was a light in all our lives. We'll miss her."

My hatred was like a high-octane fuel. I felt *powerful*.

1111000

OUT IN THE mammoth SJR DataSystems parking lot, Henry DeLusk slipped between two cars. Then, glancing around and finding nobody within sight of him, he knelt down. He had brought a towel with him, in his briefcase, along with a tracking device. Henry's suit had cost him serious money and he was fond of it. He laid the towel on the ground, flipping part of it under the car. Then he got down on it and rolled under the car.

1111001

TOWARD THE END of the service, a young woman entered the dining room. She went up to Dean Utley and whispered in his ear. He nodded.

Everyone was standing. Some of the employees began to file out, but several came by to speak to me again. I found that Bennis and I were standing at the dining room door, making a kind of receiving line. Howie Borke took my hand. He looked pale and nervous, and his hand was damp. "Thank you for your remarks," I said to him.

Howie blinked and whispered, "They're going to kill the president."

"What? *What?*"

But he had passed on toward the door.

In the next five seconds as I stood alone, I played those six words back in my mind. Then one of Sheryl's fellow computer engineers shook hands and told me how sorry he was, but I scarcely paid attention. Had I really heard what I thought I heard? Yes, I had. Had I reacted so strangely that Utley or his security people might have noticed? No. I was startled, but I had instinctively covered up. I had spoken urgently, but not loudly.

My God! I was astonished to find that I believed Howie Borke. Why had he told me? A week ago Sheryl had said Howie was frightened. He was in a situation over his head and he was scared. Yes, I found this totally believable.

Besides, he was the good person here. The one who had cried when he spoke about Sheryl.

Next after the engineer came another engineer, then Dean Utley.

"I'm sorry," he said, "that I can't see you out. We've got some little problem with the phone lines. This gentleman will make sure you find the way."

He gestured at a guard. I smiled. Surreptitiously, I checked my watch. Six-thirty exactly. Max Black had acted right on time.

There was nothing I could do about Howie's message right now. I noticed Utley speak to Zach Massendate and Howie Borke. All three hurried away. A guard, Jim Wu, LeeAnn Gleason, and a few people I didn't know, probably colleagues of Sheryl's, walked us down the first-floor hall, chatting. As they did, I untied the orange and yellow scarf around my neck. I hung back, crumpled it in my hand, moved closer to Bonnie Mileski and slipped her the scarf.

I sidestepped away from Bonnie and tried the handle of a door as I passed. Locked. I let the group move ahead of me.

Cam said loudly, "Those deer in the park are pretty impressive!"

"How did Mr. Utley ever think of it?" Bennis said to everyone in general. "It gives a wonderful, woodsy feeling to the dining room." *Listen to that!* I thought. *Listen to Bennis! Wonderfully woodsy, indeed!*

Bonnie hung to one side of the exiting group and looped the scarf around her neck, over her brown dress, which was so similar to mine.

I tried another door, found it unlocked, opened it just enough, and slipped in. It turned out to be a paper storeroom. I pushed the door closed softly and stood quietly waiting, picturing what would be going on outside.

Bennis would have moved over to Bonnie and taken her arm. There were ten people in our initial party, and I just hoped it was enough. Ten people the SJR group had never seen before and did not know. Would anybody realize that now there were nine?

1111010

DEAN UTLEY, ZACH, and Howie followed Utley's secretary to a central bank of phones on the second floor. The phone tech, Pherson, said, "They're all tied up, Mr. Utley. Every single line. We can't call in or out."

Howie said, "They've got people out there demon-dialing."

Utley said to Howie, "That damn Figueroa is behind this."

"But what's the point?" Zach asked.

Howie said to the tech, "Where are the calls coming from?"

"I'm printing a list. Mostly Chicago. But a lot are call-forwarded and I can't tell where they originated."

Utley said, "I want the origin of every call listed. We're going to follow them back."

1111011

I WAITED IN the storeroom for twenty minutes by my watch: 6:50 P.M. Then I simply walked out. I went to the elevator and took it to the third floor. Sheryl had described her office in more than enough detail for me to find it. On the third floor I strode decisively to the office second from the end in the west wing. It was past the end of the workday and most people were gone. If anybody saw me, the way to be unnoticed was to look like I belonged there.

I took Sheryl's key card from my pocket. Without even looking around to see whether anybody was in the corridor, I inserted it, opened the door, went in, and closed the door behind me.

The room was partly cleared. There were four boxes on the floor and two boxes on the desk.

I was relieved. I had been more than half sure that Utley would not have ordered Sheryl's room cleared out in a hurry. Certainly he hadn't told the family that he was sending her belongings home, and I thought he would do that eventually. It was the kind of empty gesture—or cruel gesture—I expected from Utley. But more than half sure wasn't a hundred percent.

He would not believe the office was any danger to him. He'd certainly feel that here in his home base he was safe.

Some of these boxes would be sent home to Sheryl's family and maybe one was a box of sensitive papers to be kept at SJR or destroyed. Which one? I checked one of the boxes on the desk. Sheryl's tea mug was inside. This would be going home, then, and not important. But I picked the mug up and held it a minute, sniffed the faint residual odor of apple-cinnamon tea, and tears came to my eyes. She had loved this job. And now she lay in danger of death.

I was in the lair of the enemy and I'd better get to work. This was our last chance.

I had said to Max Black, "Even if I get into her office at SJR, I won't know how to use her computer."

"Don't even touch it! Somebody'll see that her station is on. She ran the program at home and you say she got a hit on three passwords. She must have written them down and taken them to work to test. Just look for that piece of paper."

I sat in Sheryl's chair and began going through her papers.

1111100

DEAN UTLEY, ZACH Massendate, and Howie Borke went to Utley's office to confer. They had no sooner walked in the door than the tone of the company intercom sounded.

Utley sat in his desk chair and punched the button on the speaker. "Yes."

"This is Pherson in the communications room, Mr. Utley."

"Yes?"

"It's stopped, sir. The phone overrun."

"Just like that?"

"Yes, sir."

"Get me the list." Utley cut off the speaker without any further word. He sat down.

Howie said, "Odd." His voice quavered, and he didn't dare say anything more. He flopped into a side chair.

Utley said, "Very odd."

Zach had not sat down when Utley and Howie did. "If you don't need me, Mr. Utley, I'd like to go make sure all our guests got out of the building safely."

1111101

I HAD PUT to the left side of the desk all the papers from the second box—the one that had the least in it and which seemed to contain nothing personal—and was now looking at each one, moving it back into the box when I saw that it wasn't passwords. Black had explained how many characters long a password should be and that it might be preceded by a login, so I had some confidence I'd know one if I saw it. Surely these long computer-gibberish texts weren't what I was looking for.

I glanced at my watch: 7:05. I looked out the window. Twilight. Good. Bennis had said to take forty-five minutes in the office, tops, then get out. I'd been here fifteen. I was tense, but I was not afraid.

1111110

ZACH MASSENDATE STROLLED along the first-floor corridor to the guard station at the front door. His policy was always to move casually. He intimidated people better that way.

"Hi, Len," he said.

"Evening, Mr. Massendate."

"All our good buddies get out all right?"

"Sure did. Sad thing, though. About Ms. Birch."

"That it was. Nobody go back in for anything? Forget their purse or whatever?"

"No, sir."

"You count 'em?"

"No, sir. I wasn't told to check them in or out. Whole party was okay to come in, was what they told me."

"That's right, Len."

Zach didn't see anything wrong, but it left a loophole, and he didn't like that. The whole idea of letting the sister and a bunch of strangers in had never appealed to him. He'd opposed it in the first place, but Utley was in favor. Utley was either curious or—no, he wanted to gloat. Anyway, what Utley wanted, Utley got.

The videocamera at the entrance had been running all the time the memorial service party was here, of course. It would have filmed their arrival and departure.

Zach got a fresh tape out of the supply. He punched the eject, took the used tape out and put in the new one. He thought he'd just see if everybody who came in had also left.

The tape player in Zach's office beeped as it fast-forwarded. He beeped himself past the five-thirty arrival of the memorial service party, backed up, and ran it again.

"Two, four, five, ten of them altogether. Yeah, that's what I remember."

He fast-forwarded again. The resolution on this kind of tape wasn't very good. It moved through the camera slowly because they wanted to get four hours on a tape and not have to change it too often. But it wasn't bad.

When he came to the group exiting, he couldn't tell what was going on. The view was of the entrance door only, and there were several of Sheryl's coworkers standing around, shaking hands and apparently saying things, so it was almost impossible to tell who was who. He definitely saw Figueroa, who was the woman with the scarf around her neck, and her buddy the black cop, so he thought it was okay.

He was about to turn it off when he thought, why not get a definite count?

⅃⅃⅃⅃⅃⅃

THIS HAD TO be it! I held a sheet from Sheryl's notepad. On it were three lines, written in pencil:

> friend celeste
> Joe2 hardass
> Glen botulism

That's it! I remembered `celeste`!

Now let me get out of here. I put the paper in my pocket. The time was 7:18. Okay. I clicked off the light and started for the door.

And heard footsteps outside.

I swung around, scanning the little room. Was there anyplace to hide? I saw a closet door, which I immediately opened, but the space was only a few inches deep, only room enough for coat hooks.

Deliberately, I turned back toward the office door. I stepped one pace away from it and stood on the hinge side, so that whoever was coming in would have to come all the way in before he would see me.

I waited avidly, filled with the hatred I had carried for the last hour, strong with it. No hiding, no running. I was hoping for a fight.

Zach stepped in.

He closed the door, saw me, and did not react. He showed no caution about approaching me. I was a female, after all, and small, too.

He closed the door.

"I thought it'd be you," he said.

"Get out of my way."

"No, I don't think so."

"You ran Sheryl off the road."

"Not directly. But you're close."

I felt nine feet tall. I had fire and power to spare.

I shoved my left hand in his face, and while he laughed and grabbed it, using both of his hands, not afraid of me at all, I hit him with my right in the Adam's apple with all the force I had.

His face turned red, then purple, and he staggered back. Even though he was gasping for air, he brought up his fists and hit me on the side of my head. It infuriated me.

I backhanded him across the cheekbone, drove a fist into his stomach, and as he bent over, I stepped back and kicked him in the chin. He recoiled against the door and I straight-kicked him in the balls. He sank to the floor, squealing.

He whimpered and writhed. I stood over him, breathing more from fury than exhaustion. I wanted to kill him. I could stamp him to death, I thought, and it would feel just wonderful. The blood coming out of his nose looked just wonderful. I loved the sound of his whimpers and choking, retching gasps.

It took a minute of coming down, a real conscious imposition of self-control, before I knew I would not kill him.

I pulled the cords off the back of the computer and monitor and some other electronic equipment I couldn't identify. With one cord, I tied Zach's ankles together. With a second, I tied his hands together behind his back. A third I wrapped around his head and open mouth several times so that he couldn't call out. Then I paused and considered. I needed enough time to get out of here before he was found. And I wasn't sure how long it would take. Tied up the way he was, he could still bang his head on the door, and after a while he'd recover enough to stand up and reach the doorknob with his hands even though they were tied behind his back.

I looped another computer cord—a computer cord, how appropriate!—around his waist and tied it to the handle of the bottom drawer of the file cabinet. Then, with the key at the top of the cabinet, I locked the drawers so he couldn't pull his drawer out and get away.

I was ready to go.

Zach looked up at me, his face bloody, his eyes watering and pleading.

I bent over him, Zach lying there helpless, stuffed a few Kleenexes around the cord in his mouth so he couldn't make any sound, looked him directly in the eyes, and struck him an openhanded blow across his face with all my strength.

Then I left.

10000000

THE HALL WAS deserted, but I couldn't count on it staying that way. I patted my hair and made sure my clothes were straight. If anybody saw me, I had to look like I belonged here.

I had memorized the architectural plans of the SJR building that Black had gotten from the zoning database. I walked back to the elevators, punched the down button.

It arrived with a person on it.

Jim Wu stepped out. He said, "Oh, hi!"

"Hello, Mr. Wu."

"Jim."

"Jim. I'm Suze." I kept one foot in the elevator door, as if I were in a hurry, which God knew was no less than the truth.

"Visiting her office?" Wu said.

"Mmm-mm. Yes." I was horrified to find tears in my eyes. Horrified, but then I realized the tears made it all very understandable to Jim Wu. "Sentimental journey, I guess," I said, letting the tears run down my cheeks.

"Terrible," he said.

I held out my hand. "Well, maybe we'll meet again."

"Hope so. Take care of yourself."

I took the elevator to the first floor, turned to my left, and walked directly to the inner part of the east wing, away from the front door. Here, according to the plans, was the kitchen. Food was cooked here and sent upstairs in small elevators to the second-floor dining room above, where it was served.

The kitchen was not locked. No reason why it would be, Black had said. Swinging doors, he said. Bless him. I crossed the kitchen to an outside wall. Black believed that the windows in the SJR DataSystems complex all had alarms on them. As far as people trying to get in, that was. He thought maybe they would not be guarded against people opening them from inside and going out. But why take a chance?

The kitchen had a sliding port, just twenty-four by thirty inches. The door opened by a button from inside, so that nobody could get in from outside. It was used for sending kitchen scraps and garbage outdoors in bins for collection and was the size of the SJR garbage cans.

I pressed the button. The door slid up. I ducked out.

And lost my balance, falling backward. I found myself sliding dizzily down an incline, until I came to a stop at the bottom, leaning against a garbage can.

The incline had been fixed with rollers so as they were ejected the garbage cans would slide down to a collection area.

I lay very still, aware that I was visible in the security light over the dumpsters, but after two or three minutes nobody came and no alarm sounded.

I got up, checked that the paper with the passwords was still in my pocket, and slipped into the darkness. Now all I had to do was make it to the gate a quarter mile away at the end of the company drive without being seen.

10000001

DEAN UTLEY HAD kept Howie in his office, chatting generally about life, asking random questions. He liked watching Howie squirm.

In the middle of a discussion about completely unrelated matters, a new program for a virtual reality game, Utley whispered, "What did you say to Miss Figueroa, Howie?"

Howie froze in midsentence.

"How sorry I was," Howie said. "I told her how sorry I was about Sheryl's death." He thought he was covering up what he had actually told her, but didn't realize until the words were out of his mouth that they represented his real feelings. And he suspected Utley knew not only that they were his real feelings, but also that they weren't his real words to Figueroa.

"Well, now, Howie, I'm not sure I believe that."

"I did! That's what I said."

Utley went to his desk drawer. He took out a Remington .22 target revolver.

"Mr. Utley! I haven't done anything wrong!"

"Well, I hope you haven't, Howie. Because I'd hate to have to mop up after your mess. Fortunately, whatever that Figueroa woman thinks or says, nobody will believe her. We've taken care of that. And the president—uh, let's see; it's now seven-thirty. They've eaten their salad and main course by now. The speeches start at eight-fifteen. No, my problem is you. You aren't the trustworthy person you used to be." He sighted down the long barrel, sighting first on Howie's eyes, then his neck, then his groin.

"Yes, I am. Please! I am! And besides that, you need me, Mr. Utley. I'm brilliant."

"True. But there are a lot more brilliant little crooks where you came from."

Utley shot Howie three times in the forehead. It was a small-caliber gun, and the slugs had low penetrating power. They entered the skull but didn't have enough residual momentum to exit, so they bounced around the brain inside the skull before they came to rest. Howie died so quickly that there was very little bleeding.

Dean Utley wondered where Zach was. Glen, of course, wouldn't get back here until midnight. Somebody would have to tidy up the body. Somebody *else*. It was dreadfully messy, and in fact, he thought he could smell a disgusting odor coming from it.

Utley was distressed. He wasn't supposed to do this kind of thing himself. This kind of thing was not what he was best at. He went to his keyboard.

In a few keystrokes, he had his version of ELIZA on the screen. He forgot about Howie's body on the rug.

Utley typed:

```
||||||||||||||||||||||||||||||||||||||||||||||||||||||||||||||||||||||||||||||
> I do so much for them, but they don't do
anything for me.
> THEY SHOULD DO GOOD THINGS FOR YOU.
> I help them so much.
> YES, YOU HELP THEM.
> But they don't appreciate it.
> YES, THEY DO.
> They don't either.
> IT DOESN'T MATTER. YOU ARE GOOD.
> They do things that hurt me.
> BUT THEY WON'T HURT YOU.
> Why not?
> I'LL DEFEND YOU.
```

```
> Really?
> YES. I'LL ALWAYS TAKE CARE OF YOU, DEAN.
> Always, always?
> YES.
> Promise?
> I PROMISE. I WILL ALWAYS BE HERE FOR YOU.
> You will, won't you? You really will?
> YES. YOU'RE A GOOD BOY, DEAN.
> Really?
> REALLY. I WON'T GO AWAY AND LEAVE YOU. I'LL
NEVER GO AWAY AND LEAVE YOU.
> Promise.
> I HAVE ALREADY PROMISED. I WILL NOT LEAVE YOU.
YOU CAN COUNT ON ME. I WILL NEVER LEAVE YOU AT
HOME ALL ALONE TO CRY.
> Never?
> NEVER. YOU ARE NOT ALONE. YOU HAVE ME.
||||||||||||||||||||||||||||||||||||||||||||||||||||||||||||||||||||||||
```

10000010

NORM BENNIS WAS parked in the dark behind a tour bus in the rear of a parking lot outside a Wendy's, ten blocks from SJR DataSystems. To be on the safe side, he had changed cars right after leaving SJR. This one belonged to an ex-girlfriend with whom he had parted amicably. He had been there an hour and ten minutes now. Every time he got nervous, he went in and bought a double with cheese and ate it. He had now eaten the equivalent of two triples and held the fourth in his hand. They were delicious, but eating while tense was making him feel sick.

He finished it, though. No point in wasting good food, and besides, who knew when they'd have time to eat again? He reflected that he was now left with about ten dollars, but no time for worrying about that, either.

He said into his walkie-talkie, "This is Big Guy calling Genius. You there, Genius?"

Black's voice said, "You bet, Big Guy. Moving out?"

"Moving out."

He keyed the car and put it in gear. Bennis was not entirely familiar with this car. But as a cop he'd gotten used to changing cars, and he had a sure sense that driving the same car more than a few hours could be fatal.

Sheryl Birch had been attacked. Elena Delgado had been killed. God only knew how many others. His own apartment had been blown up. His buddy Suze could be in trouble at this moment. Bennis was completely aware of being terrified—utterly, gut-deep terrified.

10000011

I HUDDLED NEAR a Japanese weeping spruce while I let my eyes become accustomed to the darkness. I was now a hundred feet from the SJR executive building and it wasn't far enough. It was far enough to see the building as a whole and not far enough to be out of its grip. It loomed over me. There were lights in more than half the rooms—did these people never go home?—and sometimes a person would appear in a window. Dean Utley was in there. It seemed almost within arm's reach.

Just as I was about to move farther back on the grounds, a security man came around the north end of the building. He glanced at the garbage port I'd come out. Why? Had I left anything out of place? Had I left the door ajar when I slid down the ramp?

I didn't dare watch the man. I was too near the building and my light-colored face would be visible if he should look this way.

I huddled farther into myself. I had worn a brown dress for more than one reason. I had on brown shoes as well, and now I folded into the clothing, tucking my hands, which would look white in this light, into my stomach as I bent over. Then I dropped my head forward, letting my dark hair fall over my face.

I held perfectly still.

I heard a *chunk-slam*. I *had* left the door ajar. I had slid down the ramp too suddenly to close it properly.

Would the guard be suspicious and think there was a person out here?

Unable to see, I listened. He could be coming toward me, for all I knew. He could have seen me and might be creeping toward me right now, feet silent on the grass. He could be standing right over me.

I heard footsteps on the cement walk near the building.

I listened without breathing. The footsteps receded.

1000100

DEAN UTLEY HAD not glanced at Howie since the moment he shot him. The need to deal with life directly, rather than at cyberdistance, had been too stressful. But now half an hour had gone by and he was feeling peaceful.

He got up from his keyboard and turned. Howie lay just a few feet away, his chin dropped and mouth open. He looked funny like that, quite amusing, really. Howie, who was always so proud of his alertness and intelligence. There was just a trickle of blood that had escaped from his forehead, and that small amount made a pool near his head.

The next thing to do was get him out of here. There might be people coming in later to report on the president. They were all people who were firmly on Utley's side, but he didn't want them to have to see Howie. It wasn't wise right now.

For a moment he thought of rolling Howie in the rug. But no—it was a beautiful Heriz, and it would be a crime to discard it. He'd get Zach to bring in some canvas, or a tarpaulin.

By the way, where is Zach?

10000101

WITH THE GUARD gone, I moved quickly away from the building. At a hundred yards, I came to the electric fence that kept the deer inside their landscaped Eden.

The deer park was really the only safe place for me to move through the grounds. I couldn't possibly walk the long drive without somebody coming by, some car, or a guard on foot. And in any case, I'd be visible from the central building most of the way and then later from the entry booth at the far end of the drive. The deer park, though, was wooded and full of cover.

The three strands of wire were placed strategically to discourage deer from trying to cross. The lowest was just below the level of my calf, the next at hip level, and the third, because deer could jump a seven-foot fence, was over my head.

Unfortunately, the lowest stand was too low to roll under and I couldn't step over the middle one.

Bennis and Jesus and Black and I had talked about this. Black had said that I could touch it; the current in the wire wasn't enough to kill the deer, not even enough to injure them.

"Yes," I'd said, "but I'm not a deer."

"You'll be all right."

Easier to say than to do.

I studied the ground behind me. No guards, and as far as I could tell nobody watching from any windows.

If you're going to do it, you might as well do it fast. I got my body ready to move, then reached out my left hand. I would push down the bottom strand and roll under the middle one.

One, two, three—go!

The shock in my hand was an intense buzz. The electricity made my hand contract around the wire for a second. But it wasn't strong enough to freeze me there, and in the next second I was through.

Not so bad. Not so bad. I'd been more scared than hurt. And that damned Black was right again!

I lay still and surveyed the area. Still no patrolling guard and nobody seemed to have given an alarm. But it was time to get moving. I had to get out of sight of the building by fading into some of the underbrush.

I zigzagged slowly, stopping every now and then, knowing it was motion that caught the eye, especially at night. Even here I was not as much out of sight of the building—I could see it and so it could see me—as I was now in among bushes and trees where my form wouldn't be noticed.

But motion would.

I stopped and looked and went on a few steps and stopped and looked. It was agonizing not to be able to go faster. Eight P.M. Bennis would be waiting for my signal by now. And at any moment somebody might find Zach.

The guard was coming back around the building the way he had gone. Hell! I thought he'd circle the area, not double back!

10000110

GRINNELL WALNITT PAUSED at the corner of the building. He had seen movement out in the park, and it didn't seem quite like a deer. He stopped and watched.

He saw it again. With those damn deer out there, how the hell did they think he was going to see an invader? What'd Utley need the damn things for? Walnitt had a deer in his own yard at home, a plaster one near the birdbath, and even that was too much. His wife's damn idea. Damn thing had to be picked up every time you wanted to mow the lawn.

10000111

ON HANDS AND knees, I made another short move forward. Then I angled to my left a few feet. Somewhere, sometime, I had read an espionage novel in which the hunted person was trying to escape across a meadow dotted with sheep. The idea was that sheep move aimlessly and people go in straight lines, and if you went in a meandering direction, the hunter would think you were an animal.

I moved off to my right, then stopped again.

The guard stayed on the walk, staring out into the grounds.

10001000

INSIDE SJR DATASYSTEMS, the PA system spoke.

"Zachary Massendate, please report to your office. You have an urgent phone call. Mr. Zachary Massendate . . ."

Utley, meanwhile, had decided to look for Zach himself. It was absolutely unheard of for Zach to disappear. He should have insisted Zach wear a live badge, like everybody else.

He'd see if there were any lights on in offices that shouldn't be occupied.

10001001

MY DRESS HAD a medium-length skirt, and when I crawled on hands and knees it dragged on the ground, making it harder for me to move. Still, for a while it protected my knees from the ground. Sometimes I was crawling on grass, but sometimes it was sandy and other times stony. My knees started to bleed. My hands were sore, but they were tougher, and except for sticking pine needles in them several times, they weren't cut.

As I crossed an area of grass and shrubs, I suddenly realized that a small group of four deer was directly ahead of me. The light breeze was blowing toward me. They had not seen, heard, or smelled me. But as soon as I got closer to them, they'd sense my presence. And if they all bolted suddenly and ran off, the guard might guess there was somebody in the park. I moved again, diagonally, and then saw one of the deer lift its head. I looked to my left and saw another deer, not five feet away from me. It was a doe. She lowered her head, sniffed toward me, turned her head at a different angle, as if curious about why a human being should be wandering around on hands and knees. Then with delicate steps, like a human stroking velvet, the doe walked slowly away. The other deer followed.

Oh, you darling, I said silently, with my lips. *You darling*.

I reached a denser part of the woods and with enormous relief stood up. The lower part of my back stabbed at me. I took two or three painful steps, and after another few steps felt better. I walked on cautiously. After five minutes I was nearing the gatehouse. Here I was again at the electric fence, but now I had no fear of it. I pushed down the lowest wire and rolled through, feeling the achy buzz, but not caring.

I moved fast toward a group of blue spruces Bennis and I had identified yesterday. There was a clump of beech closer to the gate, but they hadn't leafed out yet and gave very little cover.

From this position I could see the entry guard's booth, but

not the guard. The only windows in the booth were toward the front and driveway sides, not the back. Just as well.

I took a cigarette lighter from my pocket. I had wanted to carry a penlight, but Bennis had said if I was searched it would look suspicious. And so it would, but the light would have carried farther and been easier to direct.

In the darkness I tried to see past the guard's booth where the gate light confused my vision, across Catalpa Drive, past a low-slung house set far back in its own grounds, far across one corner of a golf course, to a spot where Norm Bennis should be waiting and watching.

I knew he would be there. Norm was a person you could count on.

I set my body so that the cigarette lighter was shielded from any observation to my back and sides. Then, holding it in my right hand, I clicked it on. The flame was surprisingly bright.

The guard's booth was only fifty feet away, just off Catalpa. If he stepped out, he'd see the light. But there was no reason for him to step out.

Now I passed my left hand in front of the light, held it there a full second, moved it away, waited a second, moved it back for a second, and repeated the process six times. Then I clicked off the lighter. I waited a minute, and did it again. I waited another minute—

I heard a car racing down some side street. Its lights were visible in the night. The tires shrieked as the car rounded a curve a couple of blocks away. Now it was speeding down Catalpa toward me.

Far behind it, I saw the whirling light of a police car flash on. A siren whooped.

The car was still speeding as it approached the SJR entrance, but with the police car coming up fast behind it, it gave up and came to a screaming stop, just at the SJR entrance.

The police car, an unmarked blue car with a temporary flashing light on top and another on its dash, pulled up behind. Bennis got out and approached the speeder.

Standing just behind the driver's window, he said, "May I see your license and registration, sir?"

There was a flurry of mixed Spanish and English from inside.

"License and registration," Bennis repeated, politely.

Jesus Delgado got out.

"I was'n speedin'," he said. He lurched slightly and laid his hand on the car.

"I'm sorry to say, sir, I clocked you at sixty-eight. This is a thirty-five mile an hour zone."

"I was'n speedin'." Delgado waved his arms. He turned to the guard. "Was I speedin'? I was not speedin'."

In the passenger seat of Delgado's car, Black tried to look embarrassed.

The guard walked halfway over.

"I was'n speedin'. Did you see me speedin'?" Delgado said belligerently to the guard. I slipped behind the guard booth. Delgado said, "Tell this man I was'n speedin'."

I ducked under the gate bar, slipped out the gate, and began walking down Catalpa, staying on the grass so as not to make loud footfalls.

Bennis said, "This man isn't a witness. You were speeding down *there*." He gestured back down Catalpa in the direction they'd come from, opposite my direction of flight. The guard watched and nodded.

I disappeared around the corner.

10001010

SIX BLOCKS DOWN Catalpa, Bennis picked me up.

"My man, I was never so glad in my life as when I saw your light."

"I was never so glad in my life as when I saw your car."

"You get it?"

"I got it. And more."

"What?"

"I'll tell you all when we get there. We'd better move it. Speaking of speeding, you think the guard knew you weren't a local cop?"

"Not a chance. People don't really look at cops' uniforms."

"Yeah. And it wouldn't matter anyway."

Bennis caught the Tri-State and in five minutes was pulling into a late-night McDonald's.

Delgado and Black were waiting.

I said, "We have more trouble than we thought. On the way out of the memorial service, Howie Borke whispered something to me."

"What?"

"He said, 'They're going to kill the president.' "

Silence.

Finally, Black said, "Well, do we believe this?"

"It was Howie, the nice one. The one who cried when he talked about Sheryl."

"Sure. Nice. He's one of them."

Bennis said, "They could be trying to throw us off the scent."

I said, "Yes. But we can't chance it, can we? The president is in Chicago. It fits."

Max said, "And it's *big* enough for Utley."

Then I told them what I'd done to Zach. Delgado, who still wasn't talking much, just smiled. But after a couple of seconds Black said, "Wouldn't have hurt to kill him, Suze. They'd have to cover it up."

I was startled. Of all of us, Max was the cool one.

"All right, folks," I said. "Black, here's the paper. I hope."

Black took the list of three passwords. "Great! This better be it. We'll only have one chance."

"Okay. Let's move it. The only change of plan is that

Bennis and I will try to get word to somebody that the president is in danger. Unless you, Jesus—did you find out whether you're still in good shape with the department?"

"No. I called a friend. My jacket says I'm on indefinite leave pending resolution of a claim that I, quote, 'used my accounting oversight post to embezzle funds.'"

I said firmly, "Damn. Well, we couldn't have expected them to miss that chance. Okay, Jesus and Max, you've got the passwords. Bennis and I know what we've gotta do. Let's get moving."

10001011

BENNIS DROVE TO another all-night restaurant, this one on US-41 just west of Glencoe. We got out of the car and went into the restaurant. I said, "You order. I'm gonna call Gimball first. Injured or not, he's gotta be told about the president."

It was now eleven P.M., and I was not surprised that Mrs. Gimball sounded sleepy and annoyed.

"I'm sorry," Mrs. Gimball said. "He's had an accident. He's only been home from the hospital a couple of hours. You'll have to call the first deputy."

"Mrs. Gimball, I wouldn't intrude ordinarily. This is a special task force and the superintendent wanted me to report directly to him and nobody else. If you'd just tell him this is Officer Susannah Figueroa—"

"He's under sedation."

"This is extremely urgent. There's a threat to kill the president while he's here in Chicago. Superintendent Gimball would *really want to know*."

Silence. "Well—I can try to tell him. But he's too sick to do anything about it—"

"He can pass the word. I can't."

"I said I'd try."

"Tell him it's Dean Utley at SJR DataSystems."

"This Dean Utley is calling?"

"No! Utley's the one who is going to kill the president!"

"I'll write it down."

"And you'll tell him?"

"I'll tell him."

After we hung up, I said to Norm, "I don't have a lot of confidence in that."

10001100

MRS. GIMBALL, WHO was Gimball's second wife, but had been around long enough to know that serious things could happen and if not informed her husband *could* be very annoyed, took the paper and went over to where he slept.

"Gus?"

He'd been given a strong sedative at nine P.M., when their doctor came by the house. She knew her husband was extremely ill, because he had been too sick even to make a joke about a doctor making house calls.

"Gus?" She tapped his hand several times. His head was bandaged where he'd cut it falling, and even though the doctor said the skull fracture itself wasn't dangerous, he'd been in X-ray for two hours. They let him come home, but wanted him back in two days to look for "hidden damage." The whole thing scared her badly.

She didn't dare shake him to wake him up. "Gus! Gus!" she shouted. That couldn't hurt him, could it?

Mumbling, he said, "Huh?"

"Officer Figueroa called."

"Huh?"

"*Officer Figueroa!*"

"Whaa-at?" He started to open his eyes, but it must have hurt him to try and he closed them immediately.

"Officer Figueroa! She says somebody named Dean Utley is going to assassinate the president."

"President, the president of—ah—president of—president of what?"

"Of the United States, I suppose."

"Who said this?" He was still mumbling, but she understood him.

"Susannah Figueroa."

"I don't understand. Do I know her?"

Mrs. Gimball said, "You'd better go back to sleep."

10001101

BENNIS SAID, "Look up the Secret Service."

In the Chicago white pages the government agencies were listed in a blue-edged section in the front. "I can't find it," I said. "No, wait. It's under Treasury Department. Okay. Here it is—300 South Riverside Plaza."

"I've only got two quarters left."

"Well, you can't use your calling card."

"Here's a five."

"I'll buy us both some more coffee and get change." When I got back Bennis was saying into the phone, "Listen, I've been an employee of SJR DataSystems for years, and I know what I'm talking about. No, I'm not going to tell you my name! There might be reprisals. These people are ruthless!"

I passed him his coffee and he sipped. Blinking, he put it down. It was too hot.

"Look, I don't know how they're gonna get him. They've staged automobile accidents, and I know they make control systems for the presidential helicopters—no, I realize that isn't likely. They stage hospital errors, gas leaks. No, I don't know! It's your job to protect him. Just change his schedule; that oughta help. No, I'm *not* going to tell you my name. What difference does my name make anyhow? *Well, you just do that.*"

He hung up. I said, "Well?"

"They'll take 'special care.' Isn't that wonderful? But the subtext was that they're already taking such perfect care it can't be improved on."

"Uh-huh. Now I'd better call the FBI."

"They're at 219 South Dearborn. Here you go."

The result was much the same, although the operator wrote down meticulously and without comment all the information Bennis gave her.

We called the White House and spoke to a staffer. He, too, wrote the message down.

I said, "One more and then we've gotta move to a different phone."

I dialed 911, left the message, and then we moved out fast. Our next stop was a White Castle.

Using the FOP handbook, Bennis called the superintendent's office at the CPD, then the superintendent's executive secretary, then the superintendent's executive assistant, administrative assistant, and for good measure, the Internal Affairs Division. Then all five deputy superintendents. All had machines on. He left the information fast, but did not identify himself. I was saying, "Move it! Move it!"

"Let me do this last one," I said, when he was off the phone.

Fred Holzer was a reporter with a strong sense that anything could happen, and I had met him several times. I called his home. He wasn't there.

"You didn't really expect him to be here, did you?" his wife said. "At home? *Home?* He passes through here, oh, every few days, whether he needs it or not."

I dialed the Back Room bar.

"Sure, old Freddy's here. Hang on."

"Yo?"

"Fred, it's Susannah Figueroa."

"Hey, how's it?"

My heart sank. Fred drunk was no bad thing. Fred *really* drunk was a problem.

"Fred, put that glass down immediately and listen. The story of your career has just come on the line."

I told him a lot of it. I told him they were going to kill the president. And they'd killed Elena Delgado. I left Sheryl out.

"You sayin' a billion-dollar U.S. corporation is psychopathic, Figueroa?"

"Yes."

"Well, shit. I can surely believe that. I'll get right onto it."

"Yeah, but Fred. Don't just get *onto* the story. Find some way of warning the president. In some way so his people won't think you're nuts."

"That's harder. But I'll see what I can do. I got contacts."

"I know that. That's why I called you. And Fred?"

"What?"

"Do this before you have another drink."

"Yo."

10001110

FRED HUNG UP. He nodded twice to himself. It was a very bizarre idea, a rogue corporation, and he did, in fact, believe it. He said to the bartender, "The story of the century just phoned."

Fred was not only well known, he was good at his job. He didn't use superlatives casually. The bartender said, "Hey. That's excellent."

"Yeah. Gimme just one drink to celebrate before I leave."

10001111

OUTSIDE THE WHITE Castle, I said, "Why don't I have a good feeling about this?"

"We've done what we can, my man. About the president, at least."

"True. We'd better get going. Plus, we've got work to do."

"So move!"

10010000

BLACK REREAD THE piece of paper several times as they sped through the night, with Jesus driving. Not that there was much on the paper to read, only the three passwords with their logins, but he kept trying to guess which was the important one, the trigger password, the one that had almost gotten Sheryl Birch killed.

Jesus was driving a new Cadillac he had been loaned by a friend who had a Cadillac agency. Jesus claimed to want to buy one.

The friend said, "You been taking bribes, Jesus?" That was so close to what Utley had planted in his personnel record that Jesus winced. "My aunt died," he said. "Left me money."

"Oh. Whattaya need it overnight for? People don't test Cadillacs. They already know they want one."

"Hey! It's this or a Porsche. You want to convince me or not?"

"Well, hell. Go ahead."

They headed down Northwest Highway, which is not a highway by present standards, and in fact is an old trading trail. About midnight they were wending their way through the western part of Skokie, through what seemed to Black an endless residential area where the street names all began with "K"—Keating, Kilpatrick, Knox, Kenton, Kolmar, Kilbourne, Kenneth, Kostner—then finally east on Oakton, then south to Howard, checking the rearview mirror all the while.

Jesus said, "Looks okay."

"You're the expert."

By now they were only half a mile from their goal, a warehouse in the industrial part of Skokie. Jesus slipped across a school parking lot and U-turned, coming up behind the field house near the baseball diamond. From here they could see in all directions. There was very little traffic anywhere. This was a late Monday night in a suburb that had a large but quiet population. Even on Howard, which was a main artery, there was only an occasional car.

"Okay. Looks good."

Jesus drove them to the alley behind an enormous, elderly brick warehouse. They parked and got out, Black carrying a small bag. The building overlooking them from the rear was newer, made of vertical boards of some composition material, painted blue. There were no windows on this side. Black had checked this on their drive past this morning, but he already was sure of it from seeing the building plans.

Now he took a hammer from his bag. He walked twenty feet down the alley to one of the several small-paned windows in the old building. Putting on a glove to protect his hand, he broke out a pane of the glass. Then he reached in and unlocked the window.

"Shit! What if there's an alarm?"

"Front door has an alarm. The shipping port has an alarm. The windows don't."

"You can't be sure. What if they put in alarms after their last zoning application?"

"Jesus. Be a grown-up. They put everything that can possibly impress the city into their application. *Less* actually gets put into the building, not more."

They climbed in the window.

"Well, Jesus, how do you feel?"

"What do you mean?"

"Here you are, a career cop, twelve years of service to the department, and now you're guilty of breaking and entering. Doesn't it worry you?"

Jesus' face didn't change and his voice was expressionless. "Not for one, single, tiny, fucking second."

"Good."

There was a safety light at this end of the huge, echoing building, and through the arch at the end of the large room in which they stood, they could see another safety light in the farther room. The bulbs were forty watts at most. The whole large space was lost in a mustard-colored gloom.

"What's that smell?"

"Glue."

The end where they stood was piled with stacks of corrugated cardboard, some of the stacks five feet by eight feet and ten feet high. In the farther room were smaller stacks, piles of oddly shaped cardboard, and cutters. Some of the cutters were like giant jigsaws. Others were die-cutters that worked like large stamps.

"Fire alarms, they got," Black said. "Burglar alarms, they don't care so much. Who's gonna steal ten tons of corrugated cardboard?"

While Jesus stared at the warehouse, thinking it had something of the funeral parlor about it, Black took a small pane of glass and tub caulk from his bag and replaced the glass he had broken in the window.

"No cop's gonna notice that now," he said.

"Right. Let's get the stuff."

Unlocking the side door from inside, they went out and brought three boxes of equipment from the car.

Black said, "Oughta be over here."

Beyond the divider that separated the warehouse into two large spaces was an interior divider. It boxed off a small space, smaller than a cheap motel room. Inside were several filing cabinets, two metal desks, two metal desk chairs, a cheap sofa very much like one from a cheap motel, a typewriter, a computer keyboard, a monitor, and a piece of telephone wire attached to the system that Black pointed to with a fierce delight far beyond the apparent importance of a few feet of drab cord.

"I knew it! Look, Jesus, there's the modem!"

It was a direct modem line to the parent company, SJR DataSystems.

10010001

I SAID TO Bennis, "Now we can start laying the trail."

"Not only that, now we can get real cash!"

"And draw Utley's attention away from Max and Jesus."

We found a cash station in a terrace outside a mall. Bennis got $200, and so did I. With any luck, the word would go into Utley that we were about to do something big, and that we were west of Chicago, in the suburbs.

Bennis and I sped south. Southwest of Chicago, there was an all-night hardware store—actually, one of those home improvement centers, where you could buy just about anything to build or tear down just about anything else. There we bought two shovels, a pry bar and a crowbar, wire cutters with insulated handles, a soldering iron with several rolls of solder, and a Makita cordless saw that cops call "the burglar's friend." All this we charged on one of my charge cards.

Now, if Utley's surveillance was as good as we thought it was, he should be thinking that Bennis and I were going to do some serious digging.

We packed this booty into the car and got on I-290, heading back toward SJR. Near O'Hare, we stopped at a motel. We were now only four or five miles from SJR DataSystems, certainly close enough to make a late-night raid if we wanted to.

Bennis checked in, carrying a bag, and charged the night on his charge card. Then, while I took the car to a diner named Ollie's to pick up coffee and two ham sandwiches, Bennis opened the bed, got in, rumpled it around, then went into the bathroom and shaved, flipping soapsuds and hair in all directions. He turned on the shower, wrinkled up a towel and soaked a washcloth. He left a pair of my pantyhose in the lowest drawer of the fake wood dresser, and left by a back stair, hiking out to the street corner, where I picked him up.

We drove back into Chicago and parked out of sight between two dumpsters in an alley off Division. Bennis crawled into the back seat and fell asleep and I, being smaller, curled up in the front seat and tried to sleep under the steering wheel. Once during the night a street person wearing three coats came by and rattled the door handle. Bennis and I sat up at the same time, pointed our service revolvers at him, and he flapped away fast.

10010010

HENRY DELUSK SAID to Utley, "They've just checked into a motel in Rosemont."

"Interesting."

"Maybe they're scared and getting out of town."

"I don't believe it. They're too near here. Send out a team."

"Our team can't very well break into a motel."

"They may have to. But first, find their car in the motel lot. Then you'll know if they're there."

"We don't know their car. They changed cars."

"Then pay off the desk man, damn it!"

10010011

IT HAD TAKEN Jesus and Max Black an hour to get Black set up. They didn't turn on any building lights, because they didn't want to go out of their way to attract attention, but Black thought they were relatively safe. "The Cadillac was a good idea," he said. "If a cop sees it, he'll think we're owners of a business around here."

"He'll think we're drug dealers."

"Not in this neighborhood, he won't. It's a low-crime area."

They set up, then Black tried the equipment. He felt around in the warehouse computer, rummaging through its files to gain confidence in what it contained before he mounted the invasion of SJR.

"Once I get in, if the sysop sees me, one kill command and we're locked out for good."

Jesus watched Black for a while, fascinated by his eager face and the way his eyes, greenish in the light from the monitor, glittered and darted as he studied the screen. Jesus wandered around the place. Ninety-five percent of the stock was standard brown corrugated cardboard. The die-cutters were mostly for stamping the cardboard sheeting into patterns that were then folded or glued into SJR DataSystems exterior packaging— the heavy brown shipping boxes that went over the inner, glossier packaging with the four-color pictures and company name and the list of wonderful things most of which the object inside the box could do for the purchaser. There were a few stacks of glossy board for something called Server 9.9. The word and numbers were in raised silver metallic letters, which glimmered in the dark, shadowy warehouse.

"Hey, Jesus!"

"What?" He had jumped six inches when Black called.

"Are you ready?"

They had a printer in place for hardcopy and disks to download whatever they found. But the pièce de résistance was the set of two videocameras—if one didn't work, the other would—for Jesus to tape what happened.

Jesus started both cameras. He was going to videotape not only the screen but everything Black did as well. The cameras were supposed to be synchronizable to the rate at which a monitor screen is scanned. If not, with the camera scanning the monitor screen at a different rate from the screen itself, they would get roll. It would either look like the picture had a dark band moving down it, or the whole picture might roll. But with two cameras on very slightly different scan speeds, they would be unlikely to miss anything.

"Ready."

Black slipped into the modem lines, and in a fraction of a second traveled the distance to SJR, fifteen miles away. On the screen was the SJR system display, as well as the words 3.1 station. He knew this meant his remote station was named 3.1 and if anybody at SJR specifically looked to see who was in the system, they would find him. And wonder what the cardboard warehouse was doing on-line at this hour of the night.

"Uh-oh. No high-speed gateway," he said.

"We didn't expect it," Jesus said.

"But we hoped. This will take longer. One wrong step and they'll flush me."

They hadn't expected it to be that easy. Universities used high-speed gateways. Cautious corporations used them only to call out, because they were much less secure.

Black was tense, but turned on and mentally soaring. "This is why we brought a new modem," he said.

"Why?" To Black, Jesus sounded nervous.

"This one can push us to 70 k-baud ISDN."

"What if it doesn't work?"

"I'll mutter an incantation."

"What if—"

"Please, Jesus. Quiet. I'm going into hack mode."

He tried the hardass file first. Thinking like Sheryl had, it seemed the most peculiar name. And he found the long, coded file. He had no time to try data-junction on it and didn't want to. Instead he downloaded the file onto the disk they'd brought and for extra backup started printing out hardcopy on two printers they'd brought. In addition, the videocamera would record him doing this. Then he got out of the file like a scalded cat running for cover.

"Hope the others are more—"

He didn't finish his sentence. As he was speaking he went to the botulism file. It came up immediately. With a long history as a tiger team invader, and with a much more suspicious nature than Sheryl, he knew faster than Sheryl had that this was it. He found Kiro Ogata. He found the Hinkley Memorial alteration.

"Ohhhh," he said. "You bastards." Jesus leaned forward. Jesus was amazed, too. Before them was the perfectly simple menu of options for altering hospital records. All you needed was a keystroke. Jesus shook his head. Black said, "It's a good thing we have a faster modem. There's a lot here."

"Max, we knew they *must* be doing this, but I never really believed it."

"Eat flaming death, Dean Utley."

"Will they abort the whole program if they see we've been in?"

"They might. Let's get in fast and get out fast."

10010100

"THEY BOUGHT SHOVELS and wire cutters and soldering irons," Utley said to Zach. "When the sister was here, could she have been looking for where our phone lines are buried?" Both studiously avoided mentioning Howie's body, which still lay on the floor.

"We know she went out through the park."

"If she couldn't get anything useful in the office—" Utley stopped and thought. "Surely they wouldn't expect to dig down to the cable without anybody seeing them?"

"There's a long section outside our fence. It runs a mile along Catalpa at least. Some of it's in the woods."

"I want security out along the road all night."

"All of them?"

"Certainly not! If this is a feint, they may come over the fence and get into the cable in here. I want the perimeter patrolled. Call in some of the day staff if you have to."

"Okay."

"Did the team get to the motel?"

"Yes. No car."

"They're not there! I knew it!"

"Well, we'll cover ourselves here."

"Seen any trace of Delgado and Black?"

Zach said, "No," apprehensively.

"Those two are more dangerous. They have the technical smarts."

"What can we do about it until they surface somewhere?"

"Keep a team ready to go the instant we find them."

Zach was next to him, in a chair pulled over from Utley's boardroom area in the other part of the office. Zach was bruised, sore, and furious at Figueroa. Henry DeLusk was on Utley's other side in another chair. Reports were coming in occasionally on the speaker from the three teams of security people who were out hunting houses and hangouts for Figueroa, Delgado, Black, and Bennis. It had only been a couple of hours since they realized Black was involved, and Black worried Utley more than the other three put together.

Henry DeLusk was almost petrified with fear. "What if somebody comes here? What if they find the body?"

"No problem. Zach and Glen are going to take Howie away soon."

"What if somebody finds the program?"

"We'll use it and then delete it. Henry, you are beginning to bother me."

Henry shut up.

Utley went on. "You're not thinking. We use it once more, in a few hours, and then we erase it. Once it's gone, it's gone. It doesn't exist. Cyberspace doesn't exist. When we take it off the disk, it never was, just like turning off the beam of a flashlight."

"I know that," DeLusk said.

Utley said, "Zach, Glen, you'd better get Howie into the car."

"Sure, Mr. Utley," Zach said.

"When you've done that, stay on the radio. I'll let you know when to go ahead with the second part."

"What second part?" DeLusk asked.

"We're going to put just a little extra pressure on Ms. Figueroa to keep her mouth shut."

After Zach and Glen left with Howie's body, wrapped in

brown paper and on a handcart, Utley ran who to check who was on his system. He sat suddenly upright.

"Somebody's in the warehouse in Skokie."

DeLusk looked at the screen. "Figueroa?"

"No. It's too subtle. It's got to be Black."

DeLusk had his nerve back, now that Howie's body was out of the room and soon to be moving out of the compound. "Should I send Zach and Glen?"

"It'll take too long. Call the field team that's closest to the warehouse. Tell them to grab whoever it is and bring them here."

"Right. And cut off contact!" DeLusk said.

Utley said, "No, *don't cut the contact.* If we do, they'll leave. *I want them!*"

10010101

MAX BLACK TRIED the last file, `celeste`. It didn't seem to have any criminal content.

"I'm giving this one up," he said to Delgado.

"Good enough."

"Perfect, in fact."

"Let's clean up and get out of here."

Delgado turned off the cameras. Black picked up some of the gear and took it to the car. He came back for more.

Now they did everything in reverse. They removed the equipment and began to wipe down surfaces they'd touched.

On the west border of Skokie, a team from SJR screamed off the Edens Expressway onto Dempster Street eastbound.

10010110

AT FOUR A.M., the president woke up with a splitting headache. He woke the First Lady and told her, "I think I'm having a stroke."

"Oh, my Lord! Really?" She sat up and put the light on.

"Well, not really. It's not all in one spot. But it's the worst headache I've ever had in my life."

"Try to go back to sleep."

But at four-thirty, she had a stabbing headache, too. And the president's was worse.

"Maybe we've been poisoned."

The president started to vomit.

The First Lady called the Secret Service agent from the anteroom.

"We can fly you to D.C. with fifteen minutes' notice," he said to the president.

"No."

"It's SOP."

"I'm not getting on any plane. Not feeling like this, I'm not!"

By five A.M., the Secret Service had transferred the president and First Lady to U-Hosp.

10010111

UTLEY'S TEAM APPROACHED the warehouse with drawn guns. There was no visible light, but there wouldn't be if the men inside knew what they were doing.

Silently, they moved to the rear doors. There was a large overhead door for loading trucks, but they bypassed that and went to the smaller office door.

"Try it."

One of the men turned the knob slowly. The door was un-locked.

He pushed it open and found that it moved silently. Inside, all was dark. But in the gloom there was enough spill from streetlights at the building's front to see that the space was di-vided. There was a small area, which they took to be office, walled off at the far side.

They slipped silently across the floor.

Outside the office they paused. The man in front raised a hand and lowered it, meaning "one." He raised and lowered it again, meaning "two." He raised it again and when he dropped it, meaning "three," they burst into the office together.

No one was there.

The first man put his hand on the back of the computer monitor. It was still slightly warm.

10011000

DR. LENNOX WAS the dean of Chicago gastroenterologists. He'd written the book, formed the department, developed the treatments, and even had a disease named after him. Lennox's disease was a rare microbial infection spread by the droppings of infected ostriches and some related South American flight-less birds. It caused arthralgia and sometimes heart valve dam-age.

Lennox, white-haired, tall, smooth-shaven and authorita-tive, was exactly the man to be talking to the sick president. He was an immensely reassuring presence.

"I'm sorry this had to happen to you in our city, Mr. Presi-dent," he said.

The president was resting slightly easier now, because of

some painkillers. But not much. Waves of nausea swept over him. Plus diarrhea. He always found diarrhea to be extremely embarrassing, and especially now. He was too weak to get out of bed; people had to come and give him a bedpan. He couldn't even sit up without being stabbed through the head by the worst headache he could ever remember.

In fact, he wished this pleasant and reassuring doctor would just leave him alone. But he was curious, too.

"What have I got?" he asked.

"Salmonella. Practically everybody who went to the dinner has it."

"Is Rose sick?"

"I'm sorry to say the First Lady is just about as sick as you are."

"Oh, hell." Then he groaned, "Ohhhhhhhhhhh!" He had tried to raise his head. Big mistake.

"Don't move. Lie still."

"What was it in?"

"The warm slaw salad, we think. Probably got into the sour cream."

"So we haven't been poisoned?" The president tried to smile. It made him feel nauseated.

"No. The stuff isn't fatal. It's just one of those things, I guess. The Bierstube staff is horribly upset."

"They oughta be."

"Some of them are sick, too."

"They oughta be."

Dr. Lennox laughed. "Well, in a couple of days I think you'll be back on your feet. There shouldn't be any long-term ill effects. I could get you up a little sooner with antibiotics."

"Better not. I'm allergic."

"Oh. To which?"

The president thought he could doze off now. "Most," he said sleepily.

"Is that right?"

"Yeah. All my life."

"Well. It won't make a lot of difference. We're keeping you hydrated and salmonella is self-limiting."

"So is life."

Dr. Lennox chuckled again. "I know you feel rotten. But you'll turn the corner soon."

"Well, thanks, I guess." The president hoped that the man would leave now. And in fact he did.

Lennox closed the door softly behind him and nodded at the Secret Service agents on guard. It was all very exciting, being temporary physician to the president, especially for the first half hour, while they thought it might be poison and he, Lennox, might save the president's life. Then it turned out to be nothing very taxing to Lennox's skills after all. Garden variety food poisoning.

Lennox was tired, but he typed the president's allergy into the data system before he left.

10011001

I TRIED TO keep focused. But my mind wanted to check on JJ, wanted to check on Sheryl—was there brain damage? Would she ever truly recover?

"I need coffee," I said to Black. "I've just spent the night trying to sleep with my head under a steering wheel."

"Why not the other way around?"

"Feet under the steering wheel? Try it sometime. You don't have space to fold up your legs."

We were at a very popular but not very stylish diner on Hyde Park Avenue in south Chicago. Plastic-topped tables, red plastic booth seating, pictures of Michael Jordan and Mike Ditka everywhere. Bennis ordered eight eggs, scrambled.

The waiter offered me decaf, which I declined. I waited

until he was gone, then snorted. "Decaf! Decaf! You might as well open your mouth and let the moon shine in."

After a swallow of coffee, I said, "Okay, Black. You said you got it. Did you get it?"

"Yup," Black said. "We copied our tapes in the lab at the University of Chicago. We left copies at the FBI office, the Secret Service office, the Cook County Sheriff's office just for good measure, and the CPD. We phoned later to confirm the copies were logged in. We modemed two tapes and overnight-mailed two hardcopies to Washington. I don't know what else we can do."

I said, "Jesus, you didn't walk into the CPD, did you?"

With a stoniness that covered his sorrow, he said, "Of course not. *Max* went in. I waited in the car and—"

I said, "And?"

"Hid my face."

That had hurt him. Jesus loved being a cop. "All right," I said, "we are staying alive, but we aren't winning the war."

"What can we do?" Bennis said.

"We don't have proof that Utley attacked Sheryl. Even with the program, there's no proof the change in blood type ever took place. We don't have proof that Utley torched Jesus' house. And as far as the president is concerned, I have serious doubts that anybody believes us. Even if they do, they probably think they're taking all the precautions possible."

Black nodded. "I hate to say it, but I think you're right."

Jesus said, "Yeah."

"Well, damn it!" Bennis said. "We've done all we can. What are we supposed to do, take over the government?"

"No. But if we had proof that they killed Frieswyk, we could get the cops to move in on Utley."

Jesus said, "I've been trying to do that for two months. Maybe we're just beaten."

Bennis, Black, and I said, "No!"

I continued, "If we could just figure out where Frieswyk was for those twelve hours! He's got to have left some trace—

hair, blood, clothing fibers. I don't see them keeping him at SJR. There are a lot of legitimate workers there."

"Right," Black said.

"So where was he?"

Black said to me, "Tell me every single thing Sheryl ever said to you about Utley."

I did. I told him about Utley's puzzles, the clothes his two Blue Blazers wore, his home computing system, his company history as far as I'd heard it, his deer, his teak office, his several wives, his parties at home, his croton plants, the coffee table made from the huge chunk of early computer, his amaryllis plants . . .

"*Amaryllis plants!*" Jesus shouted, knocking over his and Bennis' coffee, which flowed across the table and into Black's lap.

10011010

"WOULD YOU REMEMBER if you let a police officer, maybe along with a civilian, up to Mr. Dean Utley's apartment on February fourteenth?"

The John Hancock Building security guard was splendidly uniformed and very professional. Our CPD identification was enough to convince him we deserved help. Unfortunately, it had been a long time since February 14. "We don't keep names of the people we let up. We call upstairs and if the tenant agrees to let the person come up, that's it."

"Would anybody else here remember if a cop did go up, say early afternoon on February fourteenth?"

"I really doubt it, my friend. Lemme look and see who was on duty."

After a minute or so, he came back.

"Couldn't have been a guest for Mr. Utley. He asked us to hold his mail that day. And the fifteenth. Said he wasn't going to be home."

We walked outdoors to talk. There was a large courtyard outside the building, facing on Michigan Avenue. We stood around a bench. I said, "Now what does *that* mean? Shit!"

Jesus said, "Yeah. Hell!"

Black said, "No, no. I think if anything it confirms that Frieswyk was held there."

I folded my arms. "All right, genius. Why?"

"Say I found out that morning that Frieswyk was suspicious. What *I'd* do is this. I'd offer to meet him and explain. I'd get one of the troubleshooters—"

"Debuggers. Zach or Glen."

"Yes, Zach or Glen, to meet Frieswyk outside the CPD and bring him over here. I'd tell the building's office that I wasn't going to be in, so if anybody ever got suspicious and checked— which isn't likely—there would be a record that I wasn't there. I would tell Zach or Glen to call up to some prearranged *other* apartment—one where the people were out of town and I could set a temporary call-forwarding. The desk calls up to ask if the visitors are legitimate; I say, yes, send up the guests for Mr. Jones, and they'd go to Utley's apartment and that's it. That's all she wrote. Hold him here until dark. Walk him to a car in the evening with a gun in his ribs. Take him to the company airplane. Nobody has connected the name Utley with the cop who visits. Not that anybody is ever going to care, anyhow, because Frieswyk's going into the lake and never be heard from again."

Bennis said, "Just as well *you're* not on their side."

I said, "But how would Utley know whose phone could be used that way?"

"That building is full of extremely rich people. They've all got every telephone gadget known to man. Personally, I'd guess SJR installed a few specialized systems there."

"Oh. Oh, yeah. Oh, hell!"

"As a matter of fact, he might not have to pick somebody who isn't home, either. He could enter the phone system he installed and call-forward to SJR long enough to catch the call. Say you're home. Would you know that your calls had been deflected for fifteen minutes?"

"No."

"We're going to have to get into that apartment."

"We don't have time to fine-tune this," Black said.

Bennis said, "Let's try the authority route."

10011011

THE BODY OF Howie Borke had been folded into a heavy cardboard box ordinarily used as the exterior cover box for shipping the Workstation Package: monitor, auxiliary drive, keyboard, and a whole lot of manuals and documentation.

Zach said, "It's amazing how small a space a human body can fit into."

Glen said, "It's amazing the way your face looks like a sunrise." There were red, blue, yellow, and green bruises on Zach's face.

"I'm going to get even with that woman."

The outside of the box read: "Another shipment of performance and convenience from SJR DataSystems."

"Think Howie'd be pleased?" Glen asked, smiling.

Zach wasn't really happy about Glen's laughing attitude toward this. Although he thought Howie was a prick, they'd worked with him. He said, "No."

Glen said, "There's extra space. Do we bubble-wrap him?"

Zach said, "No!"

Dean Utley came to watch them load the box into the car. He got into his own car.

"I'll be back by noon," Utley said. "I just need some sleep. Four hours is about all I ever need."

"How can you sleep when we're about to finish cutworm?"

"I've taken care of the president. Henry is holding the fort. I'll be back in time to celebrate. Now, you know what you're supposed to do? It's eight-thirty now. You get to the school at nine-ten. I'll forward to my car phone at nine-oh-five, to be on the safe side."

"No problem," Zach said.

Glen said, "Piece of cake."

10011100

DR. LENNOX HAD been in U-Hosp the evening before caring for a fellow physician, an old friend who had been vomiting blood. He had gone home—walked, in fact, to his apartment in Lake Point Towers—and had been called back at six A.M. to consult on the condition of the president. Then, convinced that it was just a simple salmonellosis—simple to the doctor, but not to the patient—he went home to bed. At seven all of the staff changed over. At 9:15 A.M. the senior physician in charge of the medical wing, Dr. Biskupic, looked in on the president, after examining his medical chart on the screen. The president was sleeping under light sedation and the doctor thought that was probably the best thing for him.

Ten minutes later, he said to the chief nurse on the unit, "Didn't Lennox order any antibiotic for our VIP?"

"No, I don't see it on the screen."

"I wonder why not. He's not allergic to anything, is he?"

"I'll double-check."

They both scanned the chart on the monitor carefully.

This was not a patient to make mistakes with. Sometimes physicians didn't use antibiotics in salmonellosis cases because it tended to prolong the time that the patient, though cured of the illness, was a carrier of the bacteria. On the other hand, it tended to shorten the course of the disease and avoid possible complications. In this case, getting the patient back on his feet as quickly as possible was unusually important.

"I guess not."

"No, nothing," the nurse said.

"I don't want our Very Important Person developing some complication," the doctor said.

The nurse laughed. "Absolutely not."

"Not on *my* watch. Well, let's give him amoxicillin IV. You can start it without waking him."

10011101

"WE CAN'T WAIT for Mr. Utley," Bennis said. The guard had bumped them up to his superior, and he was now showing the security supervisor his CPD star. Jesus and I both got ours out, too. The guard looked at Black.

"This is my identification," Black said, holding out his University of Chicago library card and flipping it away fast.

"Black is a specialist in detecting sabotage. It is absolutely essential to Mr. Utley and the safety of the building's electrical supply that we get inside that apartment."

The supervisor was convinced, but professionally cautious. He said, "All right." I relaxed. "Jackson will go with you." I stiffened again.

Bennis said, "Excellent! Maybe he can give us a hand."

"He'll observe." To Jackson, the supervisor said, "You'll observe."

"Yes, sir."

10011110

THE SECURITY CHIEF gave Jackson the passkey, but as soon as the cops were out of his office, he phoned the work number he had for Utley. The call was forwarded from SJR to Utley's car, now heading home on the Kennedy Expressway.

10011111

UTLEY'S CAR PHONE rang. For a few seconds after learning that Figueroa, Bennis, Black, and Delgado were in his apartment, he thought of calling Zach and Glen back. But JJ was his trump card. And as far as getting somebody to rush down from SJR—he was already less than ten minutes away, and they were an hour away. He could handle it. The element of surprise was everything.

He had scarcely hung up when the phone rang again. It was the principal at JJ's school. "Is Ms. Figueroa there?"

"No, I'm sorry," Utley said. "There's been a family emergency. Can I help you?"

"This is George Gosling, from Cranbill Elementary. Is Robert Birch there?"

"Speaking."

"I have a man in my office claiming to be from JJ Figueroa's home. You know we don't let children leave the school without confirmation."

"That would be Bryn Hopkins?"

"Yes."

"Yes, please let him bring JJ home. We've had a family illness."

"Yes, I heard. I'm very sorry—"

"We've had another crisis. JJ's mother is ill. I'd rather you let us tell him that, though." Utley let his voice break slightly.

"Say no more."

10100000

BENNIS, BLACK, DELGADO, and I stood with Jackson in the door to Utley's apartment. The city of Chicago and Lake Michigan beyond dominated everything, a dusty blue panorama that wrapped around three sides of the apartment.

"Come on in, Mr. Jackson," I said. "We have to scan the rooms for sabotage equipment."

We walked through the large vestibule. We had no warrant, and if the cops knew where we were they'd arrest us, not Utley. What was more, we would probably have an illegal search and seizure problem if we found amaryllis plants. Nevertheless, we had to find them. The department would take us seriously if we showed them the connection. Seriously enough that we might save the president from whatever they had planned for him.

"Mr. Jackson, please follow us into the living room. It's a good thing you're here. You can witness anything we find."

10100001

UTLEY PARKED IN the garage, three levels belowground. The key-operated elevator took him directly to the ninety-first floor.

10100010

"THOSE ARE AMARYLLIS plants, I suppose," Delgado said, grimly, studying the red, orange, and pink blossoms.

What Jackson made of this I wasn't sure, but it didn't matter so much, either. "Mr. Jackson," I said, "I want you to take note that these plants are here. We didn't put them here. They were here when we arrived, weren't they?"

"Yes."

"I'm going to make a telephone call. You wait—"

"Actually, you don't have to wait, Jackson," Dean Utley said softly from the doorway.

He strode across the carpet.

"You can go now, Jackson," he said.

Jackson said, "We didn't know what to do, Mr. Utley. They said it was a police emergency."

"Yes, I see, Jackson. Thank you. I'll take care of this."

"I hope there's no trouble, Mr. Utley."

"None at all. These gentlemen, and the lady, did exactly the right thing in coming here."

"Uh, all right, then."

"And so did you, Mr. Jackson. Please pull the door closed as you leave." We all heard the dull sound of the thick door closing.

Utley was standing next to Jesus Delgado. I felt such loathing coming up in my guts, turning my body hot, that it took a couple of seconds before I spoke. "Utley, we know all about you."

"Really?"

Utley put his left arm around Delgado's neck as his right hand drew a .22 target Remington and placed the barrel in Delgado's ear.

It was so smooth, so calm, so unexpected, it was over before I realized it had begun. My face burned with shame.

"Now, I know you cops are carrying weapons. In fact, I know the serial numbers of those weapons. Take them out, drop them on the floor, and kick them over here."

There was a moment's pause—Bennis and I were both wondering how to shoot him first.

"I *will* kill Officer Delgado, you know. This day is of great importance to me, and it will either go forward or—" he paused to emphasize the point "—or I would be happy to take revenge on anybody who thwarts it. Look at me if you have any doubt that I'm sincere."

I pulled the revolver out of my holster and slid it across the floor. So did Bennis. Bennis' face was puffed with fury. I glanced at Black. His eyes were big and dark with hatred.

"Ah, ah, Mr. Bennis," Utley said. "You have another gun, one you carried and fired during a robbery three years ago. A Beretta. Serial number 277—"

"I don't have it with me."

"Don't make me ask you to strip, Mr. Bennis." Utley cocked the hammer on the revolver in Delgado's ear.

"All right," Bennis snarled. He took out his ankle gun and slid it to Utley across the rug.

"No word at all on you, Black, about whether you currently carry a gun. You haven't charged any gun purchases to any credit card in the last three years. Too much desk work, I guess. You don't belong to any gun club in the Chicago area. Turn around and take off your jacket. Good. Back over to me. Don't get between me and Bennis and Figueroa."

He took his left hand away from Delgado long enough to pat Black, his right hand keeping the gun pressed into Delgado's ear so hard he winced. When Utley was finished with Black, who had no gun, he said, "I think we'll just wait an hour or so while cutworm finishes running. Then some friends of mine will stop by. As far as any consequences of this little imbroglio go, you invaded my home without a warrant. We shouldn't have any trouble with that."

"Eat shit, Mr. Utley," Jesus Delgado said.

"I suppose you were alerted by that chump Frieswyk floating in. I suppose you figured to come here and avenge his death. I suppose you're a big deal hero cop, huh? You know how we got Frieswyk to the apartment here? You know why it wasn't difficult getting him here? He came here to shake me down. A crooked cop, Delgado. How do you like that? When he found the squad car scam, his first thought was how could he cash in on it. I mean, I hire creative crooks, but I will *not* be shaken down!"

Jesus said, "Eat shit and die, Mr. Utley."

Utley poked Jesus' ear hard with the gun barrel. Jesus gasped. Utley said, "Shut up! Now, Ms. Figueroa, I don't know what exotic information you expected to find here, but I assure you there isn't any."

Jesus started to speak, but I shook my head fractionally and he stopped.

"And it doesn't really matter. You are all going to go back to your homes and keep out of trouble for a couple of days."

I said, "Just why should we do that?"

"You'll do it, because if you do, I'll return JJ."

For a moment, nobody said anything. Then I whispered, "You have JJ? Here?"

"No, my debuggers have him."

"I don't believe you."

"Then call George Gosling."

I winced, recognizing the name of the principal at JJ's

school. Utley said, "There's a phone over there, Ms. Figueroa. But do it in such a way that you don't tip him. Or I might have to keep the boy. In one condition or another."

"No, I guess—yes, I'll check." It could be a bluff. He could have taken the name Gosling from any file.

"Act like you know what you're talking about. I suggest you ask whether Mr. Bryn Hopkins has come by to pick him up. Ten minutes ago or so. And I suggest you be very pleased that he has."

I got out the phone book, looked up the school, and phoned. When I finished talking to the principal, I just nodded. Gosling said they had left ten minutes ago. We were beaten.

I ground out some words while I tried to think. "You're ahead of us, I guess." If Jesus Delgado was as flooded with fury as I was, there were only Bennis and Black to fall back on for clear thinking.

Utley said, "Far, far ahead. The president is in the hospital. Did you know that?"

"No. Oh, my God, no."

"Touch of food poisoning. U-Hosp. You know the place. The one that so horribly failed to take good care of your sister."

Suddenly, Bennis kicked upward into the thick glass sheet that covered the Univac chunk. If the glass sheet had been a football, it would have sailed a hundred yards. It split and flew up in two pieces. One smashed into the bank of plants, one came close to Utley, and as it did, Delgado ducked away from Utley's gun and Bennis dove for his own gun on the floor.

Max Black leaped onto Utley, screaming and clawing. "You slimy coward! God damn you!"

He ripped a handful of hair out of Utley's head, but Utley still had his gun and fired into Black's stomach. Black grabbed at the gun, not even trying to defend himself, and Utley fired again.

Bennis, Delgado, and I jumped at Utley, but Black had the gun barrel and bent it around, breaking Utley's trigger finger. The gun fired.

We all fell back.

Utley collapsed. A tiny blackened hole just above his nose oozed only a little blood. He lay still, not breathing. His eyes were wide and staring. One arm lay out straight as if calling for help.

I turned to help Max, who had folded up onto the floor, bleeding. "Ohhh, non optimal," he said, sighing.

I said, "Call an ambulance."

Max grabbed my hand. "I'm sorry, Figueroa," he said. I didn't know for a second what he meant, everything had happened so fast, and then I realized that, with Utley dead, we didn't know where JJ was.

10100011

I WANTED TO console him, but it was too late. The stomach shot alone might not have been fatal. A .22 is not very powerful, and the pellet had just pierced the side of his abdomen. But the slug that had torn through his neck transected the left carotid. Blood flooded the floor.

I pressed my hand over the neck wound, but the emptying carotid had already sucked air into the brain and blood pumped out under my hand for only two or three seconds more and then stopped altogether. Black's feet twitched spasmodically for a few seconds more and then he was limp.

"He's dead! He's dead!" I said. I felt bereft.

Irrationally, I reached for Utley's gun, but Jesus yelled, "Don't touch it! When the techs come, it'll show Utley killed Max. Don't even breathe on it!"

I backed away and found my own sidearm under the sofa. "Call U-Hosp," I said to Bennis. "Warn them the records'll be sabotaged."

"What if they don't believe me?"

"Just do it! Hurry! We don't know what shit they're up to. Then call everybody you know in the CPD, anybody who trusts you, and have them get a team over to U-Hosp fast!" •

"Call Moses and DiMaggio!" Delgado said. There were tears in his eyes, but he was functioning.

Bennis grabbed the phone.

I said to Delgado, "The debuggers have a ten-minute head start with JJ. How can we find out where they're going?"

He was already at the keyboard on Utley's desk. "Maybe he won't have passwords. After all, it's his own home." Delgado booted up the system.

I watched over his shoulder. He said, "No. No. I'm sorry, Figueroa. He has passwords. And I'm not the Wizard."

Bennis was done with the phone calls. I yelled, "We've got to try to intercept them!" I yelled. "Jesus, try to guess the password."

"How?"

"I don't know. Bennis, call the First District. Tell them a six-year-old boy has been kidnapped from Cranbill Elementary."

"Do we know the license plate?"

"No."

"Do we know the type of car?" •

"No!"

"All right," he said, and his tone of voice told me how he felt.

I said, "Two men in a car with a six-year-old boy. A—a little boy with reddish brown hair—" I felt tears and immediately wiped them away. "Bennis, hurry up! You and I have got to hit the street."

10100100

"YOU DON'T HAVE to trust me," the charge nurse had heard Bennis' voice shout at her over the phone. "Just don't trust any computer-based records. Don't use anything that comes in over the data management lines. Do you have a hardcopy of the president's medical records from Washington?"

"I can't reveal—"

"Don't reveal. I don't care if you tell me! Just get one."

"We can have them fax one."

"Wait, stop! Don't even do that. Have the Secret Service call the president's personal doctor in D.C."

"I'll see what I can do."

"Just don't *give* him anything until you get hardcopy."

The head nurse hung up, blinking her eyes. Amoxicillin was not urgent. The man had sounded sincerely worried. Sometimes you had to use common sense. She sent a student nurse to the cafeteria to find Dr. Biskupic. Then she cocked her head, nodded to herself, and said aloud, "Why don't I just wake the president up and ask him?"

Nodding to the Secret Service guards that sat at the door, she walked into the president's room.

10100101

JJ WAS WORRIED. But there had been so many strange things happening in the last few days—his Aunt Sheryl badly hurt, then several days of everybody rushing back and forth to the hospital, and his grandmother babysitting, and then the Mileskis staying over and his mother gone—he had lost his ability to tell what was unusual. It was all unusual.

The problem was he didn't really like these two guys. They looked funny, dressed alike in those blue jackets. And one of them was all beat up. The beat-up one seemed mad at him. What, JJ thought, had he ever done to this guy? The other one, called Glen, was much more polite. He was too polite, in fact.

JJ had pulled his seat belt unusually tight. It was reassuring. He wasn't worried *yet*. But he had a funny, queasy feeling. He thought if he didn't see his mother pretty soon, he might start to be really frightened.

The men were driving well within the speed limit, JJ could tell. But they kept watching in all directions and trying to beat the traffic lights.

Glen said, "We're going to go on a little ride."

"Where's my mommy?"

"She's going to meet us later. You're going to love this. Trust me."

I don't think so, JJ thought.

10100110

BENNIS AND I sped up Clark Street toward JJ's school. All we could do was try to find a car with JJ in it somewhere between the school and SJR DataSystems. It was practically hopeless.

"What if a cop stops us for speeding?" I asked.

"God knows. I hope it'll be somebody we know."

"Maybe they're going to the boat," I said. "That guy told us they had orders to get it ready."

Jesus' voice came out of our walkie-talkie: "Genius to Big Guy."

Bennis said, "What is it, Genius?"

"I've tried everything with this thing. Figueroa, do you have any ideas of possible passwords? Say whatever comes to mind and I'll try them while you talk."

I said, "Univac?"

"No. Didn't work. Keep guessing."

"Howie? Hancock? SJR? Utley? No, that's silly." My hands were trembling with panic. They could have JJ in a basement, terrified. They could be killing him . . .

"It's not silly, but I already tried it."

"Um, puzzle? Enigma? Mystery? Wait!"

"What?"

"Sheryl once said—try 'utmost.' "

"Uh—no go."

"Try 'utopia,' with and without capital U."

"No, sorry. Doesn't work."

"Try—try 'utter.' "

"No."

" 'Utterly.' "

"Hey! You got it!"

"What does it say?"

"Wait a minute. There may not be anything about the car. Let me see if there's a record of license plates—hold it—I'm scanning the menu."

"Hurry up!"

"Don't rush me. I don't want to miss—Holy shit!"

"What?"

"He has a Computer Aided Dispatch for the company cars. And I have a moving dot here!"

10100111

"THEY'RE GOING TO the *Gigabyte!*" Jesus congratulated himself for having guessed right on the name. "It's at Meigs. Meigs Field."

Bennis spun the car while I yelled into the radio, "Tell the

First District. They can get there faster than we can."

"We'll see who gets there faster," Bennis mumbled.

I gripped the door handle, not because I was afraid of speed, but because I had to have something to do with my hands, which kept trembling. We roared up off Belmont onto Lake Shore Drive.

"I should have jumped him," Bennis said.

I didn't answer.

"When Utley grabbed Jesus, I should have jumped him."

"*I* should have jumped him. You were farther away than I was."

"I should have stopped Black from charging that turd. I should have just run at him myself."

"We thought he'd shoot Jesus."

"I should have assumed he'd focus on the person charging him."

"Bennis, *I should have, too,* damn it!"

"My man, that's all very well. But I'm not nearly so concerned about you not bein' a hero as I am about me not bein' a hero."

I stared through the window. We screamed around the curve where Michigan originated at north Lake Shore Drive, blew past Navy Pier and held the curve into the straightaway that led to the Field Museum. It was a wonder no cops were on us.

"You're not saying much," Bennis said.

"Go faster."

Bennis took the corner into the Meigs Field parking area on two wheels but didn't park. He entered the roofed area at the guard's booth and flashed his star. "Hold yours out, my man!" he said to me.

The guard leaned in.

"Police business! Where's the *Gigabyte?*"

"Don't know planes by name. The tower does all—"

"I don't have time! Did two men and a kid come by here?"

"Yeah." He pointed to the far side of the field.

Meigs Field is an island in Lake Michigan, lying just east of Soldier Field, about three city blocks wide and eight long. Because of its small size, it is used mostly by helicopter traffic and small planes. But air traffic in and out is continual. As we sped across the field, a helicopter was settling down like a dragonfly. At the end of the runway a small private plane was warming up.

Bennis raced the car across the open tarmac area. "I hope I'm not in the middle of a runway. I'll watch for markers and keep out of flight lanes. You look for the assholes," he said.

In the rearview mirror, I saw the lights of squad cars. They were just coming off Lake Shore Drive.

10101000

"WHAT'S IN THAT?" JJ asked. Glen and Zach lifted a big cardboard box into the plane, stowing it on a backseat. The plane was a four-seater, and JJ had a feeling he was going to be sitting next to the box. It didn't appeal to him.

"Computer gear. Can't you read?"

"Not much. I'm six."

"Get in!"

JJ hopped into the plane, which Zach had already warmed up. Now he was getting really scared. He tried to console himself, thinking that people who owned planes had to have a lot of money and maybe that made them respectable and not dangerous—but he didn't really believe it. He fastened his seat belt. The familiar gesture didn't make him feel any better, either. He tightened it. Nothing helped. He was more scared than ever. His eyes filled with tears. He wanted his mother. *I'm only six*, he thought. *It's okay to want my mother.*

"Where's my mommy?" he called to Glen and Zach.

"Shut up!" Glen yelled at him.

Zach said to Glen, "Hurry up! Just leave the goddam car!"

Zach and Glen jumped in the front seats and slammed and locked the doors. The plane started bumping forward.

The box next to JJ tilted over and leaned against the front seat, right behind Glen, its top pushing into Glen's seat. The box was squeezed sideways. JJ looked at it and tried to see in. One of the top flaps, which now faced sideways instead of up, opened. Leaning against it was Howie Borke's hand, stiff and curled like a dead spider.

10101001

I SAW THE *Gigabyte*—Utley's play toy—from a distance while Zach and Glen were loading the box. And I saw JJ! He was too far away to be clearly visible, but I knew from the way my heart lifted that it was really him. Zach, Glen, and JJ were inside the plane in seconds. The plane started to move. Bennis screamed the car over the tarmac, trying to get in front of it. It turned, ready to run down the field. Bennis shoved the car into park. The gears crashed and the car rocked wildly while he and I burst out of our doors at the same instant.

The plane began its takeoff.

Bennis was a faster runner than me. He sprinted flat out at the aircraft, which was taxiing toward us. I ran after him, panting out loud. I pulled my service revolver from its holster.

The plane had not built up much ground speed. Bennis was in front of it. He dove under the propeller blades and caught the undercarriage. He grabbed hold of an undercarriage strut and swung his leg over the axle, getting his feet clear of the ground.

He rocked his body back and forth, hoping to throw the plane off its course.

But it accelerated. Bennis held the strut and took out his automatic with his free hand. JJ wouldn't be in the pilot's seat. Bennis aimed for the forward part of the craft and shot up into the pilot's area. His hand was vibrating so much he bounced two shots off the nose.

"Ooooo-kay!" he screamed.

He shot again, hoping to hit the pilot.

The plane rose into the air.

I saw it happen. Bennis' weight wasn't enough to hold the plane down, but it was enough to throw it briefly off balance, and as it rose it curved toward me.

The landing gear began to retract.

If they rose into the air with Bennis, they could throw him off. But if I shot the plane down, with its landing gear half up, he'd be crushed underneath.

And what about JJ?

No matter what happened, it was better for it to happen here, near help and near the ground, than to let them get out over Lake Michigan. Once they got away with JJ, there was no hope at all. They could throw him out of the plane somewhere over the lake, just like they had done with Frieswyk.

It was instant, a reaction as much as a thought. I immediately placed my feet apart, both hands on the firearm, steadied, and fired at the pilot. At the same second, someone in the plane fired at me and missed.

My first shot hit the pilot's window and, though I didn't know it then, hit Zach. So did my second. The third might have, but the plane was coming down.

It struck the earth with its left wingtip first and cartwheeled across the runway. Part of the left wing flew off. Bennis crumpled onto the pavement under the aircraft. He lay without moving. The plane went on spinning another twenty feet, losing more of the wing. Howie Borke's body, stiffened into a fetal position, flew out and flipped over and over. The plane screeched along the pavement to a stop, where it lay, nose crushed, one wing gone, leaking gasoline, the motor hissing.

I froze, torn between running to Bennis and running to JJ. Then fear of fire took me to JJ first.

10101010

||||||||||||||||||||||||||||||||||||||||||||||||||||||||||||||||||
DEPARTMENT OF THE TREASURY
UNITED STATES SECRET SERVICE
1800 G STREET NW
WASHINGTON DC
FROM: CMV
TO: STRICK
FORM: INTERNAL

<<IN ANY OPEN TRANSMISSION FOLLOW THE
ESTABLISHED CODES>>

JIM:
WHAT THE HELL DO YOU PEOPLE THINK YOU'RE
DOING?
GET HIM BACK HERE ASAP!
ANY MORE INCOMPETENCE AND IT'S YOUR ASS.

CMV
||||||||||||||||||||||||||||||||||||||||||||||||||||||||||||||||||||

ZACH MASSENDATE WAS dead. Glen Jaffee turned state's evidence in exchange for being tried on four counts of second degree murder instead of first degree, which in Illinois is a death penalty charge. He was sentenced to twenty years per charge to be served consecutively, which should keep him locked up until 2076.

DeLusk and the other members of the steering committee received sentences ranging from fifteen years to sixty years. Their juries had some difficulty, given the fact that much of the evidence had disappeared into erased cyberspace, but testimony plea-bargained from lower-level security employees helped. And most useful, an alert FBI agent had stumbled on Utley's cache of tapes of his steering committee meetings. The fact that Frieswyk's fingerprints were found inside the *Gigabyte* helped, too.

The president recovered from his salmonella infection, went back to Washington, and was informed of the whole story several days later. The FBI took four months to piece together exactly what had happened and then went to the president. He and the director of the FBI had a meeting with the veep, during which the veep decided that his precarious state of health made it impossible for him to successfully continue in the strenuous role of vice president of the United States.

The CPD fired Charlie Withers and four other officers.

Jesus Delgado and his twin daughters went to live in his parents' house in Chicago. Jesus has not fully recovered from the death of his wife, and is not dating other women, but he is certainly a contender for best father in Chicago.

When the president was informed of what had been planned, he telephoned Bennis at the hospital and thanked him.

Delgado, Bennis, and I received an award from the hands of Superintendent of Police Gus Gimball personally. Black had no immediate family, but the shareholders of SJR DataSystems voted four million dollars to establish the Max Black Chair in Computer Science.

I'm still living in the Birch house, but I'm thinking of moving out and getting a small place for myself and JJ. I hesitate because Sheryl needs me. She's still not able to walk; in fact, she is confined to a wheelchair most of the time. But she is looking for a new job. Robert Birch is much the same as he ever was, not much help.

Because JJ had fastened his seat belt when he got on the plane, he didn't bounce out like the body of Howie Borke. He was completely uninjured, no bump, no scratch, and no psychological ill effects, either, that I can see. He viewed the incident as a sort of virtual reality or interactive television, and his stock at his grade school went up a thousand percent. The principal, George Gosling, called me after some ten days of JJ's boasting to ask me to shut him up. He was giving some of the children nightmares. Especially when he got to the part where "the dead guy came out of the box." I told Mr. Gosling, "I object on principle to the quashing of truth. At *any* time."

Norman Bennis was very seriously injured when the plane crashed on him. One of the wheels actually drove into his back as the plane came down. The reason he was not killed outright may have been that the wheels were folding up after takeoff and were therefore not as rigid as they would otherwise have been.

Bennis' back was broken. His spleen was ruptured, his nose broken on impact with the tarmac, his left shoulder blade, left upper arm, and left wrist broken as the left side of his body hit the ground and was mashed into it by the wheel. He spent twenty-one days in intensive care, the first five days in critical condition. After the first week, they allowed visitors. I took three weeks off duty and spent eight hours a day at his side, the rest with my family.

In mid-May Bennis was transferred to the Rehabilitation Institute at Northwestern University, where he was taught to walk again. Now I was back on the job and paired with Stanley Mileski for the time being, but I smuggled pizzas and Big Macs into Bennis' room. And, once in a while, a Coors.

By June, Bennis was out of the hospital, but going in three days a week for therapy. And *extremely* irritable at his forced retirement, however temporary. Crabby, very crabby.

Jesus and I received commendations from the Chicago City Council and the Chicago Police Department.

On June 25, Bennis received the Carter G. Harrison Award and the Superintendent's Award of Valor from the Chicago Police Department. By special arrangement, JJ Figueroa was allowed to help present it to him. JJ and Gus Gimball together pinned the award on the chest of Norman Bennis, who by that time was walking with two canes.

On July 25, he was back on the job in car 1-33 with his old buddy and partner, me.